PUCK HONEY

UNINTENTIONAL PUCK BUNNY #2

DANI GALLIARO

WOLLERIN BOOKS

For those of us who are part hopeless romantic, part independent woman in need of no man, part longing to be swept away by a caretaking daddy

THE L.A. PRINCES

An Incomplete Roster

- Dylan Sorrento - captain, right wing, #11
- Jacques "Jack" Leroy - center, #29
- Chapman Beatty - left wing, #20
- Guy Stelle - left wing, #13
- Ben "Mikey" Miknevicius - defenseman, #27
- Hudson Romelski - defenseman, #56
- Nick "Obi" Oberbeck - goalie, #33

A NOTE ON TRIGGERS

Your mental health as a reader is very important to me.

While my reads are always meant to be comforting and fun, I don't shy away from difficult topics. This book is intended for 18+ audiences.

All consent is enthusiastic and this is not a dark romance. However, some content may be uncomfortable for some readers.

The full list is at the back of the book for anyone who needs it.

Take care, y'all!

PLAYLIST

Access all of Mikey's many musical tastes via the Spotify playlist for Puck Honey here.

Also, we don't talk a lot about what characters' voices sound like, but I always have a clear idea of what they sound like when I write them. In my head, Mikey sounds like Sturgill Simpson or Tyler Childers: raspy and a touch of twang. Blame it on his mom's Eastern Kentucky upbringing.

As always, there's too much Taylor and some of these are covers. They're chosen because the voice fits the story better. Sorry, Bob Dylan, you wrote it best, but Adele sang it best.

- Country Squire - Tyler Childers
- tolerate it - Taylor Swift
- Paradise - Sturgill Simpson
- Love It When You Hate Me - Avril Lavigne and blackbear
- Everlong - Foo Fighters
- Can't You See - Marshall Tucker Band
- Lady May - Tyler Childers
- Caught Up In You - 38 Special

- Amie - Pure Prairie League
- Danny's Song - Loggins and Messina
- Dancing In The Moonlight - King Harvest
- Glitch - Taylor Swift
- Untouched - The Veronicas
- I Want To Come Over - Melissa Etheridge
- New Rules - Dua Lipa
- I Think I Like You - The Band CAMINO
- Stuck On You - Lionel Richie
- C'Mon - Kesha
- First Day of My Life - Bright Eyes
- Labyrinth - Taylor Swift
- The Other Side of the Door (Taylor's Version) - Taylor Swift
- Make You Feel My Love - Adele
- For Once In My Life - Stevie Wonder

1

JESSIE

I wrapped the pillow around my head, covering my ears. At first, all I heard was the stuffing settling into place inside it. Then the strains of Mr. Brightside, loud and somewhat off-key, pushed through the fabric.

"That's it. I'm going over there."

Cole stirred next to me. "Don't be a Karen, babe. Let them have their fun. You have to get up in a few hours anyway."

"Exactly! I have to get up and go to my job where I have to prove myself so I can get a not-shitty job! They're keeping me from sleeping!"

"It's not a job. It's an apprenticeship," Cole said. I hated when he did that. I made money at it, so how was it not my job? Plus, it was a stepping stone to the kinds of roles I could dream of in L.A.

Cole went on. "And anyway, you don't even sleep when it's silent."

I growled and bopped him with the pillow. I stomped into the bathroom, or rather, wavered my way in there. The sleeping pill that didn't work to make me sleep made basic locomotion a challenge.

I glared at myself in the mirror as I washed my hands, so frustrated I wasn't sure if I'd scream or cry. I just needed peace. Why couldn't I have the peace of even six hours of sleep? I'd kill for six hours.

When I walked back in the bedroom, Cole was already asleep again, peacefully snoring. How fucking dare he.

That was the last straw.

I slid on my house flip-flops and stalked to my front door. I flung it open and made the sharp turn to be at my neighbor's door. I knocked as hard as I could, figuring those dopes couldn't hear shit over their own squalling. I knocked again and waited. I must have stood by the door for a full two minutes.

In my blind rage, I tried the door handle. To my surprise, it opened, and I found myself face to face with a kitchen full of tall, athletic men.

A few raised their eyebrows. One that was especially enormous with curly blonde hair, a missing front tooth, and an absurd number of tattoos stepped forward.

"Uh, miss, you can't be in here," he said, reading the rage on my face and trying to temper his statement accordingly. "It's a private party."

"Not anymore, it's not," I seethed. "Where's the fucker who lives here?"

The blonde grimaced and turned to the living room behind him. "Mikey, someone's here to see you."

I pushed past the men in the kitchen and headed where the blonde had looked.

"Did somebody send me a birthday surprise?" drawled a familiar man in a backward hat on the couch. I'd seen him in the hall or on his balcony a few times. Definitely my neighbor. I stood in front of him and crossed my arms. Walking aggressively across the room reminded me that I wasn't wearing a bra, my boobs waggling as freely as they wanted. I was wearing a silky white pajama set, a loose strappy tank with admittedly tiny shorts. My hair, upon last inspection in the bathroom mirror, looked insane, half of my long bob pulled up in a haphazard bun.

I stood in front of him, suddenly feeling self-conscious. The sleeping pill made confronting my neighbor seem like a good idea, but arriving half-dressed in front of a room full of men was sobering. My neighbor gave me a long look from my bare legs to my unfortunately erect nipples.

"Hey, Sweet Cheeks."

"Cut it out. I came over here to tell you to shut the fuck up," I snorted, trying to seem as mighty as I could.

A quiet "ooh" issued from the kitchen, where everyone had turned to watch whatever I had planned.

"And why's that? Since you're here, grab a drink. Stay awhile. We don't bite," my neighbor cooed. The asshole had the gall to smile and wink at me, the deep canyons of his dimples cutting down his cheeks.

Why did he have to be hot? The kind of hot that just laying eyes on them made you a little sweaty. A tuft of reddish-brown hair peeked out of the front of his backward hat, his eyes an amber whiskey to match. A dusting of stubble that would give the perfect burn along your neck and jaw in the right situation. Not that I was thinking about those kinds of situations.

And he wasn't just physically attractive. He oozed charisma. And hearing all his conquests through the walls, it sounded like he knew what he was doing in the bedroom.

The kind of hot that was nothing but trouble, so totally not my type. Cole was my type. Sensible. Practical.

"Looks like you could do to blow off some steam. Why don't you stay?" he said, filling the silence as I wobbled in front of him.

"Some of us have to work in the morning, that's why," I said. "It's two in the fucking morning and you're treating the place like a goddamn frat house. It's a Wednesday night."

"It *is* my apartment," he said. "If I want to run a brothel, I can."

"Not legally!" I snapped. He shrugged, seemingly amused by our conversation. "Your tomfoolery is keeping me, a working woman, up. Who the fuck parties on a Wednesday anyway?"

"Tomfoolery," echoed the very young-looking skinny guy sitting next to him with a chubby bald chihuahua on his lap, giggling.

"What are you, twelve? What is that thing? A tube worm on legs?"

"I'm twenty," he said, offended. "And this is Greg. Just because he doesn't fit conventional beauty standards doesn't mean he's ugly."

My neighbor squinted at me and cocked his head to the side. "Hey, haven't I seen you somewhere before?"

This fucking guy.

"I'm your next-door neighbor, dumbass!" I wavered on my feet, the damn sleeping pill getting to me again.

"Easy, killer," he said, sitting up to hold my thighs. "Don't want you to hurt yourself."

"Get your filthy fucking hands off me!" I shouted. "I'll call the cops if you keep this shit up!"

"Sweet Cheeks, I think the LAPD has better things to do than break up rich people's parties," he said, squeezing the backs of my thighs with a cocky smile. His hands were rough, and I hated that I noticed it. He was looking up at me so suggestively, basically kneeling in front of me. His eyes were full of mischief, and was that desire?

"Too bad we're not in L.A.!" I hissed. "We live in Manhattan Beach!"

"Whoa, whoa, whoa, okay, hang on." A man with a French-sounding accent stepped forward and took my arm. "I think what Mikey's trying to say is that we'll keep it down, and he's very sorry. Mikey, isn't that right? You were just going to tell," he paused to look down at me, "what's your name?"

"Jessie."

"You were just going to tell *Jessie* that you're very sorry."

"And that she's very pretty and is welcome to stay," Mikey added, voice smooth as butter.

My blood boiled. The friend trying to smooth things over let out an exasperated sigh and rubbed his brow. I leaned down in front of Mikey. What fucking adult went by the name Mikey?

"Listen up, asshat, because I'm only going to say it once. I have to hear you having sex all the time as it is." Mikey got a soft smile and gave a drowsy, drunken blink. "I am tired of staying up because you can't have the courtesy to think of your surroundings. If you do not keep it the fuck down, there will be consequences. Understood?"

Mikey's eyes made a quick visit to my breasts, which granted, were kind of in his face. "Thin walls work two ways, Sweet Cheeks. You think I don't hear you and your little boyfriend?"

He lowered his voice, his gaze flicking down to my mouth. "Let me know when you're ready for a man who can really satisfy you."

My mouth dropped open. The fucking nerve of this guy! The group of guys at large didn't hear that last part, but the mediator friend definitely did.

"MIKEY!" he shouted. He turned to me and walked me to the door. "I'm so sorry, Jessie. We'll be quiet and let you sleep."

2

MIKEY

I wandered out of my room, the sunlight feeling too bright and my head pounding. A peek into my guest room showed Obi lying on the floor, spooning his dog, Greg. Guy was sprawled out on my couch under a blanket, looking at his phone.

"*Bonjour*, birthday boy," Guy rasped. He set his phone aside. "Kitty says hi, by the way."

"Hi, Kitty," I grumbled. "Roles are reversed, huh? You're sleeping on my couch for once."

"Yeah, well, if you'd get a guest bed, I wouldn't have to pretend to be you in college and sleep on the couch," he pointed out.

My apartment was wrecked, cans and bottles everywhere with little spills trailing after them. It looked like the game of beer pong that went down at my island was successful.

I opened my fridge to look for something, anything, to touch my hangover. I settled on a bottle of kombucha *and* a bottle of Gatorade. Would those be good mixed together? Couldn't hurt to find out. I filled a glass with water for Guy. I was hungover, but still capable of being a good host.

I set the glass in front of him and flopped down into a chair.

"I think you owe your neighbor an apology," Guy said.

My head cocked back for a second. "What neighbor?"

Guy's eyes rounded. "You don't remember?"

I closed my eyes and rested my head on the back of the chair. A memory of soft thighs, white silk, and angry eyes came back to me. "Right. Sweet Cheeks."

"Her name is Jessie," Guy corrected.

"Yep. Jessie. We had good banter."

Guy guffawed. "Banter? She can't stand you."

"Impossible," I said.

I refused to accept it. Jessie was hot as hell, even when her light brown hair was disheveled and her hazel brown eyes had the wrath of the devil himself in them. I could not forget those braless wonders of breasts swinging in my face while she was cussing me out. I could not forget her strong thighs under my hands, with such soft skin. I could not forget how hot she was when she was so angry. What would it be like to have her take that anger out on me? Sounds fun.

I never heard her get angry with her boyfriend, but I heard him get angry with her. His rage was never warranted. She *should* have been angry with him. Not only did it sound like he was mean to her, but I heard their pathetic sex all the time. There was no way he was getting her there. I've dealt with a good handful of fakers in my day, and she was faking with him.

A woman like that deserves to be made whole. If she were mine, I'd make sure she wasn't faking.

But she wasn't mine. She was his, and I'd been kind of an asshole to her and should probably apologize. "Yeah, you're right," I said. "What do I do? Send a fruit basket?"

Guy chortled. "I think you can just go say sorry. But she did mention she had to work today. She's out living a normal person life. You'll have to apologize after she gets home."

After we heated some breakfast burritos that my food prep lady made, we woke Obi up.

"Can you be hung over from a gummy?" he croaked as he shuffled into the kitchen.

"Bud, I think you dominated at beer pong," I said.

"It's okay to stop early. You don't have to play the whole tournament, you know," Guy added.

"Where's the honor in that?" Obi asked, affronted.

"He's living his college experience, Stelle," I said. "Let him be. No one stopped us in college."

"Fair," Guy said.

It was Nick Oberbeck's rookie season with us, a goalie prodigy. At only 20, Guy and I took him under our proverbial wings to make sure he didn't get into too much trouble. The league can do ugly things to a man, and making mistakes at a young age on a public stage is rough. I was lucky I was still in school and then the AHL when I was his age. Guy had it a little harder, leaving his junior year and being hung up on Kitty the whole time. We were happy to let Obi cut loose in more controlled settings like our house parties, where he couldn't get into trouble. And we always made him stay over so he wouldn't get in some Uber drama or a drunk driving incident.

Who would have ever guessed that Stelle and I would be the ones to keep a kid out of trouble?

"How's the shoulder?" Obi asked.

I rotated my arm to test it. "Okay I guess? I don't know. It still doesn't feel right, but I don't think there's anything specific wrong with it. Might just be the weather making it act up."

"Old man," Obi said.

Stelle chuckled. "He called you old."

"You're the same age, dickhead!" I scoffed.

"I'm a summer baby. I'm six months younger," Stelle said with a shrug.

"You should tell PT. We don't want you out for weeks," Obi went on.

"How about you focus on what goes on between the pipes and I'll do the worrying about my shoulder, huh?"

"Sheesh. Somebody's testy," Guy said.

"I'm hungover," I said.

"But didn't we have fun?" Obi asked with a shove.

I sighed. "Yes. We had fun."

Suddenly, a knocking rhythm came from next door. Then a moan. Then a very distinct, "Oh, Cole."

All of our jaws fell open, looking between each other.

"I thought Jessie had to work?" Guy whispered.

But I knew what Jessie sounded like with Cole in that way from hearing it dozens of pathetic times. She didn't sound like that. That was an entirely different voice.

"I don't think that's Jessie," I said, my stomach twisting.

Obi grimaced. Guy stared at me.

"You're sure?" Guy asked.

I nodded. "Pretty sure."

"It doesn't really sound like her," Obi said.

"Maybe she took the afternoon off . . ." Guy suggested.

I just shook my head. Oh, God. Poor Jessie. Did she know?

She was basically a stranger, but it still made my blood boil. How could he do that to her?

IT WAS ABOUT 9 p.m. by the time I settled on my balcony with the ice pack on my shoulder and a drink in my hand. The sliding door on the next balcony over squealed and there she was. Good ol' Sweet Cheeks was watering her plants with headphones in and itty-bitty shorts on. Did this woman not know how to cover her legs? Christ.

I watched her quietly for a minute, then waved to get her

attention. She was either willfully ignoring me or really didn't see me.

"Jessie," I said just south of a scream. I didn't want to shout and scare half our building. I waved emphatically with my un-iced arm. Drips from the ice ran down my bare chest.

Ice. Good idea.

I pulled a piece of ice from my water glass and chucked it over to her balcony. It hit her square in the stomach as she turned. She shrieked, then looked up, ripping out her earbuds.

"Jesus, Jockey, you scared the piss out of me! Why are you throwing things at me?" she demanded.

"Jockey? It's Mikey or Ben, Sweet Cheeks."

"Yeah, well, you're a jock, too, so Jockey."

I laughed and tipped back my beer bottle. "Clever. I like it."

"So? Why are you assaulting me with," she kicked the ice cube on the floor, "ice?"

"I wanted to say hey. And sorry for last night."

"Oh?"

"Yeah. I feel bad that we kept you up. I promise it won't happen again," I said, trying to be contrite.

She cocked an eyebrow. "You really think I believe you're going to keep it down from now on? You've been loud since I moved in."

I clenched my jaw. "Like I said last night, I'm not the only one who's loud."

"Man, this apology really feels sincere," she snorted. She went back to tending an orchid with delicate precision.

"Jessica," I started.

"That's not my name."

"Jesserton?"

"If you must know, it's Jessalyn. Most people call me Jessie."

"I'm not most people," I said with a grin. "Jessalyn's pretty. I might call you that."

She sighed and turned more fully toward me, crossing her arms. "What do you want, Ben?"

"I feel like we got off on the wrong foot. I've seen you around but we haven't had a chance to ever talk. I want to not have my next-door neighbor hate me. Come have a beer with me."

"What if I want to hate you? You don't have to be friendly with your neighbors, you know."

I shook my head. "Don't tell my mom. She'd never stand for that. Come on. Come over. Please? I don't bite."

"I'll stay over here, thank you very much."

"Fine, let me get you a beer then," I said, shifting to get up.

"Don't," she said, annoyed. "You look . . . injured." Her eyes traveled over my chest to where the ice bag covered my right shoulder. "I'll get my own and sit on my own balcony."

"Whatever you want, Sweet Cheeks," I said with a smirk.

"Stop calling me that!" She disappeared into her apartment.

See? How was that not banter? Guy was crazy if he thought she didn't like me. She agreed to have a drink with me.

Jess popped back out on the balcony with a ball of yarn, some knitting needles, and a beer.

"Bud Light Lime? How do you drink that shit?" I scoffed.

"I don't always feel like buying limes. They can be expensive and they go bad fast," she shrugged. "What are you having, some snooty IPA?"

"Excuse you, it's a session pale ale," I said, putting my pinky up as I took a sip. "You may as well be drinking Mike's hard lemonade."

"I'd think you'd like that, since it has your name in it," she shot. I had to laugh.

"That's a good one, Jessalyn. Where's your boyfriend?"

"He's out at some work thing," she said breezily. My stomach turned.

"Did you, um, go to work today? Like all day?"

"Yes, despite you dumbasses keeping me up, I still went to work," she said, totally missing that anything was awry. How the hell do you bring up to someone that their boyfriend is most likely cheating on them? I'd never really done the whole relationship thing, so it really wasn't my place to say or do anything. I didn't know how that shit worked. She went on. "I'm surprised you're not still hungover from last night's festivities."

I brought myself back to the conversation. "I had a good sweat this afternoon. That and some healthy eating and I'm good as new," I said.

"Lucky."

"What are you knitting?"

Jessie held up the square of fabric she was working on. "It'll be a baby blanket. I'm a costume apprentice for a show. One of the characters is going to be a grandma, so they asked me to start working on a blanket for her to pretend to knit."

"Oooh, Hollywood, huh? That's a long drive, ain't it?"

"Kinda. Cole wanted to live here to be close to his work, and he makes the money, so here I am. I listen to audiobooks and podcasts on my drive," she said, her hands deftly weaving the yarn. It was mesmerizing to watch. The knitting needles made a soft clicking sound as she worked the fabric in her fingers.

"Will you make me a hat?" I asked.

A small smile curved her lips. She had a really cute smile, but she'd never shown me her teeth. Just little smirks. "Why, are you cold?"

"I mean, I get cold at work."

She scrunched her brow. "Wait, is your sport hockey?"

"Now she gets it. I honestly thought you knew since you called me Jockey. Or did you think I race horses?"

"Shut up," she said. "I thought hockey players were bigger."

"Ouch!"

"No, I mean, you're like, huge on the ice."

"Those are pads, Jessie. So we don't die every game."

"Huh. Never really thought about it, I guess. I didn't grow up with hockey."

"Oh yeah? Where are you from?" I asked.

"West Virginia."

"Seriously? My friend's fiancée is, too. The French guy you talked to last night. Maybe you know each other."

She chuckled. "Yeah, maybe in my state of a million people, I know this one person."

She had me there. "Fair. My mom's from Eastern Kentucky, though, so I know how tight knit it all is."

"So you're a blood Appalachian, huh? Where did you grow up?"

"Detroit."

"Ah yes. Hence the hockey."

"Hence the hockey," I agreed. I loved getting to know more about her, but I was still haunted by what Cole had been doing earlier that day. "So, how long have you and Cole been together?"

"Oh, a while. Since I was in college in Pittsburgh. He was all cool and graduated, a young professional. First we went to New York together. I interned with some fashion houses. Now I'm doing TV since he wanted to be out here."

Because I was feeling like an armchair psychologist, I dug into that. "Do you want to be out here?"

"I can't argue with 70 degrees almost year-round," she said.

"But do you like that?"

Jessie stiffened. "I'm sorry, do I know you?"

"No, but I want to know you."

She rolled her eyes and stood, gathering her yarn and beer bottle. "Goodnight, Ben."

"Wait, wait, I'm not trying to be creepy. I swear. Stay? I like talking to you."

She looked at me sidelong. "One more chance."

"Thank you. Sorry. I don't have many female friends. Just

my friends' girlfriends. Even with them, I don't really know how to be."

Jessie got a sly smile and a glint in her eye. "Just used to picking up girls to bring home, huh?"

"There's nothing wrong with that," I said, defending myself.

"I never said there was," she said, sticking out her bottom lip to prove her innocence.

"What's it like being in a relationship?" I asked, genuinely curious.

"I don't know. What's it like fucking random girls all the time?"

I took a drag on my beer as she eyed me for an answer.

"I'm being serious," I said. "Does it get stale?"

"What do you mean?" she asked.

Fuck, what did I mean? Obviously, Cole thought it was stale if he was stepping out on Jessie. Christ, I'd really boxed myself in.

"I mean, don't you hate fucking the same guy all the time?"

"I don't hate it," she said quietly. "In a lot of ways, you build trust over time. That's nice."

I felt sick again, thinking of how her trust was so misplaced. "Yeah. I've always wanted that. The trust thing."

"What's holding you back?" Jessie looked up from her knitting.

"Maybe haven't found the right person," I said. "Maybe I just don't know how to do it."

"Maybe you're emotionally unavailable," she suggested.

"What? I'm an open book," I argued.

"Sure. But you put on a big cocky front. If that's who you are, fine, but if it's not, you're selling yourself short. I think you're more introspective than you give yourself credit for. You've been asking me some thoughtful questions."

"Wait a minute. I was trying to psychoanalyze you, not the other way around," I said.

"See? This conversation was already too intimate for you. It's just the surface."

I took a deep breath. "How are you cutting me down so quickly, Jessalyn...?" I wanted her to tell me her last name.

"Welsh."

"How are you cutting me down so quickly, Jessalyn Welsh?"

She smirked again. "I talk to people a lot when I'm at work. I prefer to go beyond the weather. People tell me about their lives, and I listen."

"I'm impressed, Sweet Cheeks."

Her eyes shot up from her knitting. "Call me by my name or I go inside."

"Sorry. I'm impressed, Jessalyn."

"Better."

I took a sip of my beer, trying to figure out what to talk about next. "So how long has it been since Cole gave you a real orgasm?"

Her jaw fell open. "And that's my cue to leave," she said, gathering her stuff.

"So I have to be intimate for you, but you can't return the favor? That's not how friendships work."

"I never said I wanted to be friends," she huffed.

And with that, her sliding door closed.

3

JESSIE

The sun was never up when I was, at least not on my workdays. I got paid a pittance to apprentice with Glory Cats, a community college football-based sitcom out in Burbank. My hope was that the pittance would lead to my dream job, being the head costume designer for a show. Maybe even getting into movies.

My commute was about an hour on a good day, and call time was usually around 6 a.m. I had to become one of those weirdos who lays out their clothes and gets everything ready the night before work. Thankfully, they fed us breakfast and lunch at work, so I didn't have to pack my own food. A nice job perk.

But on this particular commute, my mind kept wandering from my murder podcast. Did I actually *enjoy* talking to Mikey the night before? He had a quick wit and though his questions were a bit odd, he seemed to genuinely want to know about me. Sure, I talked to people all day at my job, whether I was doing a fitting or stitching and laundering pieces. But Mikey, or I guess Ben, asked deep questions of me. I'm usually the one asking deep questions of other people.

Granted, one of the questions was deeply inappropriate. I mean, yeah, Cole hadn't exactly been a Casanova in the bedroom for quite some time. It wasn't always that way. When we met, we could have been mistaken for rabbits at the rate we were going at it.

I guess things started "getting stale" as Ben called it after we moved to New York. At first, it was exciting: the two of us taking on the Big Apple. We felt important, glamorous even. I was interning at fashion houses and working long hours. He was working long hours for his hedge fund. We had sex as often as we could, but the spark between us slowly faded.

When Cole got an opportunity to transfer to a company in Los Angeles, I knew I'd be giving up all the progress I made in fashion. Fashion and TV aren't exactly compatible. They're similar for sure, but the experience isn't the same. Dressing people for a show about a community college football team isn't quite runway-ready, cutting-edge styles. Cole told me it was okay if I wanted to stay in New York and we just parted ways. But he did point out that L.A. had better weather than New York, and maybe it would be a little less stressful for me. He picked our Manhattan Beach apartment next to Ben, and I took whatever opportunity would have me. I sucked it up and dealt with the long commute and early wakeups.

We'd been in Los Angeles for five months when I met Ben, or when Ben had his party that irritated me enough to go talk to him. And unfortunately for me and Cole, our sex life didn't improve with the West Coast ocean air. It remained mechanical. Familiar. And yeah, as Ben had noticed, unfulfilling for me.

But sex isn't everything in a relationship. Relationships go through seasons. Cole and I were in a transition. I repeated those phrases to myself over and over as I mulled over why talking to Mikey was sticking with me.

What scared me most was, Cole hadn't asked me how I felt about our lives in a long time, if ever. Sure, we talked about it before we left New York, but that was a big crossroads. How long had it been since I talked to Cole about how we felt about each other? I vowed to myself to try and restart the spark with Cole. We had so many years of history. Surely there was a reason for that, right?

But if sex wasn't everything, why couldn't I get the feeling of Mikey's hands on my thighs out of my mind? Why did I keep replaying him telling me that he could satisfy me?

Still, I wanted to try with Cole. No matter how rough things got, we always found a way to work it out. I couldn't just throw away a four-year relationship because of a few errant thoughts.

Maybe I needed to get bolder about what I wanted in the bedroom. I had things I wished he'd do, but it usually didn't go well when I asked. If I wanted to save our relationship, I might have to force the issue.

I was going to get bold. Halfway through my day, I sent Cole a text. My boss, Irina, would have had a cow if she saw me texting, but that would imply she was actually in our office doing her job. I peeked out the window to see her flirting with one of the grips and knew I was in the clear.

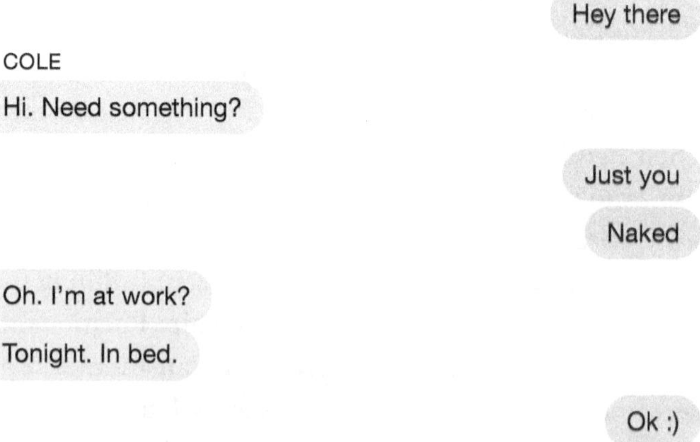

I was interrupted by the click of the wardrobe trailer's door, a friendly face poking around the corner.

"Hi! You ready for me?"

"Kitty! Come on in!"

Kitty Gatto usually just wrote for Glory Cats, but her fellow writers had written her into a few scenes on some upcoming episodes. I needed to get her measurements to start shopping and making pieces for her. I'd seen her around set, and she was always super friendly and kind. That wasn't a guarantee at work, so I was always relieved to find allies like her who wanted to make the day fun.

"If you could, just take your skirt off so I can get good measurements. Everything else can stay on. I'll lock the door," I said, stepping to take care of that.

"Great, I love the Winnie the Pooh look," she joked. "Thanks for squeezing me in. I know your schedule is weird."

"Eh, yours is, too. Are you excited to be back on camera?"

"Kind of? I said I didn't want to, but I knew I'd probably get written in at some point anyway," she said. "It's one of those 'no, no, don't make me' situations when I really don't mind. I've never acted opposite Grant before. It should be fun."

I wrapped the measuring tape around her waist. "You're probably used to this. Don't you have a wedding coming up?"

Kitty beamed. "This summer, yeah, when Guy and I are both off."

Hearing her say his name sparked a thought. "Your fiancé is French, right?"

"French-Canadian, yeah."

"And you're from West Virginia?"

"Yep, Charleston. Why?"

"I think we might have a mutual acquaintance," I said with a grin.

"No way! Who?"

"Mikey? Or I guess his real name is Ben?"

Kitty laughed. "Oh, yes. I definitely know Mikey. He and

Guy have been close since college. I guess he and I have, too, come to think of it. He's a great guy. How do you know him?"

"He's my next-door neighbor."

Kitty gasped. "Oh, you poor thing. He's the loudest creature on the planet." Then her eyes lit up. "Wait, did you break up their party the other day?"

I huffed. "Now hold on."

Kitty held out her hand to stop me. "Let me start by saying, I fully believe that they were being loud jackasses. You were right to do what you did."

"Yes. I think your fiancé was the one keeping things civil."

"That's what I heard," she said. "Glad he's not full of lies."

"You know what's funny? Mikey asked me if I knew you. Or rather, he said he had one friend from West Virginia, so since I'm from there, I must know you. Turns out he was right."

"I didn't know you were from WV! Where?"

"Bridgeport," I said. "Harrison County."

"I never knew that, Jessie! I knew I liked you. This just adds to my reasons why."

I didn't really have a ton of friends in L.A. Everyone I met was through work or through Cole, and Cole had lots of finance bro friends who were not my favorite. I was basically a homebody. Maybe I could strike up a little friendship with Kitty?

"So you're telling me Mikey's not a total piece of shit, then?"

"I can see why you'd get that impression, but no," she said, lifting her arms so I could measure her bust. "He puts up a big game, but he's really a sweetheart. I'll tell you a little story about him."

"Lay it on me." I jotted a measurement onto my notepad.

"Guy and I broke up for a while when I was in college. The long distance between the NHL and college just wasn't working out for us. Well, when I got brave and went back out to parties, I ended up falling apart in the bathroom. I never really got over

Guy. Anyway, Mikey saw me crying and held me while I cried, walked me home, made sure I had a snack and drank water. He's always been a big thuggy brother to me."

I stuck my lower lip out, picturing Mikey as this compassionate friend. "That's really sweet."

"It is. But the thug part's still there. I finally got up the courage to kiss someone new, and I started crying from that, too."

"Oh no, Kitty!"

"I was going through it at the time. Very dramatic college breakup. Anyway, Mikey thought the guy had done something to harm me and shoved the guy up against a wall and threatened the living daylights out of him."

"Oh, God, what a caveman!"

Kitty laughed. "Yeah. He's both. Total sweetheart, total caveman."

"So, nice in his own special way," I suggested.

"Mikey is nice in a uniquely Mikey way, but it's the biggest love you could ask for. He'd do anything for the people he loves. He's never found the right girl, though. But not for lack of trying," Kitty said, raising her eyebrows.

"Yes, I think I hear his tries all the time," I said.

Kitty grimaced. "I think I'll get you earplugs for Christmas." We both laughed. "Has he been hitting on you, too? He's a shameless flirt, but if he's trying to take you out and you like him, I'd go for it. I could see you two actually working."

My face went red. "Oh, he's tried. I live with my boyfriend, though."

"Shit, I'm sorry, Jessie. Put my foot right in my mouth with that one. I'm good for that."

"No worries," I said. "He knows and it hasn't stopped him at all."

Kitty gave a knowing nod. "And that's Mikey for ya. Hey, I know we don't know each other that well, but my engagement party's this weekend. It's at my house. I know it can be hard to meet new people when you're new in town. Would you like to come?"

"Oh, wow. That's really nice of you," I said, "but—"

"So you'll come?" Kitty had on a bright grin as she slipped her skirt back on.

I sighed. "Send me the details."

We exchanged numbers and she left the wardrobe trailer. Maybe L.A. would feel more like home soon.

4

MIKEY

The ride to the practice facility was cold, but it helped me wake up. I liked riding my bike to morning skate, the wind and sea air a nice way to come into the day. Southern California always had some kind of flowers in bloom, adding a sweet fragrance to even the February air.

In the locker room, I shot the shit with my teammates.

"Did you apologize to Jessie?" Guy asked as soon as I saw him.

"Uh, yeah. I tried anyway," I said, pulling my shirt over my head.

Beatty cackled, his missing front tooth adding to his goofy look. "What do you mean, tried? She hated you."

"We talked for a while on our balconies last night. But then I pissed her off again. Whatever. I did my part."

"How did you screw it up again?" Guy pushed, eyes narrowing.

"Don't worry about it. I don't need to be friends with my neighbors."

Beatty looked even more entertained. "Come on," he said, dancing his voice. "What did you say to her?"

"I, uh, asked her when was the last time her boyfriend gave her a real orgasm."

Laughter rang through the locker room. "Jesus, Mikey. You know that's not your business, right?"

"It is when I hear her faking it with him all the time!" I argued.

"No way. How do you know she's faking it?" Romelski chimed in.

"Yeah, I've never had anyone have to fake it," Beatty added. "I don't know what that sounds like."

"Shut the fuck up! You know what I mean," I snapped. "The ones who just want you to come back for more, so they put on a big show to try and stroke your ego. Every single one of you has had a faker at some point. Don't act like I'm special."

A grunt of agreement issued from the group.

"So you not only admitted that you hear them having sex, but you told her you know she's faking it?"

"I mean, yeah. She's hot. Maybe she's just been waiting for a big strapping hockey man to come make her dreams come true," I said. "Leave no stone unturned. No bone unturned."

Romelski groaned. "That was a terrible one, Mike."

Obi shook his head. "You have no filter, Mikey."

"No wonder you can't find anyone permanent," Leroy, my least favorite teammate, muttered.

"Hey, hey, none of that," Sorrento said. "Mikey's a great guy. He'll find someone."

Coach stalked in, interrupting my roasting session. "Alright, boys. We've got a big one against Vegas tonight. Get to the weight room."

❧

"Fuck."

My pads and helmet crunched as I smashed into the

boards. Vegas's forward slammed me right in the shoulder that had been acting up. I felt something pop, and that's never a good sign. Switching my stick to my other hand, I took off up the ice.

He stole the puck from me and crossed the blue line toward our goal. I gave everything I had with my legs, ignoring the sharp pain in my shoulder. Right as he got off a shot, I checked him so hard he tumbled backward.

"How'd you like that, asshole? Doesn't feel so nice, does it?"

There was an immediate whistle. It was a clean hit, and his wasn't, but of course I was going to get called on the penalty. Fucking typical. All because I had a reputation for being a bruiser. Still, I didn't argue as I was issued my two minutes. Maybe they'd feel some remorse when I went straight to the locker room after my time was up. I'd be stupid to keep playing on my bum shoulder when it was fucked up to start with.

I was out the rest of the game, spending time with the physical therapist. I didn't break anything, but some kind of strain was made worse by the hit. I wasn't likely to be heading out on the road trip that left for the next four days.

I was unbelievably pissed off. The physical therapist recommended hot and cold therapy while the team was gone, along with daily check-ins to see how the muscle was progressing.

As I sat in my car to go home, I scrolled through my DMs. I had plenty of options for beautiful women to console me, but anytime I went to reply to a message, I got a little pit in my stomach. Suddenly, my one-nights didn't sound so appealing.

I had a strict no-girlfriends policy, mostly for my own protection. I wasn't the kind of guy who people looked to for stability. I couldn't be relied on. Don't get me wrong. I'm a great friend. But whenever things got serious, I choked. It wasn't just dating. I could play great all season, and completely fall apart in the playoffs. I could have decent chemistry with a woman, but I'd forget about a date, or say the wrong name, or get distracted and determine that someone else better had to be out there.

Makes me sound like a real dick, doesn't it?

My thoughts continually turned back to Jessie. That bangin' body, her beautiful but slightly goofy features, the way I felt when I talked to her. She felt like everything I'd been looking for.

But a couple of big catches. One, I kept pissing her off. The lady doth protest too much or whatever that phrase is. I was genuinely trying to be her friend and she fought me on everything. I'm not even sure why I was attracted to her given all that, but there was some vibe with her that I couldn't ignore.

But the second catch was that she was a relationship girl, and she was actively in a relationship. I was an asshole for lusting after a taken woman.

But I knew she wasn't happy with him, and if my ears served me right, he was cheating on her.

I wanted better for her.

I wished it could be me for her.

But I was destined to forever get only part of my needs fulfilled. It was easy enough to find someone willing to fuck. And I didn't know what a real loving relationship looked like, anyway. I saw it in my friends' relationships, but my parents? No fucking way. My dad was a serial cheater, and my mom just went along with it. She pretended nothing was wrong with my dad being gone on "business trips" all week while she hung out with her bestie, my Aunt Lori. Not an actual aunt, just your mom's bestie that you call an aunt.

There was no hope for me with love.

I threw my phone in the cupholder of my car and went home alone.

5

JESSIE

I walked into our apartment, dropping my keys in the bowl by the door and sliding off my shoes.

"Hey," I called, looking into the kitchen. "Smells good."

"Hey," Cole said, glancing over his shoulder at me. "Making your favorite."

I hugged him from behind, smelling his familiar deodorant smell and eyeing the stir fry in the pan.

"What's the occasion?" I asked with a sly smile.

"Oh, you know. I got a sexy text from someone special. Thought I'd celebrate," he said, tugging me to him for a kiss. "Check the fridge."

I opened the door to find a fresh six-pack of amber beer. More his favorite than mine. Still, I didn't want to insult his efforts. "Wow. Thanks, babe."

I pushed his cutting board back on the counter and popped up to sit on the edge. "Think you want to get started now?" I asked suggestively, pulling at his shirt.

"Babe, not in the kitchen," he whined. "There's food here."

"I know," I said. "It's sexy."

"What's gotten into you?" Cole asked. "You're never like this."

"Can't a girl want her hot boyfriend?" I scraped his carefully coiffed hair out of its designated shape. I liked Cole a little mussed up. He softened at my playfulness, trying to play along.

"I'm certainly not complaining," he said, smiling into a kiss. I pulled back and looked into his eyes, the bright blue glowing. I hadn't taken the time to appreciate Cole in so long, and I felt a pang of guilt about it. Cole cut his glance to the stove. "I have to stir dinner, babe."

"Yeah. Sure," I said. What I really, desperately wanted was for him to eat me out on the kitchen counter. I wanted Cole to be so hungry for me that he couldn't wait. I tried to entice him again, squirming with my thighs together. "I thought about you all the way home. I'm already so wet, Cole."

"Five minutes to dinner," he sighed, forking the rice on the stove. I could give a shit about eating. I wanted to be eaten. But I had to respect his soft "no." "How was work?"

We talked about our days and sat down to eat. I tried not to get disappointed, but the wind was out of my sails. Since Ben had planted the idea of satisfying me in my head, I felt more turned on than I'd been in my life. Not that I wanted to cheat on Cole or get with Ben, but it made me realize how unmet my needs were.

Things were tense as Cole and I did dishes. Again, a thing I thought could have waited til later in favor of passionate sex, but he wanted everything nice.

Still, I tried my prior tactic. I hopped up on the counter and spread my legs.

"You want dessert, baby?"

Cole's face turned dark. "Are you cheating on me, Jessie?"

"What?!"

"This is so not like you. It's almost like you got this idea from someone else."

My cheeks burned, because my surge of libido kind of had come from someone else. But it's not like I was acting on it with someone else. It just gave me ideas. "No. That's not it at all."

Cole raked a hand through his hair. "I'm sorry, babe. Work's just really stressful right now and you're always up so early. We hardly see each other."

"I know," I said softly. "I just wanted to connect with you like this."

"Fuck." He blew out a breath. "I ruined it, didn't I?"

I mean, yeah, he kinda did when he rejected me three times before. It was super nice of him to make my favorite dinner and get special drinks, but I'd rather have banged on the living room floor and ordered Chinese takeout to eat naked.

But I didn't communicate that, and he was trying. I was trying, too.

Maybe it was my fault for trying.

"No, it's alright," I said. "Wanna talk in bed?"

Cole got a soft smile. "Yeah. Let's do that."

In the bedroom, Cole stripped off his shirt and tossed it in the hamper unceremoniously. As he dropped his pants, I stood in the doorway, feeling awkward.

"I was hoping maybe we could undress each other."

Cole pressed a hand to his forehead. "You're right. I'm on autopilot. Sorry, babe. Come here."

I walked to meet him by our bed, the bed we bought when we moved to L.A. Cole was excited about his signing bonus and anyway, we weren't totally sure our bed from New York didn't have bedbugs. Yikes.

"I've missed you," he whispered before kissing me and tugging at the hem of my dress. A dress that would have granted him perfect access to my pussy in the kitchen, if he'd been so inclined. I'd even considered it when I laid out my clothes the night before. I shoved thoughts of Mikey's words out of my head and focused on the man who had been there for me for the last four years.

Clothes off, Cole playfully pushed me back to the bed and offered his cock to me. With the height of our bed, it always ended up in my face. I gave him a courtesy lick and stroke, then surrounded him with my breasts. He'd always been crazy about them.

"Want more?" I asked.

"Suck me, Jessie," he begged.

"I think maybe I should go first this time," I said.

And then, he laughed, shaking his head.

My stomach dropped. The man who was supposed to love me was laughing at my request for pleasure.

"Babe, it's so hard to get you off like that," he whined, justifying himself to my hurt expression.

"So you won't even try?" My cheeks flamed. I couldn't believe I had to lay it out for him like that.

"I just don't see the point," he said.

"The point is me feeling good," I said, trying not to cry.

"Aw, Jess. Don't be like that. I'm sorry. I just feel like a failure at it."

"When was the last time you tried?" I yelled.

He held up his hands. "Baby, I'm sorry. I'll go down on you. Don't cry over it," Cole said, like he was doing me some huge favor. "Here."

He bent and lowered his tongue into my slit, no preamble. Well, something's better than nothing. I grasped his hair and rolled my hips, trying to ignore all our blunders up to this point and get in the zone.

"Too hard," I hissed as he bludgered my clit with his tongue.

He changed his pace and raised his eyebrows, looking up at me. "That's better," I assured him. I sat back, doing my best to enjoy the experience.

But the next time I looked down at him, he looked miserable. That wasn't what I wanted. I wanted him to want it with me. I wanted him to be so overcome with the need to satisfy me that he'd do whatever it took. I always did whatever it took for him.

I decided to grant him mercy.

Breathlessly, I spoke. "Fuck me, Cole."

His relief was palpable. He climbed on top of me, wiping my arousal off his face as he slid into me. Again, no preamble. He thrust into me, again and again, but I just wasn't feeling it. He was making love to a person, but it wasn't me.

"Can you push down a little more?" I asked, trying to bring his attention to me.

"Huh?" Cole seemed truly confused.

"It feels better for me if you push down," I said, trying to explain.

"Oh. Uh, okay," he said. I moved my hips with him, guiding him where I wanted him. He wasn't getting it. That's okay. I could try something else.

"Can I get on top?"

"Sure, babe," he said, as if I'd asked if we could order pizza for dinner.

Still, I tried. I rode him, watching his eyes, guiding his hands to my breasts.

"Shit, Jessie, you're too hot," he gasped, then lost himself inside me. I smiled, because I did love getting him off. But I like getting off, too. I rode him through his peak, enjoying his sated expression. "Did you go?"

"Not yet. Can I keep going? You're still hard."

"What?" He looked at me like I'd sprouted another arm. "You always get off."

I didn't have the heart to tell him that no, I didn't always get off. I brought his hands to my hips and started to move again. "What if you put a finger in my ass?"

"What the fuck is this, Jessie?" The disgust on his face was heartbreaking. "Since when do you ask for it up the ass?"

My cheeks flushed. "Forget I asked."

He narrowed his eyes. "I feel like I don't even know you right now, Jess. What the hell?"

"I wanna come, Cole. Can I grab a toy to use together?"

He scrunched up his nose. "Together? Those are . . . yours. For you. Alone. But I guess? Make it quick, though. I'm tired."

Consider the wind officially out of my sails. "Just forget it." I climbed off him and shoved a wad of tissues in my crotch. I hobbled to the bathroom to get ready for bed, stewing as I brushed my teeth. Maybe I was being unfair. He really didn't know I hadn't gotten off all those other times. That wasn't his fault.

But the fact that he wouldn't work with me to finish the job when he did know I didn't get off was 100% his problem. I seethed.

When I came back to bed, Cole was already asleep. But not me. Another long, sleepless night likely awaited me.

6

MIKEY

When I got home from the arena around midnight, I threw on my swim trunks and headed for the rooftop pool. Yeah, it was cold as shit, but that was the point. In and out of the pool and hot tub should make it at least comfortable enough so I could sleep.

I didn't expect anyone to be up there, so I nearly jumped out of my skin when I saw a figure by the pool.

Jessalyn, sitting with her phone out, playing some podcast, and working on some knitting.

"Hey, Sweet Cheeks," I said. She startled.

"Jesus, Jockey, you're always sneaking up on me," she scolded. Then with a death glare, she started gathering her things.

"Wait, wait, don't leave on account of me," I said. "I won't bother you. You can keep listening to your thing. What is it?"

"A murder podcast," she said spitefully. "I don't want it to be a group listening party."

"Suit yourself. But don't leave. Can't we chat?"

"I think the other night proved we can't," she huffed.

I didn't believe her, so I pushed past her spite and anger. "What are you doing up here so late? It's after midnight."

She looked resigned. "I come up here when I can't sleep. Which is a lot."

"Ah. An insomniac," I said.

"Going for a swim?" she asked. "You'll freeze."

"That's kinda the point. My shoulder's worse. I'm out for a few games."

Jessie's face went sympathetic. "I'm sorry. That must suck."

Her softness surprised me. Normally she fought me constantly. "Thanks. It does suck. Who got murdered this time?"

She looked alarmed. "What?"

"On your show. What murder are they talking about?"

"It's a series on the Golden State Killer," she said.

"Didn't he live here? Maybe that's what's keeping you up at night."

She laughed and her smile lingered. It was striking. She had two big front teeth that gave her a bunny-like appearance and a tiny dimple on one cheek. I liked how she wasn't perfectly symmetrical. There was nothing fake about her, unlike the women who I usually frequented.

I'd never seen Jessie smile before, not with teeth. Her little wispy brown bangs accentuated her hazel eyes. The overall appearance reminded me of a young Stevie Nicks, except with just-above-the-shoulders brown hair. She was stunning. "They actually soothe me, believe it or not."

"Stop right there," I said, sitting on the edge of her pool chair. "Stay like that."

Her eyes got big and her smile faded. "What? Is there a bug on me?"

"No. You've never smiled at me. This is a big moment in our friendship. I want to look longer."

Jessie clapped her hands over her mouth and squealed. My fingers circled her wrists, trying to pry them away.

"Who are you, Ben Mikey Jockey? What is your deal anyway?" she asked as she fought me off.

"I'm your new best friend," I said with a grin.

"No, you're fucking not!"

"Okay, maybe not best friend, but can we at least call a truce? I've been told I lack a filter, but I swear I mean no harm."

"Get out of my bubble and I'll think about it!" she barked.

"Fine," I said, standing and peeling off my shirt. I flexed my pecs. "Truce now?"

"Are you always this . . ." She frowned at me, searching for the word.

"Beautiful? Muscular? Friendly? Gorgeous? Those are all good words, Jessalyn."

She got back to her knitting and chuckled. "I was thinking more 'full of shit.' Are you always this full of shit?"

"Is that a good quality or a bad one?" I wiggled my eyebrows at her.

She just shook her head. "What are we gonna do with you, Jockey?"

"Call a truce, that's what."

"Fine. Truce."

"Great. Now you get to watch me freeze my ass off."

"I'll keep knitting, thanks."

It's no lie. I dipped a toe in the frigid water. Not ice bath cold, but ball-shriveling cold. An involuntary yelp escaped me when my privates hit the water. Jessie stifled a laugh. To combat the cold, I submerged myself completely, the noise in my head silencing. I realized how much my shoulder pain was creating a background din of chaos. When I surfaced, I let out a loud, exhilarated yell, flipping my wet hair back.

"Come on in, Jessalyn! The water's fine!"

"I'll take your word for it," she said on a laugh. "You live loud, don't you?"

"You of all people should know I do." I shuffled around the shallow end, the pain in my shoulder more isolated thanks to the cold. Silence fell between us. Jessie pressed play on her podcast and got back into her knitting. The hosts graphically detailed one of the almost-murders.

"Jesus, Jessalyn. This relaxes you?"

She smirked. "I'm not the only one. These are popular for a reason."

"I don't see why. It's horrifying."

"It's kind of like, if I know the absolute worst thing that could happen to me, anything else doesn't seem so bad," she explained.

"That's grim."

"I think it's strangely optimistic. Like well, at least I'm not being murdered."

I walked to the edge of the pool, resting my elbows on the concrete. "Jessie, you deserve more than just not being murdered. Life's more than avoiding the worst-case scenario."

Her face went stony as she considered what I said. Her eyes looked sad. "Isn't that what surviving is about, though?"

"I don't want to just survive. I want to live. Big. Love hard. Laugh often. All that shit that's on coffee mugs."

Her eyebrows went up. "Benjamin Michael Jockey, I never pegged you for a softie. You're a live laugh love girlie!"

I posed with a dainty simper. "More than a pretty face."

"I'm serious. You're cocky, but underneath it, you're hiding this . . . I don't know what to call it."

"Humanity?"

She gave me a wry smile. "Yeah. Humanity."

"Well, someone recently told me I might be emotionally unavailable. I'm pushing myself out of my comfort zone."

"Proud of you, Jockey." She studied me with curious eyes. I soaked up the attention.

From a woman who was already taken. By some guy who didn't know how good he had it. By a guy who was betraying her trust.

Jessalyn was sweet, insightful, pensive, and funny. Or that's how she was when she wasn't mad at me. Not to mention those young Stevie Nicks looks and those boobs I couldn't stop thinking about in my face.

But I was a piece of shit who didn't deserve her any more than her cheating boyfriend did.

"Hey, you were right about something," she said with a mischievous look.

My heart took off. Was she flirting back with me? This was a dream.

"What's that?"

"I do actually know your friend from West Virginia."

"HA! I knew it!"

"But in fairness, I don't know her from home. We work on the same show here. We talked about you while I was getting her measurements for something."

"You work on Kitty's show? I watch that! You do the outfits?"

She laughed. "Yeah. I do the outfits."

I bit my lip, feeling smug. "So what did you two ladies have to say about me?"

"Kitty actually said you're a really good friend. Great guy to have on your side," she said, acting skeptical.

"That's what I've been trying to tell you, Jessalyn. I'm excellent best friend material."

Jessie tipped her head to the side. "She also issued her sympathy for me living next to you."

I stuck out my bottom lip. "I'm not that bad."

"I'll record it for you sometime, Jockey. It's bad."

Talking to Jessie, I couldn't fathom having any material for her to record. In fact, it had just been me and my hand since I met her. And kind of a lot of my hand.

It wasn't my fault her bratty attitude and curvy body did shit to me. Still, I did feel a little guilty about it. Friends don't fantasize about friends' bodies, do they?

I was shivering, so I got out of the pool and headed for the hot tub. The scalding water was a welcome relief to my chilled skin and the cool night air.

"Psst," I called once I got in.

"Hmm?" Jessie looked up with a questioning face.

"It feels really nice in here. You should get in."

"I don't have my swimsuit."

"You don't need one," I said with a grin.

"Dream on, Jockey. Does that shit actually work on your conquests?"

"Honestly, I don't even have to try this hard," I admitted.

"Wow. Must be nice to be rich and swimming in puss."

"It has perks, but there are downsides, too."

We did our own thing in silence for a while, then my shoulder did a really weird thing. I'd dislocated it when I was a kid and it was never quite the same. My shoulder injury was right around that area. I was actually stuck. "Hey. Um. Jessie?"

"Yeah?"

"Can you come help me?"

"Is this a trick?"

"No, my shoulder's stuck." She looked up to find my elbow stuck up out of the water and my face contorted from the pain.

"Geez. Okay." She rushed over and stepped her legs into the water. "What do you need me to do?"

"I think it just needs to be popped back into place. Push like, right there."

Jessie's fist laid into the spot I'd indicated on my upper back and I yelped.

"Too much?"

"No, keep going."

With a shift, my shoulder was back where it should be. I breathed out hard. She didn't step away right away, rubbing the muscles. Her hands felt so nice.

"Better?" she asked, sitting on the lip of the tub behind me and putting her legs on either side of me.

"Yeah. That feels really good, right there." I leaned into her hands, head dropping back onto her bare thigh as relief flooded my muscles. Her and tiny shorts. She must have stock in them. "Fuck, these hands are magic."

"If anyone hears you say that they're going to think I'm giving out handies in the hot tub," she quipped. I gazed up at her, grinning as she continued rubbing my back. It was the closest we'd ever been since her tits were in my face that first night. Why was that suddenly seeming like the best birthday present I ever got?

"I'm serious. I think the physical therapy staff is hiring if you need a job."

"Ha. Would probably pay more than costume design."

"I thought people got rich in Ol' Hollywood," I said.

"I'm still junior. I'm an apprentice for now, so I don't make much."

"Doesn't your boyfriend cover your costs?"

Her hands slowed and she stepped away, moving to the edge of the hot tub by the stairs. "We never merged accounts or anything. I pay him rent."

"Are you fucking kidding me?" I was outraged. Not only was this guy cheating on her and not meeting her physical needs, but he couldn't even pay for her while she was working on her career? "Isn't he a finance bro?"

"I mean, yeah."

"And he can't support you while you work toward your dream."

"He helps. He covers groceries a lot. And we take turns

going to the store."

"Wow. What a guy." I shook my head. "Our rent ain't cheap, Jessie."

"I'm aware," she said, her cheeks burning.

Fuck. No filter got me in trouble again. "Hey. I'm not trying to make you feel bad. But I'd never treat a woman like that."

She rolled her eyes. "It's more equal. We both have to contribute. I don't expect him to be my knight in shining armor when I'm a capable adult."

"It shouldn't matter, Jessalyn. He should support your dreams. I'm sure you've supported his."

She went quiet again. "I should get back to knitting."

"Give me your phone."

She drew back. "What? Why?"

"I'm going to make you a playlist so you can actually sleep. And something soothing to listen to on your drive. You can't keep listening to sad murder stuff and expect to sleep."

"I'm glad you think you can fix years of insomnia with a playlist or two."

"Have you tried it, though? Music is the best."

To my shock, she pulled out her phone and handed it to me. "Knock yourself out."

JESSIE WAS SO STILL that I thought she was asleep. But when I got close, drying myself off as I went, I saw that her eyes were open. I handed her phone back.

"I think you're going to like it. Do you work tomorrow?"

"No, I'm off weekends."

"Do you ever fall asleep up here?" I asked.

"All the time."

I leveled her with a look. "And you're not worried about

getting murdered that way? Literally a sitting duck on the roof?"

"Well, at least they'd know someone from the building did it."

I sighed, grabbing extra towels from the rack by the pool and walking to Jessie's chair.

"Lay back."

She quirked an eyebrow at me but did as I asked. I covered her legs with one towel and her upper half with the other.

"Want me to tell you a bedtime story or would you rather me sing a song?"

"Seriously, Ben? What are you doing?"

"Becoming your best friend."

"Jockey," she warned. I settled into the pool chair next to her and covered myself in towels, too.

"What's the most relaxing place you've ever been?"

"No. Back up. You were going to sing to me? What song?"

"Paradise."

"Like Coldplay or like Guns N' Roses?" she asked.

"Neither. John Prine. That Muhlenberg County song from Kentucky. My mom used to sing it when we couldn't sleep."

"That's surprisingly sweet," she said, looking at me with puppy dog eyes.

"I'm going to ignore the shrouded insult in there."

"Sorry. I'm still adjusting to you not being a total jock meat-head thug."

"I know. That's why I'm being so forgiving," I said with a grin. "Now answer my question. What's the most relaxing place you've ever been?"

Jessie took a deep breath, closing her eyes for a moment. "I used to go to summer camp on a lake. Every night when the sun went down, my friends and I would sneak off for some quiet time, just watching the sunset over the lake. It was really nice."

"Okay, great. I can work with that. Keep your eyes closed."

That, of course, made her eyes pop open to give me a scathing look.

"Promise I'm just helping here." She closed her eyes and I went on. "Once upon a time, there was a girl named Jessalyn. She loved going away for summer camp with her friends. She did camp stuff all day, like capture the flag, greased watermelon contests, and cafeteria food fights."

Jessie giggled, but kept her eyes closed. She looked so pretty with her head cocked to the side, going with me as I painted her a mental picture.

"After one especially tiring day, she and her new best friend, Ben," she giggled again, "snuck away from the campfire to watch the sun set over the lake. She was so exhausted from a long day of camp fun, but she was glad to be in the calming presence of her bestie, Ben. Ben and Jessalyn listened to the wind rustling through the trees lining the lake, the bugs chirping, and the birds singing their goodnight songs."

I looked over to find Jess's face relaxed. I softened my voice and kept going.

"She had on a cozy sweatshirt and felt the warmth of her friend Ben's company. The smell of the campfire was in her hair, the taste of burnt marshmallows on her tongue. She closed her eyes against the pinks and oranges of the sunset, enjoying the final moments of a good day."

I stopped talking and she didn't move. Her breathing was long and steady. I checked my phone. Almost 2 a.m.

I knew she slept up there alone sometimes, but I couldn't in good conscience leave her up there by herself. So, I settled in and went to sleep myself.

Some time later, I was awakened by wet drops hitting my face. A rare Los Angeles rain.

"Jessie," I said, trying to wake her. Her face was spattered with rain drops, her eyelashes covered in them. I stroked her arm, but she didn't budge. "Jessie Girl."

I tried it all. She wasn't waking up. I stretched my shoulder. It seemed better than before. Jessie's magic fingers had done something to reset it. I could carry her without hurting myself, right? I lifted probably double her weight at work.

So, I slid my arms under her and carried her to the elevator.

7

JESSIE

All of this part is in a daze.

Thunder. Lightning. A jolt through my entire body. Silence.

It was one of my nightmares, but like usual, I couldn't tell that it wasn't real. It's hard to tell sometimes what's reality and what's still part of the dream, almost like they have layers.

"Baby, what's wrong?" a voice asked me. Tears poured down my face. I tried to explain it, but all I could do was cry. "It's okay, honey. It's just a dream. You're okay."

Strong arms surrounded and held me. A hand stroked my back. I sobbed as a soft cloth wiped my tears. "You're safe, Jessie." A kiss pressed to the top of my head. "I've got you. It was just a dream."

I let myself be wrapped up in the warmth. Vibrations of a familiar song shook through whatever I was snuggling. A sweet, deep voice, like honey, slowed my pounding heart and lulled me back to sleep.

~

Hours later, I actually felt *good*.

I'd slept. My muscles felt good. I was warm. My head was nestled onto Cole, something he rarely let me do because he doesn't like cuddles when he sleeps. His arm was even wrapped around me, keeping me snug and secure. Maybe all wasn't lost with Cole and me.

I hadn't slept that well in months. Maybe years? I couldn't remember the last time I slept like that — no sleeping pill, no insane sleep hygiene routine.

Except Cole didn't smell like Cole. It was cleaner, an aquatic scent. And his body felt firmer than usual. I stirred, trying to put it all together. I pressed a kiss to his neck, which was scruffier than his typical clean shave.

"Morning, babe," I rasped. "You smell good." My hand slid down and brushed over a very impressive hard-on. I moved my fingers over his shaft, thinking ahead to a morning romp. Maybe it would be more successful than the night before.

"Hey," came a deep voice. Deeper than Cole's. My head snapped up.

Oh my God. *Mikey*.

I shoved myself away, shaking. "What? What the fuck happened?!" Panic was the undertow that threatened to suck me under. Mikey reached for my hand, but I held it away.

"Hey, relax, Jess. It's okay."

"Okay?! I was snuggling in your chest and touching your dick! I kissed your neck!"

"I'll forgive it," he said with a chuckle. "But you can go back for more if you want."

"Jesus, God, no!" I shrieked.

"Okay, you don't have to act horrified."

"What happened?!"

"You fell asleep on the rooftop. I stayed up there with you because I didn't want you to get murdered. Then it started raining. I couldn't wake you up, so I carried you down here."

"Raining? Was it storming? Was there thunder?"

Ben looked confused. "No. It wasn't. Anyway, I tried to get into your apartment, but Cole didn't answer and I didn't want to dig through your pockets for your keys."

"Wha...how...your shoulder?"

"It was fine. You're not that heavy," he assured me. "And you had a nightmare. Do you get those a lot?"

Mikey was the one who helped me through my nightmare? There was so much information to take in.

"You cuddled me! With a boner!" I tucked my legs under me. I was still in my same clothes from the night before. We weren't even under Ben's sheets. He'd pulled a blanket over us on top of the duvet. That probably confirmed that nothing untoward happened beyond the canoodling I'd just initiated. Entirely on accident.

"It's just morning wood, Jessalyn. It'll go away in a minute. I was sleeping, too, you know." Ben rubbed his fingers across his forehead and yawned. "You want coffee?"

"Coffee? No. I need to leave. Where are my shoes?"

"I threw them down by the door."

I stood, crossing my arms over my chest. "Why were we snuggling?"

"That was all you, Sweet Cheeks. I put you on your side and you just came over," Ben said with a laugh.

"Why didn't you sleep on the couch?"

Ben seemed annoyed. "I'm sorry, princess. I wanted a good night of sleep, too. Seems like you slept pretty damn good, so I'm not sure why you're complaining so much. I didn't want you to wake up and freak out not knowing where you were."

My eyes must have been bugged out of my head as I processed everything.

"Shit, my phone!" I cried.

"I plugged it in. It's on the kitchen island."

I scrambled out of the room, tears pricking my eyes. Ben

came into the kitchen as I was reading my messages, looking fine as hell in a pair of gray sweatpants and a loose t-shirt. The shirt I'd just had my face nestled into.

My phone held message after message of Cole looking for me. *Where are you? Why didn't you come home? Hope you're okay, Caterpillar. Well, I'm going for my run.*

"Why are you so upset?" Ben asked.

"Cole's going to think I cheated. He's already accused me of it."

Ben shook his head. "Fuck Cole." His voice was harsh. I glared at him. Ben went on. "That guy isn't treating you the way you deserve, Jessie."

"Listen, you might think you know everything about me, but you don't know shit. Alright, Jockey? I have to go home."

I turned to go but Ben crossed the room at light speed. I backed up against the door and he put a hand on the door-frame, leaning toward me. His body's heat pressed into me, though we weren't actually touching. He hung his head to meet mine, amber eyes burning with an intensity I hadn't seen. His voice came out as a commanding growl.

"You think he's giving you what you want. You think you want nice. Stable. Boring. But how's that working out for you? He's accusing you of cheating on him."

Ben's eyes flicked between mine, and he went on. "Nice isn't what you need. You need someone who scares you a little bit. Someone who surprises you. Someone who supports you just as much as you support them. Someone who loves you so fully and completely that there'd be no reason to think you'd ever cheat. Someone who would stop the elevator to push your skirt up and feast on you. Someone who would fuck you so good in the coat closet at a party that they have to put their hand over your mouth to keep you from screaming. Someone who would treat you like the princess you are on the streets but turn you loose at home in ways you never imagined. Someone who would make you come until you can't fucking stand it and you're begging for mercy. That's what you need, Jessalyn. You need to be loved, well and thoroughly."

I trembled under him, breathless. Why was I so wet? Why were my nipples tiny hardened peaks? Why did his mouth look so tempting gaping in front of mine? Why could I feel every inch of my own skin? Why did I want to reach out and push his pants down, drop to my knees, and show him what a woman I am?

"I have to go," I managed. He stepped back to let me leave.

Before the door slammed behind me, Ben called, "You're welcome."

"IT'S NOT A GOOD LOOK, JESSIE," Cole moped. "Think of it from my perspective."

We stood in our kitchen on opposite ends of the counter. It was better that way. He was just back from his Saturday morning run and smelled atrocious.

"Yeah, I get that. But I swear, nothing happened. I just fell asleep. He tried to bring me here but you didn't hear the door."

The coffee pot beeped as the final drops gurgled into the carafe, and I poured us each a cup. I started to put cream in Cole's cup.

"I just like it black now," he said miserably.

"Oh? When did that start?"

"I started buying us better coffee. It doesn't need cream. You didn't even notice."

"Cole, that's not fair. I did notice. I just think all coffee needs cream. Sorry, I usually drink coffee at 4:30 in the morning. I'm not exactly feeling philosophical about coffee at that hour."

We fell quiet as we sipped from our mugs. His was from the

one time we took his niece to Disneyland. Mine was an ode to the biscuits from my favorite biscuit shop back home.

Cole ran a hand through his hair, his agitation building again. "That jock try to touch you?"

I focused on keeping my breathing even and remaining calm. I didn't want to give anything away to Cole, especially not Mikey's little speech against his front door that left me soaking wet. I woke up in Mikey's arms. He definitely touched me when I had my nightmare. And sang me back to sleep. But it wasn't sexual. He was just sweet. If anything, I was the accidental creep.

"No. Everything was fine. It was sleeping. That's it," I said. "If anything, I should thank him. I was rude when I left."

Cole rolled his eyes. "Don't think he's not trying to hit on you, Jess. You're so naïve sometimes."

"Jesus, Cole, I'm a woman living in this world. Don't you think I know how to handle the advances of men? Give me a little credit."

I moved to our bedroom to put on some clothes for a walk. I needed out of our apartment. Cole followed me.

"Where are you going?"

"For a walk."

"So you're just running off? We have more to discuss."

I turned to him, flailing my hands. "What else is there to say? You went for a run this morning when you thought I was a missing person. You've decided I'm cheating on you, so therefore I must be. Isn't that the long and short of it?"

"Don't get like this," he warned.

"Then say whatever it is you think I need to hear."

"Fine. It's hard for me to trust you right now. You come out of nowhere with this crazy sex stuff and sleeping in beds with other men. And you expect me to be fine with it. How are you so sure he didn't take advantage of you, Jessie?"

I shoved my shirt over my head and stomped toward him.

"Even if he had, how would that be *my* fault? Should I have not worn that dress, either? Jesus, Cole. I'm out of here."

"Jessie, you know I wouldn't blame you if he did!" Cole tried.

"Yeah, then why are you?" I had the door handle in my hand. "And by the way, if wanting you to want me or wishing you cared about my pleasure enough to get me off first is 'crazy sex stuff,' then I guess I've just been a freak all along."

I slammed the door behind me on my way out.

8

JESSIE

The air was tight in our apartment. I slid on my earrings and adjusted my wrap dress to cover my boobs better. Cole sat on the bed, pulling his socks on.

"Sorry I can't come. It was really last minute, though, and you know I've had this thing with the guys," he said.

I met his eyes in the vanity mirror. "It's fine. I can go stag."

"Come here, baby." Cole grabbed my hand, looking up at me with his big blue eyes shining. "You still mad at me?"

"I don't know. Do you not trust me?"

He chewed the inside of his lip. "I do. I trust you. I'm sorry."

He stood, opening his arms for a hug. Stiffly, I went into it. He didn't say what he was sorry for. He did this sometimes, acting like he was sorry for something but not naming it, so it was a blanket apology for whatever the fuck he did.

"I love you, Caterpillar." He used his nickname for me from when we met, which he only pulled out when he was desperate. He called me that because of how I used to crawl up on him.

"Love you, too." I said it, but for the first time, the words felt like ash in my mouth. "I'd better get going. Glendale's a long drive."

I turned to walk, but he pulled me back into a kiss. He tried to deepen it, but I cut it off. "See you later."

I STOOD against the wall of Kitty's patio. Guests mingled all around the pool, and a tent was set up over the small yard. There were a lot of exceptionally tall men, some flanked by petite blonde women and some solo. I figured that had to be Kitty's fiancé's teammates. Some faces looked familiar from Mikey's rager that I broke up.

I spotted one of the writers from work and decided to go rub elbows. Brent was a quirky guy, what you'd expect from a comedy writer.

"Jessie! Great to see you here! I didn't know you and Kitty were close."

I wasn't even sure he knew my name until that moment. "Oh, she was kind enough to invite me."

"That Kitty's a good egg," he said. A presence loomed over my shoulder. "Is this your boyfriend?"

I turned to find Mikey looking very put together in a suit. He touched a hand to my lower back. I forced out a "hey."

"Hi," he grunted, shifting his gaze to Brent.

"Oh, this is, uh, Mikey."

"This guy bothering you, Jessie?" Mikey growled, giving Brent a firm stink eye.

I drew back, affronted by Mikey's rude behavior. "What? No. Not at all. Brent Mercer, this is Mikey. Mikey, this is Brent. He's a writer from work. One of Kitty's colleagues. You know, on the show you like?"

"One of Jessie's colleagues, too," Brent added with a wide smile, trying to cut the tension.

Mikey extended his hand, gripping Brent's fingers maybe a hair too hard. "Ben Miknevicius. Mikey."

"Great to meet you. Are you one of Guy's . . . ?" Brent asked.

"Best friends? Teammates? Yeah. Both." Mikey softened, seemingly pleased by having some sort of dominant edge over silly old Brent. "I'm a groomsman in the wedding."

"Oh, how fun! Kitty asked me to officiate, so I guess we'll all have a role," Brent said, continuing to be warm when Mikey was being a real dick.

Mikey took a sip from his beer, not taking his eyes off Brent until he cut them to me. "Doesn't Jessie look pretty tonight?"

Brent's face flushed pink. "Uh, yeah, Jess. Really nice dress." He scrambled for something to say. "Did you make that dress?"

"No, no," I said, trying to lighten the mood. "I altered it, but I alter most everything I buy a little."

"We could have ridden together, Jess. Saved on gas," Mikey said, cocking his head to the side.

"Mikey and I are neighbors," I said to Brent.

Luckily, a knife clinked on a glass at that moment, and a very pretty woman with luscious long blonde hair stepped onto the small platform in the tent. She talked a little about Guy and Kitty as a couple while they stood beside her. They really were a beautiful couple. Mikey's hand touched my lower back again, steering me toward the tent.

"What are you doing?" I hissed.

"That guy likes you, Jessalyn. Be careful," he warned. I rolled my eyes.

"You're not my keeper, Benjamin."

He shrugged and kept his eyes on the woman speaking. We toasted the happy couple and Mikey turned to me, clinking his beer bottle to my champagne flute.

"Cheers, Sweet Cheeks," he rumbled in my ear before walking to the stage and taking the microphone from the woman.

"Hey, everybody. I know I'm making Kitty and Stelle sweat by having this microphone in my hand, but I felt like I should say something." His voice was deep with a rasp to it. I didn't realize how intriguing it was until he was smiling in front of a room full of people. He did have a really nice smile, and other than his little alpha male moments, he was a genuinely kind man. Not everyone would have taken care of me the way he did the night before.

A whoop went up from the crowd, presumably from his teammates. "For those who don't know me, I'm Mikey, Guy's best friend since college and Kitty's best friend by proxy. I've known them since Guy said there was a girl from West Virginia who was really special to him. Then they were just 'best friends' in college, totally angst-filled and in denial of their feelings for each other. I got to watch Guy toil away, waiting for the day that Kitty would love him the way he loved her."

Kitty pushed out her lower lip and looked up at Guy. "Poor baby," she mouthed, kissing his cheek.

"But when they came back from that fateful Thanksgiving break where her brother Frank broke Stelle's face," the crowd laughed, "there was no breaking them apart. And I was unspeakably jealous. Just ate up inside over them paying so much attention to each other. But then, Guy left both me and Kitty for the NHL to be a big hotshot star." Laughs broke again. It was fun to see Mikey be so charming. "Kitty and I were still back at Alden, and I got to pick up the pieces."

Everyone went silent. "Not like that. Not like that. Kitty and I never—uh, yeah, we didn't do that stuff. Stelle, I swear, we weren't ever like that. Never have been. Nope." Guy raised his eyebrows at Mikey and the laughs swelled again.

He pulled at the collar of his shirt and acted like he was dabbing sweat from his brow. "Anyway. I'm glad *as a friend* to *both of them* that we're all here together in L.A. and that we get to see them make this commitment to each other. I've known it was coming since college, because I can't imagine a world where they don't end up together." Kitty guffawed and wiped at her eye. "To many years of health and happiness for Guy and Kitty."

Mikey raised his glass, as did everyone else in the tent.

I realized once again how much I'd underestimated Mikey.

9

MIKEY

Jess sat at a table in Kitty's backyard, scrolling her phone and daintily sipping her champagne. What broke my heart about it wasn't that she was alone, because I understand needing a moment to breathe during social occasions. What killed me was that her eyes were so sad.

"Where's your man?"

"Huh?" Jessie looked up with those tired, sad eyes, clicking off her phone screen.

"Where's Cole?"

"He had another thing tonight. I'm flying solo."

I nodded, but my mind was alight. Hearing another woman's voice in their apartment haunted me. Not only that, but I heard their fight after she left my apartment clear as a bell. He accused her, and me, of some pretty fucked up stuff. I hated him for doing that to her.

Fuck it. I held out my hand. "Dance?"

Jess stared at my outstretched hand. "What?"

I chuckled. "Will you dance with me, Jessalyn?"

She narrowed her eyes. "I thought you hated me."

"I think that's all you, Sweet Cheeks."

Her cheeks pinked. "Don't call me that."

"Hate me all you want, but come dance with me," I said.

"No. You hate me. You think I'm stuck up and a party pooper and morbid for listening to my murder podcasts and prissy because I like being in my boring relationship and not sleeping around."

I leaned down closer to her. "Maybe he says that to you, honey, but that ain't me." Her eyes rounded. I'd hit a nerve. "I wanna be your best friend, remember?"

Jessie sputtered, trying to find some words. I held out my hand again. "Come on. One dance. I don't bite."

She smirked, putting her hand in mine. "You keep saying you won't bite, which makes it seem like that's exactly what you'll do."

I laughed, shaking my head as I walked her to the dance floor in the tent. "I don't know where you got this idea that I'm out to get you, Jessalyn."

I squared us up, holding her right hand and slipping my other hand to her waist. She put her left hand on my shoulder, but kept her distance, not leaning into me. It was a slower song, so we could talk. But she was quiet, her eyes searching my chest.

"I never said thank you. For last night." Her gaze stayed fixed on my shirt, but she quickly flicked a glance up at me.

"You're welcome. Sorry it caused unrest in your house."

Her cheeks burned again. "That's—it's—he'll get over it. We're working it out."

I clenched my teeth. I wasn't going to have molars if Jessie stayed with Cole much longer. He was cheating on her. He didn't deserve for her to 'work it out' with him. He deserved to dine on my fist for fucking dinner and spit up chiclets for dessert.

"Nice party," she said. "They really are a great couple. Rare."

"Why rare?" I asked.

She rubbed her lips together, looking at the white fabric draped over us. "Not every love is that all-consuming, do-anything-for-you kind of love, you know? It's the stuff of love songs and movies and novels, but it's rare to see it in real life."

"What do you mean?" I asked. "You don't think it really exists? You're the one who believes in long commitments."

"It exists. It's just rare. Not everyone gets that lucky."

I originally thought Jess was a hopeless romantic, or assumed people who were good at relationships were. Instead of being a full beating heart, it now seemed like hers was made out of crumbly, dry-rotted elastic. What had Cole done to her? This beautiful woman in front of me didn't believe in love the way it was meant to be felt. Or at least, how I hoped it would feel. "It might sound weird coming from me, but I believe in it. I think it's out there for everybody. We've just gotta keep looking."

"Well, we've established that you're a live laugh love girlie, Mikey," she said with a sad smile. "You gave a nice speech, by the way."

I laughed self-consciously. "I don't know if I give speeches so much as public verbal diarrhea."

She cackled, a musical sound, her head dipping into the space between us, then throwing her head back. "You're funny, you know that?"

"Funny. No filter. I've gotten 'em all," I said. She laughed again, then studied my eyes. What was she looking for? What was I looking for looking back at her? Whatever it was, it felt like I found it. Her hazel irises were fascinating in color alone, but it was how she looked at me. She was waiting for me to say more, to keep brightening her day. I wanted to give her that, because when I could make her laugh, it made everything better for me, too. Tension pulsed between us and I felt something that didn't come often to me: attraction. And not the more familiar "you bounce on my cock" attraction, though that was there, too. It was more "I need to know everything about you and this is probably dangerous but I want to breathe the same air as you for the rest of my living moments."

I felt that way for a woman who was in a relationship, just dancing with her once and looking into her eyes. And snuggling her in my bed. And talking late into the night with her.

Christ. I was a piece of work.

The song ended, but we still stood together, our arms up in the classic partner dance pose.

"I should get going. It's late for me."

I swallowed and nodded. "Right. Sure. I probably have to stay a while. Groomsman and all that."

"Oh, yeah. Of course."

"Walk you to your car?"

"I think I'll make it, Jockey. It's just out front." She walked back to get her purse at her table and I followed.

"This neighborhood, Jess," I warned.

"Is what, really safe?"

I rolled my eyes. "Just make me feel better. This is for me, not you."

"Oh, well, since it's about you, you want me to wait until you can tailgate me home, too?" she scoffed. "I'm going to go say bye to Kitty."

Kitty's eyes lit up as Jessie and I approached. "Look at the two neighbors, making peace!" she teased. Jessie and Kitty hugged and promised to have lunch together Monday.

Jessie's car was way up the street, almost a mile it felt like. "How old is your car?" I asked once I laid eyes on the ancient red Honda.

"She's antique," Jessie said, touching the hood defensively.

"Seriously, Jess, is that thing safe?"

"It's gotten me through many-a commute and she's still got plenty of life in her. I bought it when I moved out here. I never needed a car in New York. Used cars are expensive right now."

The rage fire reignited in me. "And Cole couldn't—"

"Jockey. Stop it." Her tone was firm.

I chewed the inside of my cheek. "Text me when you get home?"

"Ben, are you my dad?"

"You had a drink or two!" I huffed.

"I'm also a grown-ass adult and I don't need a fucking babysitter!" she barked. "I don't even have your number."

"Yes, you do."

She squinted at me, waiting for an explanation. "I sent my playlist to myself and programmed it in."

"Lord God," she muttered. She shifted her voice to a childish whine. "Am I allowed to go now, Daddy?"

My eyes widened, and so did hers. Her breathing quickened. I drew a half step closer. What was my plan? Was I going to kiss her? Her eyes rounded, then softened. Oh, merciful God, it seemed like she wanted to kiss me, too. She was in a relationship. But he was cheating! And what's a kiss? I was just thinking of seeing if her lips were soft and she tasted good, not ramming my dick in her. Though—

She pulled the handle to open her door. "Goodnight, Jockey."

She drove off, leaving me standing stunned in the street.

10

MIKEY

I felt like shit after Jessie left. I was no better than my dad. Why couldn't I respect that she was in a relationship? Why was I so insistent that she needed to be with me, when I knew deep down she was way out of my league?

Jessie is a relationship girl. I'm a fuckaround boy. Those two don't mix.

And I'd caused her to fight with Cole. All of his arguments weren't valid. I heard the whole thing. That dude is lucky she puts up with him at all. Still, it was fundamentally my fault. I'd never heard them fight before I got involved. I heard him pick on her. I heard her deal with it and try to talk him out of it. And I heard their sad, pathetic sex where only one of them was getting anything out of it.

I didn't want to be a homewrecker. And there I was, wrecking homes.

I was hopeless.

Back at the party, I saw other women seemingly attending alone, but I didn't have the heart to strike up a conversation. I tried scrolling my DMs, willing myself to find someone good enough for that night. It was useless. I wanted to connect with someone like I connected with Jessie, even if our connection was fiery and tenuous. I liked that fire. It made me feel alive, getting burned by her. She was different than the women who found me through hockey. Jessie didn't defer to me. She challenged me.

I ended up leaving the party an hour or so after Jessie did, telling Guy my stomach was upset. He knew how sensitive my system is. I wasn't fully lying. It just wasn't upset from food.

And still, I stopped for a six-pack of Bud Light Lime on my way home. Just in case.

When I got home, the fighting was well underway with Jessie and Cole.

He blamed her for falling asleep. For even talking to me. For leaving after some fight they'd had before I saw her. And then she dealt the big blow.

"You haven't gotten me off in years."

I heard it loud and clear in my kitchen. The silence that followed was so long, I wondered if I'd dreamed it. Then the rage came.

"What do you want me to say to that, Jessie? You've been lying to me all this time? How long?"

I was torn. Should I leave? Stay and keep being nosy? I was rooted to the spot. If they heard me pour a glass of water or shut my refrigerator door, they'd know I could hear them. Jessie probably thought I still was at the party. I couldn't make out what she said back to him.

Then the yelling started. "We moved here for you, Jessalyn!"

"Oh, don't kid yourself. It was for you. Stop gaslighting me! You were ready to leave me in New York."

He yelled. And yelled. I heard her quiet, "I'm going to leave," and his loud, "If you leave, don't bother coming back."

Then their front door slammed, creating a suction breeze in my apartment. Then the elevator dinged. I had a feeling where she was going. It was chilly out that night. I waited a few minutes, then grabbed the six-pack, a sweatshirt, and a blanket, and went to the roof.

I heard her before I saw her. "I don't know, Mom. I think I just need to come home. Yeah, to West Virginia. I can't afford New York."

Sniffles, and sobs. "No, I only have my purse. I'll get clothes when I get home. I don't have my laptop. Can you book me a flight?"

I rounded the corner from the elevator bank and saw her, face puffy with tears, sitting in a pool chair on the phone. Her nice party makeup was smeared, her sweatshirt pulled down over her bare legs. "I need to go, Mom. Can you send me the flight options? Appreciate it. Love you, too."

She hung up and leaned her head into her hands. I approached her, knocking the cool beer bottle into the backs of her hands. She gave a thick laugh, taking it from me. She popped it open with her sweatshirt sleeve.

"Thanks," she said. "I thought you hated these."

"Felt like you needed one," I said, trying to sound sympathetic. I spread the blanket over her lap. I popped open a bottle and sat in the chair next to her, planting my elbows on my knees. "You okay?"

She took a long drag on the beer and stared at the pool. "I don't know."

We sat in silence for a while. I was good at this. I was good at being the breakup friend. I'd done it before for Kitty and was pretty proud of my performance. Sometimes, you've just gotta sit in the misery.

"I guess you heard," she said.

"I heard," I confirmed. "Are you going home?"

Jessie's breath shuddered. "I think so. I don't even know what I'm doing out here."

I wanted to reach out and touch her, but I was part of the

problem. I needed to give her space. "You're working toward your dream, right?"

She nodded.

"Do you want to do this or go back to New York and do fashion?" I prayed the answer was the former. The thought of Jessie moving away was disturbingly upsetting. I shouldn't be that upset at the thought of her leaving.

"This." A sob broke loose.

"Don't go then," I said.

"I don't have anywhere to go," she said. "He threw me out."

"You pay rent, Jessalyn. He can't just throw you out," I started.

Jess blew out a breath. "I'm not going back down there tonight."

There was no way I was letting Jessie sleep on the roof with everything she was going through. "You can stay with me. As long as you need."

"What?" She looked at me like I had three heads. "Mikey."

"I'm not even home a lot of the time. I've got an extra bedroom. There's no bed in it, but I can take care of that. I need to get one for guests anyway."

"Mikey, no. It's too much. I just need to rethink everything. I just need somewhere for tonight."

"You probably can't quit the show mid-season, can you? I know Kitty talks about stuff like that."

She raised her eyebrows and rubbed her forehead. "Yeah, you're right about that."

"And look, I know I was, uh, a little . . . aggressive this morning."

Jessie was clearly not trying to react, but that was a reaction in itself. She rubbed her lips together and stared at the cement between us.

"I promise, this is purely from a friend perspective, okay? I'll leave you alone. I just don't think you should go home without seeing where your job is going."

She nodded and sniffed, considering my offer in silence. "When did you buy Bud Light Limes?"

"I had some left over from that party," I lied.

Her eyes flicked to the full six-pack minus our two bottles, but she didn't say anything. She shivered.

"Stay with me tonight, Jessie. It's cold up here."

She scowled. "I need to think."

I sighed. "Think all you want, but sleep at my place, okay? Don't sleep up here."

"I'll come down. I just need some time to think."

"Arms up," I said.

Her brow furrowed until she saw me holding out the sweatshirt for her to slide into.

"I'm right downstairs. My door's open and you have my number. Don't stay up too late."

She gave a sad laugh. "Okay, Daddy."

I laughed, my stomach tingling again. "You're a real brat, you know that?"

She caught my hand before I could walk away, peering up at me with the tiny dimple next to her lips showing. "Thanks, Ben."

I squeezed her hand, noting how nice it felt in mine. I didn't do a lot of hand-holding on hookups. Something about it was so simple and sweet. Intimate. Trusting. A gesture you make with your body when you're really connecting your soul to someone else's.

And yet, I couldn't leave well enough alone.

"Anytime, Sweet Cheeks."

11

JESSIE

My hand shook as I raised my knuckles to knock on the door. It was all getting real.

It didn't take long for it to swing open.

His voice was soft. "Hey."

"Hi," I whispered. A sob shuddered through me.

Then he took my hand, pulled me inside, and closed the door. Without thinking, I thrust myself into his arms, wrapping myself tight around his neck. He responded by pulling me in at my waist, letting us be together again. My tears were hot, melting into his shirt. This wasn't how I wanted the evening to go, but it felt like it would be okay anyway.

"Hi, roomie," Ben said with a quiet chuckle. "Welcome home."

We sat on the couch with a bowl of popcorn between us, watching a nature documentary. Ben was trying to take my mind off things.

"Which would you rather have as a pet: a baby ocelot or a baby bobcat?" he asked.

"I mean, bobcats are native to North America, but ocelots have those cute spots. I think I'd have to go ocelot, but I'd feel bad about it."

Ben sat looking pensive. "What if I get the bobcat and you get the ocelot and they can play together since we're roomies?"

I gave a soft laugh. "Do you get a pet with someone for one night? And was that not your mutant chihuahua here?"

"Huh? No. Greg is Obi's dog. He just doesn't like to leave him home alone."

"Okay, so say we get these feral cats. What happens when you're on the road and I've got to work long hours?"

"I'll hire someone to walk Aussie and Robert."

I cackled. "Okay, let me break that down. Aussie for ocelot, Robert for bobcat?"

"You're quick, Jessalyn."

"You're quicker. You came up with it."

He shrugged. "I'm being generous. You're going through a thing."

I sighed. "Yeah. I am."

He studied me, then threw a piece of popcorn at me. "You wanna talk about it?"

"Not really. Do you want me to?" I asked.

"I don't know how to talk about stuff like that. But I feel like it's my fault, Jess. I'm really sorry."

I scrunched up my nose. "How would it be your fault?"

"I never heard you fight until I came into the picture."

A lump formed in my throat, a thick swallow clearing it as tears rose in me again. Ben reached across the couch and put his hand on my forearm.

"I'm so sorry, Jess. If there's anything I can do to help you fix it . . ."

I shook my head. "It's not that. I think we never fought before because we were just on autopilot."

Something flared in Ben's eyes, his jaw flexing. He looked away, running his tongue over his teeth. "I got nothing. No advice on the topic. But I can listen. I'm here for you."

I stared at the TV for a while, not really seeing what we were watching. "I think I'm tired of thinking," I said with a yawn.

"You ready for bed, Jessie Girl? I tried to get a bed delivered tonight, but apparently no one delivers beds at 2 a.m."

My stomach did a somersault. "What? When?"

"While you were still upstairs and I came back down here."

I groaned. "Ben, don't order a spare bed for me. I have an air mattress next door, but..."

Ben looked at me sympathetically. "You don't have to go get that right now. Stay in my bed tonight? I won't be all over you."

"Absolutely not," I said. "I'll sleep on the couch. And I'll be out of your hair in the morning."

Ben cocked his head at me. "Do you have anywhere else to go?"

"That's what tomorrow's for. It's Sunday. I'll have all day to try to find a place."

"Jessalyn."

"Benjamin."

"Just stay, Jessie. For a week. A month. Two years. As long as you need."

"Wouldn't I be getting in the way of you getting ass?" I asked skeptically.

He got a funny look on his face, unreadable. "Let me worry about that on my own time."

"Is this just a guilt thing? Because you think you ruined my relationship?"

Ben sat up and put the popcorn bowl on the coffee table. He faced me. "Jessalyn, here's what's going to happen. Tonight, you're going to sleep in my bed, because it's more comfortable and you need a good night's sleep. In the morning, we're going to go next door and get your stuff. We're going to move you into my spare bedroom, and you're going to be my roommate."

I studied him. His eyes seemed earnest, the amber color glowing in the light of the TV. He was taking charge with me. I was so exhausted.

"What are you getting out of this?" My voice was dry and crackly.

"Being your best friend," he said with a smirk.

I leveled him with a look.

"I'm serious. I kinda hate living alone. It'd be nice to have someone to come home to."

"So, like a girlfriend for you?"

Ben shivered. "That word terrifies me, Jessie. I think we might have fun if we just tried being there for each other."

"As friends," I clarified. The last thing I needed was to leave one questionable relationship and jump right into another one.

Wait, was I having thoughts about getting into a new relationship with Mikey?

I wasn't even entirely sure things were over with Cole. He just told me not to come back, and he'd never said anything to me like that before. Ever. Maybe he'd ask me to come back tomorrow.

"As friends," Ben agreed.

12

MIKEY

I sat at my kitchen island, grinding my teeth. It had been five minutes since I heard Jessie crying next door. Asshole Cole had exchanged some harsh words with her and left. She'd left the living area, because her cries were more faint. How much longer could I listen to her sob like that?

She'd spent the morning combing apartment listings, which I let her do even though it killed me. I didn't get why she wouldn't just stay with me. Before she went over to her apartment, she told me she found a place a little out of budget and farther from work for her, but she'd go look at it in the afternoon.

I couldn't let this go on. Jessie was losing her mind in the drama of it all. I could be the strong one. I just needed to put my foot down.

I stood, ready to take over. Her and Cole's apartment door was unlocked and I walked in. I found her on the bedroom floor, a half-packed duffel bag open next to her. She gazed up at me with bloodshot eyes, waiting for me to talk.

"You're coming with me."

"I found a place, Ben."

I crouched next to her. "It's too expensive and it's farther from work for you. Do you really want to do that?"

"I don't want to be near him. I don't want to see him. I don't want to hear him."

Now that was a fair argument. If I laid eyes on him in my present state, I'd probably knock his teeth out. "I'll make sure he stays away from you. Just stay with me. It's free. It's no further from work for you."

"I can't live with you for free."

"Jessie, money's not an issue for me. I don't want your money."

Her face arranged into a sneer. "I have to earn my keep, Ben."

"Let's worry about that later. Right now, I'm going to help you pack up and we're moving your stuff into my place. Okay?"

She looked at her crossed ankles in her lap. "I hate this," she mumbled. I sat next to her and put my arm around her.

"I know, hon. Show me what's yours and I'll carry it to your room. Then we can order some nasty takeout. Sound good?"

She sniffed and rubbed her fingers under her eyes. "Alright."

Jessie had been living with me since Cole broke up with her, and it was Wednesday. She usually came home before I did and shut herself in her room. I knocked at her door sometimes when I heard her crying, but she either pretended not to hear it or to be asleep. But I knew she'd been awake because she'd pop out to use the bathroom.

Sunday night, after we moved her stuff in there, blew up her air mattress, and got her settled, she claimed she wasn't hungry.

Monday and Tuesday, she got home from work and disappeared into her room. She claimed she ate on her way home. Through the door. She wouldn't even open the door for me.

I was about five seconds from demanding she eat with me like the Beast in Beauty and the Beast.

Wednesday, I was clear to play again, but we didn't have a game. I cooked dinner, making enough for two. Nothing fancy, just tacos. It was actually Valentine's Day, but I didn't know how to handle her feelings around that. Was she depressed? Would she accept roommate flowers? Better to ignore it altogether. I even planned to make a joke to her about it being Taco Wednesday if she came out of her room.

I perked up at the sound of her bedroom door. She shuffled through the kitchen with her head down and her phone in her hand.

"Hey, Jess," I tried.

"Hey. I'm going to talk to Cole."

"Oh. Cool. Um, good luck, I guess?"

She gave a weak smile, then stalled at the front door like she realized she should say something else. "Work okay for you? You get to go back yet?"

"Yeah, yeah. Shoulder's doing a little better."

"Good."

"Everything okay for you?" I spooned up some of the taco meat I was stirring. "Hungry?"

"I ate on the way home." Then with her hand on the door-knob and a wry smile, she said, "Don't wait up for me, Daddy."

And then she was gone. Why was I relieved that she had a two-minute conversation with me? And why did I like it so much when she called me Daddy, even if it was a joke? I heard Cole greet her, his tone sounding flat.

Their voices grew faint. I'm sure she knew that I could hear them and they went deeper into the apartment. I can't not be nosy, so I cracked open the window hoping to hear more. I had the TV on and muted, so I could quickly pretend like I wasn't being absolutely invasive.

I was desperate for any scrap of her because honestly, I was worried about her. She was crying alone in her room and wouldn't let me in. I suspected she wasn't eating.

I fell asleep on the couch absolutely 100% waiting up for her. I wanted to be there when she got home. I startled awake when she came in. She went straight for the freezer.

"Lookin' for something?" I asked.

"Do you have ice cream?"

"Sorry. Lactose issues," I said. "Makes my tummy upset."

She muttered something. "Goodnight, Mikey."

"Jessie, wait."

She turned in the hallway, looking back at me with a sadness that was deeper than tears, bigger than just getting dumped. Or at least, I thought. I'd never been dumped. I didn't know how big that could feel.

"Is it over?"

She sighed. "Yeah."

She stood, frozen.

"I'm sorry," was all I could cook up.

"Someday, I'll tell you 'don't be,' but I'm not there yet."

I nodded.

"Goodnight, Ben."

That night, her sobs leaked into my room as I sat up in bed, worrying about my roommate.

"I think my roommate's depressed."

It was Thursday, and the team was due to leave for another road trip Friday morning.

Guy stuck out his lower lip. "Why?"

"She's been just in her room crying."

"Didn't her boyfriend just dump her? Like Sunday?" Sorrento asked. I may or may not have texted a few guys to let them know I was getting a new roommate.

"I mean, yeah. Saturday night after the party. I don't think she's been eating. The only time she came out last night was to go fight with her ex. Then she was looking for ice cream, which I don't have. I told her it makes my tummy upset."

"You said 'tummy' to the hot girl living in your house?" Leroy asked. "That's why she's not fucking you."

My cheeks flamed. "I didn't say she needed to fuck me. We're friends."

And I just said she was depressed. What kind of monster would it make me if I were even thinking about sex with her when she'd been like that the whole week? Even I had limits.

Sorrento raised an eyebrow. "You're friends with that girl with the huge boobs that you were waltzing around at Stelle's party? *Just* friends?"

"I mean, yeah. She's fuckin' gorgeous. But she's still kinda cranky with me."

"So get her the ice cream," Obi said, cutting through the chatter. Everyone went silent, waiting for him to go on. Despite being the youngest guy on the team, he somehow always had wise things to say. His name is fitting. He's got a Jedi-like way about him. Sometimes I imagine a cloud of mist around him as he delivers his little proclamations and nuggets of wisdom. "She's going through a breakup. She's sad, and she wants ice cream. Give her what she needs."

"That's not his job," Leroy said. "He's already housing her. She's not his charity case. She should be nice to you, Mike."

"She's going through a breakup," Guy emphasized. "She's probably cranky with everyone. I agree. Get her the ice cream. Try and feed her. Show her you're there for her. Be a friend."

So on my way home, I stopped for boba, Thai takeout, and ice cream.

13

JESSIE

I wish I could say that I thought I was better off without Cole. I wish I could say I was a strong independent woman right away. That I felt confident and capable. That I knew he didn't define my self-worth.

But four years with someone will do ugly things to a woman. Particularly when that someone blames the end of your relationship squarely on you.

I tried suggesting that maybe we were just growing apart, that maybe we needed to work harder.

He countered with the suggestion that I didn't love him the way I used to and he fell out of love with me because of it.

Ouch.

Some people eat when they're sad. Others don't. I was in the don't category. I ate just enough not to get the shakes from all the coffee I drank to stay afloat. It was a necessity thing, not a pleasure thing. I hardly tasted the food anyway.

I was a robot at work that week. I made carefully penned lists of what I needed to do and plowed through the tasks without emotion. I would not let my work suffer because of him.

But then there was home. Or whatever I was calling home for that moment. An air mattress in Mikey's spare bedroom. I hated to admit to him that I loved Cole, because I knew how much he hated him.

But did I really love Cole? The brain tends to only remember the good stuff, sweeping the bad stuff under the rug. I was playing the highlight reel from our relationship when there were plenty more scenes where things were just plain bad. Had I confused our years together with a genuine bond?

Either way, I wasn't fully sure why, but Mikey had a vendetta against Cole. So when Mikey came to check on me every night, I couldn't face him.

But it meant everything that he tried. I just didn't have the energy to tell him.

~

"H'LO?"

I held the phone away from my ear as a cacophony of dogs barked. I was on my way home from work Thursday and calling my mom for a little bolstering.

"Jessalyn? You there?"

"Yeah, Mom, hi. I was just waiting for the dogs to stop."

"You'll be waiting all your life, then," Mom said. "How's the new place?"

I sighed. "Fine. Cole and I officially broke up last night."

"Cole, Schmole. Start working on that rich roommate of yours."

"Mom," I chided.

"What's the big deal, Jess? He sounds like a real gentleman. Go for him. He's single, right?"

"Mom, you called Cole a gentleman once upon a time. Look where that got me."

"Yeah, well, guess I was wrong, huh? Cole also wasn't a big hunky hockey player, anyway."

I should have known better than to expect my mom to actually provide what I was looking for out of a phone call. What I wanted was "I'm so sorry you got dumped! You're better off without him!" What I got instead was "Jump in bed with your roommate!"

"How's Da—"

"Thurston! Stop humpin' him! He's just a baby!" My mom always had a chaotic mix of dogs at the house. Ever since I moved away for college, the collection grew. My dad just put up with it as long as one of them was a hunting dog for him. "Your dad? He's good. He's already snoozin' with his hand down his pants. Hey, does your new man know about your nightmares?"

I clenched my jaw and rolled my eyes. "He's not my new man. And unfortunately, he does."

She softened her voice. "You gonna see about getting that medicine again?"

"The last three didn't work, Mom. The dreams are just bad when I'm stressed. I can't always control how stressed I am."

"You know, Carolyn's daughter started doing yoga and she said it really helped her. She's one of them banking types, too," Mom said. "And Carolyn tried it and said it made Howard ask if she got a new puss—"

Lord God. My mother was almost as bad as Mikey with the no filter. "Okay, Mom, I'm pulling up to the grocery store!" I lied. "Gotta go!"

14

MIKEY

Jessalyn was already home when I got there, so I knocked on her door.

"Jessie? You hungry?"

Her sewing machine thumped. I knocked again and cracked the door open. Jessie looked up, but while doing so accidentally ran the side of her finger under the needle.

"Ah! Fuck!" she hissed, sucking on her finger.

"Shit! I'm sorry. Let me see," I said, rushing to her side and crouching in front of her. I pulled her hand into mine to examine her wound. A little drop of blood sprang out of the side of her index finger. "Fuck, Jess, I'm sorry. Let me get you a Band-Aid, hon."

I jogged into my bathroom, grabbing ointment and a Band-Aid out of a drawer. When I got back into her room, I put a dot of ointment on the wound, then unwrapped the Band-Aid.

"I can put it on, Ben."

"Just hold still," I said. "Your hands are shaky. When was the last time you ate?"

"I get food from craft services at work."

"I hear ya, babe. But when did you eat last?"

She thought back. "I had a bagel this morning."

I closed the bandage around her finger and gave it a little kiss. "There. It won't get better unless I do that."

She cracked a weak smile and blushed, making me blush, too. My stomach got some stupid flutters at how cute she was, despite being pale and wan. The Jessie I knew was feisty and full of fire. This wasn't my Jessie, and it broke my heart.

But I had a plan.

I still had her hand in mine, and I rubbed my thumb softly over her injured finger.

"I got you some dinner. Wanna come eat?"

"Ben," she started.

"Come eat. I'm not taking no for an answer." I pulled her to her feet and dragged her into the kitchen. "I got you tofu pad thai in case you're a secret vegetarian or something. But if you're allergic, I can order you something else."

"No. That sounds great. I'll Venmo you."

"Jess, I'm an actual millionaire. If I buy you something, it's because I want to, and I don't want to hear anything else about it."

She rubbed her forehead. "How about a thank you?"

I grinned at her. "I'll accept that."

She was quiet at first as we ate, seemingly embarrassed. Whether it was from the injury incident, or me feeding her, or that she hadn't been feeding herself, I wasn't sure.

"Work's been stupid busy," she finally sighed, breaking our silence.

"Yeah? Are y'all like . . . filming more?" I didn't know shit about how filming TV worked. I cursed myself for having not asked Kitty more about it.

She sighed. "It's the normal amount. About one episode per week, but a lot of on-location stuff and my boss kinda doesn't do shit."

I was thoroughly confused. "Isn't on-location good?"

"Sorry. That means we're actually not at the studio. Backwards, I know," she said.

"Gotcha. But your boss doesn't do anything?"

She had a mouthful of pad thai, so she didn't answer right away. "No. It's just me and her in our department, and she's supposed to be leading me. But I just end up doing everything. She strolls in like two hours after I do and does whatever she wants. And when we got in trouble for not having something ready on time, she ended up giving me a pay cut to show that at least we were under budget."

Oh, that I could not handle. "She did what?"

Jess nodded grimly.

"Did *she* take a pay cut?"

She shrugged. "I doubt it. But I'm the junior one."

I ground my molars. "What's her name?"

Jess's face finally broke from its frowny state and she giggled. She sat back and crossed her arms. "Irina. Why? What are you gonna do to her, big hockey thug?"

Okay, yeah. I was being a little ridiculous. "Top secret hockey thug stuff."

That got more laughs out of her. Each laugh was a little reward, and I hung onto them like a lifeline. I was desperate for Jessie to be okay. I finished my food and put on a Fleetwood Mac record.

"Never pegged you for a vinyl guy," she said.

I shrugged. "I love music. It's the best way to hear it."

"So I've heard. It just seems kinda...hipster-y? Do hipsters even exist anymore? But you do drink IPAs."

"Pale ales. IPAs give me headaches," I joked. I took a slurp of my boba. "Ah, so fucking good."

"I've actually never had it."

"Seriously? Here. Take a drink." I held out my cup and she recoiled. I shook it, the ice clattering. "Come on. I don't have cooties."

She quirked an eyebrow at me. "You forget that I hear your conquests through the walls."

Wow, way to punch me in the stomach, Jess. "I always wrap it up. And I get tested for diseases. I'm clean. Try it."

She took the cup and sucked in a tiny sip of the tea. "Happy?"

"No! Get a bubble! They're the best part."

She laughed. "Fine." She pressed the straw to the bottom of the cup and slurped up one of the bubbles. "Okay, yeah. That's pretty good."

"See? So good, right?" She finally cracked a genuine smile.

"Yeah. Like a tea-flavored gummy bear."

"I'll get you one next time." She'd finished her food and put the leftovers in the fridge. "Do you have to get back to work for evil Irina, or can you hang out and have dessert?"

"There's dessert?" she asked.

"Check the freezer."

Jess narrowed her eyes at me but opened the freezer. She gasped. "I thought it made your stomach hurt."

"It does. But it doesn't for you. I didn't know what flavor you liked, so I got a few."

Her mouth flapped open and shut a few times. "Ben, you have to stop being nice to me."

I just grinned at her. "I won't."

15

JESSIE

I had to get my shit together.

Having Mikey away on a road trip was the first time I'd been truly alone in years. I always had Cole. And technically, Cole was next door if I had an emergency or something, but it would have to be pretty dire for me to bark up that tree.

Strangely, I was sleeping harder than I had in years, despite being alone. Was the air different in Mikey's apartment? Was I that weighed down by Cole? Cole hadn't been the whole reason I'd been a shit sleeper for most of my life, though.

I was both grateful for and embarrassed by Mikey force-feeding me and picking up the slack where I wasn't taking care of myself.

I looked down at the bandage on my left index finger, thinking of the kiss he left there. Why did I keep replaying him kissing my boo-boo? Why did it surprise me so much?

Friday, I decided to pretend I had it together as a method of trying. I picked up ingredients to make a healthy dinner, plus a fancy fizzy water as a treat. There would be no wine-soaked garbage food benders to get over my garbage relationship.

I was settling in to watch some deliciously trashy TV when my phone buzzed.

BENJAMIN MICHAEL JOCKEY

Game just ended. Checking in on my favorite
roomie. Did u eat today?

I had two options. Answer honestly, or fuck with him a little bit for fun. He was genuinely being kind, but that was scarier than joking. I'd rather make the tone light.

Yes, Daddy. I made myself a healthy dinner
and cleaned it up. Now I'm having water. Do I
get my gold star?

PS you need water glasses that don't sweat so
much. Or coasters. My ice water keeps trying
to leave a ring on your coffee table

Bad attitudes don't get gold stars, Jessalyn

Good girls who eat and drink their water do

I guess I had started the whole Daddy joke early on in our... roommateship, but he was taking it to another level. Kitty had said he was a shameless flirt. He was just flirting like he would with anyone else. Right?

I'm being good! What more do you want?

Start contributing to this family and get us
some coasters

I snickered, thinking of the girly coasters I could crochet. He'd regret that request.

For real, u good?

My stomach turned. I hardly knew Ben and he was pretty

worried about me. I'd met him, what, a little over a week before? And I was squatting in his apartment while he wasn't home. What the fuck was I doing with my life?

> Yeah, I'm fine. Thanks for checking. You good? Y'all win?

The three dots appeared and disappeared multiple times. Then nothing. The amount of disappointment I felt told me everything I needed to know.

This situation wasn't sustainable.

I needed to make a plan to leave.

16

MIKEY

I got back late on Sunday night, almost missing the pink crocheted coasters on the coffee table in the low light coming in. I got goosebumps thinking Jessie had made those per my request. I couldn't wait to talk to her about it. But right away, I mostly needed sleep.

The first scream must have been what woke me, pulse racing and breaking a sweat instantly. The second had me bolting from bed.

I tore into Jessie's room to find her thrashing on her air mattress.

Seeing her in the middle of one of her nightmares on a half-inflated air mattress was enough for me to step in. Sweat dampened her shirt and made her hair stick to her face. Her eyes were open but not really seeing. It was spooky, exorcism-like. She screamed again, cowering as tears streamed down her cheeks.

"Jessie Girl, can you hear me? It's Mikey. It's Ben. You're okay, Jessalyn."

I felt so helpless. Something was wrecking her from the inside and I couldn't stop it. She didn't deserve whatever was making this happen to her. I went to sit on the edge of the air mattress, but it just had a see-saw effect because of its half-inflated status. I wasn't leaving her in there to suffer alone.

I scooped her up in my arms and carried her into my room. She looked at me, confused.

"It's okay, Jessie. I've got you."

She didn't say anything, almost like she was sleepwalking. Her eyes were still a weird unseeing haze. She curled in closer to me, tucking her head into my chest. I sat on the edge of my bed and held her there, feeling her sniffs and sobs.

"You want me to sing?"

Jessie didn't answer, but wrapped her arms around me with a boa constrictor's grip. I started to sing Paradise, feeling self-conscious, but it was what put her back to sleep the time before. As her body relaxed, I pulled down the comforter on the not-me side and shifted her into the sheets. I went around to my side of the bed and got in, continuing to sing. I was afraid if I stopped, she'd start crying again. I couldn't stand to see her so torn up like that.

I turned to face her, noticing a wad of pink and blue yarn around her neck. I was afraid she'd get strangled on it in her sleep, so I pulled at it. Jessie quickly yanked it back and draped it across her neck. I didn't bother trying again. She seemed to know, even in sleep, that she needed that yarn wad. I'd ask her about it in the morning.

Jess nestled into my body, nuzzling her face into my chest. Was it wrong for me to hold her back? Was she going to wake up in the morning and freak out like she had a few days before?

I decided it didn't matter. Sleepy Jessie needed me, or someone, and I was the someone there.

～

"MIKEY!"

Jess's voice was a rude awakening. Her hair and yarn wad were partially in my face, whipping around as she tried to get out from under my arm. Seems we moved to spooning in sleep.

"Morning, Sweet Cheeks," I rasped, noticing that my cock was actually lodged between her cheeks. Oops. Clothed, but still, that's where it was. It was still dark outside. "What time is it?"

She jolted her butt away from me and I lifted my arm to let her out.

"Again?!"

"You had a nightmare, Jess. I couldn't let you keep sleeping on that uncomfortable air mattress."

"I can't live here," she coughed out. "This was a terrible idea. I can't do this."

I scrubbed my hand over my face. "Why?"

She panted, considering that.

"Jessie, you have insomnia, right?"

"Right."

"Except when you're here, right?"

She tossed her head from side to side. "Yeah."

"Just let it happen. I'm not trying to get you to fuck me. I'm just trying to be your friend. If that means sleeping in my bed, that's fine. If that means we get close to each other, also fine. It's not a big deal."

She narrowed her eyes at me. "This is feeling more and more like you're trying to be my boyfriend. I'm still, I don't—"

"Jessie, it's not like that," I groaned. "Wait, seriously, what time is it?"

I flopped over and looked at the clock, then flicked on the lamp to make sure I was reading it right. "Four fucking thirty?"

"I have early days and a long commute, Ben." She stood and smoothed the sheets on her side of the bed.

"You hardly slept last night. Are you sure you can drive?"

She scoffed. "Nice of you to care, but I'm used to this life. Little sleep and straight to a forty-five-minute commute."

"I'll drive you," I said, rolling out of bed. I chugged the glass of water on my nightstand, just like I did every morning.

"It's way out of the way for you. Don't you have practice or something?"

"I have a workout this morning, but that's it. It's not until nine. At this rate, I'll be back way early."

Jessie stood in my doorway with her yarn wad in her hand, looking mystified, then disappeared to get ready for work.

I padded out to the kitchen to start some coffee. I'd never admit to her how late I got in and how bad I was really going to need that caffeine.

Within 10 minutes, she was in my kitchen, dressed and ready for work.

"Damn, that was fast," I said. "Let me brush my teeth and I'll get us out of here."

She was at the door grabbing her keys. "You really don't have to drive me. How am I going to get home?"

I shrugged her off as I headed for my room. "I'll order you a car or come get you. I need something to do today."

When I looked back, her eyes were rounded like she was about to cry. Something stirred in my gut. I wasn't sure why, but I knew I'd do just about anything for that firestorm that walked into my life.

17

JESSIE

Ben's car was nice. Like, really nice. I'm not sure why I was surprised. He's a professional athlete. Of course he'd have a flashy car. New car smell mingled with the hazelnut coffee he'd made for us.

"Sorry, Sweet Cheeks. I'm not listening to a murder podcast on the way," he said, pulling up a playlist on his phone.

"Your car, your rules," I said, typing in my work address on the massive touch screen.

A Marshall Tucker song came on as Mikey put the car in gear and we left the garage under our building. I couldn't afford the garage, so I did street parking, and thus had a solid sheet of bird shit all over my car at all times.

"You would like this song," I teased.

"What's that supposed to mean?" Mikey said, flicking his eyes to me.

"It's a beer uncle song. You are 100% a beer uncle."

"I feel like that's not a compliment. I could leave your ass on the side of the road if you get too uppity, you know."

"I mean, beer uncles are really fun. You're like the loud, fun uncle who brings a case of Bud heavy to your nephew's wedding reception while wearing a cut-off t-shirt."

Ben's shoulders shook for a moment, and I wondered if he was having some sort of medical event. Then his boisterous laugh erupted, filling the cab of the car with its warm sound.

"That's a really vivid picture, Jess."

"I didn't come up with it, but it's totally who you are," I affirmed.

"I guess you're right. And beer uncles like classic rock?"

"Oh, totally. And that's you. Do you have nieces and nephews?"

Ben blew out a breath. "Yep. One of each. And maybe some illegitimate half nieces and nephews, too."

I winced. There was some pain there. "I'm sorry, Ben."

"It's fine. My dad just sucks. I'm the miracle baby of the family. My sister and I were five years apart. I was the 'let's fix this marriage' baby."

"Ouch. Did it work?"

Ben scoffed as he merged onto the empty highway. "No. They're still together, though. My mom refuses to admit defeat and my dad refuses to quit cheating."

I didn't quite know what to say to that. It was still before five a.m.

"Anyway," he said. "You can put your seat back and sleep if you want. It says forty minutes."

"I'll keep you company," I said, not wanting to just knock out on him after he revealed that his dad was a serial cheater. A little ping in my gut told me that had something to do with his own promiscuous ways, but it was way too early to be digging into that. "The coffee's good. Cole never let us have flavored coffee, but I love it."

I felt foolish for bringing up Cole. Even though Mikey and I were just friends, it felt weird to be talking about my very very recent ex.

Ben shook his head. "Does that guy like anything fun?"

I hoped Ben would laugh at my next Cole fact. "He said flavored coffee is the opiate of the masses."

Ben snorted. "He's a card, that one."

"A card?" I repeated.

"Look, I don't want to talk too much shit. If you end up getting back together, I don't want you to hate me for all the mean stuff I said about him."

"Why do you think I'm getting back together with him?" Hadn't he seen me after our final fight?

A muscle ticked in Ben's jaw and his fingers shifted on the steering wheel. "That's just what I see relationship people do."

"Relationship people?"

"Yeah. They break up, then realize maybe it wasn't so bad and that person might be their only chance, and then they get back together and get married and buy a golden retriever and put up the white picket fence and send smarmy Christmas cards of them and their perfect little kids."

Shew. I was taken aback by all the hostility packed into that one statement. Ben sucked down a sip of his coffee to fill the silence.

"We were never getting married. Cole listens to those men's podcasts where everything is a conspiracy to take the white man down. He thinks marriage is a social construct designed to trick people into government surveillance."

"Are you fucking kidding me?" Ben was incredulous, bordering on outraged. "That man had no intention of putting a ring on it?"

"Is that a problem?"

"A woman like you deserves to be celebrated, Jessie. He should have been throwing a goddamn parade every day that he had you." He took a long rip on his coffee, then muttered, "Social construct."

My stomach fluttered. Did Mikey *like* me?

Oh, this was bad. Really bad. I was trying to leave because this was looking like a messy situation, and that was before this comment. The longer we continued this cohabitation experiment, the sloppier it would get.

And yet, I pressed on. "What do you mean, a woman like me?"

"I mean, you have ambition. You're driven. You're talented. You don't give up because stuff's hard. You've got guts. You don't deserve to be minimized. You need to hear every fucking day that you're amazing. And for a man to have the nerve to not meet your needs . . ." he trailed off.

"Why do you keep going on about the orgasms?" I asked.

"It's not just the orgasms, Jessie. You need someone who won't live in an expensive place and charge you rent when you make less money. Instead of supporting you, he just added obstacles. And because he knew you're tough, he knew you wouldn't back down."

I was furious, mostly because he was right. But also, the audacity. "And what, you're going to give me what I need? You're back on the sneaky boyfriend train again."

"No, I'm not. Am I right, though? Did I get it right?"

"Fuck off, Ben!" I snapped.

Ben stared through the windshield like the empty road itself made him mad, while I stared out my side window. He swore under his breath.

"I'm sorry, Jessie. I went too far. I don't know how to do this right."

His apology caught me off guard. I expected him to keep slinging hurtful truths my way.

"Yeah. It's uh, it's okay." And surprisingly, I did really forgive him. For someone so cocky, he was especially willing to show me his shortcomings, *and* own up to them. He trusted me in a way I didn't anticipate. Mikey did everything 110%, it seemed.

It was still dark outside and would be for the duration of our drive together. A soft folky love song played.

"Is this the playlist you made for my drive?"

A sad smile played on his lips. "Yeah."

"This isn't very beer uncle of you."

"I have a variety of musical tastes, thank you very much. The goal was to ease you into your day. I go from gentle to party."

"Who would've guessed you had a gentle side, Mikey? You slam people around for a living."

"Excuse you, I also chase a frozen piece of rubber around and run on metal blades."

"Oh, yeah. That reminds me," I said, rifling around in my work bag. I'd started a hat for Mikey a couple days before. I could get some stitches in since I wasn't driving. "I hope you like dark gray."

Ben gasped. "Is that for me?"

"It will be when I'm done. I should be able to finish it between these two drives."

"Seriously? Jessie, I love it. Thank you."

"Maybe hold your applause til it's done. It might still come out lumpy," I laughed. "Fiber arts aren't my strongest craft."

Dancing In The Moonlight by King Harvest came on and Ben hummed into our comfortable silence, punctuated by the soft click of my metal needles.

"Oh, come on. I know you want to sing," I said. "Let it out."

"I'm trying to be less loud. I've been told I'm too loud."

"Aw, did I break you, Mikey?" I asked, squeezing his shoulder. He hissed and squirmed away from me. "Fuck, sorry, that's your bad shoulder, isn't it?"

"It's fine," he said.

"Are you still hurting that bad? How are you playing?"

He just grumbled, turning his attention to the road like I

didn't ask the question. Touchy subject, okay. I tried to soften him up again. "Come on," I said. "Sing. You have a nice voice."

"Really?"

"Yes, really! Let's hear you. I'm knitting for you. You can sing for me," I pushed.

"I'm also driving your ass to work, Jessalyn," he pointed out.

"Don't hold that over me! I could have driven myself. Stop distracting. Sing."

"Only if you sing with me."

Joke was on him because my voice is god awful. I got him to join me in the chorus as we belted out the song together. Mikey wore a huge smile. I got a little chill. I hadn't gotten close to someone new in a long time. I'd spent so long being a dull piece of linen, and Mikey was this bright, sequined disco dress. Colorful threads were stitching us together, binding us to each other and making me brighter from being associated with him. This guy did truly everything big and it was the most fun I'd had in a long time. The last week had been hell with Cole, so actually enjoying myself was a stark contrast. When was the last time I had fun on my way to work? Never?

"You sound good, Jessalyn," he said when we were done.

"Anyone ever tell you you're a terrible liar? I sound like a dying swan."

"Well, I like singing with you."

Despite him pushing too hard about Cole, I was sad to leave his car when he pulled onto the studio's parking lot. The end of the playlist was upbeat K-Pop. It was impossible to hold back a smile.

"What time are you done today?" he asked.

"I never really know. I'll just order a ride when the time comes."

"No you won't. Just give me as much heads up as you can. I'll come get you."

I growled my distaste.

"Jessalyn. I just have practice and PT today. Give me something to do. You owe me that for getting me up at 4:30."

"I told you not to hold that against me!"

He cackled. "I knew that would piss you off. Just text me, okay?"

"Fine."

"Have a good day, Sweet Cheeks."

"Thanks for the ride, Jockey. Be careful going home."

18

MIKEY

"Be careful going home."

It was a simple phrase, something my mom would say. But I knew from Mom's Kentucky raising that it was a mountain people way to say "I love you." Almost everyone from that side of the family said, "be careful" instead of "I love you."

Jessie, like Kitty, was a mountain person.

I didn't think Jessie loved me, and she didn't love me like *that*, but she cared about me. That was a change from our rocky start.

And what did she mean by home? Our home? Was she acknowledging that we shared a home? Or was it just my home?

I was all tangled up. I had no business having a crush on my roommate. None at all. Still, I started the playlist from the beginning before leaving Jessie's work parking lot, reflecting on everything we'd talked about on the way there.

When I got home, I made more coffee and got ready for practice. My body was tired, but my mind was wide awake, and

I couldn't wipe the smile from my face. It was still stuck to me when I strolled into morning skate.

"Morning!" I chirped.

Guy narrowed his eyes at me. "Morning? You're awfully cheerful."

"Yeah, he's like . . . smiling," our captain Sorrento said. "More than usual."

I shrugged. "Don't know why. I'm pretty tired, actually." I knew that would get me more questions.

"Somebody got laid," Leroy taunted.

"Actually, no."

Guy had fully stopped what he was doing to examine me. "What's going on with Jessie?"

Figured that he would be the one to know me best. "She actually talked to me—"

"Well, yee-fucking-haw," Leroy said.

"While I drove her to work this morning."

Stelle wasn't giving up. "What do you mean, you took her to work?"

"She had bad sleep, so I took her to work so she could rest."

Guy shook his head. "Mikey, she just broke up with her long-term boyfriend. Go easy."

"Who says I'm not going easy? I haven't touched her! I mean, other than snuggling in my bed."

Guy widened his eyes at me. "And taking her to work. And taking her dinner. I know you like her, Mikey."

In my head, I added *and kissed her boo-boo on her finger, and did anything and everything to get a second of her attention.*

"No, I don't. I mean, she's hot—" I protested. "And you were the one who told me to take her dinner!"

"Mikey."

"Yeah, okay. I hear you."

"Just be her friend. She needs a friend right now. Put the

other stuff out of your head. Be safe for her. If you try to put the moves on her, she'll pull away. Give her space."

"Bullshit," I said. "You gave Kitty space and you guys were broken up for years."

"Yeah, well, now we're getting married," Guy said. "The long game works. I know a thing or two."

I ENDED up having to order Jessie a ride home because I was at the practice facility still when she texted that she was done. The physical therapist had me do extra conditioning and get a massage.

While I was on the table, I ordered a special delivery on rush to my place. She wasn't comfortable in my bed, and that air mattress wasn't doing shit for her. Jessalyn deserved a real bed, and I refused to be a bad host.

I rushed home to intercept the mattress people. But there was a little hitch in my plan. Apparently her new bed had to "off gas" or some shit before she could sleep in it. I guess memory foam stinks. As an apology, I ran to the store to get stuff to make for dinner. The other guys on the team had wives and girlfriends to make their meals. I had my meal prep lady, too, but I was also pretty decent in the kitchen. Plus, chicken breast, rice, and broccoli didn't sound like an apology dinner.

She flumped through the door, looking exhausted as she slid off her shoes and put her purse and jacket on a hook behind the door.

"Hey," I greeted her.

"Hey," she said, surprise in her voice. "Second time this week I've caught you chef-ing."

"I made enough for two," I said with a grin.

"Mikey, you don't have to cook for me."

"But you didn't eat yet, did you?"

"No."

"Okay, before we eat, I have a little surprise and a little apology. Go look in your room."

She squinted at me as she passed through the kitchen to the hallway.

"BEN!"

"Yes?"

She stomped back into the kitchen, looking half like she wanted to cry and half like she wanted to slit my throat. "Why is there a bed in my room?"

"I couldn't let you keep sleeping on that air mattress, Jess. This is your home."

"Stop being nice to me!" she shouted. "I'm not pitiful! I'm not your...your child!"

"You're right. You're not. But I want you comfortable here so you don't rush out."

Her chest was flushed red. "So what's the apology? That it's embarrassing that I'm a grown woman who's relying on the charity of her rich athlete roommate?"

"No," I said over my shoulder as I stirred the sautéed vegetables. I tapped the spoon on the edge of the pan. "Apparently the bed has to, like, off gas or something? Like they said it stinks and you have to let the smell come out for a few days."

A few emotions passed over Jess's face. The final one she settled on was anger. "So let me guess, we have to keep sharing a bed."

I grimaced. "Hence the apology dinner."

"Ben, I just needed to duct tape the air mattress. Stop fucking meddling!"

"Jess, come on. I'm trying to help."

She closed her eyes and took a deep breath into her hands. "I didn't ask for your help. I don't want an apology dinner. I don't want to share a bed. I need to find my own place."

I felt like I'd been slammed against the boards. Somehow,

this hurt worse than physical pain. I was trying, and she flipped it back in my face. I ground my molars as I turned off the stove. "Why?"

"I can't rely on you for everything, Ben."

"Why not?"

"I just walked out of a four-year relationship and right into, where am I, my neighbor's apartment? I met him a couple of weeks ago, I sleep in his bed, he drives me to work, pays for my ride home, buys me furniture, cooks me dinner, and doesn't let me pay rent. Is that an accurate assessment of where we are?" she raged.

"I don't see why it's a problem, Jessalyn," I said carefully, trying not to let my own temper show in my voice. "Seems a 'thank you' would be in order."

She stormed toward the front door. "Is that what you're doing it for? The applause? What the fuck is this even about, Ben?"

I couldn't exactly tell her that I knew Cole was a lying cheater. She might tear my skin off and make a skin suit out of me for being the messenger. I couldn't tell her that I was a selfish bastard who wanted her instead. I had to keep playing the friend. I tried distracting her.

"Can you just eat? I feel like you need to eat," I said.

"I won't eat until you tell me what the fuck you're doing and why! This is so fucking bizarre! I've lost my fucking mind for even being here. I should just go home." Jessie paced by the front door, chewing her thumbnail. It looked like she might bolt at any moment.

"Don't go home," I said, staring at the floor between us with my arms crossed. I dug my fingernails into my forearms. Nerves passed through me, making me shake slightly.

"Why. Not." She stalked toward me, eyes wild. In that moment, I realized just how much I didn't know her. She could be a murderer herself and I'd have no clue. I hadn't even googled her. I only knew her last name because I asked her when we talked on our balconies.

"I'm just trying to be nice," I said, but my words were limp.

"Nope. That's not it. Are you trying to fuck me?"

"Jesus, Jessie—"

"Well, what then?" she seethed, now standing right in front of me, all five foot whatever of her somehow seeming enormous in her rage.

I couldn't tell her the full truth. She couldn't handle it in her present state. I went with the easy out.

"I feel like I broke up your relationship!" I burst out. "I feel like it's my fault that you left him, and I have to do something about it."

Jessie's face reddened, then she curled her lips. "Don't flatter yourself, Mikey. You think you can just press your giant cock against me and sex-face me against your door, and that'll make me walk out on my partner of four fucking years? I may have walked out but he called it over anyway."

She said my cock was giant, thought the teenager who ruled half my brain. Not the time, teenager.

"No." I said it low, quietly, with conviction. She'd been heaving a breath like she was ready to lob more insults at me. The breath hissed out of her like a pin in a balloon as she waited for me to say more. Her eyes darted quickly between mine. "I don't think you left *for* me. I think you left because of what I said. I think you were perfectly happy pretending with him until I pointed out the obvious. And I feel like an asshole for pointing out the obvious and taking away your bliss."

She rubbed her lips together, then gnawed on the bottom one. Her gaze traveled up and down the horizontal stripes on my shirt.

"You don't owe me anything, Ben."

"And you don't owe me, either. We're even."

"No. We're not," she said, getting impassioned again. "I'm *living* in your apartment. You bought me—"

"Sweet Cheeks, you're breaking the deal."

"What deal?" She spit that phrase at me like a gangster holding brass knuckles in front of my face. God, she was feisty.

I grabbed her shoulders and walked her backward until her low back was pressed into the counter. Jessie's breath caught as I leaned over her and opened the cabinet behind her to get down plates.

"You said if I told you why, you'd eat," I said. "I told you why. Dinner's getting cold."

I held a plate out to her. Her ears turned red as she took it.

"Right."

"Hope rice bowls are good with you."

After filling her plate, she stalled, not knowing where to sit. She stood by the dining room table. "Should I go to the other end like we're mortal enemies and have a stare-down?"

I cracked a smile for the first time since we'd been arguing. "Wait, are you implying we're *not* enemies?"

"Hmm, good point."

The banter that I loved so much was back. Had we just had our first real fight?

She ended up sitting across from me. "I'm sorry I got so . . . loud."

I chuckled. "Don't sweat it. You're fun when you're loud."

"That's demeaning!" she cried, her cheeks getting pink again. "That means you don't take me seriously!"

"I take you seriously."

She bristled. "Not if you think I'm 'fun' when I'm communicating a problem."

Jessie was winding up for another rampage, but I swear, the woman just needed to eat. I stood as she prattled on, walking to her side of the table.

"It's so classic for a man to think that a woman is being

'cute' when she's mad, like her anger is just a child's tantrum." She stopped short as I took her fork from her hand, which she had just been using as a weapon to gesticulate at me. I rested my hip on the edge of the table. "What are you doing?"

I forked up some rice with the sauce I made and held it in front of her face. "Open."

"Excuse me?"

"Are you going to open nicely, or are you going to make me shove it in when you're cussing me out?"

"This is exactly what I'm talking abou—"

I pushed the fork past those plush lips and she bit down. Her eyes went from a disbelieving shock to a new softness as I removed the fork.

Then.

She fucking moaned. Her eyes rolled back and her head tipped. "Fuck me, that's good. Did you really make that?"

I bit back a laugh. "If you want me to fuck you, Jessalyn, all you've gotta do is say 'please.'"

I was being crass, but in reality, my stomach clenched. Why was the act of her enjoying my food so sensual? Why could I feel that moan at the base of my spine?

She rolled her eyes. "Dream on, Jockey."

"Want more?" I asked, forking up another bite. "Open wide."

She went right back to furious, giving me a glare that would have killed a weaker beast. She pressed her lips into a line, snatching the fork back from me and taking a bite.

"I'm not a child," she snapped.

I leaned down close to her. "Then don't play games. If you're still mad at me after you eat, you can yell at me some more. But right now, you're gonna eat, Sweet Cheeks. No more arguing until you're full. Got it?"

She batted her eyelashes and gave me a simper. "Yes, Daddy."

This woman. She really had no idea what she was doing to me. How much I wanted to pin her bratty ass to the dining room table and have her screaming for Daddy.

But that wasn't where we were. She was upset with me for trying to help.

I returned to my side of the table, somewhat defeated. "I take you seriously, Jessie. I really thought I was being helpful."

She dropped the attitude and gave me a morose smile. "You are. You're just too nice."

I poked my fork around my plate. "I just think you're not used to someone treating you nice. You're suspicious when someone's nice to you. That happens when someone's mean to you a lot."

"Ugh, don't remind me," she groaned. "I don't know what the fuck I'm doing. Everything feels so out of control."

I nudged her foot under the table to get her to look at me. She was starting to spiral. "You're eating dinner with your friend."

"Yeah, at his apartment that I currently haven't paid for. That's next to the apartment I shared with my long-term boyfriend."

"Jessie, you're not paying me to live here. This is your home. You don't need to pay me for it to be your home."

She scowled. "I will pay you, because I have to pull my weight."

I tapped my lips, thinking. She really wasn't going to let it go. "What if you make me a suit instead?"

She gave me a blank stare.

"You're a seamstress, right?"

"Correct."

"Well, I usually have some weird guy make my suits. I'd rather give you the business. And it'd probably be cheaper than paying rent and I'll get a dank suit out of it."

"Do you really wear suits that much?" she asked.

I totally forgot that Jessie was in fact *not* a puck bunny and knew jack shit about the NHL. "We're required to wear them on game days, to and from the game."

Her expression finally lightened. "Holy smokes, Jockey. I had no idea. I could probably get rich off your team alone."

"Make me a good one and you know I'll put in a good word for you, Sweet Cheeks. I'd market the shit out of you."

She sat thinking for a moment. Her next words were quiet. "Because you feel guilty?"

God, was it Cole that made her so unsure of herself? When Jessie was at her most fiery, she was a force to be reckoned with. But vulnerable and self-doubting? I hated seeing that in her.

"Because you're my friend and I assume you do good work."

"This is actually not a terrible plan," she said, taking a bite of her dinner.

"I'm full of good ideas. I'm excellent best friend material. And," I said, gesturing to her rapidly emptying plate, "I'm a remarkable chef."

"Alright. Deal. I'll make you a suit in exchange for living here."

"Great. So you'll measure me tonight and have it done tomorrow, right?"

Jessie flopped her head down on the table.

19

JESSIE

I insisted on doing the dishes since Ben cooked. I wiped down the kitchen counters, but really, he'd been a surprisingly neat cook. I don't know why I had such rock-bottom expectations of Ben. I really wasn't being fair to him. He was nothing but nice to me, albeit a little bossy about it.

I grabbed my measuring tape from my sewing table, glancing at the new bed that indeed did carry a strong odor. I knocked at Mikey's open bedroom door.

"Jockey?"

The en-suite bathroom door swung open, steam coming out around him. There was Ben, buck naked and rubbing a towel over his hair. Muscles. Glorious, corded muscles, miles of them stretched over his whole body. Veins. And, "Holy God!"

I screamed and flattened myself against the wall, covering my eyes. His dick. His actual dick. Was that *soft*? I mean, I'd felt the thing pushing into my backside when we cuddled, but Jesus, was it really that big?

"Shit, my bad," he said. "Need something, babe?"

"Babe?!" I shrieked. "You're naked!"

"In my own room!"

"With the door open, Mikey!"

"Well, sorry, I'm not used to having a roommate yet."

I sputtered. "I knocked! The door was open! You just came out of there like that!"

A waistband snapped. "There. I got on some pants. You happy?"

I stammered, unable to come up with anything to say.

"Jessie? Did you need something?"

My hands were still cemented over my eyes. Mikey's footsteps came closer and his fingers closed around my wrists, pulling my hands off my face. I pinned myself against the wall behind me, gasping.

"Hey. Didn't mean to embarrass you."

My face flamed. "It's— it's just your body. Bodies are fine. I'm sorry I barged in here."

"It's fine," he said, his tongue darting out to wet his bottom lip. "I'm sorry I got you all flustered."

"I'm not flustered," I breathed.

The measuring tape in my hand unrolled, dropping to the floor. Mikey didn't take his eyes off my face. Our faces were just inches apart, and he still held my wrists. His voice was low and calm. "What do you call what you are, then?"

The humid warmth of his skin from the shower pulsed into my space, a manly body wash smell surrounding me.

I found my words. "Surprised."

He gave a little chuckle, a smirk playing on his lips. "Is that what you call it?"

Was he putting the moves on me? Worse, was I liking it? I had that same could-morph-into-a-puddle feeling that I had when he gave his little speech about fucking me in a coat closet.

My chest heaved as I forced a breath. "Yeah."

His thumb passed over the inside of my wrist, and my stomach clenched. "I'm too used to letting it all out in locker rooms. I'll do better."

I flicked my eyebrows up. "At least a towel would help."

He still held my wrists, my elbows tight to my sides. "You gonna measure me?"

My cheeks boiled anew thinking of that monstrous thing I'd just seen bouncing between his legs. Mikey gave a soft laugh and let go of me. "For the suit, Jess. Get your mind out of the gutter."

My jaw flapped and I cleared my throat. "Yes. I need to get your measurements so I can make a drawing. Might help to see what your favorite suits look like, too."

"You got it, hon."

He took a step back and stood with his arms extended. I followed, wrapping the measuring tape around his bare pecs. I pulled my phone out of my back pocket and marked down the number. I slipped the tape to his waist, sliding a finger between his skin and the tape for a little breathing room.

His breath coated my shoulder where he dipped his head to watch me. The hairs on the back of my neck rose and I fought a shiver. If he had put a hand on me right then, I would have thrown it all away. Been ready to beg him to throw me on the bed and have his way with me. When did I become such a perv? I was taking a non-sexual situation and making it sexual. It was just taking measurements! I had to gain control of the situation, for my own sake.

"Stand up straight, please. Do you gain or lose a lot during the season?"

"Usually my butt gets a little smaller over the summer, but gets big once I'm skating more again. It's probably at its biggest about now. And I bloat when my stomach's pissed off or I forget Lactaid."

I puffed out my bottom lip. "That sucks."

"It's life. People have bigger problems."

His hip measurement was indeed much larger than the actors I worked with, but I never comment on peoples' bodies.

We all have enough to deal with without comparison. I put the tape off-center so I wouldn't have to make direct contact with an area of his body that would haunt me for the rest of my days. I was mortified that I'd seen him naked. It was just bad timing and not a big deal, but . . . ugh.

I knelt in front of him to get his inseam and outseam. These were measurements I took every day. No bother for me, right? We were silent. I picked up my phone to punch in the final measurements, staying on the floor. When I glanced up, Ben looked down at me with his hand out to help me up. My breathing quickened as I stood, chest to chest with him for the second time that night. We stared, locked in an uncomfortable battle of the wills.

His eyes flicked over every part of my face. "I'll show you the suits."

MY TEETH WERE BRUSHED. I'd taken my evening shower and done my hair so it would be easy to style in the morning. I'd laid out my clothes. It was just a matter of consciously getting in Ben's bed. The other two times I'd ended up there, I'd gotten there by him carrying me in while I was asleep.

I didn't know how to feel about that.

I stood by his bed, my book and blankie in hand. Yes, I was twenty-five and still carrying my childhood blanket. I have no shame about it. That thing is the most comfortable scrap of fabric that exists on this planet, and was my companion through countless sleepless nights.

"You don't have to go to bed when I do, Ben," I said. "I'm a shitty sleeper."

"Yeah, well, maybe I can help."

I closed my eyes, searching for patience on the inside of my eyelids. "Ben, I appreciate everything you're doing for me, but please don't smother me. Go to bed when you normally would."

"Well, if I want to drive you to work tomorrow, I should go to bed when you do," he said.

I sighed, putting my head into my hands. "I can drive myself. As long as I sleep half-decently tonight, I should be fine."

He pressed his lips together. "What if you have a nightmare?"

"Apologies in advance if I do, but it's better if you don't wake me up, okay? Just ignore it if you can."

Ben's eyes rounded and he seemed upset. "It's so hard to see you like that."

I pulled back the sheets and got in, draping my blankie around my neck and sliding on my glasses. "Sorry about that. Two more days, and then I'll be in my own room, right? And if you need me to move out, I'll start looking. You've already done too much."

"I want you to stay," Ben said. He said it so firmly. Resolutely. No questions asked. He wanted me to live with him. "Nice glasses."

"Thanks?"

He snorted. "No, they look good on you. Hot librarian vibes."

I glared at him. "Fine, *pretty* librarian vibes," he said.

I guffawed. "I love that you think that's better."

"What's up with the yarn wad?"

"What?"

He bent over and shook my blankie on my shoulder. "That's my blankie. What did you call it?!"

"Yarn Wad. I think it's a good name. Because it's a yarn wad."

"Look, I don't need your mockery," I huffed, turning on my side away from him.

"Aw, come on, Jessie. I wouldn't pick on you. I think it's cute. But it is definitely deserving of the name Yarn Wad."

"But did I ask for your opinion?" I bit out. "I have a hard enough time sleeping as it is."

He blew right past my irritation. "What's your plan with that book?"

I flipped over to face him, where he still sat on his side of the bed. "If you'd ever stop cajoling me, I'd fucking read it so I can go to sleep!"

"Okay, okay, geez," he said, scooting off to the bathroom.

Okay, but one serious issue: my annoyingly persistent and eager and infuriatingly attractive roommate and all of his back-and-forth banter had me all kinds of tense. With no room of my own and very little private time for the next 48 hours, I had nowhere to manage that tension. He'd have heard me in the shower. Did I have enough time while he was in the bathroom getting ready for bed?

I just needed to take the edge off. The way he stood over me in the kitchen had me melting. His gentle touch when we danced together at Kitty's party. How ridiculously good he looked naked. How he held my wrists against his wall. That tiny stroke of his thumb over the tender skin. How he licked his lip. He smelled so goddamn good and he got this look in his eyes like he'd just love to show me how it's done. And "it" was mind-blowing sex.

I did *not* want to get involved with Ben. Yes, Cole and I were through, but I needed recovery time. And Ben was my roommate for Christ's sake. And anyway, he was a player. I'd done my share of messing around before Cole, but I wasn't thrilled with the thought of being with a love-em-leave-em kinda guy. I was already sleeping in his damn bed. I didn't need to add anything more physical to the already tense equation.

Still, I was pretty sure if I just said the word, Ben would do any combination of fun and exciting acts with me. The thought had my hand drifting under the covers. His women *did* always sound satisfied. I wanted to be satisfied, so very, very badly. My hand moved faster as I let my mind explore what those strong hands would feel like on me, how hard he'd grab, whether he liked to be a little rough or more tender. My breathing hitched as my back arched. A tiny whimper escaped my throat. God, I needed release so bad it hurt.

The bathroom door slammed against the wall. That meant the bathroom door had already been open for a few seconds at that point. It was too fucking late. Ben was already in the bedroom.

I ripped my hand out of my shorts. Fuck, my fingers were wet. Jesus. That went far, fast. Fuck fuck fuck. I wiped them on my stomach and rubbed my shirt over it, because I wasn't about to put them on his sheets.

"Oh. I, uh," Ben's face went beet red. "Sorry, I can, uh, give you some space."

"It's not what you think," I squeaked. "I just—"

"Nope, nope, no problem. I'm gonna go, uh, watch TV," he said, gesturing to the living room with his thumbs.

"No, it's nothing. Um, come to bed?"

Ben stood in the doorway to the hall. He swallowed hard and held his hands over his crotch, not looking directly at me. "You're right. I should let you get to sleep on your own. I'll, uh, see you around."

Mortified. Medically. Physically. Metaphysically. Mortified.

20

MIKEY

This was all Guy Stelle's fault. He was all "give her space" and "be her friend." If I were typical me, I'd have had my hands under the sheets and my fingers covered in Jessie. But no, I had to behave myself under extreme circumstances.

Jessalyn Welsh had been touching herself in my bed. I heard what she sounded like when she was actually turned on. I saw the flush in her cheeks before she realized I could see her. Her hand was under the covers, but I could tell what she was doing. God, she was fucking gorgeous.

I sat in the living room with the TV up way too loud, shell-shocked with an aching hard-on. My sweats were fucking wet from my tip leaking. My dick was literally crying for attention, and I'd already jerked it in the shower after dinner. Christ. How did she have that kind of power over me?

Because she was Jessalyn, and I was obsessed with her. That's how.

Fuck it. I couldn't get in bed with her with my dick like that. I couldn't stop thinking about the way she breathed. How it caught the slightest bit when I leaned over her to get a plate from the cabinet. What would that feel like against my neck, deep inside her, making her beg for me? How would she taste? She wore this perfume or lotion or something that made her have this soft peach scent. Would I smell like that after we fucked? Would she be as feisty in bed as she was when we bantered, or would she let me take the lead? Would it be "take me, Daddy" or would it be "fuck me, Ben?" Maybe ten strokes later, my hand was a mess. I'm not sure I'd ever come that hard, that fast.

As I came down, I realized it was Florida playing Toronto on the screen. We were playing Toronto in a few days, so it would be smart for me to watch. Yep, I could give Coach notes and show how much value I added to the team by checking them out. It was already debatable whether we'd be snagging a wild card spot that year. We needed all the help we could get.

I had to get my head on straight. I couldn't keep living in this Jess-centric la-la-land.

It was no fault of hers. I just hadn't been this way over a woman, I don't know, maybe ever?

Would giving in make it better? Or would giving in make me more of a shithead for inviting her into the lion's den only to be devoured by the lion himself?

When I crawled into bed with Jess a couple of hours later, she let out a quiet hum in her sleep. Her breathing was downy soft. I was usually a side sleeper, but I couldn't help myself. I stayed on my back in case she'd want to curl up on my chest like she did that first night. Thinking over the day, I relished how for the first time in my life, I'd started and ended an entire day with the same person.

21

JESSIE

"So, I kinda have a new roommate."

I shifted down the craft services line with Kitty, picking out breakfast before shooting started for the day.

"So I've heard!" Kitty said, her face lighting up. "I didn't want to say anything in case you'd already left or something. How's that going?"

My face flushed as I thought back on the self-love incident in his bed the night before. "It's whatever. We're adjusting to each other. He's kind of all over me, wanting to hang out constantly."

Kitty laughed as she poured cream in her coffee. "Mikey always and forever wants to hang out. He's like a lost puppy sometimes, God love him. He's so sweet, but it can be a lot. I'm sure he's glad to have your company."

I raised my eyebrows. "That's one way to put it. He decided my air mattress was inadequate and ordered me a bed. But it has to off-gas, so I have to bed share with him. It's been a whole thing."

Kitty fought a spit take of her coffee. "Did he purposefully orchestrate that? Are you okay with that?"

"Well, I didn't imagine he did it on purpose. I don't think he premeditated me becoming his roommate."

Her eyes were wide. "Just know, if you ever need a break, my door is open. Whether Guy's home or not, you're welcome to stay at my place. Even if you just need to sit in Mikey-free silence for a while, you can come over."

"Appreciate it, Kitty." But really, I was spiraling a bit. Why was I twenty-five and relying on everyone in my limited social circle for housing?

"And maybe all four of us can get dinner when they're back from the next road trip. We can make the boys come up this way or we can go out around me and Guy in Glendale."

"That sounds awesome," I said.

I was taken aback by how nice she was. A writer and actress was just opening her life to me. We were sort of around the same age. I'd only briefly met her fiancé, between the sleeping pill incident and the engagement party, but still, the hockey crowd was surprisingly kind of amazing.

Three weeks before, my life was boring as shit. My job was still exciting, but I only ever hung out with Cole and his friends. Suddenly, I had this expanding world. I kept waiting for the other shoe to drop, but there was no indication that either Mikey or Kitty was going to cut me out of their lives.

The day finally came where I'd be able to sleep in my own bed. The second night in Mikey's bed was less tense, mostly because he wasn't home and didn't even come in until after I was long asleep. I only had to give him a dirty look for making some ridiculous grumbling noise that woke me up when he got in bed Tuesday night.

Had I known I was going to be alone Tuesday, I would have kept my damn hand out of my pants Monday night. Still, I didn't dare attempt masturbating again, though I'm pretty sure that's what Mikey had done after he left me alone that night. You don't turn the TV that loud just because. Thinking that me touching myself had made him have to touch himself made my whole body flush.

We weren't childish enough to build a pillow fort between us. We're grown adults. We could share a sleeping surface without touching, right?

Wrong.

Both mornings, I woke up curled up on his chest, his arm holding me to him. I decided to just enjoy the snuggles. He barely stirred when I got up, probably because I'm a considerate human being and am quiet. He mumbled a "have a good day" from the bed when I left each morning.

When I got home Wednesday night, I was so looking forward to crashing in my own bed. I spotted a familiar face when I was walking into my building: Cole's coworker Sheila. I'd always suspected there were feelings between them, but never wanted to push. I got a text chime as I walked to the elevator.

BENJAMIN MICHAEL JOCKEY

Hey, r u almost home

Walking up now

I'll meet u outside. Something came up

"Jessie?"

"Oh, hey, Sheila!"

She was dressed very nice, obviously not in work attire. More like date attire. Had she put salad dressing on her legs to make them that shiny?

"I didn't know you still lived here!" she said with a too-big smile.

"Oh, yeah," I said, fearing where our conversation was headed.

The elevator dinged and we walked in together. I pushed the button for my floor and she didn't press any other floor. There were only two units on our floor: Cole's and Mikey's.

My stomach sank. Was this what came up for Mikey? Not only was Sheila a temptress for Cole, but she also was seeing Mikey?

"Are you . . . here to see Mikey?"

"Who?"

"Oh. You're here to see Cole."

"Uh, yeah. He told me you two were, ah—"

I gave a tight smile. "Yep. We are."

My mind took off at a sprint. He wasted absolutely no time in getting with Sheila. I always knew he liked her. I joked with him about it once, but he got suspiciously defensive about it. Though it wasn't a surprise, it still stung. Had they been involved before we broke up?

"So how long have you two been . . .?" I asked, carefully arranging my face to be pleasant.

"Oh, you know. A couple of months now. Nothing too serious, though," Sheila said, like that wasn't a big detail.

I could have vomited on my own shoes. He was accusing me of cheating, which I hadn't, while he was actually cheating on me. Why a couple of months? What made him start? I was too shocked to even cry.

The doors opened on my floor, and there stood Mikey and Cole in their respective doorways. Mikey's eyes bounced between Sheila and Cole, then to me, assessing the situation. I rounded my eyes at him, a silent plea for help that I hoped he understood. Recognition flashed over his face and he jumped into action.

"Hey, honey," Ben said. "How was work?"

Ben Miknevicius. Mikey. The guy who would do truly anything for me, doing something for me yet again. I was overwhelmed by the role he instantaneously assumed, pretending to be my boyfriend without question. I cracked a smile at him and gave out a breathy, "Oh, ya know."

I stepped to him as he reached for me. Our eyes met for a slight beat before we both knew what was going to happen. He bent and his mouth was on mine for what was supposed to be a quick hello kiss. But once we were in the kiss, there was no way either of us was backing out. Because even what was supposed to look like a routine kiss felt like the most monumental kiss of my life. The first kiss was quick, but we hardly pulled away. He hovered at my mouth with a slight smirk before going back in. Ben tugged my bottom lip between his teeth, sending a jolt of lust through me. I had to taste him, and he damn well knew it. Could he read my mind? He dropped his jaw open and slanted his mouth to give me the access I wanted. His chest was firm under my hands. I already knew that his body was rock solid from all the snuggles we'd shared but combining it with the kiss had a synergistic effect.

And the kiss itself. My God, I hadn't been kissed like that in far too long. There was both restraint and wildness as his tongue roved over mine, my stomach a tickled-up mess. I played with the ends of his long-ish hair that reached just above the nape of his neck, the stubble around his mouth grazing my skin. Realizing we'd been at it probably a hair too long, I pulled out. Ben stroked his hands over my hair and held us nose-to-nose, giving me another soft kiss.

"Missed you," he whispered.

"You, too," I said, feeling Cole and Sheila's eyes boring into us. My senses returned. I smelled the curry that Cole usually made special for me. I turned to look at my old apartment's doorway, finding Cole pushing Sheila inside and glaring at me.

"Fucking whore," Cole murmured before he slammed the door.

Mikey's eyes rounded, lunging like he was going to go after Cole. I instinctively held him back, which snapped his attention back to me.

"You okay?" Mikey asked. He wrapped me in a tight hug as Cole's harsh words broke over me. "He's a liar, you know."

That's when the tears came to me. Ben released me and wiped his thumbs under my eyes. "I'm so sorry, Jess. You know that's not true."

"He's been cheating," I croaked.

Ben pulled me to him again, squeezing me hard. He murmured in my ear, "Hon, I know this is a bad time, but we have guests."

"Hi there!" came a cheerful voice. I leaned around Mikey to see the source, a short red-headed woman with Mikey's dimples and a taller blonde woman who looked like she spent a lot of time in the sun.

"Jessalyn, meet my mother, Debbie, and my Aunt Lori."

The red-headed woman stepped forward with a look of sheer delight. "I've heard so much about you! Ben didn't mention that you two were an item!"

Ben put his arm around my waist and brought me inside. I looked at him for help.

"It's all very new," he said pleasantly. New was an understatement. A scheme hatched up when I stepped off the elevator was more like it. "Mom and Lori are going to stay with us for a couple of days. We were just about to head out for dinner."

"Oh, well, I can let y'all go catch up," I said as graciously as possible. I really wanted to go sob in my bed, but it seemed my bed would still not be mine.

"Nonsense, sweetie. Come eat with us! You're part of the

family," his aunt Lori said. Never have I ever loathed Midwestern hospitality so much as I did right in that moment.

Ben kissed my temple and squeezed my side, where his hand still hadn't left. "Yeah, hon. Come with us. Unload from that bad day at work."

He was covering the Cole situation for me by blaming my upset on work. Not bad, Mikey.

I forced a megawatt smile that I hoped looked authentic. "I guess if you insist! I'm just going to go freshen up and then I'll be ready. That okay, baby?"

"Of course, darlin'," he said, stifling a laugh. As I left the kitchen, I glared at him over his mom and Lori's shoulders.

"DARLIN'?" I mouthed. He just shot me a dimply smile and a wink. I stepped into my room to find two suitcases already in there. Christ. I fired off a text to Kitty.

> SOS. Mikey's mom and aunt are here and they're staying in my room. They think we're a couple. There are other complications. I might need to take you up on your offer

I took off my blouse and bra, waving fresh air under my boobs and analyzing the situation. Ben had kissed me. I'd kissed Ben? Why was it such an amazing kiss? But it wasn't real. Right?

Cole was seeing Sheila. That was real. He *had been* seeing Sheila. I'd been cheated on. I was shaking. Another wave of nausea passed over me. How had I not known? How could he do that to me? No wonder he was so eager to find a reason for us to split up.

And now I had to keep up the ruse that Ben and I were dating because his mom and aunt saw us kissing? I had to go to dinner with them. Sleep in his bed *again*. Unless Kitty, who I also didn't know that well, could offer me an out.

I applied a fresh layer of deodorant as sweat broke out in every fold of my body. My phone pinged.

KITTY GATTO

OMGGGGGG you poor thing!

Yes of course. Come on over. Let me know when you're on your way

THANK YOU so much!! I'll keep you posted. I'm headed out to dinner with them now. This is insane.

There was a knock at the door. "Can I come in?"

"Hang on," I said, scrambling to hold a shirt to my front. So much for airing out my boobs.

The door creaked open and Ben stepped inside. "Shit, sorry," he said as he realized I was topless.

"I said 'hang on!'" I hissed.

"Sorry, I thought you said 'come on!'"

"Well, your mom and your aunt think you've seen it all before anyway, huh?"

Ben sat on the bed and put his hands over his eyes, leaning his elbows on his knees. "I know, Jessie." He sounded some mixture of guilty and defeated.

"What the fuck is going on here?" I whisper screamed as I looked through my drawers for a clean shirt.

"I'm really sorry, Jessie. I forgot they were coming to visit. I'm really bad with scheduling stuff. I'm lucky the team tells me where to be all the time."

I gave some sort of harrumph. "Also where are we even going? I don't know what to wear."

"I thought I'd help you with the Cole situation, but then Mom and Lor saw and well, you are kind of an ideal girlfriend, so I just went with it. And we're going to my favorite taco place. Casual."

"You just went with it?!"

"Sorry, Sweet Cheeks, how else was I supposed to explain why I was passionately kissing my roommate? And you're welcome, by the way. I think we pissed Cole off plenty."

Tears flooded my eyes as I jammed on a band t-shirt to go with my ripped jeans. "I shouldn't have kissed you. Now he's really going to think I was cheating."

"Who gives a fuck what he thinks? He actually cheated on you! He deserves to feel like shit because he is a piece of shit."

"You knew?" I snapped, loud enough to make Mikey flinch and uncover his eyes to look at me. His mouth opened and closed, and he stammered, trying to find his words. "You fucking knew. This whole time. Is that what all of this has been about?"

"Jessie, honey, Sweet Cheeks," he started. I glared at him. "I didn't want you to feel worse than you already did. Either way it was over between you. Trust me, I hate that guy as much as you do. I just didn't want you to have any more reason to doubt yourself."

"So noble of you!" I hissed.

"Why are you mad at me? He was the one cheating on you!" Ben massaged his temples. "I wanted to help you live a happier life, Jessalyn. He hasn't been taking care of you."

"Because you seem to know so well how I sound when I orgasm? Christ, Benjamin."

"Well, you certainly sounded different in my bed the other night!" he blurted out, then clapped a hand over his mouth.

Disdain ripped through me. How fucking dare he. I was beyond done with this man and his allegedly altruistic meddling.

"I don't have to stay here for this," I said finitely, opening my drawers and grabbing a duffel bag.

"Jessie, please, no."

"Oh, you need me to stay so your mom can think you have a girlfriend?"

"You wanted to pay me for living here. This is one way you can do that."

My jaw dropped as I shoved socks into my bag. "I am not for hire, Benjamin. My body is not for hire."

"Jessie, you know that's not what I meant. All of this is so out of hand. You know I just say shit sometimes. I don't mean to."

"Actually," I said, gesticulating to him with a bra before slamming it into my bag, "I don't know that. Because I hardly fucking know you, Ben. We've known each other for two weeks. But still, you think, you think, you think . . . you know everything about me."

I was afraid I was going too far, but he went too far with me. My life was crumbling, not his.

"This is my life, Ben. It's not some game. I just got dumped after years with someone. He's been cheating on me. We've lived together in three different cities. And all you can focus on is that I make you look good in front of your mom and that you know how I sound when I come."

"Honey, I never should have said that."

I dabbed at the tears on my cheeks with the back of my hand and was filled with a new wave of rage. "But you thought it. Why not say it? Have anything else you want to tell me about my sex life, Ben?" I stalked toward where he sat on the bed, chucking the bag down. "You know my favorite position? You know just how I like it?"

Ben stood suddenly, our chests brushing again. His height and size humbled me in my tirade. He breathed heavily, looking down at me. Tension pulsed, and a shot of desire passed over me. The memory of our kiss thundered through my body, his lips a permanent impression on mine. Without him even touching me, I could feel him on me.

His eyes cut to my mouth, then back to my eyes. He had to be thinking the same. His demeanor softened. He lifted his hands, then started and stopped a few motions, like he couldn't decide how to touch me. The tips of his fingers skated down my forearms, to my wrists. I trembled, the raw emotions of the last twenty minutes erupting. His fingers laced in mine, holding both of my hands.

"I don't want to fight with you, Jessalyn. I'm really only trying to help. I think maybe I'm doing it wrong. But I care about you. I'm so sorry about all this. This has to be so hard."

His eyes were so sincere, his hold on my hands steady and gentle. He was right. I was misdirecting my anger. He was actually being pretty patient with me, to his credit. I blinked back more tears.

"I hate him so much right now," I said on a gulp of air.

"I know, honey," he said, pulling me into a tender embrace. His hand passed over my hair, idly gathering it into a tiny ponytail at the nape of my neck and twirling it around. The fact that he was calling me little pet names behind closed doors struck me.

"I don't have time to cry. Your mom and aunt are still outside."

"They'll be fine. I'll tell them you had a rough day. And hey, I wanted to help you when I kissed you. I wasn't trying to be weird."

I nodded against his chest. "I know. That was really nice, Ben. Thanks for doing that." My arms circled his waist and I leaned back to look at him. "I want to pay it back. I'll be your fake girlfriend."

He shook his head. "You don't have to. That's a ridiculous thing to ask."

"No. It's not a big deal. You helped me with Cole. I'll help you. We'll make it fun."

"You don't owe me anything, Jessie. I shouldn't make it seem like you do."

"I know," I said. "I want to."

He twisted his lips to chew on them. "So you'll come eat with us? I'll buy you as many margaritas as you want," he offered, thumbing over the moisture on my cheeks.

"Can we get queso, too?"

Ben cracked a smile. "Queso, guac, that chorizo and cheese stuff, anything you want, baby."

"Okay."

With a kiss on my cheek, he stitched our hands together and walked us out of the bedroom.

22

MIKEY

Jessalyn was a heartbreaker. As in, it broke my heart when I saw the desperation in her eyes getting off the elevator with Cole's new chick. I was only standing out there to warn her about my mom being there, but I ended up being needed for more. The good news is, I'd been dying to kiss her anyway. That was as good an excuse as any. My years of reading situations and thinking quick on my feet for hockey came in handy.

It was such a relief to finally feel her lips on mine, to taste her, to have her wrapped up in my arms. I'm known for my casual encounters, but I needed her kiss more than I needed to get off with other conquests. It made me realize how empty most of my hookups were. Kissing was just a means to an end with them.

I actually felt something for Jessie. I wanted to keep kissing her until she felt how special she is. I wanted to do other things with her, too, along with plenty of kissing. I wanted to know what she thought about everything under the sun. I wanted to protect her. I wanted to have her tease me and sing along to songs with me. I wanted to hold her hand because I liked how it felt.

What was happening to me?

I couldn't stop replaying the wildness in her eyes the moment she realized we were actually going to kiss, like it was what she needed, too. The sweet softness of her body pressing into me. Those fucking tits. God.

Well, anyway. I was out to dinner with this powerhouse of a woman and . . . my mother and her best friend.

Jessie was good-natured fielding Mom and Lori's endless questions. When Lori asked how we met, we both gazed at each other lovingly. "We were," I started, and she finished my sentence, "Neighbors."

I love a girl with a good appetite, and Jessie was absolutely laying into the chips and salsa. Eating her feelings about Cole, I supposed. Or eating her feelings about me. Or both.

Either way, I was happy to see her eating again.

What were her feelings about me? The kiss was a fake, obviously, but damn did it feel real. I can't deny that I enjoyed it, that I wanted it with every fiber of my being. Maybe I just needed to get laid.

But tonight wasn't about me. She'd been dealt a serious blow by her ex, and I didn't need to make it any more about me than I already had. She was cool enough to put up with dinner with my family.

"Jessie, how are you liking Ben's games?" Mom asked.

"She actually hasn't been yet, Ma. She doesn't know a thing about hockey. Can you believe that?"

"It's true," Jessie said. "When I found out what he did for a living, I told him I thought hockey players were supposed to be bigger."

Mom and Lori cackled, eating that up. Peach margaritas lubricated the situation.

Jessie looked over at me with her tiny little dimple out and went on. "He informed me that those are pads that make them so big. How was I supposed to know?"

Mom patted Jessie's hand on the table. "I like this one, Benny. You should keep her around."

Jessie blushed and I squeezed her thigh, looking at her all moon-eyed. My stomach even did that dippy feeling. A mousey squeak of a voice in the back of my head screamed to stop, that this was dangerous, but it was too late. I was genuinely enjoying pretending like Jess was mine, so much so that it didn't feel like pretending. "I plan to try."

The waiter came by to ask if we wanted drink refills before our food came.

"I do!" Mom chimed in.

"Me too!" Aunt Lori said.

"Not me. I'm cut off," Jessie said. I also gestured that I was good, since I'd be playing the next day and I was DD for those clowns.

"Aw, come on," Mom whined. Lori booed. Man, they *really* liked Jessie.

"I have to work early, and I'm going to head out to Kitty's for the night tonight."

"What do you mean, honey?" I asked. I didn't know she and Kitty were close enough to be having girl slumber parties.

Jessie waved her hand. "No, y'all need to catch up without me in the way."

"Jessalyn, we're not prudes. We don't mind if you two shack up together. We weren't born yesterday," Mom said.

"Mom," I sighed.

"What? You're grown adults. You can have all the sex you want," Mom pushed.

Lori cackled. "Deb, you're making them turn beet red!"

Indeed, Jessie's gaze was locked on the empty chip basket, her face a deep crimson.

"*Mom*," I whined. "Let's leave our sex life out of this discussion, please."

"Oh, you kids. So uptight. Your father says hello, by the way. You should call him sometime."

"Yeah. Yeah, I will," I said tersely.

"I'll just slip out to the ladies," Jess said. I scooted out of our booth to let her leave.

"I'll join you," Lori said, leaving me and Mom some privacy.

"Mom, I don't want to talk about Dad. I'm glad you came to visit. Let's just enjoy this time, okay?"

"Benjamin, when are you going to forgive your father? I forgave him years ago," she said, rolling her eyes. "Not like he'd change."

"That's what makes me mad. He'll never change."

"Well, I'm glad to see you're not like him, Benny. Jessalyn is such a catch for you! So pretty and sweet. I know you did your fair amount of sowing your oats—"

"Mom," I protested again. What was wrong with my mother?

"Mikey, is that you?" The timing couldn't have been worse. A busty blonde woman whose name escaped me but whose body I had definitely been inside approached our table. At that moment, Jess came back from the bathroom, laughing over her shoulder with Lori.

"Hey there," I said, trying not to show off exactly how much I had no clue what her name was.

"Is this your mom? And . . . sister?" She gestured to Jess.

I stood to let Jess back in, but grabbed her before she could slide back in and kissed her cheek. Jessie laced her fingers with mine on her hips.

"Not my sister. This is my girlfriend, Jessie."

The blonde looked Jess up and down with an expression like she was smelling a bad smell. "I thought you didn't do girlfriends."

"Yeah, well, the right one came along. Ain't that right, hon?" I nestled my nose into her neck and planted a kiss there. Jessie leaned into me and giggled, pressing her hand to the side of my face.

"That tickles," she sighed.

"More where that came from," I mumbled in her ear. Her breath caught. Jesus, what was I doing?

My old friend was not amused. "Cute. Well, let me know if you change your mind and want somebody more your type. You have my number. Have a good night." She disappeared in a flash of blonde hair.

Jess pasted on a smile, but I could tell she was uncomfortable. Like she was my actual girlfriend, I tried to smooth it over with an arm around her shoulder and a kiss to her temple. It was the kind of shit I saw Guy do to Kitty, so I figured that's loving boyfriend stuff. Luckily, our food came right then.

"Actually, sir, could I get another margarita?" Jess said. Her voice was calm and sweet, but her eyes had absolute anguish in them. I turned to our food.

"Not going to Kitty's after all?"

"What's another marg?" she asked with a grimace of a smile, to Mom and Lori's excited whoops.

"Dig in, everybody," I said, desperate to shift the mood.

Jess didn't talk while we got ready for bed. Pissed off radiated from her like a black cloud. She was in the white silk pajamas she wore when we first really met, with the tiny shorts that gave her the Sweet Cheeks name. I had to focus not to stare at her boobs, because that was not going to help my case.

As she put on maybe the fifteenth step in her skin care routine, I spoke.

"I'm sorry, Jessalyn."

Her fingers stopped moving over her skin and she stared at me in the mirror for a second. Then she continued her meticulous skin care application. When she finished, she turned to face me, crossing her arms.

"What exactly do you think you're sorry for, Ben?"

I wanted to reach out and touch her, to hold her hips while I spoke to her. But we were not actually dating, and that was also part of the problem. I looked very pointedly at her eyes as she rubbed some cream into the skin over her boobs, doing my best to have some decorum when I really wanted to bug out my eyes and pant like a dog.

"For upsetting you. For dragging you out to dinner. For making you uncomfortable."

She studied me, blinking slowly as she took off the headband that held back her bangs. "Hmm. Okay."

I was not sorry for touching her as much as I did, because goddammit, I liked it. And, she'd agreed to the fake girlfriend thing. Touching was part of it.

Why was I feeling defensive about the touching? Was it because I liked it so much and I wasn't sure if she felt the same? I didn't want her to be uncomfortable. I wanted her to want to touch me, too. Did she?

"Not sorry for not telling me my boyfriend was cheating on me?"

"Jessie, see it from my perspective. If I were in a relationship, and you thought I was being cheated on, would you have told me?"

Her mouth went into a narrow line. I had her there. She moved on to the next thing. "You're not at all sorry that you didn't defend your fake girlfriend in front of your old hockey whore? Is that the term? It's something cutesy and demeaning like that, isn't it?"

I slapped my hand over my face and croaked out a humiliated, "Puck bunny."

"Ah yes! How could I forget?" she said sarcastically, heading into the bedroom.

"I felt like I stuck up for you, Jessie," I argued. "What more did you want?"

"She was the second woman and third person this evening to look at me like I was trash, okay? Maybe that wore me down a bit."

"Jess, she was jealous of you. Take it as a compliment."

"She was jealous because I fake have something she wants! I don't even know why I'm worked up about this. What we're doing isn't even real. Soon enough, you'll be right back to women like her so things won't be 'stale' for you anymore," Jessie ranted, plopping down on her side of the bed.

God, I could never imagine things being stale with Jessie, but I *knew* it was the wrong time to say that. "Honey—"

"I don't even have a real boyfriend, but Cole is dating someone else. He just thinks I am."

She wasn't facing me, but her shoulders shook as her tears came. I moved to sit next to her and put my arm around her.

"Let it out, babe."

Jessie wailed, leaning into my chest. "Four fucking years," she spat, her teeth chattering with how hard she was crying, "and who knows how long he's been cheating."

I cradled her head as she cried, feeling awful that Cole had put her through so much pain, and that I didn't lighten the load that night like I'd intended.

I could have asked her to be my real girlfriend right then. But I didn't want her to date me out of desperation. I was the desperate one. I didn't want to be her rebound. I wanted to be the one she wanted. The knife twisted in me, too.

Her crying slowed.

"You've gotta get up early, Sweet Cheeks. You wanna try to get some sleep?"

She nodded, and I pulled back the sheets for her, tucking

her in. I wanted to do anything I could to make her feel cared for, to make her life a little easier. I draped Yarn Wad across her neck.

She looked at me, mystified. "Thanks."

"Will you let me drive you tomorrow?"

"Why?" she asked.

"I want you to have fun on your way to work. Just the two of us. Otherwise, Mom and Lori'll be here, and there's a game, and then I'll be going on the road. Can we have Jessie and Ben friend time tomorrow morning?"

Her breath shuddered as she dabbed her face with a tissue. "That'd be really nice."

"Okay. Do you need reading time?"

"No, I'm exhausted," she said with a sniff. I opened my arms just expecting a hug, but she tangled her legs with mine, burrowed her face in my chest, and fell asleep within a couple of minutes.

I didn't object.

23

JESSIE

It turned out that being Ben's fake girlfriend wasn't as hard as I imagined it might be. Thursday morning, he drove me to work. We sang and laughed, drinking coffee. He really was doing everything he could to cheer me up about the Cole situation. For brief periods, I'd forget how much I was betrayed. It was nice.

Thursday night, Mikey had a game and I was in bed when he got home. I briefly woke up as he thumped into bed, groaning so loud it could shake the earth. Sweet as he can be, he's still the loudest man in the world.

"Tired?" I asked, rolling over to look at him.

"Wiped," he moaned, then wiggled his eyebrows. "Can I score a snuggle, girlfriend?"

I laughed, worming my way over to him. I supposed we were just accepting of that physical part of our relationship. Friendship. Whatever it was. "Sure." But when I got close, I got a whiff of him. "Ugh, you smell like a bar."

"We went out after the game," he said. "Mom and Aunt Lori are bad influences. I left my car at the arena."

"I should have known you three couldn't be trusted. Your shoulder do okay in the game?"

"Sore, but okay. Look at you asking questions like a real girlfriend," he joked, jostling me gently.

"I think we're actually friends now. I'm comfortable calling it that."

"Really, Jessie?"

"Really. Now shut up and go to sleep."

When my alarm went off a mere three hours later, I had to pry Ben's heavy arm off my middle. As I scooted to the edge of the bed, he tried to pull me back.

"Tell them you're sick," he mumbled.

"No. I'll see you tonight. Be careful out there," I said. He was already knocked out again by the time I got out of the bathroom. I had to smile at his form in the bed: one arm dramatically draped over his eyes and the other stretched out to the side. Who was this loud, snuggly, big-living creature that had blown up my life?

I got home from work on Friday to find a big black box with a shiny purple ribbon on the counter with my name on it. I couldn't go to his Thursday game, but I had no excuse for Friday. I'd be going to the game with Mikey's mom, Aunt Lori, and Kitty. He'd been so sweet about everything that I felt like I owed him the favor. And professional hockey is supposed to be fun, right?

"We can skip the WAG suite. I had Guy get us all some seats down low," Kitty said. "It's hard enough that you have to pretend to be his girlfriend while his mom is there. No sense subjecting yourself to WAG scrutiny."

Opening the box he'd left for me on the counter, I found an explosion of Princes gear: his jersey, 27 with MIKNEVICIUS across the back, a Princes pajama set, and a round neck long-sleeved tee, plus a big water tumbler thing. He left a little note inside on Princes' stationery.

You'll look great in these. You can't wear the jammies to the game, though. Your legs'll get cold. Anybody hates on you, they answer to me. See you tonight, Sweet Cheeks. -Jockey

The note was Mikey in a nutshell: protective, thoughtful, silly, sweet, and somewhere in there, thuggy.

DEBBIE, Lori, and I met Kitty outside the arena. Debbie and Lori wore Mikey's jersey, and I had on the Princes long-sleeved tee he'd gotten me with some jeans. It was a hair too tight, but Kitty told me it would be a faux pas to wear Mikey's jersey as his girlfriend. Thank God for Kitty Gatto.

"It's so nice to finally meet you! Ben's said so much about you over the years. I'm a little starstruck," Debbie gushed to Kitty as she hugged her.

"And how wild that you and Jessie work together!" Lori said after introductions were made.

"Shall we go in? I could use a Friday night beer," Kitty said.

We fought through the crowd, and someone from the Princes' staff stopped by our seats to get our drink orders. I'd never been to a hockey game, much less with VIP treatment. I could get used to that. He returned with a tray of drinks, one of which had a lime in it. I scrunched my nose in confusion when it was handed to me.

"Miknevicius specifically requested that you get Bud Light Lime, which we don't have, so you get a Bud Light with lime," he explained. My stomach jumped and my ears grew hot. Mikey had thought of me enough that he wanted me to have my drink of choice.

We thanked the man and cheers'ed our drinks. "Don't you think we should do a shot?" Debbie asked.

"I heard y'all went out last night and got a little wild," I said skeptically. "Mikey smelled like booze when he came in."

"That was yesterday. This is today!" Lori said.

"Alright, then," Kitty said, going along with it. "When they come back around, I'll have them bring the WAG intermission shot early."

I widened my eyes at her and she just patted my leg. I squeezed my lime into my beer as Kitty perked up. "Here they come!"

Pucks were knocked off the wall by the benches and players poured out of the tunnel. I surprised myself with how proud I was when I saw number 27 hit the ice. There was Mikey, as big as I hadn't expected him to be. I mean, yeah, he's big anyway, but still, I don't know what to call it, narrower than I thought hockey players were? And there he was being all broad and padded up and big. Debbie and Lori let out a long yell when he sank his first practice shot into the net.

"It never gets old," Lori said, grasping my hand. "We watched him grow up and now here he is. It must feel wild for you! You've never seen him play."

"I, just, there he is," I managed, actually getting kind of emotional seeing him work. What the fuck was that? He was beautiful. And like, really fast? While he waited for his next practice shot at the back of the line, he found me and made a drinking motion. I shot him a thumbs-up. He blew me a kiss and waved at his mom and aunt.

While the rest of the team did various drills, he skated over to the glass. We were a few rows back. Debbie and Lori ran down to him and dragged me with them.

Debbie babbled with him about some technical whatnot about his shots and the game. She was, I assumed, a hockey mom through and through. Mikey listened to her but kept cutting his eyes to me. As soon as he could get a word in edge-wise, he turned to me.

"You look nice in the team colors, Sweet Cheeks," he said, all heart-eyed and simpy. I thought I was immune to his charms, but not so. I got butterflies from the compliment. His expression was so believable.

It was just the beer, right? Sometimes a single beer could make me feel all in love.

"Thanks. You look...big," I returned. Debbie cackled.

"Told you I would," he smirked.

"Let me get y'all's picture!" Debbie crooned. "First hockey game with a hockey boyfriend and all!"

"Oh, okay. Sure." I handed her my phone.

I put my back to the glass, looking to Mikey through it for guidance. He kept going with his enamored expression, reas-suring me with his eyes. Debbie must have snapped one with us like that, because then she said, "Now look at me!"

We posed. "Let me get one of you three!" I said to Debbie.

"Oh no, a selfie with all of us! Laura's going to love seeing Benny's girlfriend," Debbie insisted. "Benny's sister would love you, Jessie. I hope you get to meet her soon." Kitty jumped up to take our picture.

Whatever googly-eyed feelings I was getting from the hunk of a man on the other side of the plexiglass were muddled by the inclusion in Mikey's family. People I didn't know would think we were together. Ben's sister would think we were together. Kitty shot me a nervous grimace followed by a big smile, a show that I wasn't insane and this situation was just insane.

So I went along with it, but also made Debbie, Lori, and Mikey pose solo. That way, when I was out of his life, they'd still have this memory.

Mikey banged on the glass one more time and beckoned me close. I walked down.

"See ya later, darlin'."

"Have a good game, Jockey," I said, physically unable to stop smiling when he was being all cute with me.

"Kiss for Daddy?" he asked.

"I am not kissing this nasty glass, Benjamin. But thanks for my beer order."

"Anything for my woman," he said with a wink. "Thanks for coming. I'll see you after."

Then he pulled off his helmet, gave the glass an exaggerated kiss that left a smear mark, laughed at my horror, and skated off to sign a puck for a kid. My face and ears were on fire.

At that point, there were many, many people I didn't know who thought we were together.

MY FIRST HOCKEY game was generally a success. Debbie and Kitty went out of their way to tell me what was going on with various plays and calls. I focused on Guy and Mikey when they were in. It was easier to focus on the game through the lens of one or two players. Much less intimidating that way.

"Guy's a forward, so he's more of an offensive player. Mikey's defense, but he can still score goals if the opportunity comes up," Kitty explained.

I still didn't understand what icing was, but in general, I knew if there was a whistle, somebody was in at least a little bit of trouble.

In the second period, Mikey got in big enough trouble to go to the penalty box. I thought Debbie would be disappointed in her son for being reprimanded, but she was on her feet letting the officials have a piece of her mind.

Mikey didn't look sorry in the least, chattering at the player he'd fouled even after the whistle. The next thing I knew, both helmets were off and Mikey was engaging in some sort of wrestling match. Debbie wasn't alone in unleashing her fury. Half the crowd was cheering Mikey on in his quest for blood. With all their gear, it reminded me of those blow-up sumo suits people wrestle in at team-building events. And the official just let them do it? And his coach was unbothered about it? The sport was so bizarre to me.

By the time Mikey skated off to the penalty box, he was holding a cut on his cheek and still cussing out the player also headed to the other team's penalty box. Ben spat almost constantly while he served his two minutes, occasionally reigniting the argument with his opponent and yelling across the layers of plexiglass. Between that and the smooch smear he left on the glass by our seats, I had to laugh at the passionate man who did everything big, including fighting. I couldn't help thinking of him as an overgrown little kid.

The Princes ended up winning 3-1, so Mikey's fury was not in vain. Kitty led us to the Wives Room, where we got a cold reception.

"Hey, Sydney," Kitty greeted the person who appeared to be the Queen Bee. "This is Jessie. She's Mikey's girlfriend."

Sydney cocked her blonde head to the side. "Mikey doesn't have a girlfriend," she said, matter-of-fact and with no smile.

"I'm his mother, and yes he does," Debbie said, stepping up and putting her arm around me.

"My apologies, Mrs. Miknevicius," Sydney said with a saccharine smile. "It's good to see you again!"

"What was your name?" Debbie asked. Damn, Debbie. Way to put ol' Sydney in her place.

"I'm Sydney Leroy."

"Huh, I didn't see Leroy play much tonight. He getting ready to retire?" Debbie asked. I instantly knew where Mikey got his diarrhea mouth. I stifled a laugh.

"If you'll excuse me, I've got other wives to chat with," Sydney said, turning and walking back to her group.

"Don't worry about her," Kitty said with an eye roll. "She still doesn't fully accept me because Guy and I aren't married yet. She tried to start a rumor that I was still seeing my ex from SNL. Anytime I miss a game because of work, she goes on about it again. He doesn't even live here and I haven't spoken to him since we broke up."

"Jesus, Kitty," I gasped. "That's awful. How do you stand it?"

She shrugged. "Guy's worth it. We've been meant for each other since we met as teenagers. And half the time I don't come in here until right before they're out of the locker room so I don't have to socialize."

"Well, now you'll at least have each other," Debbie said, putting an arm around each of us. I felt like I could crap my pants from that statement. Everything I was doing was a ruse. The reason I was even standing in that room was so contrived, no one could ever believe it.

To review: My apparently cheating boyfriend of four years threw me out. I moved in with his next-door neighbor who happened to be an NHL player. I slept in his bed, snuggled him, let him buy me things, let him take me to work, kissed him to make said cheating boyfriend jealous, and was fake dating him to make it all believable for his mother.

I didn't have too long to dwell, because another arm wrapped around my shoulders and a whiskery kiss met my cheek. Mikey inserted himself between Debbie and me, dressed in a gorgeous bright blue suit, his hair slicked back from the shower. I had to swallow down a "wow." Obviously, I know that clothes make the man, but I'd only seen him in a suit before at Kitty's engagement party. He stunned in a suit.

"My ladies," he cooed. "Y'all have fun?"

"Look what you've done to yourself, Benny," Debbie scolded, touching her fingertips around the cut on Mikey's cheek. "But did you get him good?"

"Yeah, Ma," he laughed, then turned to me. "What'd you think of your first game, Sweet Cheeks?"

"You're a nut, but I already knew that," I said with a grin.

"You like me that way," he said, yanking me to him and running his thumb along my jaw. My stomach tingled at the touch, my heart taking off. He sure did have a way of making me feel special, whether it was fake or not. It had been so long since Cole had been so affectionate with me. I linked my hands behind his neck. Mikey lowered his voice to a mumble, bringing our faces to almost touch. "You gonna let me have that kiss now?"

In a breathier voice than I anticipated, I said, "I think you've earned it."

Despite the beers and shot, my nerves were off the charts. Kissing Mikey, there, in such a public venue, with people judging us everywhere. We had to make it count.

Before I could overanalyze, Mikey's lips were on mine, first a quick smooch, then coming back for more. He bent me backward slightly with a tight hold on my back, a deep kiss with a tiny hint of tongue. That first kiss wasn't a fluke: Mikey knew how to kiss, pushing the boundaries of propriety in a way that was thrilling.

I wasn't supposed to be liking this. I was supposed to be moving on. This wasn't supposed to feel magical. I wasn't supposed to be giddy down to my toes, which were kicking up behind me like in an old movie. I wasn't supposed to be wishing we were alone so we could keep going.

We pulled back, exchanging a dazed look. "I bet you're tired," I said.

"You woke me right up, Sweet Cheeks," he said with a smirk and another peck on my lips.

"Hey, lovebirds," came a French-accented voice. "You wanna go out and get drinks?"

Mikey looped his arm around my waist. "Jessie, you remember Guy."

"I do. Hi."

"I'll try and not disrupt your sleep this time," said the tall, dark, and handsome man with his arm around Kitty.

"Disrupt your sleep? Benny, are you having your loud parties while Jessie's trying to sleep?" Debbie asked.

Eyes cut between Guy, Mikey, Kitty, and me as we worked out how to explain it all. Mikey blurted an answer. "My birthday party might have gone a little longer than what my Jessie Girl can handle. I've made it up to you, haven't I, hon?"

Mikey pulsed a kiss to my temple. Our height difference was almost perfect for him to be able to do that, his lips right at my hairline. The booze had me all gooey-feeling. "Sure have, babe."

"Debbie, Lor, you coming to the bar?" Kitty asked. "First round's on me."

Lori groaned. "Oh, Deb, I don't know if I can do two nights in a row. We've gotta be at the airport so early tomorrow."

Debbie chuckled. "I wish we could hang like we used to, but I think we're going to turn in early. We're still on Eastern Time."

"And hung over," Lori added.

"We'll take you home, then," Ben offered.

"No, we'll catch a ride. Y'all go have fun. Dad's been waiting on my call anyway."

Ben's body tensed under my hand, so I gave him a reassuring squeeze. We bid Debbie and Aunt Lori goodnight, and made our moves to a dive bar by the arena, aptly named The Stadium.

"What are you drinking?" Kitty demanded when we walked in.

"Oh, I'd better not," I said.

"Come on, babe. You can cut loose. I'm driving," Mikey said, his thumb stroking absently over my ribs. "You girls can have your fun. Stelle and I'll make sure you get home safe."

I leaned closer to Kitty and lowered my voice. "I'm afraid if I drink too much I'll give away our little secret to the others."

Kitty waved a hand like it was nothing and threw her arm around my shoulder. "I'll keep you safe. Come on. Let's be stupid for a night."

Kitty and I split off to a high-top table in the corner by the bar, and an hour later, I was blissfully buzzed. Okay, probably more than buzzed. We talked shit about office politics, and Kitty agreed that I was doing more work than my boss, Irina. I rarely let myself go like that, but I had a lot on my mind.

I actually kinda liked Mikey. Like not as my friend. Watching him across the room talking to his teammates, sipping a single beer because he was driving, he just looked perfect. And I knew he looked just as perfect clothed as he did with almost nothing on. All those veins—

"Earth to Jessie," Kitty laughed, waving her hand in front of my face as I twisted the straw from my water glass between my fingers. "You watching your boyfriend over there?"

"I mean, he is kinda cute, right? Like he's a good-looking guy." He looked up at that moment and held my gaze, his dimples framing his smile.

"Well, yeah," Kitty said, like it was a simple matter of fact.

My stomach dropped. "You didn't used to have a thing with him, did you?" I blurted it out so quickly, I didn't have time to think about how desperate it made me sound.

"Relax. He's always just been a friend. There have been times I thought he was hitting on me, but I think that's just how he relates to women."

"So, he liked you?"

Kitty cocked her head to the side, narrowing her dark eyes. "Oh my God, you really like him, don't you?"

My face warmed. "Shut up. No, I don't."

"Oh, Jessie!" Kitty shrieked, grasping my hand. "It's all like I planned!"

"You planned for my boyfriend to cheat on me and throw me out?" I sniped, trying to get her to lower her voice.

Kitty blew right past that. "Jessie, oh my God. He's so into you, babe. I mean, just look at him right now! Look!" She grabbed my cheeks to turn my face toward Mikey. He stood chatting with the team's goalie and Guy. "He's looking at you like you're made out of fucking gold."

And he was. His mouth was in a little simper, his dimples popping, eyes shining, just at me. He looked back to the guys like he was trying to get out of the conversation.

"Ooh! Dance time! Come on, I love this song!" Kitty said, pulling me off my stool toward a circle of WAGs in the middle of the bar. There was no dance floor as it was just a dive bar, but they danced on the chipped hardwood like it was one. I wavered as I stood, grabbing the table for balance. No more drinks for Jessie.

I joined the group, singing along to the girly hit like it was my karaoke jam. I shook and swirled my hips, feeling just loose enough to have a good time. Gone was the nastiness from the Wives Room, all women uniting under the force of Dua Lipa.

A corded arm snaked around my waist from behind, a cool beer bottle on the back of my arm. I knew from his scent that it was Ben. He followed my lead, then twirled me around and hooked my arm around his neck. We were front to front, our thighs interlocked, his forehead lowering to mine as he sang a few of the words to me.

"Didn't know you were a Dua Lipa fan, boyfriend," I said.

His face jumped in surprise. "I'm obsessed with her! She's so fucking—" he stopped himself as I raised my eyebrows at him. "Talented."

"Talented, huh? Then what does that make me?"

He hiked me up so I was straddling his thigh more fully, balancing me on his leg. "You're mine, baby."

I climbed up his body and wrapped my legs around his waist to his cocky chuckle. "You like being mine, don't ya, hon?"

In my tipsy haze, I couldn't think of a witty thing to say, so I just held on tight and pulled him in for a kiss. Ben gripped my thighs, slanting his mouth and coaxing mine open. His mouth was cool and malty like the beer he drank. I locked my ankles behind his back, drawing us closer together. I was consumed by the fire of Ben, his firm hold on me and the way he closed his eyes so tight stoking the flames. His kiss got more aggressive, scraping my lip with his teeth to my moan.

"Get a room!" came the call from next to us. I pulled out of the kiss, realizing what a fool I was making of myself.

"Put me down, please," I said, dropping my feet to the floor. I fanned my face, shame washing over me. "I'm hot."

I wobbled on my feet, and Ben steadied me by my elbows. "You need some air, hon?"

"I think I need the bathroom."

"I'll take you."

24

MIKEY

I helped Jessie into the bar's all-gender bathroom.

"Are you gonna be a peeping Tommy?" she slurred.

I chuckled. "I won't look. You just seemed like you'd need help. You're a little wobbly."

"I'm fine," she said, yanking her jeans down without unbuttoning them first. I averted my gaze. When she was done peeing, I didn't hear any movement.

"You sure, Sweet Cheeks?"

Jessie leaned over her thighs, her head propped up on her fist. She was falling asleep.

"Come on, Jessie Girl. You've had a long day. I'll take you home."

"Huh?" she snapped awake, still in a daze.

"It's okay, baby. I've got you." I knelt in front of her, pulling her jeans up to her knees.

"Benny, what are we doing?"

"We're getting you ready to go home."

She grabbed my wrist, swaying on the toilet. "No, but what are we doing?"

I looked up into her eyes, and though they were drunk girl

eyes, they were also quiet and pleading. She knew what she meant, and I did, too.

"You really kissed me out there," she went on.

All the air left me, the room a vacuum of oxygen. "You . . . really kissed me first?"

We sat in a stare-off, and I thought she might kiss me again, sitting on the toilet with her pants down. "I'm really drunk, Ben."

"I know, honey. I'm trying to get you home. Can you stand up for me?" She held my shoulders as I pulled up her underwear and pants, taking care not to look at things I wasn't supposed to see. "Why didn't you have to unbutton your pants?"

"I'm losing weight," she sighed, putting a celebratory fist in the air. "Yay."

"You haven't been eating," I stated.

"Getting brutally dumped'll do that to ya."

"You need to eat, Jess."

"I guess you're right. I can't afford a new wardrobe."

We were headed for the sink so she could wash her hands, but I turned her to me. Her eyes struggled to focus on me. "Uh-uh. Don't do that. You don't need to lose weight. You need to eat because you need to take care of yourself. And if you won't do it, I will."

She gave a lazy blink. "You're not the boss of me, Ben Miknevicius."

I blew out a breath. "Got that right."

JESSIE FELL asleep on the way home. I was a little afraid she'd puke in my car, so I had a bag at the ready. Fortunately, that didn't happen.

I was going to have some choice words for Kitty Gatto. I told her to get Jessie loose, not to get her completely hammered.

In the parking garage, I rubbed her arm to wake her. "We're home, baby. You ready to go to bed?"

She mumbled something. I went around to her side of the car and opened her door, unbuckling her seatbelt and helping her out. She stumbled into me. "This is so embarrassing."

"Nah. It's just me. I told you to cut loose tonight."

In the elevator, she leaned against the wall, resting her head back while she gripped the handrail.

"Did you and Kitty have fun at least?"

"Yeah, and I had fun with you," she said with a little smirk. I reached for her hand and squeezed it.

"Me too."

She closed her eyes and slumped into me with her mouth tipped up, and I realized she was fishing for a kiss. It was just the two of us. No pretense for other people. And she was drunk. But it was what she wanted when she was drunk? But it felt gross, like I'd be taking advantage of her. I wanted her all the time. She just wanted me when she was drunk. All I wanted was her, really wanting me, no faking.

I wanted those lips, wanted that kiss so bad, but I couldn't do it. I had to let her down easy.

I took her chin in my hand and traced her lips with my thumb, admiring the curve of her cupid's bow. I had kissed those lips before. As bad as I wanted to kiss her again, this wasn't the time. So I said, "Hi, beautiful."

She giggled, grinning up at me like a fool. "I think you're pretty, too, Benny."

She was so, so drunk and also so, so very cute. "Mikey, Ben, Jockey, *and* Benny? These are really adding up, Sweet Cheeks."

"I think it's cute that your mama calls you Benny," she said.

"What's your mama call you, Jessie Girl?" She was pressed into me, all her weight leaning on me, looking up at me with her eyes barely open and a blissed-out grin on her face.

"What do you wanna know about my mama, Jockey?"

The elevator dinged at our floor. "Come on. Let's get your sloppy ass to bed."

In the kitchen, she opened every cabinet. "Do you have any tuna? I'm hungry."

I laughed at her. "Who wants tuna when they're drunk?"

She got a snarky look on her face and put on a mocking voice. "Cole," she dragged out his name with a sneer, "never let me eat tuna because he said it stank. But I love a tuna salad sandwich. With the toasted bread, Ben? Mmm, a delicacy."

I couldn't stop smiling at her. Who used the word "delicacy" when they were as drunk as she was?

"Whatever, I'll just go to bed in this snack-free hell." She ambled toward her room. I dove in to stop her from opening the door.

"Not your room tonight. Come on. You're with me tonight," I whispered, redirecting her to my room.

In the bedroom, she shoved her pants down, her bare butt exposed. She shook her butt, looking over her shoulder at me. I cursed whoever invented the thong, making it possible for my fake girlfriend to be both covered up and so naked at the same damn time. I walked around to her front so I wasn't ungentlemanly.

"Didn't you say you could satisfy me, Ben?" Her voice was deep and velvety.

I laughed it off. "Not right now, Sweet Cheeks. You need to sleep it off."

"You know what would help put me to sleep, don't you?" She looked at me from under her lashes. I swallowed, heat flashing over my body. Of course, I wanted to tear into her. I wanted all of her. And if it had been any other girl I didn't care about, I'd have done what she asked. Well, not if they were as drunk as she was. Not exactly consenting territory.

But either way, I knew it wasn't right with Jessie that night.

It could fucking crush me if she decided it was all a bad idea the next day—if she even remembered it the next day. My body fucking ached for her. But I couldn't settle for scraps of her. I needed all of her, or nothing.

For once, I took the smart route. "Not tonight, hon."

"Why not? You scared?" she drawled, tugging at the hem of her shirt and dragging it up her body with a little smirk.

"You don't do casual, babe."

"I could with you." She did a little dance with the bottom of her shirt almost over her boobs.

"What if I don't want that?" I asked.

Heartbreak fell over her face. Oh my God, she thought I meant I didn't want her when every spare fucking thought was about her. "Jessie—"

"Oh. Yeah. I guess I'm probably not your type."

"That's not what I meant. You're fucking gorgeous."

"But you don't want me."

"That's not what I said—"

She was stuck with her shirt over her head, stumbling around. She fell, folding in half over my arm. That's when I saw the scar on her lower back. It looked like a fern had been burned into her skin.

"Jessie."

"What?" she snapped. "I get it if you're not fucking me, but are you going to help me or not?"

I blew past that, tracing my finger over her scar. "Who did this to you?"

She gasped and straightened, wobbling as she bolted upright and pulled her shirt back down. "No one."

"Jessie, I need to know who did that to you." Rage burned inside me, not with her, but with whoever did that awful thing that left a mark on her beautiful body.

"No one!"

"Did Cole do that?" I was getting angry. Why was she hiding it from me? Why was she trying to protect this person?

"No!"

"Then who, Jessalyn? They'd better be in fucking jail."

She laughed, fully guffawing and snorting.

"This isn't funny, Jessie."

"I don't think you can put Mother Nature in jail, Mikey."

I shook my head. "What?"

She sat on the edge of the bed and wrestled with her shirt again. "I was struck by lightning."

I yanked her shirt off once it was over her head. I guess the Princes shirt I got her, though amazing-looking on her tits, was a bit too tight. I'd get her a bigger one. "Seriously, Jessalyn? You survived?"

There she sat, shrunken and slumped forward on my bed, in just her bra and underwear. And her socks, randomly. She was stunning, but she was so sad that I wasn't focused on how much of her I was seeing. "I survived. My best friend died."

My mouth fell open as a sob choked her. "Oh, Jessie. That's terrible. How old were you?"

"13. At summer camp." I sat next to her and wrapped her up in a hug. She shrugged me off. "I hardly ever cry about it. I'm usually fine. I usually just try not to show my back."

"You don't have to be fine with me, hon. And your back is beautiful," I said, squeezing her shoulder. "Is this why you have nightmares?"

She nodded, wiping her tears with her hands, then on her legs. "Always storms. I always lose her again. It's part of why I like living here. Fewer storms."

She sucked up her tears, but the sadness hadn't left her. I knew it probably took a lot for her to share that with me. I thought about how she said the most peaceful thing in her life was from summer camp, too. Probably from before she lost her friend.

Poor little girl Jessie.

I went into caretaker mode. I'd been a breakup helper for Kitty in college. I'd helped Jessie with her feelings about Cole. I could be a childhood trauma helper, too, right? This was a thing friends did, right? "Which of your little jammie sets do you wanna wear?"

Her tear-stained eyes met mine. "Can I wear your shirt?"

25

MIKEY

Jessie actually slept in. I woke up to her arm and leg thrown over me, her face tucked into my shoulder. Her breath was fucking awful but she was so cute cuddled up to me that I forgave it.

It had taken me a while to fall asleep. I was buzzed off the day: all of Jessie's kisses, her trauma with the storms, and I couldn't stop fixating on how mean Cole was to Jessie. My mind stewed the same few facts over and over: him calling her a whore, her not being allowed to eat tuna in his holy presence, him picking on her for wanting flavored coffee, him not wanting to marry her, and worst, him cheating on her. If she hadn't stopped me, he was in to get knocked out by a Mikey knuckle sandwich. No one gets to treat my Jessie that way and get away with it. I plotted my revenge instead of counting sheep.

While I waved my mom and Aunt Lori off at 5:30 a.m. and put them in an Uber, I noticed Jessie's car on the street, covered in bird shit. I mean like solid lines of bird shit all up and down her car. That just wouldn't do.

Trying to move fast before she woke up, I went back

upstairs and got her keys off the hook by the door. I took her car through the car wash and filled up her tank. I went to my favorite coffee shop and got us each a coffee and a breakfast sandwich. I stopped by the grocery store when it opened and found a cheesy card, plus some items I needed for my revenge plot.

I got back and stopped by our building's office to get one more thing for Jessie, then headed up to pack for the team's road trip.

With a little pit stop next door.

I knew Cole went out for his stupid weekend run on Saturday mornings, a fact Jessie had confirmed when she was complaining about him at one point. Running isn't intrinsically stupid, but Cole is, so it's his stupid little run. Either way, he was due to be out of his apartment. I unpacked what I needed from the grocery bags, listened at the door, and used Jessie's key to go in. If I got caught, I was screwed. I had plans to tell him I was grabbing something Jessie forgot as a cover. But if I succeeded? He got every last thing he deserved.

Jessie was starting to wake when I got back home. I placed her hazelnut latte and breakfast sandwich on the nightstand, along with two ibuprofen. She grumbled as I sat them down.

"Morning, sunshine."

"Hey," she croaked.

"How you feelin'?"

"Pain."

"Here." I placed the two pills in her hand and gave her the Princes water cup I'd gotten for her. She always complained about her glass sweating when she put ice in it, so a stainless steel monstrosity seemed to be the cure.

"Thanks." She flopped back on her pillow. "I was pretty bad, wasn't I?"

The corner of my lips lifted as I sat on the edge of the bed.

"You were fine. I wanted you to cut loose for a night. You're always so uptight."

"Oh God. Did I kiss—? Was I all over you?"

My stomach panged. There was the regret I feared. "It was fine, hon. Promise."

She sat up, examining her shirt. *My* shirt. "Did you . . . get me dressed?"

Damn, she really was drunk. I didn't think she'd blacked out. It made me more glad that I didn't give in to her special requests at bedtime. And in the elevator. I wanted her to want those things with me sober. And if she didn't, I couldn't keep getting played with when she was drunk.

"Yeah. I asked if you wanted jammies, and you asked for my shirt."

"Oh my God. I'm so sorry." Little did she know how much I liked her snuggling me and wearing my shirt. She wiped under her eyes, examining the mascara streaks on her fingers. "Did I cry or something?"

"You told me about the storm thing."

Her eyes rounded, panic setting in.

"It's okay, Jessalyn. I'm glad you told me. I hope you're not too upset."

She nodded, not meeting my eyes.

"Do you think about it a lot?"

She sat back on the pillows. "Sometimes more than others. When I'm under a lot of stress it comes up. Which between work and Cole and . . . everything, it's been a lot lately."

I grabbed her hand. "Know that you have me if you ever want to talk."

The corner of her lips lifted and she squeezed my hand back. "Thanks, Benny." We exchanged a long glance. I could get lost in those hazel eyes, even when they were tired and bloodshot.

"But hey, this is yours," I said, handing her the hazelnut

latte. "And this." The breakfast sandwich. "Felt like you could use some caffeine and grease."

She lunged at me, throwing her arms around my neck. "Where did you come from, Benjamin Michael Jockey?"

I laughed, returning her hug. "Next door."

She was napping on the couch when I left for my road trip, some trash show on the TV. She wore my shirt still but had added her own sweatpants. She was curled in a tight ball, so I threw a blanket over her. She stirred, cracking an eye open.

"Thanks for the blankie," she mumbled.

"No problem," I said with a laugh. "Get some rest. I'll be back late Wednesday night."

"K. Have a good trip, Jockey."

I turned to go, but she spoke again, sitting up.

"Ben?"

"Yeah?"

"Thanks," she said carefully, "for last night. I don't know what all I did, but I think you did a lot. So thanks."

"Anytime, Sweet Cheeks. No benders while I'm gone."

A pillow from the couch flew my way.

26

JESSIE

I moved into my own room. Finally.

My bed was really mine, and honestly, it gave me some space from Mikey. If I'd stayed in his room while he was gone, I'd just have been surrounded by reminders of him.

He, who was really nice to me when he didn't need to be. He, who I'd embarrassed myself with before he left. He, who got me coffee and breakfast anyway.

With him gone, the reality of how absurd my life had become settled in. It was too much. I really needed to start plotting my exit.

I honestly will never know what all happened Friday night after the game. I remember talking to Kitty. I remember dancing. I have some flashes of Mikey helping me in the bathroom, telling me to eat. After that, nothing. I woke up in his t-shirt that carried his delicious scent.

Kissing Mikey. Like, really kissing him. Not for show. He told me I was his and I couldn't tell if he was faking or being real. I wanted it to be real, so I pretended it was.

But the thing is, he kissed me back just as hard. If we'd been at home and sober, there's no way that wouldn't have ended with us in bed together. Or on the kitchen counter. Or on the living room floor. Or one of the twenty-nine places I had little flash fantasies of us getting it on.

I had to get a grip.

I was still reeling from Cole cheating on me for God knows how long. And yeah, that was over, but I was in a fragile place. I couldn't just be flitting around pretending to be a professional hockey player's girlfriend.

Even if that professional hockey player was kinda dreamy. And sweet. And protective. And yeah, loud.

He texted me Monday to make sure I recovered from my hangover (I had, thank you). He sent me a picture of a stray cat and asked if maybe that could be our ocelot pet. I found a prop cat on set and sent him that as a counteroffer.

But as much fun as we had together, he was also someone who didn't take relationships seriously. He didn't *do* relationships. Relationships were stale, and Mikey had to keep it fresh.

I got a nasty reminder of his need to keep it fresh Monday night. There was a knock at the door, which I found weird. Only people from our building could get in, and Cole was the only other person I knew in the building.

I opened to a blonde woman in an open trench coat and some very fancy lingerie.

"Um, can I help you?" I asked, trying not to laugh in my surprise.

"Who are you?" she asked.

What the hell? "I'm sorry, what are you doing here?"

"I'm looking for Mikey." My stomach dropped as she narrowed her eyes at me, taking in my sweats and messy hair. "Are you his cleaning lady or something?"

"No. Is there something I can do for you?"

She tried to walk past me into the apartment. I put my arm across the doorway to stop her. "I don't think so, missy. This is my apartment. How did you get in the building?"

"Where is he? And who are you?"

"He's on the road. And I'm his girlfriend." I crossed my arms over my chest. I was his fake girlfriend, but she didn't need to know that.

"HA! Mikey doesn't do girlfriends."

I squinted at her. "If you were truly diligent, you'd have known he was on the road."

She tossed her hair over her shoulder and pulled her trench closed. "Whatever. Tell him Hannah came by."

I gave a weak smile. "Hannah, I'd suggest you leave before I call the building's security."

She scoffed and turned toward the elevator, muttering a "bitch" as she went.

I sat with the TV on, too rattled to pay attention. Was I wrong to tell her that I was his girlfriend? Did I just ruin something for Mikey? Probably not, right? It's true, if she had been talking to him she'd have known that he was gone. Maybe just some stalker?

A stalker with a real hot body. A hot body that looked nothing like mine. She was toned and firm in all the places that I was soft.

That was the second of Ben's "type" that I'd met. Busty blondes with tight little bodies. I had the busty thing going, but not the blonde, and certainly not the gym physique. Any muscle I had was from crouching and standing at my job, plus sewing and knitting.

Ben was on Eastern time, so I didn't want to bother him late. I'd tell him the next day. It made me sad to think of Ben talking to other women while we were in our fake arrangement. Was he kissing other women? He had a right to take care of his physical needs, I supposed. But somehow the thought of Ben cheating on our fake relationship hurt worse than Cole cheating on me after four years. He'd built up so much trust with me, saying he'd never treat me bad. This felt pretty damn bad, though.

But he had chosen me publicly, right? I was the "ideal girlfriend," his words, not mine. That had to mean something. I'd been wearing his shirt to sleep, but suddenly that didn't seem so appealing. His scent had been comforting to me while he was gone, but now it just seemed sour.

Almost as sour as the gross smell starting to emanate through our apartment. Almost like rotten seafood.

"WHAT THE FUCK DID YOU DO?"

My phone rang at work around 8:30 a.m. Tuesday. Cole was on a rampage. I happened to have a spare second, so I made the mistake of answering.

"Excuse me? I'm at work, Cole."

"It smells like shit in here," he bit out. "I know you and your stupid little boyfriend had something to do with it."

"You're going to have to fill me in," I said. "I have no idea what you're talking about."

"I found the tuna can in the kitchen, Jessalyn," he hissed. "But that's not all of it. Where did you hide the rest?"

"What tuna can? Why would I have anything to do with a tuna can?"

"You're the only weirdo I know who likes fucking tuna salad! Who else would have put an open fucking tuna can on top of my kitchen cabinets, Jessalyn?" he raged. He rarely called me Jessalyn. I was pretty sure he'd just heard Mikey calling me by my full name through the walls, which made me even happier. I had to bite back laughter. Whoever did it was a genius.

"Well, maybe one of the women you cheated with decided it was time to pay you back."

"Oh, whatever, you little puck bunny. Hope you're enjoying the jock's diseased cock."

I hung up right then. He didn't deserve another second of my time. Brilliant as it was, I didn't do the tuna can stunt. I didn't need to take his abuse. If anything, finding out he'd been cheating made it easier to move on. He went from being a vanilla human in my mind to being an actual menace.

But it still hurt. And what I really wanted was a hug from Mikey. Mikey, who left me flowers and a "hang in there" card with a picture of a kitten hanging on a screen door. Mikey, who washed my car, gassed it up, and got me a garage pass.

Oh, fuck. Mikey'd had my keys Saturday morning. It totally could have been him.

Why did that somehow excite me to think he'd commit light vandalism on my behalf?

> Commit any petty crimes lately?

BENJAMIN MICHAEL JOCKEY

Not that I'm aware of officer

Do I need to step out of the vehicle?

> Seems kinda "fishy" that you had my keys
> Saturday morning

Only to treat my favorite roomie to a few things

> Like vandalism?

Jessie, you know everything I did

> So you're confessing?

I'm entitled to an attorney

And a 5 minute phone call

My phone buzzed in my hand as his call came in.

"Hello?"

"Hey, Sweet Cheeks. Miss me yet?"

I chuckled, picking up a pair of football pants I was working on. "What did you do to him?"

"Nothing he didn't have coming."

"Ben, he just called me in a rage. He thinks it was me."

"Give me his number. I'll set his ass straight," Mikey fumed. "He doesn't get to talk to you like that, Jessie."

"Well, he did, so he thinks he does."

"He's lucky I'm not in town right now," he said through clearly gritted teeth.

I sighed. "Mikey, leave him alone. I appreciate you sticking up for me, and yes, it's funny. But let me handle him, okay?"

He huffed. "Fine. If that's what you want."

"It is. How's...where are you today?"

"Tampa. It'd be more fun if I had my fun roomie with me."

I couldn't help but grin when he did shit like that. I never imagined I'd be friends with someone who was so all over the place: sweet as honey, big bear protective, but also with big soft emotions. "What would we do together if I was there?"

"Go to the beach, of course," he said without hesitation. "I'd make you play beach volleyball and get popsicles from a popsicle guy and drink beach beers."

"You know we live by the beach, right?" I said, tucking my phone to my shoulder so I could get back to work while talking.

"Then I guess we'll have to go when I come home, huh?"

My smile leaked into my response as my stomach fluttered. This was bad. I hated how smitten I was with his attention and affection. The flutter turned to a nauseating churn when I remembered the guest appearance I'd had the night before. "Maybe. Um, someone came by for you last night, by the way."

"Oh, God. Was it Hannah?"

I furrowed my brow. "How did you know?"

He sighed. "Not her first rodeo. She shows up every now and then when she decides she'll try to bag me again."

"How does she get in?"

"Honestly, I think she shows the security guard her tits. She wouldn't be above it. She's not well, Jess. I'm sorry you had to deal with that."

"I, uh, told her I was your girlfriend. Hope that's okay."

He chuckled. "No, it's perfect. Thank you. Maybe she'll finally go away."

"So I didn't ruin your shot of getting back together with her?"

"Absolutely not. I was never with her to begin with. I blocked her number a long time ago. I'm really sorry she showed up. You should have called me."

"It was late. I didn't want to bother you."

"Always bother me, hon. I don't want anyone making you feel uncomfortable in your own home. I'll talk to the building management when I get home. She can't keep getting in like that." My heart warmed a little at that. "I hate to do this after all that, but I wanted to ask you a favor. Since you're the best girlfriend ever."

"Oh, God, what?"

"I've got this benefit thing on Friday when I get back. Since you don't have to work the next day, would you be my date?"

I pricked myself with a needle on the garment I was sewing. "Date?"

"Yeah. You know. Dancing. Drinking. Merriment. Hors d'oeuvres. Handshaking and shit. Kitty'll be there, if that helps."

"And I have to be your fake girlfriend again?"

He lowered his voice. "Well, according to these people, you're my real girlfriend. I realized I can't tell the team you're fake without them leaking it to their wives. Guy knows, but that's it."

I sat, blinking rapidly and analyzing how I felt about it. My stomach jumped. Being Mikey's date! But being Mikey's fake date. But maybe that's all we could ever be. "I'm gonna need more tacos and queso to deal with this."

"I'll be home late Wednesday night. Can I take you out Thursday night?"

"I'll accept that. What do I have to wear for this benefit thing?"

"How about I have a few things sent over? What's your size?" he asked. "I just guessed on the Princes stuff. Let me put you on speaker so I can write this down."

"Mikey! I'm not just announcing my size over speakerphone for whoever is with you to hear! Besides, I do what I do for two reasons, and they are my right and left boob."

The line went silent. "Mikey, are you alive?"

He coughed. "Yep. Yep. I just didn't know what to say about your boobs without getting myself into trouble."

"It's okay, Ben. I know they're big." It's true. My body is what it is. I learned to work with it as soon as my boobs made their presence known in middle school. The straight and narrow clothes for girls my age just weren't working for my body type and I refused to wear baggy clothes. So, I learned to sew.

You could say puberty really changed my life, more than most people's. My boobs ended up choosing my career path, and I'm not in sex work. As such, I'm very comfortable with that part of my body and talking about it. If I don't talk about it, someone else will behind my back.

"So, you became a seamstress so you could make clothes for your boobs?"

"Pretty much. Nothing ever fit growing up, so I learned to tailor my own clothes."

"Remember what I said about you not backing down from challenges, Sweet Cheeks? This is just another example."

"Are you calling my boobs a challenge?" I teased, knowing I

was making him uncomfortable and kind of loving it. Our roles were reversed for once.

He let out a choked sound that made me cackle. "It's challenging for me to have this discussion. The event is formal. If you want me to have somebody send you some dresses, I will. Or pick out whatever you want and tailor it, I don't care. I left a credit card in the silverware drawer just in case."

"Yeah I saw that. You really must trust me, Jockey. I'll find out what Kitty's wearing and adjust. Anyway, I have to get back to work. They're about to change scenes and I need to tape somebody's hem."

"Alright. Have a good day, Sweet Cheeks."

"You, too."

I was about to end the call when I heard his voice again. "Oh, and Jessie?"

"Make it quick, Jockey!"

He paused. "I kinda miss you."

I sighed, a little tingle passing through me. "I kinda miss you, too."

27

MIKEY

I tried to be quiet coming in Wednesday night. It was almost midnight, and Jessie would have been long asleep if she wasn't having an insomnia episode.

The smell coming from Cole's apartment was pretty foul, but luckily it didn't leak into my bedroom too bad.

I was disappointed to find my bed empty. Part of me wished Jessie would have been there waiting for me. I'd gotten so used to my strange bedfellow that it looked sad without her there.

I moped while I brushed my teeth. We were just faking. I didn't deserve her in my bed.

That didn't mean I didn't want her there. Selfishly, all I wanted was her warm, soft skin against mine after the long road trip. Her sweet peachy scent. The ultimate welcome home.

Unlike when she shared my bed, I just got down to my underwear, too bummed out to even jack off. I got in bed and turned out the light, almost instantly conking out in a mixture of loneliness and self-loathing.

A LOUD BOOM startled me from sleep. I struggled to orient myself in the dark. That happened sometimes after road trips.

Then a flash of light illuminated my room around the blackout shades. A muffled cry came from across the hall.

Oh God. Jessie.

I bolted out of bed and ran for my door, throwing it open and tearing across the hall to Jessie's door. I didn't bother knocking, pushing my way into her room. She sat curled into her grandma's chair, her face streaked with tears and Yarn Wad around her neck. Her blinds were open, her gaze fixed on the storm. She had her phone in her hand, the weather radar continually cycling. I went straight for her, another boom shaking the windows and making her jump. I knelt in front of her, wrapping my arms around her trembling frame.

I kissed her cheek, the salt of her tears staining my lips. "You're coming with me. Come on, hon."

She nodded and stood as I did, letting me guide her into my room. I walked to her side of the bed and pulled down the sheets, fluffing a pillow for her. I kept a hand on her through everything. She didn't seem to want to let me get too far away. "You're okay, honey."

Before she could get in the sheets, she clung to me, pressing her forehead to my bare chest. It took me that long to realize I had my mitts all over her while I was just in my underwear. It was irrelevant. She needed me. I held her tight to me, peppering the top of her head with kisses. She still hadn't said anything even though she wasn't dreaming. Her whole body shook. I hated that she was going through this, and I hated even more that she hadn't come to get me when she was scared.

"Let's get you in bed."

I tucked her in and climbed over her to get on my side, sliding into the sheets next to her. I turned her to face me in the dark. "Always come get me, honey. You belong in here. You hear me? You don't sit in there and suffer alone. Not for storms, not for anything. You come to me."

Jessie's voice was quiet and broken. "Okay."

I had my hand on her shoulder, rubbing my thumb over the muscle and bone. "Get over here, Sweet Cheeks."

"But you're . . . naked."

I chuckled. "I have on undies. I can put on a shirt if that'll help."

Thunder rumbled, and the sheets rustled from her quivering.

"C'mere, Jessie Girl. I've got you."

She rested her head on my chest and I put my arm around her shoulders. I patted her arm with my other hand.

"This is embarrassing," she said between sobs.

"Never, Jessie. It's just me. You're always safe with me."

"Thanks, Benny," she whispered.

There was more lightning and thunder. I reminded her that I was with her and that I had her. I rubbed her back, and kissed her hair, and hummed to soothe her.

When the storm slowed, she spoke again. "I'm glad you're home."

I was so thrilled and touched that I almost felt like crying. I dipped to put a soft kiss on the tip of her nose, and another on her forehead, then pulled her in tighter. "Me too, hon."

And then we were asleep.

In the morning, Yarn Wad was on my pillow, proving it hadn't all been a dream.

28

JESSIE

"A delivery for Miss Welsh at the gate."

The page came over my headset. Hardly anyone ever paged me.

"On my way," I croaked, knowing time was shy before I was next needed on set.

Lead trudged through my veins, but I hurried so I wouldn't miss my cue. I had to sub out a shirt with a comically-placed stain on it for that particular scene. It was around 2 p.m. and the lack of sleep from the storm was really catching up to me. A large cup of coffee waited for me at the entrance desk. A handwritten note on the side told me that was my delivery.

Here's to sunnier skies today. See you tonight.
-Jockey

I thanked the desk attendant and took my still surprisingly hot coffee. The sticker on the side said it was a hazelnut latte.

Did Mikey drive two hours round trip to bring me a coffee? It could have been a delivery service, but it looked like his handwriting. I'd slept so heavy once I was in his bed. I took a sip off the top of the latte as I hustled back to set, my breaths shallow.

Mikey was my fake boyfriend, but who would he have been faking for at work? The only person who knew about him was Kitty, and she knew we were faking.

For that matter, who were we faking for at all? I hadn't seen Cole since the jealousy-inducing kiss, and Mikey's mom was back home in Detroit.

And was it faking for him to hold me through the storm the night before?

After the stain scene wrapped, I sent Mikey a quick selfie of me sipping my drink with a thank you. Like the devil from a puff of smoke, Irina materialized.

"When you're done posing for the camera with your coffee break, we've got a new scene to shoot," she spat.

"The pieces are already prepped," I said with a forced smile.

"I was unaware we were leaving for a coffee run," she said, glaring at my cup.

"Actually, my boyfriend brought it," I said, cocking my head to the side and turning for the wardrobe trailer.

She followed in step behind me. "It's really unprofessional for an apprentice to be getting visits at work from her boyfriend."

And it's really unprofessional for you to not do your job, I almost shot back. My blood boiled, but then I remembered that I had an NHL player waiting at home to take me out to dinner. Did it matter that he wasn't my real boyfriend?

Kind of. I oscillated between being nervous and feeling giddy on my whole long commute home. What was forty minutes at 5 a.m. was an hour and twenty minutes at 4 p.m. When I finally walked into the apartment, Mikey sat at the kitchen island, scrolling his phone. By that point, whatever stink he'd put in Cole's apartment was most everywhere in

Mikey's. He had an ocean-themed candle lit and the windows open, but the faint seafood stench prevailed.

"Welcome home, Sweet Cheeks," Mikey said, dropping his phone and looking up with a grin. He jumped up to greet me as I put my bag and keys behind the door. He chewed his lip with his hands in his jeans pockets, looking surprisingly shy as he waited for me to empty my hands. He had on a backward hat to go with his t-shirt and jeans, which pumped up his sex appeal. After the latte worked its way out of my system, I went right back to my exhausted state at work.

But being in Mikey's presence again was like a shot of intravenous caffeine. He was happy to see me. We turned to face each other and he opened his arms for a hug. As his much less seafood and much more sea breeze scent enveloped me, I relaxed in his embrace, both of us swaying from side to side exaggeratedly. The urge to kiss him again kept going through me like tiny jolts of electricity, each little lightning bolt saying "DO IT." But I couldn't. I was too nervous. If we kissed alone, it was real. Did he want it to be real?

Still, I enjoyed it when he mumbled in my ear, "Missed you, roomie."

I laughed and squeezed him a little tighter. It felt like in college when you're randomly really touchy with the people who live in your dorm because you're all just far from home and essentially lost souls looking for somewhere to land. "Thanks for my coffee, roomie."

"No problem. Thought you might need it after last night."

I blushed and pulled out of our hug. I hated to admit how vulnerable I'd been getting with him. I was eager to change the subject.

"Let me go change and we can go get tacos? You can tell me all about your trip."

"Yeah, I'll order our ride. Can you be ready in ten?"

I nodded and ducked in my room. Fuck, I really wasn't

expecting to be so thrilled with Mikey coming home. He was essentially waiting by the door for me, and the way he looked nervous made my stomach all first-date melty. I hadn't felt this way since I met Cole, and even then, it was such a calm affair. There was a spark, we pursued it, and we stayed together.

But with Mikey, it wasn't just sparks. It was a mouthful of Pop Rocks. And it scared the shit out of me. I had no business getting invested with anyone, much less with a womanizer like Mikey.

And yet there I was, carefully choosing my outfit to try and show off for him.

I put on a burnt orange tee that didn't show too much cleavage (a hard feat with me) and tucked it into a short vintage corduroy green skirt, matching his laid-back vibe but letting him see a little more skin. I put a leather jacket on top for the evening's chill, and I was pretty happy with my look.

Ben was, too, giving me a long look up and down with a simpy smile when I came back into the kitchen. "You dressed up," he said.

"Ah, not too much. I wanted to look as cool as you," I said, dismissing him.

As we headed out the door, he said, "You one-upped me, though."

A FEW TACOS EACH DEEP, Ben and I officially had a case of the giggles. We sat at the bar at his favorite taco joint, the same place we'd gone with his mom and Lori. We had two seats on the end where it was a little more private.

"Wait, but really, tell me what you did to make it smell so bad," I pried, resting my hand on his knee to recover from my laughing fit. He traced circles into the back of my hand, a tiny movement that sent a shiver through me.

"If I tell you, you have to promise not to help him," he said, looking down at his finger's workings, then back at my eyes. "I'm not sure I trust you not to tell him."

"My lips are sealed," I said, mimicking a zipper over my mouth. He squinted at me, seemingly determining if I was trustworthy. "Come onnnnn! I've had to smell it more days than you have."

He waited for me to stop laughing, looking me dead in the eye. "Shrimp in the curtain rods."

I almost pissed myself. "Mikey! He'll never figure that out!" I started off on another laughing jag and he joined me. I snorted, making him laugh harder, throwing his head back and banging his hand on the bar. "He'll have to move out!"

"Aw, shucks, that's too bad," he said, setting us both off again. Mikey's dimples were endearing under normal circumstances, but they were deeply carved into his face when he laughed. We hadn't stopped laughing in a while.

Those damn dimples made me daring.

"But if he moves, you won't have to fake kiss me for him anymore."

Mikey's face went serious, like he was considering what to say. "We're pretty good at faking, don't you think?"

Our gazes locked, my heart pounding. Our laughter had firmly stopped. It took a lot of strength to stay looking at him, to not look away because I was scared. So much hung in the space between us. Did he want me the way I wanted him? "I don't know. I think we could probably use more practice."

The corner of Ben's mouth quirked up as he moved closer to me. "Are you asking for more kisses, Jessalyn?"

"Is that a problem?"

He laughed a little, then put one hand on the outside of my thigh. "No, it's not a problem."

His other hand slid along my jaw, a delicate touch like he was handling a Faberge egg, coming to rest with his fingers in my hair and his thumb by my ear. His eyes bounced between mine and to my mouth, my hands coasting up his arms to rest on his biceps. The soft puff of his breath met my open lips, a lit match to my powder keg. The want, the need, the touches we'd exchanged that had brought us to this point came to a head as our lips magnetized, a connection that was finally just ours.

We were doing it. We were kissing for real. We were kissing for us. For everything we saw in one another. For all of our fears. For all of our hope.

My whole body was sparkling, a shimmery feeling grounded by a bass-like rumble: low, velvety, and earth-shaking. His lips were a little spicy from the hot salsa he'd slathered on his tacos, adding another sensation to the experience. Just like before, he worked in a tiny hint of tongue, just enough to make my thighs clench and have me craving more. We both kept trying to pull away, knowing that we weren't being restaurant-appropriate, but struggling to stop.

We finally broke apart, smiling.

"That fake for you?"

I shook my head. "I wasn't faking."

His stare lingered on me a little longer and he turned to the counter. "I'm in so much trouble with you, Jessie."

"Why?" I thought it was solved. Sealed with a kiss. No going back to platonic pretending.

He folded his arms on the bar and stared down at them, then turned his head toward me. "I like you, Jessie. A lot. But I don't know how to do this. You talked about me going back to the type of women I used to date, but I don't want to go back. I want you. And I don't know if what you mean is that you want this, too. But if you want this, I don't even know if I'm qualified. I'm twenty-eight and I've never had a real girlfriend. I want it all. But I don't even know how to do it all. I only know how to fuck and leave, to the point that I think it's all I'm good for. And so do you."

I was taken aback. Like always, Mikey just blurted it all out there.

"Ben," I said, struggling to find my words. "I don't think that's all you're good for. You're such an amazing person. I mean, yeah, you're bossy with me sometimes, but it's all because you care. And I've never had somebody care like you do."

His brows knit as he considered my words. I took a deep breath, terrified of what I was about to spill out.

"If I'm honest with myself, I've wanted this for a while. But I've really been scared. I just got out of a relationship where I got treated like trash. Being around you has made me realize how much all that messed me up, made me think less of myself."

"I know that," Ben said. "And I don't want to be your messy rebound that you leave for some better relationship guy. You could wreck me."

"I don't want that either," I argued. "I want whatever this is to be real."

He shook his head with a sad smile. "You want me to be your post-breakup good dick guy. But the good dick guy doesn't get the girl. He just gets to be her best sex and show her that she wants more than good sex."

"Mikey, that's not true. You're more than that to me. We haven't done any of that stuff, and I still get excited when I think about you."

He sighed, hanging his head over his forearms on the bar. "That came out shitty. I don't think you'd mean to do it or anything. I just don't know how to do relationships and you're going to figure it out sooner or later anyway. We're different kinds of people. I'm not a relationship guy."

I thought about the throwaway comment he made about his dad being a cheater, and knew this was coming not from a grown man, but a hurt little boy. I put my hand on his leg.

"Do you want a relationship with me?"

He nodded, not meeting my eyes. "Yeah."

I grabbed his hand and squeezed. "I hear what you're saying about the rebound, and I want to respect that. But there's no magic bullet that makes you a relationship person or not. There's just communication, being honest with each other. And you're really good at that."

He swallowed hard and glanced at me sidelong. I went on.

"I can't make you trust me, or yourself. But I know you trust other people. Look at your team, your friends. Those are real relationships, too. Don't count yourself out."

His eyes traveled over my face, processing. Then his mouth went back to that smirk. "You should be a coach, Sweet Cheeks. You give one hell of a pep talk."

My heart fluttered. "Does that mean I get the prize?"

He cocked an eyebrow. "Prize?"

"You. Us. We've both got reasons to not do this, but what if we just did it anyway?"

He chuckled and gestured to his body. "You think you can manage all this?"

I smirked at him. "If anyone can, it's me."

He rolled his lips between his teeth, considering. He reached in his back pocket, pulled $100 from his wallet, and threw it down on the bar.

"You ready to go?" he asked, holding out his hand.

"Let's go home," I said, lacing my fingers through his as he led me out of the restaurant.

29

JESSIE

Outside the restaurant, Ben ordered our ride home.

"Six minutes," he announced, then turned back to me. "What do you wanna do with that time?"

"That's up to you. Are you in or out on this?" I asked, gesturing between us. Nerves wracked me as a little voice in my head told me he could be doing this with any number of other women at the same time.

He pulled my hips to his, gazing down into my eyes. "It might be a mistake, but I think you know I'm in."

"Are you? No other girls? Because some girls are probably okay with sharing, but I'm not that kind of girl."

He rubbed his lips together nervously and put his head back, sighing. "I probably have no game for telling you this, but you know I can't keep my mouth shut."

"Oh, geez," I said, fearing for whatever was about to come from his trap.

He smiled at me, but his eyes were serious. "There hasn't been anyone since I met you. Since you stomped over to my place in your tiny pajamas. Since you raged at me and tore me open and told me what was what. No one else could ever bowl me over like you do. It's just you."

A warm wave of joy spread over me. He was choosing *me*. Not Sheila. Not some other woman. He just wanted *me*. Someone who was with me for four years couldn't choose me, but Mikey did. "Not even on the road?"

His thumb stroked my cheek. "Not on the road. Not at home. Not on a plane or a train. I've been stuck on you, Miss Jessalyn."

I was elated but struggling to wrap my head around it. "So you're not pretending?"

He looked down into my eyes, fingers brushing some hair behind my ear. He chuckled self-consciously, blushing like he was embarrassed. "Honey, I was never pretending."

I launched myself at him, throwing my arms around his neck and jumping. He caught me around the waist and pinned me against his body, laughing as his head dipped for a wild and unrelenting kiss. His lean muscle pressed against me as his tongue danced with mine, surrounded by Ben. I loved how big his hands felt holding me up, safe and protected as we were real with each other. Raw. Unleashed from pretending and fully going for it.

This man had stormed into my life, taken me in, done anything and everything to make things easier for me, to support me. And I couldn't be happier to have him.

He tried wrapping my thighs around him, but that would involve flashing half the neighborhood with my bare ass.

"Skirt," I mumbled into his mouth as a car tooted its horn. Our ride had arrived anyway.

The Uber home was tense. We didn't want to be the weirdos making out and making it weird for the driver, so we told terrible jokes and laughed way too hard at them. I kept coming up with reasons to laugh and grab his arm or lean into him. Eventually, he kept the touch going.

"You're silly tonight, Sweet Cheeks," he said, squeezing my thigh. But then he left his hand there. I put my hand on top of his and scooted it farther up my leg. Maddeningly, his index finger stroked my inner thigh, sending shockwaves to my core. It wasn't a long ride, so it wasn't long before the driver let us out in front of our building.

I pressed the button to the elevator with Mikey creeping up behind me. He gripped my hips as we waited, breathing into my neck. His lips ghosted over my skin, making me moan. I didn't care what I sounded like or who heard. I was with a man who valued me, who turned me on, who made my whole body feel alive.

The elevator dinged and the doors opened. Thankfully, it was empty. I took Mikey's hand and led him inside. He pressed the button for our floor. The second the doors shut, his body was on mine, pinning me to the wall. His mouth covered mine, tongue sliding, heart pounding, like we'd die if we didn't taste each other. His hand rode up my skirt to my bare hip, searching for fabric and finally finding it at the top of my hip bone.

"Christ, Jessie, these feel sexy," he growled. "Do you want me to touch you?"

"Uh huh," I mewled. Without hesitating, he reached back to push the stop elevator button and dropped to his knees.

"You've been wanting this real bad, haven't you, Jessie Girl?"

"You're really going to do this?"

"I made you a promise, honey, and I keep my promises."

I spread my legs for him, ready to cash in on any and all of Ben's promises.

"That's it. Let your man take care of you." He pulled my thong to the side and kissed my sensitive inner thighs. "Goddammit, Jessalyn."

I clamped my thighs around his hands, panicking. "What? Is something wrong? Is it gross?" I mentally cursed myself for not changing my underwear after work.

"Not at all, hon. It's fucking beautiful." He looked up at me, brow furrowed. "Can't believe you've been keeping this from me."

My cheeks burned, not accustomed to getting compliments on that part of me. "Oh?"

He kissed around his hands on my thighs and I relaxed again. He wasted no time, putting his tongue on me before I could think any more, amber eyes watching me. The pleasure was so intense I could hardly stand, legs shaking.

"Your taste, Jessie," he said before diving back in. I grasped his reddish-brown strands and tugged. He moaned into my skin and looked up at me with the most salacious grin.

A click resonated through the elevator. "Is everything okay in there?"

Fuck. The security guard. I looked around for a camera but didn't see one.

Ben stifled a laugh.

"Oh. Yes. We must have bumped the stop button," I said brightly. "Do I just press it again to restart the elevator?"

"Yes ma'am."

"Okay, thank you!"

Mikey looked up at me. "To be continued." He put my underwear back in place and pulled my skirt down. He stood and leaned into me.

"I feel like we're going to the principal's office," I whispered.

"We are, you bad girl," he laughed into a kiss. "You got us in trouble."

"Me?!"

The doors opened on our floor and we slinked out, hand in hand. I leaned into the doorframe as he unlocked our door and tugged me inside. Even the process of toeing off our shoes was foreplay, his predatory gaze combing over me. I was everything: nervous, excited, terrified, exhilarated. Ben's hands were reaching for me within an instant of getting inside, his mouth covering mine. I walked backward until I was against the kitchen counter. Like he read my mind, he lifted me up, setting me on the edge of the counter.

"I've wanted you everywhere in this apartment, Ben," I breathed as he laid kisses on my neck.

"Tell me where you've wanted me."

"Right here," I gasped. "And the living room floor. And bent over the couch. And . . ." I trailed off as he lifted my shirt to unveil my breasts, moving his lips over the cleavage that my bra displayed.

"All those places sound good to me, baby," he said. "You know what's been eating away at me?"

He ran his hands down my sides as my shirt hit the kitchen floor. "How fucking gorgeous you were that night I caught you."

Renewed embarrassment sent heat through me, but I pressed on. I wanted this, wanted him. I peeled his t-shirt off and circled my legs around his hips to pull him close.

"I wondered what you were thinking about, what you would have looked like without all the covers on you, what you do to make yourself come."

"You wanna watch me?"

He cemented us together with his arms. "I want everything with you, Jessalyn." His amber eyes darted to my lips as he devoured me in another deep kiss, his hands skating under my skirt to cup my ass. "But first, I want to watch you and have you tell me what you were thinking about when you were playing with yourself in my bed."

I cocked my head, considering. "What's in it for me?"

His voice was low and husky. "What do you want from me, honey?"

"I want to see you, too. And to know what you thought about when you fucked yourself in the living room after you caught me."

A wolfish grin spread over Ben's face. "Bed?"

"Bed."

He hoisted me up, which put his face between my breasts. He gave me a sheepish smirk and I had to laugh at him. "Go on," I said. "I know you want to."

"What, this?" He placed a delicate kiss on each breast, making puppy dog eyes up at me. I cackled.

"That's all?"

His smile was face-splitting. "Nope." With exaggerated nibbling noises, he laid his face into my breasts and shook his head, leaning forward to tip me back to my squeal.

"See? You do bite. All that time of saying you don't? It was a trap."

"Well, I caught you now," he laughed, carrying me away to the bedroom.

He laid me back on the sheets and stood between my legs.

"I like you like this," he said. "Half undone for me. But I need more skin. You gonna take this skirt off, or do I have to tear it off you?"

"Hands off! This is vintage!" I unzipped the skirt, dropped it to the floor, and kicked it away, sitting on the edge of the bed. "Take your pants off, big boy."

He leaned down to kiss me with amused eyes, his hands tented on either side of me. "You think you're calling the shots?"

I would have never been so confident with Cole, but with Mikey, I had to match his cockiness or be taken under by it. "If you want to see me come, you'll let me take the lead. Pants off."

"Jessie, I don't give up control easily. I have half a mind to make you take my belt off so I can paint that ass red with it."

"I believe it. But you'll give up control for me."

He unbuckled his belt, shaking his head. "I always knew you were a brat." And yet, his pants were on the floor, joining the pile with my skirt. "Now get on your back and show me how you make yourself come."

Not taking my eyes off his, I spread my legs and tugged

my thong to the side, still sitting up. I put my fingers to his lips and obediently, he opened. His tongue circled my fingers as I slid them out of his mouth and drew them down to my pussy. "You forgot the deal. You've gotta show me, too."

"Oh, I'll fuckin' show you." He lowered the band of his boxer briefs to free his burgeoning erection. If I thought it was big the last time I saw it, this was a whole other affair. My breath caught at the sight of it. "Like what you see? You like my giant cock?"

I smirked, his words snapping me back into my confident, take-charge mode as my fingers started to circle my clit. "Get over yourself."

"You get over it," he teased. "You're the one who called my cock giant."

"Fine. I like your giant cock. Now fuck your hand for me."

"Jesus, Jessalyn."

I laid back and dipped my fingers into my soaking slit. Ben stood over me, jacking his cock and feeling my leg with his other hand.

"Look at you," he rasped. "So fucking perfect."

"You like watching me?"

"Never seen anything more beautiful in my life. You've never done this with anybody else, have you?"

I shook my head and bit my lip.

"But you've always wanted to, haven't you?" he went on. "You've been waiting on me to let yourself loose. Anything you want, Jessie. I'll make sure you get it."

My hand sped up around my clit as the other went to my breast.

"That feel good, baby? You like having your tits grabbed?"

"Mmhmm."

"You gonna show me one of those pretty nipples?"

I grinned. "Why don't ya beg for it?"

He shook his head and let out an agonized groan. "Such a brat."

"I'm waiting," I said. "I don't have all day."

"Please let me see you, Jessie. You're killing me."

I held his eyes as I lowered one bra cup. "Like this?"

"That's it, honey. Good girl."

My face screwed up. I hadn't known he was serious with the Daddy/good girl text exchange we had. "What am I, your dog?"

He cracked a cocky smile. "No. When you do what I say, you're my good girl. Now, why don't you be a good girl for me and tell me what you were thinking about when you did this without me?"

My eyes widened as I bit my lip.

"Don't be shy, now. We're way past that, hon."

"I wondered whether you'd grab hard or be more tender. I thought about your hands on me, your thick fingers. Your cock filling me up, my mouth, my pussy. The taste of you. I wondered what made all those women scream so loud and whether you'd think of me as a fucktoy or something more."

"Fuck, Jessie." His hand made small circles at the top of his strokes, working the head of his cock. "You'd be all that and more. There's so much I want to do with you."

I trailed my other hand down to my pussy, sliding two fingers inside. "Why don't you tell me what you'd want?"

He sucked air through his teeth as he put his head back, eyes remaining on me. Then he bent over me, his hand on his cock skimming my stomach. "I'd want you screaming my name when you come on my cock, my tongue. I want to brand you with my cum, claim you with my cock. No one else. And when you come for me, you'll belong to me. Because now that you're with me, you're never faking again."

I whimpered, his words turning me on more. "What about if I come for you now? Will I be yours?"

"Not yet, honey. You'll come when I say so. And when you

do, you're gonna look at me. I need to know how gorgeous you are when you come."

My nipples felt tighter as his words washed over me, my breasts heavier. All I wanted was more, and him, and now. I could have easily reached out to touch him, but I liked the game we were playing. "What did you think about when you jacked off to me?"

He hummed. "I thought about what your breath would feel like on my neck. Whether I'd smell like you when we were done. Whether you'd be a little brat or a good girl. Whether you'd let Daddy take control or take matters into your own hands. How that hot, tight little pussy would feel gripping my cock."

"Ben," I whined.

"That's it, baby. Beg for it. I'm gonna let you have it, but you've gotta show me you want it."

Where had Demanding Jess gone? When did I become so submissive? Why was it turning me on so much? A rush of moisture coated my hand, his face going to a thrilled surprise.

"Ben," I squeaked. "Did I just squirt?"

"Fuck yeah you did, honey," he growled. "Now you're gonna come for me. Eyes on me and tell me who's turning you on."

My eyes squeezed shut, but I remembered to open them as my edge inched closer. With a final twitch of my fingers, I came, hard, his name falling from me.

Ben nodded with the greatest admiration in his eyes. "That's my girl."

"Come on my tits," I pleaded. "I need it."

"You got it, baby. Sit up a little for me."

He knelt over me as I sat up on my elbows. The fierce motion of his hand and his abs flexing told me he was close.

"Fuck, I could go again," I gritted out. "You're so hot, Ben."

"Do it, Jessie," Ben said. "Be a good girl and come when I do."

Before reaching for my pussy again, I pulled my breasts fully out of my bra. Ben's breathing quickened and his eyes went wide.

"Say my name, too," I said. "If I'm yours, you're mine."

"I've been yours, Jessie." With a yell that was something like my name, a hot spurt hit my chest, followed by a few more. Ben panted over me, running his finger through the mess on my tits. I looked down to see what he was doing and found the word "MINE" written there. In his cum.

I whimpered his name.

"You're mine now, Jessalyn. You're so fucking beautiful and you're mine. Don't you be scared of it. I've got you in every way, honey."

I'd never had someone go all in so hard in my life. Mikey didn't hesitate to call me his own. And he said he'd *been* mine. He was putting me first.

Could anything be hotter? To be so wholly desired?

Holding his gaze, I dragged my fingers through his cum and rubbed it onto my peaked nipple, then into my clit. He kissed my neck as I touched myself, whispering in my ear how gorgeous I am. It was then that I fell over the edge again.

"You did so good, honey. I love seeing you lose control."

My eyes flitted all over his exposed skin, feeling self-conscious realizing I'd just orgasmed twice, and squirted, in front of someone new. "We did that."

"We did. It was really fucking hot." He bent down and kissed me. "Stay here. I'll get you cleaned up."

I scooted to the top of the bed and looked down at the mess we'd made. Ben came back in the room in just his boxer briefs and an ear-to-ear smile. He used a warm washcloth to wipe first my pussy, then my breasts. His face faltered to a more polite smile.

"You are on birth control, right? That was really hot and it's not likely that you'd get knocked up from that, but I don't like to tempt fate."

I gritted my teeth. "Yes, I am. Sorry. I didn't mean to make you uncomfortable."

He kissed me and stayed over top of me. "I'm clean, too. I get tested, so we're good there. I'd have told you before, but we weren't touching each other."

"Oh, yeah, I got checked up while you were gone. No issues despite being cheated on," I sighed. "But . . ."

"What, hon?"

I rubbed my lips together. "Have you been tested since your last partner? I know you have lots of other options."

His face softened. "One, yes I have been tested. And I always wrap it up. I've never been bare with anyone. And two, Jessie, I'm not talking to anyone else. Haven't been for a while. You can go through my phone if you want."

"Sorry. Yeah. You told me all that. It's just, you know."

I didn't want to say his name. Mikey got it, though.

He settled on his side facing me, patting my cheek. "I know. I would never do that to you. And what we just did? That was my first time doing that, too."

I nodded. It was the first sexual thing we'd done together, and it was still the freakiest thing I'd ever done. Still, someone treating me the way I'd been treated for the past four years, I had trouble believing it all. I looked at my nails, running my fingertip over a jagged edge. "You do still get messages from girls, though, right? Like, nudes and stuff?"

He chewed his lip but didn't look away. "Yeah, I do. But I never found what I was looking for with people like that. With you, I want something deeper. I genuinely like you. All of you."

I twisted my lips with a little snort. "Not just my killer rack?"

"Definitely not just your killer rack," he said with a kiss. "I also like how you don't take any shit, and your smile, and your laugh. I like this little dimple," he said, touching my cheek and waiting for me to smile so it would show, "Thank you. And I like how somehow, you like me, too."

I stroked my thumb over his cheek. "This is all really unexpected, you know."

"I know. I'm fucking terrified, but I'm going with it. I hope you will, too."

I raised an eyebrow. "You told me not to be scared of being yours."

He chuckled. "I feel good about you being mine. That doesn't mean I'm not afraid I'll screw it all up."

"Interesting contradiction, Mr. Miknevicius." We shared a tender, delicate kiss and then he moved to the bottom of the bed. He put a towel where I'd made a bit of a mess.

"Sorry about that," I said with a grimace, getting up to head for the bathroom.

Ben's brow furrowed and he scrambled after me, tackling me back to the bed. He lowered his voice to a growl.

"Don't you dare apologize for being sexy as fuck and squirting on my bed." He nuzzled my nose, making me giggle. "That was hotter than actual sex. You're perfect, Jessalyn."

I yawned, patting his side. "Thanks, bubby. Now get off me so I can go pee and brush my teeth. Some of us have to get up early."

He laughed as he rolled off me. "You going all mountain mama on me?"

"Reckon I am."

He followed me into the bathroom to do our evening business. When we headed back for the bedroom, he was wrestling me into bed again.

"What gives, Jockey?" I asked, laughing.

"I can finally touch you and mess with you like I've wanted to," he said, clinging to my side. "You ready to go to sleep?"

"Yeah, but let me get this bra off. I can't sleep in them."

"I've noticed," he said with a skeevy grin. I rolled my eyes and reached for my bra clasp, but he beat me to it. "Can I hold your tits while we sleep? Though they aren't the only thing I like about you, I'm still kind of obsessed with them."

"Sure." I pulled back to look at his face, then kissed him. "Hey. We're kissing in your bed. Not just sleeping or snuggling."

"We are. And I think it's our bed."

My heart fluttered at how readily he included me in his life. "Is that weird?" I asked.

"If it's weird, I like weird."

With an arm wrapped around my waist and a hand on my boob, he sighed out one last "mine" before we drifted off to sleep.

30

MIKEY

essie's alarm went off at 4:30 as usual, but this time, her mostly naked body was nestled into mine. My left hand was full of her right breast.

This was paradise. Even if it was too damn early.

"Morning, Sweet Cheeks," I said, stroking her nipple.

"Not a bad way to wake up," she murmured. "Minus like no sleep."

"Can you be late today?" I asked, pressing my rapidly hardening dick into her backside. "I could go for more Jessie and Ben time like we had last night.

"I wish. I'm actually in more of a hurry. This is my last chance to shower before your thing tonight."

"We could skip it," I said, rubbing my hand down her hip.

"Or will there be a coat closet there?" She turned to face me with a mischievous smile.

"Good memory, Sweet Cheeks. I'll see what we can pull off. But I'd rather our first time not be in a coat closet. That's later stuff."

"Oh, is that part of the Mikey Formula?" She said it sarcastically, but I could hear her insecurity.

"No, ma'am. What I told you against the door were my wildest fantasies of what I wanted to do to you." She was halfway to the bathroom but gave me a little smile. How long would it be before she trusted me not to cheat on her?

I mean, yeah, a guy who didn't have dozens of women in his DMs cheated on her. I guess I could see where she'd get a little gun shy.

But whatever nerves she had didn't stop her from giving me a kiss in bed before she left, her wet hair brushing my cheek.

"Have a great day, Jockey. See you tonight."

~

> Can't wait to see you

JESSIE GIRL

Getting my hair and makeup done now by the girls on set! I feel like a star

> U r my star

Stop. You're a schmooze

> Seriously. Can't wait to have u on my arm. Ur a star to me

> Saw ur dress hanging in the closet. Very excited to see it on you

> Or off you?

(smirk emoji)

~

"Will you zip me?"

Jessie had walked in from work looking stunning in her fancy hair and makeup, something she said Kitty did, too. I poured her a glass of prosecco and sent her to go get dressed. We were kinda pressed for time, even with a fashionably late arrival. Her dress had this high neckline that of course made her rack look amazing. The red glittery fabric went to the floor with a slit that let one whole leg out. As I stepped in the bedroom to zip her as requested, I had an open view of her back.

"What if I'd rather get you out of this dress?" I asked, kissing her neck from behind.

"I don't want to mess up my hair just yet," she said with a wink over her shoulder.

I groaned, rubbing myself into her ass. "Jessie, it's almost worse to know that you're kind of a freak."

"That's what you think. What if I turn out to be the most vanilla you've ever had?"

"I don't see that happening. You were begging me to come on your tits last night."

She tossed her head from side to side, weighing that. "Fair."

Slowly, I zipped her dress. "You know, we're getting a limo to the event. And it's a good twenty minutes away."

My hand dragged from her knee to the slit at the top of her dress.

"Is twenty minutes enough time?" she asked innocently.

I nibbled under her ear and slipped my hand into the slit of her dress, petting my finger over her panties. "We can make it enough time for a little fun. Take the edge off."

My phone buzzed in my pocket. Jess whined as I looked at my phone, removing my hand from her. "That's our driver. I'll tell them we'll be right down. Can I do anything to help you get ready?"

"I'm almost done. Just need my earrings and to touch up my lipstick," she said breezily, taking a sip of her Prosecco. I turned her to face me and ran my thumb over her bottom lip.

"Maybe don't bother with the lipstick, darlin'."

She arched an eyebrow. "What exactly do you think is going to happen in this limo, Jockey?"

"This sassy, pretty mouth wrapped around my cock if I'm lucky," I said.

Her arms went around my neck, pressing herself into me. "Hmm. And what do I get out of the deal?"

"You're my girl now. You know I'll take care of you," I cooed, holding her waist. We melted into each other for a kiss so intense, I came away with swollen lips and a semi.

"I want to fuck you right here on this dresser," I said, scooping up her bottom and setting her on the edge.

"How long til the driver leaves?" she asked, running a finger down my chest and pulling me in by my tie. As if on cue, my phone buzzed again. I growled, checking my watch. We were late.

"We should go," I said miserably.

It turned out that the driver was a very sweet old man who apparently wanted to talk the entire time, and we had a town car, not a limo. Neither Jess nor I were in the mood to shut down an old man so we could fool around in the backseat. We exchanged many tense glances and hand squeezes, her dimple almost constantly out from where she was trying to keep from laughing.

That meant by the time we got to the venue, we were both frustrated as fuck. I had to mentally pour cold water on my dick and try to pretend every touch from Jess wasn't sending my body into overdrive.

She adjusted my tie before we went in and undid the top button of my jacket. "Button this when you get out of the car, babe," she said.

The driver got out to open our door and she burst into laughter. "Well, that didn't go as planned."

"No, it did not," I said. "And look at you, fixing me up like your little Ken doll."

"Sorry. Old habit. It's what I do all day. You ready to be fancy?"

"Ready. There's photographers, so smile big."

She looked momentarily terrified but steeled herself with a deep breath and a smile. I pecked her cheek. "Don't worry. You look gorgeous, baby."

We stepped out into the flashes and cheers of fans waiting on either side of the red carpet.

Jessie tugged on my hand and I bent down to listen. "Jesus, Jockey. I didn't know you were this famous."

I grinned at her and squeezed her hand. I stopped and talked to a reporter. Jessie tried to step out of the camera's view, but I wrapped my arm around her waist to keep her close.

"Mikey, why do you think it's so important to help disadvantaged youth?"

I rattled off some answer my PR rep had told me to give.

"And who's this with you?"

"This is my girlfriend, Jessie. She's a brilliant costume designer. I'm very glad she came tonight to make me look sharper."

She gave me a goofy grin. I went in to give her a kiss on the temple, but she turned her face up and well, I just full-on kissed her. Quick, nothing nasty. Her face went bright red. I thanked the reporter and walked Jessie on down the carpet.

I signed a few autographs for fans that had stuff waiting and snapped selfies with a few. Someone asked to get a picture of me and Jessie, which I thought was a little weird, but we went with it.

"Sorry about the kiss. I didn't mean to make you uncomfortable," I said as we walked the last few feet to the door.

"I'm flattered. It was a surprise, but you're always full of surprises."

"I might be a teensy bit excited about having you with me," I admitted.

"It's nice to have someone excited to be with me," she said, her eyes kind of sad. My stomach turned a little, both for her sadness and because she was thinking about Cole. I didn't want her thinking about that douchebag when I was the one bringing her out places. Oh well. I guess I looked amazing by comparison.

We walked into a grand hall and were immediately flagged down by Guy and Kitty.

"Look at your dress, Jessie!" Kitty said, her jaw on the floor. "Miss Jessica Rabbit in the building!"

"Doesn't she look incredible?" I said, taking the opportunity to look my date over from head to toe.

"A-thank you," Jessie said, pretending to flip her hair over her shoulder when really it was slicked back in a low bun. "You also look fantastic, Kitty."

"Well, someone made my dress fit like a glove," Kitty said, tapping Jessie's arm. "Grab a drink before cocktail hour's over. I think they're about to seat everyone for dinner."

I got Jessie's drink order and went to the bar, meeting her at the table. We sat through the program, quietly passing around rolls and having our salad course. Whenever we weren't eating, I held Jessie's hand in my lap. It was simple, but it felt so nice to have her close, someone who wanted to be there because she liked *me*. Jessie wasn't into me for my money, or for hockey. She liked hanging out with me, and I more than liked hanging out with her. She caught me staring at her, but instead of looking over at me with judgment or scorn, she just smiled back at me and patted my leg.

I was so smitten with her. So royally fucked. How did I get that lucky?

I was supposed to be paying attention to the presentation, but I couldn't focus with Jessie looking so gorgeous sitting next to me.

Last night was really fun

Jessie took her phone out of her tiny purse in response to the buzz. Her cheeks went pink.

JESSIE GIRL

I'm still thinking about it. Not sure how I'll wait til we get home

Fuuuuuuck. That had me ten kinds of fired up. I looked around and determined that there wouldn't be much to miss for the next little bit. I snuck out to the bathroom and texted her again.

Meet me at coat check

I tipped the teenager working at the door $200 to make himself scarce and keep people out of the closet. He almost started to ask questions, but I pointed to the money. He shut his mouth immediately.

"Knock five times if someone's coming in, you hear me?"

The kid nodded.

A few minutes later, Jessie appeared at the wooden double doors with a suspicious look on her face. "Seriously?"

"Do you want this?" I countered. Her eyes went lust-filled. "Please."

I grabbed her by the waist and hauled her into the coat check room, shutting the doors behind us. It was dark except for the hallway light peeking through the crack in the door. I brought us into the far corner of the closet, protected from view by a layer of coats. I stripped off my jacket and took her purse, throwing it over a rack of coats. Before I could pin her to the wall, she pinned me, her mouth hungry as my head fell back. Jessie knew what she wanted and was taking it. I'd never had a woman battle me for dominance before and it was hot as fuck.

Her hand met my crotch, rubbing fiercely against my already hard cock.

"This for me?" she asked.

"Every inch," I said. I pushed her back against the other wall, lifting her leg over my forearm and sliding my hand over her ass. My fingers crept along the split of her until I found what I wanted: her drenched center through her thong.

"All this for me?" I asked as my finger met her wetness.

"You wish," she teased. Our old dynamic of hate-you-love-you was in her tone, but she wasn't fooling me. Her fingers groped at my tie, loosening it and undoing the top buttons to touch my bare skin.

"You know it is," I rasped as I undid my fly and button and shoved my pants and underwear below my butt, still not releasing her leg. "How long have you been hot for me, Jessie Girl?"

"Since you pushed me against your door. I wanted to drop to my knees right then and show you how bad I wanted it."

"Why don't you show me right now?"

Her strength was surprising as she shoved me back against the other wall, sucking on my neck before lowering to her knees and taking my cock in her hand. I couldn't see her very well, so I felt everything: her hot breath on my dick before the warmth of her tongue, then the cool of the wet she left behind. I struggled to stay quiet, but knew I had to. Her mouth surrounded me, taking me all the way in, a quiet gag leaving her before her tongue flicked my underside. *Christ.* A hum as she tasted me. I didn't want to mess up her hair, so I held under her chin, her vocal cords vibrating as she hummed again. Her hands, one on my balls and the other around my base. Her mouth, working absolute sorcery. I wasn't going to last, and I still had a promise to keep.

I pulled at her arms to get her up. Then, cradling her head, I pressed her back against the other wall. It was a game of ping-pong we were playing between the walls of the corner. I kissed her deeply, my salt still on her tongue. My fingers drifted under her skirt, sliding her thong to the side. She sighed into my mouth as I rubbed over her sensitive nerves, suppressing her scream with my kiss.

She stopped and tugged her skirt higher on her hips, giving me more room. I couldn't resist just a little taste.

"I could spend my life on my knees for you and it would never be enough," I breathed. "I was born to taste you."

I tossed my tie over my shoulder, dropped to my knees, and lapped at her pussy, her smooth skin and tangy taste a welcome sensation. Her leg fell over my shoulder as I went deeper, burying my face and making a huge, delicious mess. She writhed into my face, rolling her hips against my tongue as I drowned in her. My cock was so sensitive I was afraid to touch it, the whole experience so deeply erotic. She pulled up on the back of my head.

"Now," she whispered. "I need you to fuck me now."

"I don't have anything with me," I whispered back. Why the fuck didn't I think about condoms?

"I trust you," she said, bringing my hand to her breast. "I'm protected and we're both clean. If you want it, I'm in."

I could just make out her face in the faint light as she lifted her leg back over my arm, nodding to push me on. Did she remember that this was such a big moment for me? Not just sex with her for the first time, but my first time bare with anyone? I didn't want to ruin the moment by bringing it up, but I absolutely, 100% wanted it to be with her.

I used my hand to guide my cock through her wet, soaking up what we'd made together before notching myself and sliding in. We both breathed out hard as I went in. I dropped my forehead to hers.

"Christ, Jessie," I whispered, surrounded by her wet heat.

"You're really big, Mikey," she whimpered.

"You can take it, baby. Squeeze me tight with that pussy. It'll help." Her muscles tightened around me and I groaned. "There you go. Do it again. Better, hon?"

"Yeah," she said. "Hey, it's your first time bare."

"I'm glad it's with you, baby." I gave her gentle kisses as I felt her get wetter and relax more. Then I leaned into her ear. "Now shut the fuck up and take this dick like a good girl."

The dark, throaty laugh she unleashed at my dirty words almost broke me. I could give her my worst and she'd giggle with delight. Who was this woman? I clapped my hand over her mouth, fulfilling the promise I made up against our front door. She moaned into my palm.

"Can you breathe okay?"

She nodded under my hand. Then I started to move, thrusting into her, the sequins and beads on her dress rattling as I filled her. I moved her leg higher on my forearm, spreading her so I could reach her clit with my thumb.

"That alright?"

"Mmhmm," she responded.

Her eyes were gorgeous in the low light, eyebrows pinched in pleasure. She thrusted along with me, tiny affirmations issuing from her throat. Her walls fluttered around me, her hips bucking wildly with me, and I knew neither of us would be long. She held my shoulders, clawed my chest and back, drew me in closer to her.

"That's it, baby. Feels good, doesn't it? Having a real man fuck you senseless," I gritted into her ear. She wound the leg that wasn't over my arm around my leg, completely held up by me and the wall.

She whimpered out my name under my hand. A muffled

sound like "coming" came out of her as she squirmed up the wall.

"There you go, honey. Come for your daddy." She released around me, her pussy grabbing me, and my God, there must be nothing better in this world. Her breathing was so heavy that it wet my hand over her mouth. I spread my fingers to give her more room to breathe.

"Can I finish inside you?"

Her stifled "yes" vibrated against my hand. I came into her, hard, my release feeling like it was draining my entire spine. I must have made a loud noise, because her hand came over my mouth and she let out a little laugh.

Both of her hands held my face as I came down, holding her up but struggling to stay standing.

"Jessalyn," I sighed into her neck.

"Benjamin," she said as I released my hand from her mouth.

"How are we supposed to function after that?"

She laughed quietly. "I'm not sure. Can we get a light on and you can fix my hair and makeup, though?"

I kissed her. "Not yet."

I pulled out of her, sliding my fingers inside to her moan. "You feel that? That's us."

I withdrew my fingers, lifting them to her mouth. "One for you. One for me."

I put my index finger to her lips, and she opened, sucking our taste off my finger. "Good girl."

I did the same with my middle finger, tasting what we were like together.

"We taste pretty good," she said before sharing a kiss with me.

I grinned. "I've always wanted to do that."

"Me, too," she said. Gone was her sad, vanilla relationship.

She had me now. We could be as nasty as we wanted together, and I had every intention of making all her dreams come true.

We returned to our table as dinner was served. I'd done a pretty bang-up job on her hair and makeup if I do say so myself. I scooted her chair back in, but as I went to put her napkin back on her lap, I saw the white streak going down her leg. My cum was rolling down this perfect woman's leg. Without anyone noticing, I gave it a quick wipe before dropping the napkin in her lap. I sat and she widened her eyes at me. Her cheeks were flushed, and I'm sure mine were too, but I didn't give a shit.

I'd just fucked the most wonderful woman on the planet in a coat closet.

After dinner, we drank, we danced to the band, and she was good-natured with even the cattiest of the wives. Jess was an unstoppable ray of fucking sunshine. She danced along with them to Barbie Girl like she knew everyone and belonged there. Her dimple peeked out at me whenever I put her out for a spin on the dance floor. It made me so gushy inside I could have died. My teammates clapped me on the back to congratulate me on such a catch. Guy and Kitty kept dancing over to us and making a fun group of four. I'd always wanted it: a girl to have fun with me and my friends. I'd never had such a fun date, ever.

I held her hand and let her put her head on my shoulder on the car ride home. We got out of our fancy clothes and passed out tangled up naked together.

It was, perhaps, the best day of my life to date.

31

JESSIE

He fucked me in a coat closet. Not just fucked me: he held his hand over my mouth and railed me against a wall in a coat closet. He did what he said he would do.

Ben watched me all night with stars in his eyes. I'd known Ben's horny look since the night I broke up his party. This was different. It was enamored, dreamy, completely moon-eyed. Like he couldn't wait to hear what I'd say next or see what I'd do.

Waking up together, naked, surrounded by a man who truly appreciated me? There's nothing better.

"Hey, gorgeous," Ben crooned as I woke up.

"Oh, good morning."

He hit me with a kiss, just lips, his massive hand resting on my cheek.

"We both have morning breath, but I don't care," he smiled into my lips. I kissed him back. "I'm kind of obsessed with you."

The sheets gathered just below his hip bones and at my lower ribs. I was exposed, but it didn't feel scary-exposed. I was there with someone I trusted.

"You're beautiful like this," I whispered, thumbing over his hip bone. Ben looked genuinely touched.

"I can't believe we get to wake up like this, Jessie."

I grinned, overcome with the need to have him. I pushed him onto his back and climbed on top of him.

"My God, Jessalyn," he gaped, taking my breasts into his hands.

"What, you like?" I gave him a coy smirk.

"Yes. Yes, I like." He scrunched my boobs together and rubbed his tongue between my nipples. "I don't even know where to start."

"You're on a good track, baby."

He sucked, drawing out one nipple, looking up at me. "So perfect, Jess. Is this real? Are you really my girlfriend now? No more faking?"

"I don't think the coat closet was fake, or did I just dream that up?"

"Hmm, it's a little fuzzy. You'll have to remind me."

"Well, I think I sucked your cock, you ate my pussy, and then you fucked me raw in a coat closet at a benefit thing for your hockey team. And then you had me eat our cum, and you wiped your cum off my leg at the dinner table with all your friends. But I could have made it all up. That sounds improbable," I said, shrugging. His cock was hard between us.

"Sounds like a dream, but it's one I want to have."

Ben drew me in for a deep kiss. When we came up for air, he spoke again.

"But here's the thing. You're way behind on orgasms, and it's my duty to apologize for the male sex. I need to get you off before I fuck you, then get you off again. Sound like a good plan?"

I beamed. "Prove it, Jockey."

Ben flipped me on my back, pinning my hands under one

of his, the calluses grating against my skin. He hovered at my ear, whispering in a husky voice.

"Don't you dare fake it for me, Jessalyn. We're not finished until it's real. I don't care how long it takes. Got it?"

I nodded. "Be warned. It might require a toy."

"Didn't require a toy last night," he drawled.

"Yeah, well, you'd kinda built up the experience in my mind. Here, it's in a bed, the pressure's on, ya know. Different scenario. Don't want your ego to deflate if I need a little assistance."

He got a glint in his eye. "Honey, you know I'm going to want to see how hot you look using a toy, but I'm a competitive man. I'm going to do my best to beat the machine this time. You give me a challenge, I'm going to do anything I can to beat it."

His lips traveled down my neck, taking his time on me.

"Was that the equivalent of telling you to skate twenty laps as fast as you can?"

His warm laugh rattled my ear. "Something like that."

He worshiped my breasts with his mouth, caressing, stroking, sucking. But he didn't stay there as long as most men did. Strangely, that made me feel more seen and appreciated. My boobs are something of an attraction. Everyone's always in a hurry to get their dick between them or stare at them blankly, but Mikey was dedicated to keeping the focus on me. Me as a whole, and not just me as a vessel for giant boobs.

"You are a fucking goddess, Jessalyn," he cooed as he settled his shoulders under my legs. "You tell me if you like it harder or softer, okay? This ain't about me. It's about you feeling good. I want you to have exactly what you like."

He kissed softly all around my slit, building the anticipation. I let out an unintentional whimper that made him look up at me with apology in his eyes, like he couldn't believe he'd tortured me like that. He grasped my hand as his tongue sank into me, eyes going devilish. I rested back on the pillow, letting myself take in the sensation. A brief thought flashed through my mind of how much better he was than Cole, not just in skill, but in actually caring what I thought about what he was giving me. Wanting me to have what *I* wanted. I rocked my hips, matching the work of his tongue to his pleased hum. A glance down showed him truly making love to me with his mouth, immersed in the experience. He gave a long suck, making my back pull taut like a bow. Then he went back in with soft side-to-side flicks. I felt impossibly turned on, a feeling bigger than most orgasms I'd had in the past, and this was just the build-up.

"Ben, Jockey, baby, it's—" I broke off with a cry as my lower belly tingled and hollowed out. He gave and gave, nodding to encourage me. My words came out as a squeak because there was hardly any air in my lungs. "Just like that, baby, please, yes, I'm gonna—Ben!"

I made a sound that was downright pornographic, something I never imagined could actually come from my body as I released, little tears at the corners of my eyes and my ears ringing.

"I can't, you made me, you did it," I blurted as I came down, truly disbelieving. He continued lapping at me, long and light strokes with little kisses in between. I combed my fingers through his thick hair. He ran his tongue around his lips and wrinkled his nose in a gleeful grin.

"How was that for twenty laps?"

I laughed out loud. "I think you did it in under twenty, baby. Holy fuck."

His precum wet my stomach as he crawled up to kiss me. His smiling eyes met mine. "You said my name when you came. You know what that makes you?"

I twisted my lips, knowing what he was getting at. "Nah, no way."

"Yes way."

"I'm a good girl for you?"

"You're the best girl, Jessalyn."

"I bet I could be even better," I said, taking his cock in my hand. He put his head back.

"Wait just a second. I have an idea." He grabbed a blanket from the end of the bed and put it on the floor in front of his closet mirror. "You game for the floor?"

I laughed. "We're never gonna do it standard missionary, are we?"

"If I have my way, we'll do 'em all, Jessie Girl. Is that what you want? Standard?"

"I think I like your ideas better," I said. I was genuinely thrilled, going from the most vanilla sex life to someone who actually wanted to play like I did.

"Then get those sweet cheeks on over here."

He stood by the mirror, reaching for me. I felt wanted down to my core, not just for my body, but like Ben wanted me. All of me. He wasn't rushing, but he was still fervent somehow. Savoring. That's the best word for it. Ben was savoring the experience, taking it all in with hyperaware senses. Our kisses were slow and drugging, a dance of teasing and sampling. I took my time dragging my mouth down his body, pinching his nipples, playing my fingers along the lines of his muscles.

I met his eyes as I knelt before him, admiration glowing in his gaze. I stroked his cock while I spoke. "You want this?"

"Anything you're willing to give me, honey. I'll give you anything you want, too," he said with a grin and a thumb over my lips. "You look pretty on your knees like that."

I couldn't help but smile before sucking his thumb between my lips. It was so new to me to relish in sexuality with a partner who loved it as much as I did. I gladly took him into my mouth, his hand tangling in my hair and a sigh on his lips.

"So fucking good, Jessie," he praised me. I alternated

working him deeper into my throat and playing with the head, rewarded by little bursts of his precum. I'd always enjoyed turning men into putty that way, but it felt more gratifying to have someone appreciate it so deeply—and be so eager to give it back. I pulled off to speak but kept my hands moving on him.

"What did you have in mind with the blanket?"

He smirked. "Get on your tummy, baby."

I did as he asked and he knelt behind me, kissing up my back.

"Face the mirror," he said, "and lift your hips."

He slid a pillow under my hips. "Your back feel okay if you go up on your elbows?"

I nodded. He sat between my spread legs behind me, rubbing my ass cheeks and kissing the base of my spine. I rolled my hips into the touch, already needing relief again.

"I thought you'd look real pretty like this, and we could watch each other," he said.

"I'm into it. You gonna fuck me or what?"

He chuckled. "Damn, Jessie, I don't even have to ask you to beg today."

He lined himself up and pushed into me, then leaned over my back. The friction was sublime.

"That feel good, dirty girl?" His hands met my breasts, rubbing and squeezing.

"How's that pussy?"

"Fucking perfect, Jessalyn. I love how you dirty talk, too. Christ."

His speed increased, positively railing me, my breasts jolting with the motion. Feeling good but not good enough, I moved my hips along with him. I thought back to his words from the coat closet and thought I'd test a theory.

"Daddy, I need more," I whined.

He got a similar shocked and thrilled look to when I

squirted during our first time messing around. "Tell me what you need, honey. Daddy'll take care of you."

"My clit."

His hand slid between the pillow and me, finding the pulsing point. "This needy little thing?"

"Yes," I sighed. "Right there."

His fingers worked magic while he continued pounding me, one hand full of my breast, the other working my clit.

"Choke me," I spit out. His hand moved from my chest to my throat, meeting my eyes with a smile in the mirror as he squeezed.

"Good girl. Tell Daddy what you need and I give it, baby. Keep talking to me."

I'd never had someone so willing to give, and I wanted it all, a two-person gang bang. He watched me with a lurid fascination, mouth agape.

"Fuck, you look pretty in pink," he said, releasing his grip on my throat. "I need you to come for me. What do I gotta do to get you there?"

I met his eyes in the mirror, more red creeping into my cheeks. I'd only tried asking Cole for this once, and it didn't go well. This was deepest, darkest cobwebbed corners of the brain territory.

"Don't you do that, baby. You tell me what you need. I'm game for anything but you gotta tell me."

"My ass," I whispered.

He bit his lip in concentration as he took his wet fingers from my clit, spit on them, and gently pushed them into my ass. He looked to my reflection for confirmation. "How's that?"

I cried out, the pleasure so intense as I tightened all around him.

"Oh, fuck, Jessie."

I pressed my hips up from where they rested on the pillow,

which he took as an invitation to switch to doggie. "Jessie," he warned again.

"I need," I started, pulling away and flipping onto my back. I tugged him down and shoved him back inside me, pancaking our bodies together. "Pound me."

I gripped his shoulders and he gripped mine, using the leverage to give me everything he had. Our names spilled out and my orgasm was sudden and fierce. He buried himself to the hilt with one final thrust as he jerked inside me, pulsing with my walls.

Ben held his face over mine, locking our mouths together, whimpering in relief.

"Jessie, how am I supposed to not be obsessed with you?"

I grinned up at him. "I think you might be my new favorite thing. But I made you do missionary."

Ben let out a loud laugh. "You are not vanilla, darlin'. Rest assured. Anything but."

"Why thank you," I said, beaming up at him.

He stroked my cheek, still deep inside me. "You're not gonna run off on me, are you? Take all this away?"

His question caught me off guard. I didn't expect him to be so vulnerable after sex. My mind swirled.

"I don't think so?"

"You keep saying that you might leave L.A. I just want to put in a formal request that you . . . not do that," Ben said. He was trying to make a joke, but his eyes were wounded.

"I wasn't planning on making any big decisions at the moment," I said, not sure what to think. "But things are a little chaotic right now. This is all happening pretty fast."

The hurt was all over Mikey's face. "Right." He couldn't meet my eyes. "I'll just, uh," he said as he pulled out of me and pushed the blanket up to the mess. He stood, getting a look at the clock.

"Fuck! I've got morning skate in like thirty," he said, stomping to the dresser to get out his clothes.

"Oh. Can I help? Coffee?"

"I'll just grab something at the arena," he grumbled.

I was already tired of his shit. "Ben, you're not doing this."

He slammed open his underwear drawer. "Doing what?"

"Pulling away because you're scared!"

"I'm not pulling away, you are!" he objected. "You keep acting like you've got one foot out the door!"

I rolled my eyes. "When was the last time I said anything about leaving? Were we together?"

He stopped with his shirt halfway over his head. "I guess not."

"Jockey, I'm not trying to leave. But you have to know, this is all a lot for me. I might need some space to deal with that."

"What does space even mean, Jessalyn?" he shouted.

I blinked twice and bristled.

"I'm sorry I yelled. You don't deserve that."

"Thank you," I said.

"But clue me in. All I've ever wanted is someone to care about me like what my friends have, but it's fucking terrifying. I don't know what I'm doing. I like you so much, Jessie. I don't want to screw all this up, but I also don't want to get all tied up just for you to decide I'm not worth it."

His words were heartbreaking. Such a big, sweet guy was so full of sadness deep down.

"That's kind of the risk of love, Mikey," I said, pulling the blanket up to cover me. "But from what I've seen so far, you're worth it. What are you so afraid of?"

"Nothing. Forget it," he said, sitting at the end of the bed and putting his socks on.

"Ben. Remember what I said about communication? Please don't shut down on me."

"Yeah, and I'm not ready to fucking talk about it, alright?"

I shot him a death glare. That kind of shit was not going to fly with me. He softened, approaching me and crouching down to where I was still on the floor. He held my chin and looked deep into my eyes. "When I have the right words for it, I'll tell you. Okay, hon?"

He kissed my cheek and stood to leave. "I'll see you later."

32

MIKEY

"So, you and Jessie seemed to have a lot of fun last night." Guy watched me carefully as we got changed for practice.

"I guess," I grumbled.

"Yikes," Sorrento said. "Trouble in paradise."

"What happened? You two were having a great time!" Guy said, sliding his pads over his head.

"Nothing."

Guy cocked his head to the side. "Come on, man."

"She's just gonna leave anyway," I said. "It doesn't matter."

"Oh?" Guy said. "Did she say she was going to leave?"

"Every time we fight, she starts packing a bag." That was partially true. She did that the night that we first kissed. She really hadn't done it since. A few guys laughed.

"The old bag trick," Sorrento said knowingly.

I turned back to him, incredulous. "Wanna clue me in?"

"She wants you to beg her to stay, bro," Sorrento said. "Give her a reason to stay. Don't get all butt hurt. She wants to know you want her there."

"She said she needs 'space,'" I said. Another "ooh" rippled across the locker room.

"That's more complicated," Guy said. "Sometimes space means come closer, and sometimes it actually means space. But she's kinda going through a lot, isn't she?"

"Yeah, she ran into her ex's not-so-new girl. He'd been cheating for a while," I said. I didn't mention her trauma with the storms coming up just a few nights before. That didn't seem like locker room fodder.

"Oof," Sorrento said.

"If her ex has been cheating, she's probably pretty scared of getting burned again," Obi said. "He probably wasn't exactly tending to her emotional needs either. Maybe show her you can handle it with her."

"What makes you the expert, Oberbeck? It's not like you've had tons of experience," I snapped.

"Actually, I do—"

"Cool it, Mike," Stelle warned. "We're trying to help."

I closed my eyes, knowing they were right and I was really in the wrong, with them and with Jessie. "Fuck. I yelled at her earlier."

Guy grimaced, and the other guys wouldn't meet my eyes. "Then it's time to grovel."

~

ON THE ICE, I was distracted. Guy had to pry me off a bike during warmups because I was so zoned out. My stomach hurt, threatening one of my episodes from the stress. All I could think about was getting home and apologizing to Jessie. Her question kept ringing through my head: what are you so afraid of?

Her leaving. Not being good enough for her. If I was asking her to be mine, I needed to be able to stick with her. I needed to not be like Cole and my dad. Could I trust myself to be like that?

I needed to be honest with her about how I was feeling. She was right. Communication was the only way we were going to work.

Mercifully, practice was short. We had a game that night, and I hoped Jess would come. I wouldn't be surprised if she didn't after how I treated her that morning. I decided to shoot her a text before I headed home. I also chugged a little Pepto Bismol to settle my furious digestive system.

> I'm really sorry about this morning. I have some stuff to tell you. Wanna get lunch? Picnic on the beach?

JESSIE GIRL

> Okay

> Bring the blanket from the hall closet. It's a good beach one. See you soon

JESSIE GOT in my car in a sweatshirt and some leggings, looking winter beach day ready. Her hair was up in her usual half-bun, the rest of her short-ish hair left out. She was so goddamn cute.

"Hey," I said, reaching for her hand before I put the car in gear. "I fucked up."

"Yeah," she sighed.

"I'm really sorry, Jessalyn. That wasn't okay. I think I'm so afraid of losing this that I accidentally do stuff that would push you away."

She was half turned to me in her seat, leaning her elbow on the console as she listened to me. She nodded. "Thank you for saying that. That's the kind of honesty I meant. I know this isn't easy for you, and I appreciate you trying to make it right."

My heart jumped into my throat. "You're willing to just . . . accept my apology?"

"I mean, I don't like how you talked to me and stormed out when I was just trying to help you. That hurt. But I know this is all new for you, and I like you enough not to give up just because it's not picture perfect."

I thought back to the fights I'd had with my friends over the years. The time I was especially mean to Guy about dating Kitty, and how they're both still my friends today. My friends didn't think in absolutes, and neither did Jessalyn. They were people who could see my flaws and still see the good in me, too. I felt that way about my friends and about Jessie, too.

It was just hard to believe that someone would see that in me. I'm a known fuck-up. I've seen what fans have said online when I choked in playoffs. And I've heard it firsthand from my dad.

Was she forgiving me too easily? Did she give Cole such easy outs? I didn't want her being a pushover for me, but this felt like the wrong time to bring it up.

"I don't like how I talked to you either."

"I'll be honest and say that if that became a pattern, you might have to worry about me leaving. I've put up with shit for too long."

"Understood. I appreciate the second chance, Jessie."

We watched each other, my thumb stroking over her hand.

"This is the hard stuff, but it's what makes the good stuff, Ben. When you stop talking about this stuff, that's when things fall apart."

Up to that point, I'd just been some version of obsessed with Jessie. But in that moment, something way deeper started to take root. I had deep friendships, but I'd never experienced the depth of falling in love with a partner.

Was this what it felt like? Like flying without wings? Like

the roller coaster never stops dropping? Like she's made of liquid gold, shining in the sun and blinding in her beauty?

"Kiss for Daddy?"

"You're ridiculous." Jessie blushed and laughed before leaning in to kiss me.

I smirked at her. "I liked when you called me that."

Her dimple popped out. "Thought you might, since you called yourself that in the closet. And when you asked for a kiss."

"I do want to be your Daddy though. I want to take care of you, Jessalyn."

She gave a soft snort. "I don't need a hero, Ben. I'm not a damsel in distress."

I kissed the back of her hand. "I know you don't. That's why it's even more fun to pamper you. You could do it yourself, but I want you to feel what it's like to be spoiled."

I put the car in gear and headed for the beach.

"Who spoils you, though?" she asked.

"You."

"I don't spoil you. I haven't done hardly anything but accept all your gifts and favors and generosity."

"You ask me about my day. You make me smile. You care about me. You believe in me. That's spoiled enough for me."

She was quiet for a minute. Her voice was crackly when she spoke. "You deserve the world, Benny."

A chill went through me. Whatever force of fate brought us together deserved a thank you card. My heart felt like it was radiating fucking sunshine.

I spread a blanket on the sand and pulled out some things I grabbed at a deli, particularly a tuna sandwich for her. We talked and laughed while we ate, spotting orcas out in the distance. We speculated on what kind of mayhem they were getting into, making each other laugh. After we ate and packed our trash back in a bag, I sat with my arm around Jessie, her head on my shoulder. I kissed her temple and she turned to smile at me. I could see so much in her eyes, and I felt ready to tell her about the hard stuff.

"I'm a mess, Jessalyn. I'm afraid of screwing all this up."

She didn't say anything, just gazed at me curiously and waited for me to go on.

"When I was a kid, my mom found this robin's egg that had fallen out of a tree in my Kentucky grandma's yard. It wasn't broken. I knew it was so special, and I got terrified when she asked me to hold it. I held it so carefully, but with all my nervousness, I dropped the egg on the pavement."

Jessie's eyes went straight to heartbreak. She turned so she was facing me, legs crossed and her hand holding mine. "That's so sad, Ben. You must have been so upset."

"Oh, devastated. Embarrassed. Mad at myself. She trusted me and I got so nervous I screwed it up." I swallowed and went on, turning to face her and mirror her posture. "I feel like you're my robin's egg, Jessalyn."

She winced. "I'm not that fragile."

"Yeah, but you're going through a lot. And I don't know if I'm going to handle it all right. I want to be good enough for you."

She laced our other hands together and shook them. "You're putting too much pressure on yourself. I don't expect you to cure me from a rotten relationship. And I'm here for you just like you're here for me, okay?"

I pressed my mouth into a line. "This might be rude, but you said we needed to communicate."

She gave me a nervous look and took a deep breath. "Bring it on, Jockey."

"Why did you fake with him? I don't want you to get into a place where you just suck it up with me, too. I want you to be vocal about what you need. Not just in bed."

Jessie looked out at the water, considering. I was so afraid she was going to shut down on me, but she started talking. "It started one time, you know. I was tired and just wanted to be through with it so I could sleep. Not like I didn't want to, I just wasn't as into it that time as he was. But then he just seemed so relieved that I came when he did that I realized maybe I'd been doing it all wrong before. And then I couldn't get off. Then I started to feel like I was broken. And that didn't seem like his fault. It seemed like mine. So I just ... kept pretending."

My lips went into a pout. "You're not broken, baby."

"I know. But it took you calling me out for me to see that. You got me all interested in sex again, you hornball."

I laughed. "Aren't you glad, though?"

"Yeah, I'm glad." Jess's face went more serious. "Now do I get to ask a question?"

"Open book, baby. Fire away."

"What's the deal with your dad?"

I blew out a breath. Honesty. "Well, my parents had a weird relationship when I was growing up."

She studied me. "Weird, how?"

"My dad started cheating on my mom, and then he got some woman pregnant when he was on a business trip in Kansas City. She showed up with the baby when I was nine, and I just hid out for weeks. Aunt Lori moved into the guest house in our backyard around then, too. Dad started spending Monday to Friday with his Kansas City family and coming back on weekends. Aunt Lori basically became my stand-in dad. And then when Dad was around, I just felt the pressure to make him stay somehow. It was just ... really tough on me. I felt like he gave up on us, all because he couldn't stop lying and cheating. I don't know what good relationships look like. That's part of what scares me about us."

She squeezed our joined hands. "That's a lot, Benny. Definitely a weird situation. I know that wasn't easy for you to say. I'm glad you shared it."

I hung my head between us. "This is all pretty intimidating, Jessie."

"You scared of me?"

"No. Scared of me. I don't want to end up like them."

She pulled back so I had to meet her eyes. "If you get scared, just squeeze my hand."

I pulled her into a crushing hug. "What if I just squeeze you?"

She laughed into my neck. "That works, too."

I held her face in my hands, her soft smile dissolving the training wheels that held me back from love. I wanted to grow into a person who could give and receive love, and not just hide from deeper commitments. I needed to be that for Jess, for myself. I brought her in for a kiss, sealing my trust in her, in the delicate new bond we shared. We kissed for a long while on the beach, not even giving a shit that it was the middle of the day. This beautiful, wonderful person was giving me a chance to love her, and I was damn well going to give it my best shot.

33

JESSIE

Ben handled me with a new tenderness after our beach date. Thus far, our sex had consisted of a lot of chatter and urgency. But after the beach, Ben took me home and took it slow.

He held my hand in the car all the way home, drawing it to his lips for kisses every so often. His amber eyes shone with hope, and promise, and honor. When we got to our apartment, we took our shoes off at the door.

"What time do you have to be at the arena?"

"Around four."

I glanced at my watch, a thin vintage metal piece I'd found at a shop in Encino. "Don't you need your nap?"

He stepped toward me, cupping my cheeks in his hands. "No." His lips met mine, soft and deferential. "I need you."

He'd been sweet all afternoon, but this made my stomach jump. "Me?"

"You, Jessalyn. It's hard for me to say everything I'm feeling right now, because it's all so big. You make me feel so much, and I just want to show you. I want my body to be yours for a little while."

My eyes jumped between his, completely caught by his admission.

"That okay?"

I grinned up at him. "Very okay."

"Come on, gorgeous." Mikey took my hand and brought me into his room, closing the door behind us. "I'll eat you on the kitchen counter another time. He doesn't get to hear this. The way I make you feel is all for me. He missed out on you, and I'm not sharing a single scrap."

I wrinkled my nose. "Let's not talk about him."

Mikey cursed himself. "My big mouth again. I really am trying to talk less."

"Your big mouth is part of you, though. And I'm into you."

"I'm beyond into you, Jessalyn," he said, pulling me into the bathroom. "My every hope and dream is wrapped up in you. I look at you and see things I wanted but never thought I could have. I see myself becoming a better man because I want to be that for you."

He shoved my leggings down and hoisted me up on the bathroom counter between the two sinks. As he peeled my leggings off my feet, he continued talking. "I see you by my side for all the events I have to go to. I see you getting to know my ridiculous friends. I see your snuggles after I get home from a road trip."

He shucked my shirt off and followed with his own, kissing the space where my neck meets my shoulder. "I see me driving you to work when you're tired, and bringing you coffee. Summers off together where I can take you to Italy or Japan or wherever the hell you want to go. Fucking Disneyland if that's what you like, and I'll ride those stupid teacups with you all fucking day just to see you smile. I see myself facing my fears so I can be enough for you."

I pulled back and grinned at him. "You said you couldn't put it into words. Seems like you found a way."

He chuckled self-consciously. "You know me. Can't stop talking."

I pulled out foreheads together and held his cheeks. "Promise me something."

"What?"

"Never stop talking. Not when you're going to be like this. You're perfect, Ben."

He assaulted me with an overjoyed kiss, a whimper escaping him as he cradled my face and waist. "No one's ever called me that in my whole life, Jessie."

"That's their loss."

Ben locked our bodies together, binding me in his arms and holding the nape of my neck with an unprecedented tenderness. His kisses were full of fire, like he'd never quench his thirst for me. He kept a hand at my neck as the other explored under my bra, down my side, up my thigh.

"I don't know how to make you feel all the things I feel for you, Jessie."

"Just keep going," I said, scraping my hands over the planes of his back and grabbing a fistful of his rock-hard ass. His kisses traveled down my body as he pushed my underwear aside, rubbing gently over my clit.

"I need you to feel how much I need you." His brows knit in desperation as he sank to his knees. "How much I'm helpless for you. You have all of me tied up in you, Jessalyn."

How was he so poetic, so vulnerable with me? How was I falling in love again? It was easy. He gave me everything. He was fearless in that moment. He bared himself to me in every way.

He pulled my legs gently to scoot my ass to the edge of the counter, sinking his tongue into me.

"I'm at your mercy, Jessie. I won't be happy until I give you every single thing you deserve, and even then, it'll never be enough," he said, diving back in to devour me. He was eating me out, but it was so much more than sex or physicality. This was spiritual. "For now, give me all this pleasure. Let it belong to me. Give this part of yourself to me."

"Christ, Mikey," I managed, on the verge of tears. "It's yours. I want you to have it."

After a long suck, he said, "Say it again."

"It's yours, Ben. I'm yours."

He rewarded me with the frenetic pace of his tongue, and I pushed my hips into his face, grabbing hold of his hair. The bathroom counter bit into my ass, only held up by it and his strength. The pinch of pain and the intense pleasure of his mouth melded together until I was dancing at the edge of heaven. Ben's thick fingers slid inside me, and he looked up with a salacious grin. Where I would have been scared to move Cole where I wanted him, I knew Ben could take it. I fisted his hair and showed him where I needed him.

Ben raised his eyebrows at me as he sent his tongue over my clit again and again. I thrust against his face, his tortured groan sounding. And there I was, coming in my new boyfriend's face on the bathroom counter. I hit my head on the wall behind me as I slumped back, Ben giving me a concerned yet amused look. He stood to kiss me, pulling me forward.

"That okay for you, Jessie?" He smiled between kisses.

"Yep. Real okay."

He laughed, a delicate, shy kind of laugh.

"Okay if I haul you over to our bed and get inside you?"

"More than okay."

Ben laid me down on our bed, crawling on top of me to kiss me deeply. I reached for him between my legs, letting him push into me without interrupting our torrent of kisses. He pulled back and looked down at me as he pushed in the final inch, eyes rounded.

"Jessie, I," he started, "I feel like I . . . you're just so perfect. I don't know how I've been without you my whole life."

Yeah, we were in the middle of having sex, but Mikey was

feeling something big. I was, too. But I couldn't tell him that kind of thing while we were having sex, and I didn't want him to confuse sex with love. But it did feel right in the moment.

"I know," was all I could manage. He planted his face in my neck, curling into me slow, deep, and hard. "I need you, Ben."

"Not near as bad as I need you."

His hands slipped under my back as he raised us upright, scooting to sit on the edge of the bed with me facing him in his lap. Admiration flowed between us as I rode him, his hands exploring every inch of my skin. Most men I'd been with just stared at my tits in that position, but Ben watched me. My face. My eyes. It got so intense that I felt like I might cry, the gravity of what passed between us overwhelming me. We were falling, hard. And while I wanted it, and felt the same way, I wasn't ready to be so serious.

I pressed his face into my breasts, guiding a nipple to his mouth. He closed his eyes reverently as he sucked, then moved to the other breast. He moaned out my name as he dropped kisses all over my breasts, my chest, and my collarbones.

"Please never leave me," he blurted out, then got a distant look as his brain left the present.

"Daddy," I begged, bringing him out of his head. Ben snapped back into action.

"I got you, baby. Just hold still." He gripped my hips and thrust up into me. His name tumbled off my lips and I pushed him back on the bed. He rolled us so he was on top again, surrounding me with his embrace.

"Ben, I need everything." I didn't even know what that meant, but I knew that I needed to feel like we were one, not just our bodies joining, but every single part of ourselves.

"It's all yours, Jessalyn," he managed before he shouted a curse word and lost it inside me. I twitched my hips, trying to meet him there, but I still had a little bit to go before I could come.

Ben breathed heavily into my hair, kissing under my ear. "You didn't go, did you?"

"No, but it's no big deal."

He pulled back to look at me, smoothing his hand over my hair and bringing our foreheads together. "You know that's not how it works with me, Jessie Girl. What does Daddy do for you?"

I blushed.

"Come on, baby. What do I do for you?"

"Take care of me," I said with a grin.

"That's right. What can I do to help you get there right now?"

My blush deepened. "Jessie, don't hide. You need my fingers?"

I struggled to meet his eyes. "Really, I'm good."

Ben played with my bangs. "Are you good, or are you afraid to ask for what you need?"

"I..."

"Do you need a toy? Butt stuff? Me to lick your feet? Eat you out? You know I'm good with anything."

"Fine! Get a toy."

34

MIKEY

I stared into Jessie's underwear drawer, a sea of different sex toys facing me. Stuff shaped like a U, dildos, little bullets, and some giant wand thing. I grabbed one of each and walked into the bedroom.

I held up one of the U-shaped ones. "This one?" Then I held up a dildo, which jiggled in my hand for dramatic effect. "Or this one?"

Jessie giggled, watching me. "I didn't expect you to be such an enthusiast."

"If it involves you, Jessalyn, I'm an enthusiast. Now which one?"

She pointed to the giant wand contraption, which made a lump form in my throat. "That's huge! Does it go . . . inside?"

"No! Come here and I'll show you," she said.

I threw the other toys at the end of the bed and crawled up to meet her. She flicked the power switch and handed it to me. The vibrations were pretty strong.

"Hold it right there," she said, putting her hand over mine and moving the head of the toy to her clit. "And kiss me."

She arched her back as our lips met, moaning softly. She

closed her inner thighs around the wand, rocking her hips.

"You need me to move it a little?" I asked.

"Sure," she said. I used small circles around her, and she got much louder.

"That feel good, hon? Am I hitting it right?"

I expected her to respond with words, and all she could manage was a breathed "uh huh." Her breath hitched.

"Can you put your other fingers in?" Her voice was so desperate and God, it was better than the night I caught her. Her nipples were drawn into tiny peaks, her low back miles off the bed, her lips tucked into her teeth and her eyes pinched shut. I slid my fingers just inside her, pulling back toward me.

"That it?"

"Yes, Ben. Holy shit. Keep going."

I was positioned with my face at her hips, watching her writhe and cry. She didn't even have words anymore, just frantic yelps.

"Ben, it's—"

Like that, a jet of fluid shot out of her, a big spurt followed by smaller ones.

"Yeah, baby, that's it. Fuck, you're incredible."

"I'm—" She dug her heels into the mattress and lifted her bottom, then her pussy contracted around my fingers. Jessie let out a scream as her body shook. I growled along with her, so fucking thrilled that she was coming that hard.

One thing was for sure: I'd be buying every toy on the market if it made her act like that. And a lot of changes of sheets. It would be worth every penny.

"There's my girl," I cooed, moving up to kiss her down from her high. "See? You can always tell me what you need. I'm here to help. We're on the same team."

"Your team might have something to say about that. I'm no good on ice," she joked.

I laughed. "They'll get over it."

35

MIKEY

I had the thing I always wanted. I had a honey who cared about me.

The next few weeks were bliss. Jessie waited for me after weekend games. She laughed at my jokes and told great ones of her own. When I was home without a game, we had quiet dinners together in sweats. We had beers and talked about our days, sometimes at home, sometimes at the little neighborhood bar down the block. I loved the moment that she got home from work, because then I could smell her so strongly, a change in the air in the room. It's not like she wore strong perfume or anything. It was just my Jessie.

Jessalyn actually cared what I thought about stuff. She snuck me cute texts during the workday and when I was on the road. I left her little treats before I left.

I went with Sorrento and his kids to the zoo on a day off when she had to work, and I ended up buying Jessie a stuffed animal. But I mean, it was an ocelot. I had to.

If you'd told College Mikey that I'd be voluntarily doing cute stuff for a woman . . . actually, I might have believed it. I always craved that connection. I just never let myself have it. I went for all the wrong kinds of girls, but that was fine. Whenever there was inevitable fallout, I was unaffected. I knew deep down that they weren't lasting connections. They weren't it for me.

Jessalyn was it. It took some convincing for both of us, but we really were a good match.

After one particular road trip in late March, I got home after she'd gone to bed. Jessie is very dedicated to her pajama sets, but she went to bed naked for me that night. And yes, it was *for* me. She sent me a string of racy texts to get me excited. And yeah, it worked.

But when I got home, she was completely knocked out. I had to laugh. She was taking up more than half the bed with one leg out of the sheets, one boob out, and snoring like an old man. When I lifted the sheets and confirmed that she was, in fact, naked, I tried lightly to wake her. After all, she'd talked a big game. She didn't budge. I got ready for bed and crawled in next to her, hoping maybe I'd have better luck when she got home from work the next day.

I must have woken a little at her alarm, because her butt pushed up against my hard cock.

"Welcome home, baby," she cooed. "You up back there?"

"I am now. I missed you, hon." I nestled my face in her neck.

"I could tell from your texts," she giggled.

I slapped her butt and pulled her hips in tighter to me. "You were quite the Shakespeare yourself, Sweet Cheeks."

"Yeah, sorry I wasn't conscious when you got in last night. I didn't even hear you."

"It's fine, baby. You need your sleep. You don't have to wait up for me." Her ass traveled up and down my shaft. "You fishing for action right now?"

To date, we'd never done anything before she went off to work. It was always too damn early. But I missed her and her ass felt so good against me.

"If we can make it quick," she said.

"I could get down for a quickie." That meant I needed to warm her up first. I sunk my head under the sheets, teasing up Jessie's inner thigh with my teeth. She wasn't messing around, lowering herself right onto my face before I could get there. "Damn, baby, just getting right to it."

Her hand raked into my hair as I devoured her. She flipped the covers back to watch me, the first I'd seen of those hazel eyes since I got home. Her sighs got louder and more desperate, then she was calling me up to her.

"Need you now, Ben," she panted. She turned to her side again, inviting me behind her. "This one good for you?"

"Sweet Cheeks, I've wanted this one every single time I woke up with my cock between your cheeks."

She feigned a gasp. "You said you didn't want to fuck me all those times."

I laughed into her neck, where I left a trail of tender, wet kisses. "I lied," I growled.

I pressed into her, overwhelmed by her velvety heat. I reached a hand around to massage her clit. "Good God, baby, you feel amazing."

"Keep going," she begged. "Give me more."

"Who you askin'?"

"You," she sighed.

I slapped her clit, not hard, but enough to give her a rush of pleasure hopefully. "But who am I, baby?"

She turned to look at me with a smirk. "Give me more, Daddy."

"That's more like it." My hand went to her throat, propping myself up on my bottom elbow to watch her. I rocked into her ruthlessly. She smiled as I squeezed her throat, shoving her hips closer to me. "Got my girl back. Were you a good girl while I was gone?"

"Maybe," she said with a look that told me she wanted to provoke me. This was a game.

I pulled out of her to her whine. "Face down. Ass up."

Shockingly, she obeyed, swaying her hips from side to side in the air. I settled my hands on her ass. "I'll give you one more chance. Were you a good girl while I was gone?"

She looked over her shoulder to challenge me, arching her back to push her ass out more. "No."

I spanked her, first on one side, then the other, rapid fire. She cried out as her ass cheeks went red from my hands.

"You learn your lesson yet, baby?"

"No."

I gave it to her again, her response getting louder, and louder still when I rammed back into her sweet pussy.

"Ben," she breathed. "It's too good." I slipped my hand into her hair and pulled her up from where her chest was pressed into the mattress. I leaned over her back, growling in her ear as she went on all fours.

"You forget you were mine?"

"Never," she grinned, following up with a satisfied hum, dropping her mouth open further. She was loud as hell and I loved every second of it.

"Only a slut would moan around my cock like that. Are you my good little slut?"

"Always." Then I sat back on my heels, thrusting into her and holding her hips as she glanced at me over her shoulder. "How's the view?"

"Fucking. Gorgeous," I panted. "I wish you could see how pretty you look like this, taking it so good for me."

"God, Ben. So fucking dirty."

"You love it, don't you, baby?" My pace picked up again, her ass rebounding as she took everything I had to give. "You love being nasty for Daddy."

"Yes."

I pushed her back down until she was laying flat and I was over her back. I lowered onto my elbows, going deeper and kissing behind her ear. "That's right, you do. Because you're my dirty little slut, and you love it when I rail you and tell you what a good fuckin' girl you are and how perfect you are."

Jessie whimpered and pulled my hand back to her throat. "Take me. Please. Hard." I didn't know how much harder I could feasibly go, already at my edge. "Tell me," she whispered.

"That's my good girl," I bit through clenched teeth. "You're gonna make me come."

She let out an anguished yell. There is truly nothing sweeter in this world than talking and fucking my woman over the edge.

"Fuck, I feel you coming, Jessalyn. Come all over that cock. Tell me who fucks you so good."

"You, Daddy."

And with a grunt, I buried myself inside her as I met my release. I breathed hard through my nose, sinking my head to her shoulder and kissing her there.

"You're so beautiful, Jessalyn. So perfect. I can't believe I found you."

She smiled, sweaty hair sticking to her neck. "I'm glad you asked me to move in."

"I'm glad you stayed, honey."

I insisted on driving her to work so we got to spend a little more afterglow time together. I caught her staring at me and smiling, my hand on her thigh and her hand covering mine.

"Whatcha thinkin' bout?" I asked.

"Why do you call me honey?"

I shrugged. "It's just a nice name. You're sweet."

"Yeah, but you called me that before I was sweet to you," she said. "It's kind of an old-school endearment."

I looked over at her and squeezed her thigh. "Because you're my honey. I've always wanted a honey to call my own, and when I met you, I guess part of me knew that you'd be mine."

"No way," she laughed. "I thought you hated me. You picked on me for being uptight."

I rolled my eyes. "I specifically told Stelle that was banter. We were bantering."

"We were fighting. Bickering," she said.

"Are you gonna fight me on everything forever?" I asked with a laugh.

She gave a self-satisfied smile. "If you're lucky."

36

JESSIE

"You're late."

I walked into the wardrobe trailer nine minutes late, but on cloud nine. Irina wasn't wrong, she was just far later than nine minutes every single day. Why was she there this one day?

She always shaved off her eyebrows and drew them on, constantly touching them up throughout the day. They typically looked good, but on this particular day, they made her look severe, like she'd used her whole fist to draw them on.

"Sorry, Irina. There was a slowdown on the 105."

"A slowdown that makes you smell like sex?"

I bristled. It had been well over an hour since Mikey and I got it on. She was just trying to get under my skin. "Call time's not until 6:30 today," I said.

"Yeah, well, we're under the microscope. The network's got some big wigs in today, and I don't think they've forgotten our last issue."

Ah, yes. Our last issue, that was partially my fault and mostly Irina's. Don't worry, though. She put the blame squarely on me. She failed to communicate with the writing staff about a character change, and a guest actor showed up on set with no pieces to wear. She said I was the one who misplaced the brief about the character. In an effort to not cause a stink, I swallowed it down. Cole had encouraged me to suck it up.

"She's your boss, babe. No one's going to believe you if you don't take responsibility. We all eat shit at our jobs sometimes," he'd said.

But part of the problem was, I didn't just "eat shit" and "suck it up" at work. I did the same shit at home with him. It happened gradually, but over time, I pushed back less and less over things I didn't agree with.

I didn't start sticking up for myself again until the night I decided to give my loud next-door neighbor a piece of my mind. The awakening was gradual, too. I felt empowered when I talked to Mikey. I could tell him what I thought, and he'd take it seriously, even if he got silly about it immediately after. He acknowledged that he'd heard me. He listened to me in a way that Cole never did, not even at the beginning.

Normally, I'd have been fighting tears from Irina's nitpicking. But here, I felt confident. If she was going to stay on for next season, I'd go get experience somewhere else. Surely Kitty could put in a good word for me somewhere. I didn't feel as trapped as I did a month ago. Funny how having someone listen to you and respect you at home boosts you up elsewhere.

Mikey didn't even offer any great advice for dealing with Irina other than his vague threats. He'd listen when I crabbed about work. He knew he couldn't actually do anything about the situation for me, but he believed me. And I knew his thuggy threats were his way of showing support.

Plus, I'd forbidden him from putting shrimp in anyone else's curtain rods.

Even though having network big wigs on set made me nervous, I was sure I could perform under the pressure. Maybe they'd even notice how I carry our little wardrobe department.

The day was long and grueling, but I had nothing but smiles when Mikey's car waited for me in the parking lot at the end of the day. Not only that, but he leaned against my door, waiting to open it for me.

His "Hey, Sweet Cheeks" and getting wrapped up in his scent with a kiss was the best homecoming I could ask for.

37

MIKEY

"You're awfully quiet today." Sorrento rode the stationary bike next to me. We had a half hour before we had to hit the ice for warmups. "And smiley."

"He's in love," Obi said.

For once, I really didn't have anything to say. I was pretty sure they were right. Something had shifted with Jessie. I'd stopped counting the times that I looked at her and the L-word was on the tip of my tongue. I've got a big mouth, but I knew that wasn't the kind of thing you just blurted out.

"Damn, you know it's bad if Mikey's struck silent," Guy said.

"I don't know what y'all are talking about," I said with a grin.

"Never thought I'd see the day," Sorrento laughed. "This woman brought you to your knees."

"Sure did," Leroy said. "Should be the other way around, though."

"Your poor wife," Guy said, rolling his eyes.

"I gave her the kids she wanted. I gave her the house and all the stuff she likes. It's the least she can do."

"Again," Sorrento said. "Your poor wife."

Coach wandered in. "Mikey. My office."

An "ooooh" echoed around the locker room. "Ah, shut up. He's not in trouble."

Coach waited for me to wipe my sweat before patting my shoulder and escorting me into his office. I sat in the chair across from his desk.

"You've been playing really well lately, Mike. And working well with the other guys. I'm glad to see it after your rough patch last year."

I nodded. I'm a good player. I know that. But I also know that I've constantly battled choking under pressure. It's what kept me from getting drafted during college. I'll play well all year, but then when the playoffs come, I make stupid mistakes. When I know the stakes are high, it's like I forget how to function.

"We've got Detroit coming up. I know your folks are from there. I just wanted to check in with you and make sure it wasn't going to be a problem."

And truthfully, I felt better than usual going into the Detroit road trip. Things were going really well with Jessie, and it made all the shit my dad gave me while being a piece of shit himself feel less powerful.

I shook my head. "No, Coach."

He hesitated. "That came out wrong. We have resources if you need help, son."

My cheeks warmed. "Thanks. I know. Anything else?"

I hated that my coach knew that my dad was a dick. It was embarrassing. I didn't like my personal and professional life crossing.

His ice-blue eyes studied me, stalling like he thought there was more to say. "Don't go after Riki so hard tonight against Dallas. The refs are going to be watching you for that shit after last time. You've got a new girl, don't you?"

"Yes, sir."

He twisted his lips. "Wouldn't be surprised if he tries to make it personal. Ignore it. We don't need you getting suspended so close to the playoffs."

Anders Riki had been my archenemy since Alden, a real tool who played for Princeton. He had a terrible reputation, and I took it as my personal responsibility to make his life hell on the ice. I'll admit, I almost gave him a concussion the last time we met. Oops.

"Noted."

"Los Angeles number 27. Two minutes for tripping."

I ripped off my helmet, skating for the ref making the call. It was the third period and my second trip to the sin bin. It didn't feel coincidental.

"You gotta be kidding me, man!"

His face betrayed no emotion. "Serve your time, 27."

"What about what he did to our goalie?"

"Are you looking to get thrown out?" His eyes challenged mine.

"You can't let people fuck with our goalie!" I shouted back.

My gaze snagged on Jessie's between the benches, her eyebrows almost in her hair and her hands over her mouth.

Riki circled us. "Better serve those two minutes, Mikey. Your new bunny with those huge tits ain't gonna blow you if you don't be a good little boy."

I lunged for him and the ref let me. I yanked him in by his jersey, grinning as I dealt the first blow.

"Bet she's got huge nipples, too, huh? Wonder if she'd let me take them for a spin. Are they real? I know how these L.A. girls work. You meet her at a strip club?"

I couldn't be held responsible for what happened next. I

pulled him down face first onto the ice, flipping him to straddle his chest and spit in his face. Stelle and Sorrento appeared in seconds, tearing me off him. That gave Riki a chance to get a good jab up at me, splitting my lip.

"You're both out of here!"

"Don't fucking talk about her!" I shouted as I skated toward the tunnel, Stelle and Sorrento ushering me there. "This isn't over!"

"Yeah, won't be over til those tits are in my mouth."

Guy took one look at me with his eyebrows up, and we both went for him. Coach's voice rang out over the chaos that ensued.

The last thing I saw before leaving the ice was Jessie, brows drawn and tears forming.

38

JESSIE

Kitty patted my shoulder. "He's known for being a fighter. I'm sure it's nothing."

"But Guy's not," I said, biting the inside of my lower lip to keep it from quivering. I was shaky from the coffee I had before the game so I could stay awake. Friday night games were not my favorite since I had work earlier in the day. But Ben always made it up to me if I came to his games. He'd let me sleep in and bring me a fancy coffee and make good breakfast.

Kitty stared ahead. "It's probably just shit-talking that got out of hand. Guy got into one after he moved here because someone talked about me, though."

The gears in my head turned. "But how would they know about me? I'm a nobody."

Kitty's face stayed blank, but she squeezed my shoulder. "It's probably nothing."

I knew she was lying. "His lip was bleeding."

"I've known him a long time. He's a tough boy."

I pulled out my phone.

You okay? How's your lip?

BENJAMIN MICHAEL JOCKEY

Fine. Doesn't need stitches

Probably won't be a good kisser for a couple
of days tho

I chewed my thumbnail waiting for Ben to come out of the locker room. I could have just met him at home, because I was pretty tired, but I was worried about him.

I could tell he was pissed by the set of his shoulders leaving the locker room. He gave me a weak grimace as he approached. Instead of his usual "hey, Sweet Cheeks" and a kiss, he just gave me a silent hug, cradling my head to his chest. I pulled back and looked him over: tired, defeated.

"You wanna go home?" I asked.

He hesitated. "It's Obi's birthday, and Dallas treated him pretty shitty on the ice. I should at least go for one drink. Will you come?"

I really wanted to go to bed, but Ben's sad eyes would always break me. I took his hand and squeezed it. "Yeah, I'll come."

We drove my car to the bar. He was quiet but clingy. "You want to talk about it?" I offered.

"Nobody's . . . contacted you about anything, right? Like no hockey people have reached out to you anywhere?"

My brow wrinkled. "Not that I know of. Why?"

He shook his head. "No reason."

"Was your fight about me?"

We parked outside The Stadium, and he turned to me as I turned the car off. His eyes combed over my face. "No. No. But you'll tell me if anyone bothers you, right?"

"Yeah. I'm alright, Ben. I'm worried about you."

"I'm good as long as you are, Sweet Cheeks." He leaned in

for an attempt at a kiss, wincing as my lips brushed his freshly battered ones.

"Oof! Sorry!"

"It was worth it," he said with a grin. "Let's go give this kid a good twenty-first birthday."

~

KITTY and I had been chatting with Sorrento's wife, Jeanine, when I decided to check back in with Mikey. He had a twinkle in his eye as I walked his way, reaching for me as soon as I was in range.

"You having fun, hon?"

I nestled into his side where he sat on a barstool. "Yeah. You didn't tell me that Jeanine was cool. I'm offended."

"Yeah, well. She puts up with Sorrento, so she has to be cool." Ben shook hot sauce onto a potato skin and shoved the whole thing in his mouth. "Thanks for being here, Jessie. I know you're tired. You're a good sport."

I gently kissed his bacon bit and jalapeño-flavored upper lip. "How are you eating spicy stuff with your lip like that? You gonna tell me what happened out there?"

A muscle in his jaw ticked and his eyes went dark. "They were fucking with Obi. Not only is he our goalie, but it's his birthday."

The way he wouldn't meet my eyes had me thinking that wasn't all, but I let it go. On cue, Ben's youngest teammate stumbled into him. "Mikey, buy me a shot."

"Whaddya want, birthday boy? You gonna be able to skate tomorrow?"

"I'm fine," he grinned, turning to me. "I'm Obi. I'm twenty-one today. Can I have a hug?"

I chuckled at the slurring mess of a man in front of me. He seemed to have forgotten that we met when I shut down Ben's party. "Sure." Obi hummed into my hair and gave my cheek an exaggerated kiss.

"Mikey, you have the best girlfriend. She's pretty and she smells good. And she gives good hugs," Obi said, pulling out of the hug but staying close to me. "I used to have a hot older babysitter and she looked just like you."

"Okay, kid, take it easy," Ben said, handing each of us shot glasses. "To you, wise Obi-Wan Kenobi."

"To me!" he giggled. Obi tossed back the shot, wiping a dribble of it from his chin. "You think I can get that bartender to give me a birthday whooping?"

The woman behind the bar looked like she wouldn't be taking any shit from anyone, much less a twenty-one-year-old punk.

"Good luck trying," I said. "Is someone looking after you tonight, Obi?"

With dreamy eyes, he turned to me. "You could be my mommy."

"Alright, that's it. You got your shot. Get out of here."

Obi staggered back to a table with some other players and their wives. "Someone should really look after him."

Ben gave out a heavy sigh. "It's been a long time since I've had to deal with that level of stupid."

"Liar. I saw you on your own birthday, and you're how old? Twenty-eight?"

"Okay, I was a little high, too. I got these really good gummies."

"And that makes it better, how?"

Ben chuckled. "I guess it doesn't."

Obi's hyena laughter rang out at that moment. A blonde woman sitting next to him looked like she was being tortured. Sorrento swooped in and scooped him up to make him play Golden Tee.

"It looks like he's in good hands. Does that mean we can go home?" I asked.

Ben was quiet as we got ready for bed, just a few soft touches while we brushed our teeth. We lay facing each other in bed, my hand stroking his arm.

"What happened out there, Benny?"

He gave a weak attempt at a smile. "You know I get in fights."

"Yeah, but this one was different."

He took a deep breath. "I don't want you to worry."

I planted him with a look. "That's a recipe to make me worry more."

He wouldn't meet my gaze.

"Was it about me?"

A small nod. "I hated it, Jessie. I'll do anything to keep that from happening again."

"How did they even find out about me?" I asked.

"Probably pictures from that benefit. I love taking you places, but I hate that this is the result of it."

"You don't think he'd actually do something to hurt me, do you?"

Ben shook his head. "Unlikely. I just don't like that asshole talking about you."

I ducked my head to meet his eyes. "Hey. I'm not too worried about it. I mean, I don't like it, but I did have my sexy boyfriend throw some sick punches on my behalf. Did you spit in his face, too?"

Ben grimaced. "I might have."

"Not very classy, Benny. But thanks for sticking up for me. And know that you don't have to. Okay?" I ran my thumb over his busted lip. "I need these lips."

He pulled me close and nuzzled the top of my head. "I get why in the fairy tales they locked the princess away in a high tower. I just want to put you in a bubble so no one can mess with you."

"Don't forget, babe—they're messing with you. Not me. I probably don't want to know what he said."

He shook his head. "You don't. It was disgusting, and he can't just get away with it."

"I'm sorry, Jockey." I yawned. "No shrimp in his curtain rods, okay?"

"Oh, I want to do worse than shrimp in the curtain rods."

Ben held me extra tight that night as we fell asleep.

39

MIKEY

On Saturday morning, Jessie and I had a little date day before I had to leave town. We fucked in the shower when we got up, and man, did we get adventurous. I know Jessie likes a little ass play, so I rimmed her until she was a screaming, whimpering mess. But then, she returned the favor and I was shocked at how much I liked it. Who knew I was a butt guy? But even more, the whole relationship thing was taking me by storm. I didn't realize that even sex brought you closer when you stayed committed to one person. It felt amazing. I loved my dirty girl so damn much.

Oops, there I was thinking, nay, knowing, that I loved her. But it seemed wrong to tell her I loved her for the first time right before I went on a long road trip. I wanted to be able to take her to dinner, to celebrate, to spend hours in bed solidifying it. And what if she didn't feel the same way yet? I didn't want my brain to be messed up for an entire nine-day road trip. I needed to be locked in.

We got take-out coffee and she took me to her favorite fabric store to pick out material for my suit. My only requirement was that it had to coordinate with the hat she made me, so I could have a complete J. Welsh ensemble. She didn't let me see what she got when she was looking over the silk for the liner, saying it was a surprise. I loved seeing her in her domain like that, describing why certain materials were better than others. She got emotional looking at a certain green velvet, her fingers delicately touching the fabric.

I walked up beside her and took her other hand. "You want some of that, hon?"

She sniffed. "No. My best friend just had a dress for a middle school dance made out of this material. It just took me back unexpectedly."

I tucked her into my side and kissed her temple. "You want me to get you some?"

She turned to me quickly with a tearful smile. "No. It just felt nice to see it. Let's go check out."

After we had lunch, she headed to drop me off at my car at the stadium. I always hated to leave Jessie when a road trip came around, but I really hated this one. Even though Riki and the rest of the Dallas team were long gone, I felt like I needed to be Jessie's bodyguard. I just had this sneaky feeling like something was going to go wrong while I was gone, but I needed to shake off my jitters. It was an important time for our team.

The road trip would be our longest of the season, and right before the playoffs. You're always due for one hellish road trip per season, and apparently, they'd saved the best for almost last for our team. We were sitting pretty in the number one wild card spot for the Western Conference, but we really had to focus to make sure we secured our spot in the playoffs.

And plus, we were going to Detroit. That meant a visit with my parents, which always carried some baggage. To say I was dreading it is an understatement.

Adding to my anxiety, Jessie's car sounded like it was on its last legs.

"Hon, your car sounds kinda bad. You wanna drive mine while I'm gone and we can put yours in the shop?"

She rolled her eyes. "You are always on about my car."

"It sounds like there's a beehive under the hood and anytime we hit a pothole, it feels like something's going to fall off!"

"Don't talk so bad about her!" she quipped. "She can hear you!"

"Jessie, I just want you to be safe."

"I know, Daddy," she said, patting my leg. "I just got an oil change and they didn't say anything."

I threw out my arms. "Because you go to that janky place on Pine! They barely keep you street legal!"

"Just because I'm frugal doesn't mean I'm getting bad service," she huffed.

I sighed. "You are stubborn as a damn mule, Jessalyn. If I ever meet your parents, I'm going to have some words."

She grinned a little. "You wanna meet my parents?"

I hesitated, my stomach swooping. "I guess I did say that."

"Look at me! I got the commitment-phobe to want to meet my parents!" she cackled. "Call the L.A. Times. They'll want to do an exclusive."

"You are the biggest brat, Jessalyn Welsh."

"Yeah, you like it." She pulled into the lot at the arena and turned to me. "You gonna miss your little brat?"

"So fucking bad. You'll be good while I'm gone?"

She just smirked at me, her little dimple popping out.

I took her chin in my hand and traced her lips. "The correct answer is 'yes, Daddy.'"

"We'll see," she said with a giggle. "I'll miss you. Tell your mom and Lori hi for me."

"I will, hon. Kiss for Daddy?"

"Get over here, Jockey."

40

JESSIE

Work was absolute hell while Mikey was gone.

Irina seemed to be protesting my very existence by decreasing her contributions to almost zero. I asked her to help me on Tuesday during a particularly hectic scene change and she told me I'd never learn if I didn't do it myself. Then she had the nerve to saunter off to eat lunch, when I hadn't even had a chance to eat breakfast.

I FaceTimed Mikey when I finally got a minute for lunch. "Hey, Sweet Cheeks."

"Hey. Sorry, I'm stuffing my face."

"S'okay, hon. They working you too hard?"

I lifted my lip in a snarl. "Fricking Irina."

"My threat still stands," he said. "I'm sure the grocery store has some manager's special seafood I could take off their hands."

I giggled. "How's Columbus?"

"Fine. Other than work, everything okay at home?"

"As far as I know. I've hardly been there. Kitty and I are going to the watch party at Sorrento's after work. Big wives get together, I guess."

Ben looked thrilled. "You're doing the whole girlfriend watch party thing?"

"Yeah, is that wrong?"

He took a breath, looking away from the screen. "No, hon. It makes me really happy. I've never—never mind."

"What? Tell me!"

He rolled his lips. "I've never had someone who would watch for me like that."

"I watch most of your road games, Jockey. As long as it's not messing with work."

"I know, but I've always been jealous of the guys getting cute texts from their girls while they watched together. And the fact that it's you makes it that much better."

I puffed out my bottom lip. "I really never saw this side of you coming."

"Don't tell anyone my secret," he joked. "What else are you girls going to do? Drink wine? Gossip? Paint your toenails? Test out each other's vibrators?"

I cracked up. "You're demented. You went straight from being the sweetest human to being a middle schooler."

"Well, you didn't answer the question," he pushed. "What are y'all gonna do?"

"Drink beer, fart, and talk shit about you guys."

I stood by the untouched veggie tray, decked out in my Miknevicius jersey and staring blankly at the game. Were these things this hot when they wore them on the ice? No wonder they called them sweaters. Or maybe it was because the cliques seemed already established and I was lurking on the outskirts.

Sorrento's wife Jeanine was one of my allies in the Princes WAGs group, but she was hosting and couldn't devote all her time to me. I was impressed with the group as a whole. Babies

were balanced on hips and passed around, and older kids wrestled in front of the TV that showed the game. I'd just recently
surrendered the smallest Sorrento baby, who I was using as a
social security blanket of sorts.

Kitty saw me standing alone and swooped in. "Okay, I'm
going to get you a glass of wine, and you're going to tell me why
Irina hasn't been fired yet. Red or white?"

"I'll come with you." I poured myself a short glass of red
wine and Kitty and I wandered back toward the viewing area.

"So what's the deal with her, anyway?" Kitty asked.

"Honestly, she's awful, Kitty. I feel bad complaining about
her, though. I don't like to attack other women."

"Oh, come on. It's just us. It's not an attack when you do
90% of the work and she just flirts with the crew all day and
runs to Russ whenever things don't go 100% her way."

"That is an accurate assessment of how it is," I agreed. "It's
frustrating. I'm working my ass off. I've asked if we can hire
someone else so I don't have to work so hard, and she says it's
not in the budget."

"I could pull some strings, you know," Kitty said. "I have a
fair bit of influence over these people."

"No, please don't say anything. If I ruffle any feathers, I'll be
the one blamed for everything. You know how it is for women."

Kitty scowled. "Sure do. That's why we've got to stick
together."

"But Irina's one of us," I pointed out.

"Yeah, but she's not exactly being a good sister in the cause,
is she? She's taking credit for your work while you get paid less
and work longer hours."

I hesitated. "Still. Don't say anything."

A blonde head whipped around from a chair behind the
couch. Sydney Leroy, who I recognized from my first night as a
WAG, while I was still faking. "Can you two pipe down about
your petty work drama?"

"We're no louder than your rugrats," Kitty shot back.

"Sydney," Jeanine warned, turning to talk to us. "Has work been busy for you?"

Kitty and I both nodded. "And Jessie's boss sucks," Kitty added.

"Poor Jessie," Sydney said, flicking her hair over her shoulder but not turning to face us.

Jeanine mouthed a "sorry." Fortunately, Mikey and Romelski were just taking off up the ice in a two-on-one against Columbus's goalie. Romelski's wife reached for my hand as we both got loud. Mikey knocked the puck to him as the goalie prepared for Mikey to shoot, and Romelski effortlessly popped it to the upper part of the goal. His wife and I high-fived and clinked our glasses as cheers erupted in the room. For that moment, I felt good. Included. Part of something bigger.

Then it all came crashing down.

I pulled out my phone to text Mikey a congrats for his goal, like I always did. I knew he wouldn't read it til after the game but he'd told me how much he liked it. At the same time, Sydney scooted her chair back as the game went to a TV time out, knocking into me. Red wine splashed down the front of my jersey and into her hair. She gasped. "Look what you did!"

I started to apologize, but Kitty tapped my arm to stop me. "It was just an accident, Sydney. And you scooted your chair!"

Jeanine appeared next to me with two wads of paper towels extended, rushing to the drinks table for some club soda.

Sydney patted the paper towels over her hair. "What are you even doing here, anyway? You know he's not going to marry you, right? He's just doing this to look better in the press."

My stomach sank. Was that true?

"Can it, Sydney," Kitty hissed.

"Everybody knows that Mikey doesn't do girlfriends. He gets bored too quickly. He'd have a new pussy every day if he could. He probably still does," Sydney said, stepping closer to me.

"Sydney, there are kids here!" Romelski's wife cried. God bless that woman. I could safely add her to my allies list.

"Does he still cry when he comes? He did when he shot it down my throat. Said I was the best he ever had. That's why it doesn't make sense that he's with you."

"That's enough, Sydney," Jeanine said definitively.

Sydney lowered her voice. "Did your man fail to mention that I was first? You thought you were special, didn't you? You shouldn't even be here. You're still fucking around with your little Hollywood job, but look around. This takes dedication. And he knows you don't have what it takes."

My jaw was clamped shut so tight it hurt. I could not cry in front of this monster. No matter if what she said was true, it was too much. Just the fact that she was trying to get under my skin hurt.

"You need to leave," Jeanine said, rounding up Sydney's diaper bag and pouring out her drink.

"It's fine. I'll go," I said.

"The hell is wrong with you," Kitty spat at Sydney, following me to the door.

"You can stay," I called over my shoulder.

"No, I'm with you," Kitty caught up to me. "Are you okay?"

We made it outside and I turned to her, tears blurring my vision. "Is it true? Was she really with him?"

Kitty's eyes were round and sad. "I don't know. We've only been here a few months more than you. It would make sense as to why he and Leroy hate each other so much. But hey." She put her hand on my shoulder and leaned so I had to look at her. "Mikey loves you. Even if she did sleep with him, it doesn't matter. He's obsessed with you, Jess."

"He's never said he loves me," I said, trying not to go into complete hysterics.

"Yeah, well, he will. He's in it because he likes you. Don't listen to her shit."

I swiped at the tears on my cheeks. "I don't like being blind-sided. He should have told me."

"He probably didn't tell you because it wasn't important to him. But you'll have to take that up with him. Why don't we go get some takeout and we can finish the game at your house?"

COULD THINGS GET ANY WORSE? Kitty and I walked to the elevator in my parking garage only to find that we weren't alone.

"Hey, Jess." Cole, sounding way too friendly for how I felt toward him. "How's it hangin'?"

I kept my expression blank. "Cole."

Kitty gave him a grimace.

"Oh wow, are you Kitty Gatto?"

"In the flesh," she said curtly.

"Jess, I didn't know you were that tight with Kitty. We should all go get a drink."

"I don't think we'll be doing that." I narrowed my eyes at him. "You were supposed to come with me to her engagement party, if you'll recall."

"Why are you being so nasty, Jessie? I thought there were no hard feelings."

I drew back as we all walked into the elevator. "No hard feelings?! You cheated on me and blamed the demise of our relationship on me! You made me feel worthless. You constantly went out of your way to show me how unimportant I was to you."

His face reddened. "I didn't put smelly-ass fish in your apartment. I had to pay a fine for that smell, you know. I almost got evicted. I still haven't found the last of it."

"Maybe if you paid any attention to detail you'd have figured it out by now."

He got closer to me. Kitty's whole body stiffened, ready to attack. I was extremely glad she was with me. He couldn't gaslight me out of this one.

"I could have had your little boyfriend arrested for vandalism, you know. He broke and entered. I still could. You made my life hell."

I got right in his face as the doors opened on our floor. "Maybe you've had just a little taste of how you made me feel." I looked to Kitty, who nodded, and we walked to my apartment door.

Right before I got inside, "I'm sure the police will be really sympathetic to you when I call this in."

I wheeled around. I'm a pretty reasonable person. I don't like making enemies in my life, and somehow I'd encountered both of mine in the span of an hour. "What do you want, Cole?"

He sighed. "Tell me where the last of it is."

I hadn't talked to Mikey yet. We were going to have plenty to talk about aside from this whole encounter. He'd told me not to tell Cole where it was, but if it was tell Cole or have Mikey arrested, I'd tell him.

"If I tell you, you're not going to the police, right?" Cole was a shithead, but he wasn't fully diabolical. If he said he wouldn't, I believed him.

"Yeah," he said. "I'll drop it."

"Check your curtain rods. And don't even think of being friendly with me again."

I slammed the door behind me.

41

MIKEY

When I checked my phone after the game, I had my usual post-game string of texts from Jessie. Except, these weren't entirely typical.

I laughed at that one. The thought of "smacking" someone in hockey was a fun idea. There was a picture of her looking genuinely happy in my jersey, holding someone's baby and smiling with some of the other wives. I didn't expect to feel some kind of way about her holding a baby, but she looked like a natural. We hadn't talked about kids. I hadn't even thought about wanting kids until I met her, because it didn't even seem like a possibility. I didn't hate the idea.

But the next text froze my blood.

Ohhhhh, fuck. So much for her blending in with the wives.

As I was reading through the messages, Leroy approached me.

"Hey, Mike," he snapped. "Tell your stupid girlfriend to stay the fuck away from my wife."

I turned to face him. "Excuse me?"

"Your little bimbo got Sydney kicked out of the wives' party."

Stelle was already rushing to get behind me, sensing the mayhem in the air. "Hey!" he warned.

"What did you call her?"

"And while you're at it, you stay the fuck away from my wife."

I laughed. "You're deranged if you think I want anything to do with her. She's all yours, bro."

"Oh, I'm deranged, asshole?" His voice boomed. Guys gathered in various states of dress. It was about to go down. "It's your little whore that bullied Sydney and made her feel bad about fucking you."

"That's not what I heard," Romelski said, shaking his phone as if to prove he had receipts from his wife.

"Did you call Jessie a whore?" I shouted, climbing over the bench behind me to shove Leroy.

And then the wrestling match began. In seconds, Leroy and I were battling on the locker room floor. I had him pinned under me, pummeling his cheekbone, when Coach demanded Sorrento and Stelle pull me off him.

"Both of you, in the office, NOW."

We sat in two chairs across from the desk, not looking at each other.

"One of you had better start talking. We can't have this bullshit right before the playoffs."

"I haven't talked to my girlfriend yet, but it seems Leroy's wife harassed her at the party back home."

"Sydney wouldn't hurt a fly," Leroy exclaimed. "It was your scrappy little bitch."

I stood, ready to pound his face again, but Coach pulled me down.

"Leroy, quit being a dick. Mikey, settle down. Whatever this is, it ends right this second. You don't have to like each other, but you have to have each other's backs out there. Out there, we are one big happy fucking family. Got it? I don't want to hear another goddamn thing about your wives fighting."

"She's my girlfriend," I corrected in a mumble. Coach glared at me and I raised my hands. "You're right."

Things were tense as I got changed in the locker room and got on the bus. I texted Jessie as soon as I got out of the meeting.

> I'll call you as soon as I'm back in my room, honey. I'm sorry.

I felt like I was riding to my funeral on the bus back to the hotel. Instead of grabbing food with the guys, I went straight to my room. I could order room service later. Jessie needed to come first. My throat was dry as I dialed her number.

Jessie's voice was tearful. "Hello?"

Already off to a bad start. Not her usual "hey, Jockey," or "what's my favorite thug doing?"

"Hi, Sweet Cheeks. You wanna tell me what happened?"

She sniffed. "Everything's awful."

"I'm so sorry, babe. Some of the guys caught me up, but I want to hear it from you."

"Seems like you should tell me. I'm apparently the last to know that you fucked your teammate's wife."

I sucked in a breath through my nose. "It was a long time ago, Jess. Before they were together. I was really young. She wanted more with me, and when I said no, she moved on to him."

"She said . . . some awful stuff. In front of everybody. About me. About you," Jess sobbed.

"Aw, honey. I'm so sorry. She doesn't mean anything to me. Nothing. You're so important to me."

"Why didn't you at least warn me? I got completely blind-sided. How many other women are lurking, just waiting to remind me how much I don't belong with you?"

There was the knife in the gut. The reminder that Jessie was a relationship girl, and my fuckaround ways were only ever going to hurt her.

"I don't know, hon."

The line was quiet, punctuated by her sniffles.

"Jessie, if I could undo it all and have met you first, I would. But that's not how life works."

"I know that. And I don't blame you for being who you are, but . . . you do want me, right? Just me? I'm not stale?"

"Of course, I do, honey. Just you. And I said that stale thing before I had you. Before I knew how good this could be."

She gave a little cry. "Things aren't so good right now, though."

I scrubbed my hand over my face. Even I felt like crying. A gnawing feeling chased me that I wasn't good enough for her. But the only reason I was feeling that way in the moment was because of Sydney fucking Leroy. But I couldn't let Leroy's mean-ass wife ruin my relationship. "I'm not going anywhere, Jess. I'm in this. Okay?"

"Okay."

"But I can't guarantee no one else is going to pop up and try to make you feel like shit because they're jealous."

"Yeah. I get it." She didn't say anything for a minute. "She said she was the best you ever had."

I chuckled. "That's rude. And untrue. Because I hadn't had you."

"She acted like I can't have my job and be your girlfriend."

"Don't listen to her, honey. You belong there. You're mine, remember? But if you don't want to go to that stuff, you don't have to do it for me."

"You said it made you happy that I was going," she objected.

"Well, I don't want you to go if you're just going to get bullied, Jess. That doesn't make me happy at all," I said. "You're enough for me, okay? You do know that, right? I'm so proud of you all the time, Jessie."

"Thanks, Ben."

"I'm really sorry that my past keeps fucking with you, Jess. I hate it."

"She said," Jessie said, sucking some snot, "that you got bored easily and you were probably cheating on me. And that you were only dating me because it made you look good."

"Jessie, you know that's not true." I wanted to tell her that I loved her right then, but I really didn't want to tell her because of something bad happening. I wanted it to be joyful. "I'm dating you because I really, really like you. I'm crazy about you. And I could never cheat on you, honey. Never."

"Okay," she said, seemingly steeling herself. "No other team wives, right?"

I hated that she even had to ask that. Sydney had made it seem like Jessie wasn't good enough for me, but in reality, I wasn't good enough for her. She deserved better than me. "No other team wives. Feel better, Sweet Cheeks?"

She coughed. "That's not all. I ran into Cole. He threatened to have you thrown in jail if I didn't tell him where the shrimp was."

I really thought I'd hit my peak of feeling bad, but I suddenly felt worse. Not only had my former promiscuous ways come back to bite us, but my little crime added to her hard day. The gnawing feelings I'd been fighting broke through. How could I keep putting Jessie through misery?

"I'm sorry, Ben. I told him. I didn't know what else to do."

"Oh, honey, don't blame yourself for that. It's not a big deal. I didn't mean to put you in a bad position. I was trying to get back at him, but yeah. It's pretty illegal what I did."

"Okay."

"I feel like it's my fault you had a bad day, Jess. I feel terrible."

"It's fine."

She said that, but I knew it wasn't fine. I was ruining Jess's life. She was going through a tough time anyway: bad stuff at work, bad stuff at home, her limited free time being taken up by people from my life being rude to her. Everything was my fault. Everything I touched turned to shit. The opposite of the Midas touch.

We were both quiet.

"I just really don't want to see Cole anymore, Ben. I might have to move."

Panic washed over me. "I hear you, baby. Can you wait until I get home and we can figure something out together?"

"It's a little early for us to be fully moving together, don't you think?" she asked.

"Well, yeah, but . . . we already do live together," I said. "And I don't want to stop."

"Really?"

"Yeah, babe. I like living with you."

She gave a little whine. "I miss you, Benny."

"I miss you, too, hon. I'm real sorry about today. I wish I could hold you."

"Me, too."

"I can't wait to get home to you. Kiss for Daddy?"

"Yeah," she said with a sad chuckle. "Kiss for Daddy."

42

JESSIE

Well, Tuesday had been a shit show. I was determined to make Wednesday better. Mikey seemed equally determined. He had coffee and flowers sent to work for me, garnering an embarrassing number of squeals as an admin carried them through set.

Kitty laughed as my face boiled when the flowers were handed to me.

"Is it your anniversary?" one of the other actors asked.

Kitty snatched the note. "No, it's just her boyfriend's cute way to say sorry."

I swiped the note back, scowling at her. "Mine!"

"You know I'm just nosy and want to see Mikey being cute," she said.

"You're lucky you got one that says sorry at all," the other actor cracked.

The note read, "Sweet Cheeks, Hope today is better than yesterday. I'm sorry again. Gonna give you the biggest hug when I get home. Heart, Jockey."

My stomach dipped as I took a whiff of the flowers. Irina

stood off to the side, distaste apparent in her expression. I grinned as I walked them to the wardrobe trailer.

Ben called when he was getting in bed that night in Detroit. They didn't have a game but got there a day early. He'd been out with Guy and his best friend, who was also Kitty's brother. He lived in Detroit and they apparently had a grand old time getting caught up. Ben was nervous about seeing his family the next day, but otherwise, he seemed fine. I'd had some time to cool off and didn't hold all the stuff that happened Tuesday at the party against him. He, however, seemed to still blame himself for all of it. I told him not to sweat it, and after a steamy little dirty talking session, I went to bed thinking that all was well between us.

THE LIGHTS WERE on when I walked into the wardrobe trailer Thursday morning. Usually, I was the first one in, with Irina sauntering in two hours later. Russ, our producer, sat in the middle of the room in a folding chair.

"Yep. She's here now. I'll call you back when I know something," he said, hanging up the phone. "Hi, Jessie."

"Hey, Russ. What's going on?"

"Have a seat," he said, then realized there was nowhere for me to sit. He pulled his chair over to my worktable and I sat. "How are things going for you here?"

My heart pounded. Was I about to get fired? "Good. I've learned a lot. We've been really busy, too."

"I don't think it was 'we', Jessie. We noticed that Irina wasn't pulling her weight. She'd been warned before, but we let her go last night."

My mouth fell open and I coughed out an involuntary laugh. "Oh, wow."

"I know it's not ideal timing with the on-location coming up next week, but if you're interested, we'd like to promote you to Costume Director. I know that leaves you not a lot of time to hire your replacement. But the sooner you can get someone hired, the sooner you can have help."

"Russ, wow. I'm honored."

"So you'll accept?"

"Yes, yes, of course," I stammered. "Thanks for the opportunity."

"You earned it, kid. Sorry you had to work so hard while we didn't notice. Hopefully your job will get easier now."

I felt like crying. I was elated, but overwhelmed, too. Where the hell would I find the time to look for a replacement? I gave him a simper of a smile.

"Twenty minutes to call time, though. Figure I should get out of your hair. Scarlett will send an email with your new salary and the budget for your replacement."

I put my nose to the grindstone and got to work. I'd have to tell Mikey later, but I was sure he'd be happy for me. He'd been pep-talking me for weeks on dealing with Irina, and trying to encourage me to leave if things didn't get better soon.

Still, I was so excited to share the good news with him. I shot off a quick text at lunchtime, so mid-afternoon for him. He was in Detroit that day.

> Got some big news. Can't wait to share

I didn't get a response.

43

MIKEY

It was like my body was revolting to touching down in Detroit. My dad was going to come be my guest for team lunch, and I had a pit in my stomach about it. I purposefully didn't keep in touch with my dad, even though he and my mom were still together and I talked to my mom all the time.

I'd never get over how he spent so much time away from us growing up. Laura and I didn't deserve it. Mom didn't deserve it. Aunt Lori had been more of a dad to me than my actual dad. She was the one who picked me up from school when Mom couldn't. She threw a ball with me in the backyard when Mom was cooking dinner. Hell, she even moved into the guest house in our backyard when I was nine, effectively becoming my mom's live-in bestie.

To Dad's credit, he did spend the long Saturdays at the rink with me. He came home from his business trips late on Friday nights, but he was always up for those ridiculously early wake-ups to drive me to play hockey. But when he was there, he was always critical. And I felt pressure to perform well so he'd keep coming to my games. That was the only time we got, so I had to make it count.

On this day, I spotted Dad in the stands during morning skate, watching me in the same posture he always had: standing with his hands folded behind his back, brow furrowed. He'd asked if he could come visit while I was in town with the team, and I couldn't find a good reason to say no.

My stomach had been a fucking mess that whole road trip. My IBS was really having a field day with all the stress I was under: seeing my dad, fighting with Jess, fighting with Leroy about his evil wife, and trying to figure out when I could move us out of that apartment. Jess and I had mostly made up, but I hated that my actions made her feel so insecure. How was I any better than Cole? I was the shitty one, not her.

So my stomach raged on: cramping, digesting shit weird, and generally not doing its job. I did all my little tricks to try and get it back to functional, but it was what it was. I couldn't afford to miss games because of it. Not after the fight with Leroy, who continued knocking me around any chance he got during practice. I was sure Dad would have something to say about that, too.

Dad met me in the tunnel after I got changed. "You looked a little sloppy out there, son."

My jaw clenched, as did my stomach. "Hi, Dad. Good to see you again, too."

He had the good sense to look at least mildly chastised. "I'm not saying it to be rude, Ben. I'm worried about you's all. Is your stomach giving you trouble again?"

Funny of him to care now. He didn't seem affected when it started, when a woman with a baby showed up on our front porch saying she wanted me to meet my little brother. I was nine at the time.

"I'm fine, Dad. Let's go eat." I shuffled him off to the lunch-room Detroit provided. The catering was at least pretty good that day. I stayed away from anything with my trigger foods in it, sticking to stuff that was easy to digest. I got a second smoothie from the table and put together a very bare bones sandwich.

"How's everything going for you?" I asked when we sat. "Haven't heard from you in a while."

"Phones work two ways, Ben," he said. "I really don't understand why you don't like me so much. I provided you with everything. The hockey camps, the clubs."

A quiet went over the room. Dad and I sat alone. Stelle, Obi, and Sorrento were at the next table. Stelle gave me a sympathetic grimace, and Obi launched a loud new conversation. My friends were deeply familiar with how hard things were between me and my dad.

"Giving money doesn't make you a father," I hissed. "You were never there. You screwed Mom over."

Dad had the nerve to roll his eyes. "This has nothing to do with your mother, Ben. Your mother and I have an understanding."

"It has everything to do with her! Aunt Lori had to be my substitute dad while you were out fucking around with your other family that you chose over us. Or families. I don't even know how many there are."

"There's just one. Don't be so dramatic," Dad snapped. "Your mom broke my heart. Made me look like a fucking fool."

"What the fuck are you talking about? Mom wasn't the one stepping out on you."

"Wasn't she?"

My stomach cramped in response to the shit Dad brought into my life. "What are you saying?"

"Your mother stopped being interested in me . . . intimately. She met Lori and decided that's who she wanted."

My head spun. The room felt small. "Mom's gay?"

"Not so loud," he said, yanking me up by the arm and pulling me into the hallway.

"Aunt Lori is Mom's . . ."

"Partner. Yes. Your mom and I were on the rocks, and I wanted to work it out. While we were working on it, we had you. I was so in love with her and we were still best friends, but she wasn't interested in me that way anymore. I started travelling more for business. She encouraged me to see other people. One of those people got pregnant. Lori and Deb got closer, and we agreed to keep the arrangement going. She didn't feel comfortable coming out and we didn't want to split the house for you kids. I also had obligations in Kansas City, so I spent weeks with them and weekends with you."

My lungs felt oxygen-starved, having to remind myself to suck in a breath. My phone buzzed in my hand, "Jessie Girl" showing on the screen. "How do I know you're not lying?"

He sat forward. "Look, son, I know it's a lot. I probably should have clued you in sooner. But it hurt to see your mom moving on without me, so I moved on."

I wanted to slap him. "It wasn't just Mom that you had to worry about! You had me and Laura! How could you just leave us because you couldn't get over your shit? You picked another family over us, why, because you got your feelings hurt? Get over yourself."

He scrubbed a hand across his face. "Ben."

"You know what's the most fucked up? I'm standing here today because I thought if I just played hockey good enough, you'd stay. There were times I wanted to quit, but you and I always had hockey. I pushed harder because that was the only way I could get you to love me."

"Son, that's not—"

"I need to go," I said, gesturing to the lunchroom. "Don't call me again."

"Hi, brother of mine," Laura crooned on the other end. "To what do I owe this honor?"

"Hey. Um. I just saw Dad." My older sister and I didn't talk as much as we should, but I always knew she was there for me.

"Big Benny!" came a shout from the background. My nephew was three, and I was thrilled he still remembered me enough to get excited when I called.

"Hi, Mason," I said. "You being good for your mama?"

"He can't hear you. He's just yelling," Laura said. "What's going on with Dad?"

"Laura, I—" I couldn't say more without crying, something I really didn't have time to do.

"Aw, Benny. What happened?"

"He told me something really fucked up."

"Like what?"

"Did you know? About Mom and Lori?" I didn't want to just blab it if she didn't know. I didn't want her finding out like I did.

"What about them?"

"That they're, you know, partners?"

Laura was quiet for a long while.

"It's fucked up, right?"

"Benny," she started. I could tell from her tone that I was the last to know.

"What the fuck! You knew? How long have you known?"

"Ben, it's complicated," she said.

"How. Long."

"High school," Laura said, "but don't take it personally."

"How the fuck am I supposed to not take it personally? Everyone else has known and I've just been stuck out here, because why? Because everyone thinks I'm some kind of bigot? Because I can't handle the truth? Because Mom and Dad are both pieces of shit and no one wanted me to know?"

"Ben, that's not fair. I caught Mom and Lori, ya know, doing stuff."

"Easy for you to say it's not fair. You've been lying to me. Pretending I was right whenever I said it was all Dad's fault. Is this why Dad still comes to visit you? You two are so chummy?"

"I have kids, Ben. They deserve to know their grandfather. And their uncle, for that matter, but you're always so busy," Laura huffed.

"Oh, you want me to know your kids, but you don't want me to know the truth about our parents? Fuck off, Laura."

I hung up.

I WAS FOLDED in half on the toilet, absolutely miserable, when my phone rang again. Jessie Girl. We hadn't talked much about my stomach issues. She knew I needed Lactaid, but otherwise, I tried to hide it from her, using a different bathroom if I had an episode. I'd only had one rough day since we got together. I guess being happy is good for digestion or something. A few times I had bad gas in front of her, though I just laughed it off. One night, though, she did rub my arm and ask if I was okay. I should have told her. I was pretty sure she loved me. But it's something I wish didn't happen to me, and I wanted to shield her from the less savory parts of myself.

I let the call go to voicemail. I couldn't deal with Jessie. I loved her, but I was reeling from my family drama. My parents and sister had been lying to me my whole life.

My mom and Aunt Lori were supposed to meet me after the game, too. I'd purposely put them after my meeting with my dad, because I don't like dealing with the strained dynamic between my parents.

Why didn't my mom feel like she could be out with me? Hockey isn't known for being the most accepting sport, but I wasn't part of that. It's fine if people are gay. Why was my dad so hell-bent on keeping it a secret? Why would Mom let me blame

Dad all those years without bothering to correct me? Only recently had she asked me to forgive him, and that was without explanation.

And what kind of partner could I be if my own family didn't trust me? How could I ever love someone if the only love I'd ever known was a lie?

My phone rang again a few minutes later. Jessie again.

I chose to answer. "Hello?"

Her voice was shaky and quiet. "Hey. Can you talk for a minute?"

"I'm kind of in the middle of something," I said.

"Are you okay, Ben? You don't sound good."

"Yes," I grunted as a cramp passed through me. "I'm fine. What's up?"

"Oh. Okay. Well, I, um, work's just really crazy and—" she started to cry. "I just wanted to talk to you."

I broke. I couldn't be a support to Jessie and deal with my parents' lies and my traitorous body and my past coming back to bite me all at the same time. All I'd brought Jessie was pain, and mess, and complication. I would never be worthy of her. She was better off without me. "Jessie, I can't deal with your work right now."

"W-what?" She sounded stunned. "I mean, okay. Did you get to see your family?"

"Look, you need someone better than me, Jessie."

"What are you talking about?"

"Just do yourself a favor and leave me alone." I hated myself for saying it. I knew I was hurting her, but it was either hurt her one last time or keep bringing misery into her life. The old flings showing up. Assholes talking shit about her on the ice to piss me off. My own teammates' wives making her feel like shit for being who she is, for things I've done.

"Ben, did something happen? This isn't like you. I'm not letting you do this. Something's wrong."

She was far, far too good for me. All I'd ever do was ruin everything for her, and she was too blind to see it.

"Go, Jessie!" I had to tell her before I changed my mind. "I can't deal with all this! I can't deal with you, and them, and everything else. Go find your relationship guy, because it ain't me."

I hung up.

44

JESSIE

It was a night of celebration. And misery.

Kitty and I were a bottle of wine deep and screeching out breakup songs at the top of our lungs by her pool.

Yes, we were having an impromptu wine night in honor of Mikey hanging up on me. And me getting a promotion, I guess.

"This is how I got through Guy and I breaking up that one time."

"That one time?" I asked.

"Okay, we were actually broken up for like, years," she said with a little hiccup.

I stuck out my bottom lip. "That must have been awful. Did he screw you over?"

She looked wistful. "No. I broke up with him. Long distance was too hard between the NHL and college. We were living in two different worlds. I was shredded, though. I was really successful those years, but I wasn't fully me without him."

Tears pricked my eyes. "I don't want it to be over. We were really good together. I was upset about the Sydney thing, but I really don't blame him for whatever he did five years ago. This came out of nowhere."

"Oh, honey. It probably isn't. Mike just has a hot temper and no one's ever held him accountable for his bullshit. And if you don't want to deal with that in the long haul, I totally get it. But I think he really loves you. You can't change him, but if you can be patient with him, I bet he can learn to communicate better. Especially for someone he loves."

I wished Kitty would stop saying love about me and Mikey. I felt really close to him. I was happy with him. I was thinking about testing the waters and telling him I was falling for him when he got back from this road trip, but I knew how scared he got about commitment. I had to be careful how I told him.

And well, it seemed like it didn't matter because he ended things in a three-minute phone call.

I was trying not to cry. I was so sick of crying. Irina. Cole. Sydney. Nightmares. I just wanted to be free of all of it.

Kitty had called me honey, just like he did. I always thought that name was cheesy until he said it. Then it felt so natural. I was his honey. He'd wanted one for so long, and I came along.

Oh, God. Did he want me, or did he want just any honey? Was I just a placeholder?

"Oh, babe." Kitty leaned across her pool lounger to mine, giving me a hug. "It'll be okay. You got a new job today!"

"I know, I know. Head costume designer. It finally happened." I put my glass up in celebration and Kitty clinked it. "But he's not happy for me."

"Fuck him. This is about you. Tonight, we celebrate you."

Her phone chimed. She flicked a glance at it, then flipped it over.

"What was that?" I asked.

"Nothing. Let's go raid the pantry and make some messed up dinner."

We put together a feast of popcorn, pasta, and a random steak Kitty had, then put on a movie. All the while, Kitty's phone kept dinging.

"The game?" I finally asked.

"The game. They're winning for what it's worth."

"You can watch them," I said. "It's been a long day. I think I'm gonna hit the hay."

Kitty winced at me. "You sure?"

I nodded. "Got another long day of work tomorrow. Gotta put out an ad to hire my replacement."

With a hug, Kitty sent me off to their guest bedroom.

45

MIKEY

"Get in, Mikey!"

Coach had been shouting at me from the bench basically the whole game, and that's how it had been on every shift.

I turned over the puck every single time I got it. I swear I heard the crowd laugh when I did it the last time.

I tried not to think about my dad, and how he would blame all these fuckups on me. And yeah, I'm an adult, and he wasn't the one in pads and skates, but he fucked with my head. Plus everything else that had transpired that day.

The game was a blow-out, no thanks to me, with us taking home a 3-0 win. Obi had a hell of a game, maybe just to spite all my shit. After the game, Mom and Aunt Lori waited in the reception area. They were both all smiles, talking to Stelle when I got there like nothing was wrong. Like they hadn't been responsible for imploding my entire world.

"Benny!" Aunt Lori cried, sweeping me into a hug. I hugged her back, but half-assed. "Tough game, kid, but you pulled through."

I forced a smile and hugged my mom. "So proud of you, kiddo."

"Should we go get a drink? Celebrate? Commiserate?" Lori offered.

I stared at my shoes, struggling to figure out what to say. Fuck it. I met my mom's eyes. "Why have y'all been lying to me?"

"Lying? About what?" Lori asked.

Mom seemed to get it. "Lor," she said quietly. "Benny, maybe we should talk about this somewhere else."

Guy leaned in. "You good?"

"Great," I gritted. He clapped me on the shoulder and headed for our bus.

"Please, Benny," Mom said. "Can we go home?"

"No. You give me a ride to my hotel, and you tell me on the way."

I sat sullen in the back of their stinky-dog car. Neither of them spoke. I didn't feel like it either. They had three Saint Bernards, which is like three too many. So many things clicked into place. How they'd gotten dogs together. How sometimes, it looked like Aunt Lori hadn't "gone home" to the guest house at night when Dad was gone. Mom washing the sheets between Dad being gone and coming home.

Mom was openly sleeping with someone else while Dad was gone. I guess Dad was, too. What kind of fucked up shit was that?

We got to the hotel and Mom turned off the car.

"Why did you do it?" I asked.

"We wanted you and Laura to have a normal childhood."

"What's normal about your mom and dad both having affairs, one of whom is a person we know as an aunt?" I blasted. "What's normal about not telling your children who you are as a person, and then continuing to lie after they're grown up?"

"Benny, you know we love you so much—" Mom started.

"You're fucking selfish, Mom! You made a choice to give me some weird fucked-up idea of what relationships look like, and then expect me to function like a normal person?"

"How is Jessie, anyway?" Aunt Lori asked.

"I'm not talking about Jessie right now, Aunt Lori!" I barked. My stomach cramped. I'd be lucky if I ever shat normally again after the stress of this trip. "For the record, the problem isn't you two being gay. The problem is you two, and Dad, lying to me for my whole life. All this time I thought you were the hero, Mom. Turns out you and Dad were both the villains."

I got out of the car and headed through the snow flurries into the hotel. A glance at my phone showed a message from Jessie.

JESSIE GIRL

Hope you're okay. I'm here if you want to talk

A PERSISTENT KNOCKING CAME from my hotel room door.

"Ay, Mike!"

Guy. I looked at the clock and realized how royally fucked I was. The team was supposed to be on the bus to the airport ten minutes ago. I threw open the door on my way to the bathroom.

"Fuck, Mike, it smells in here," Guy said, waving his hand in front of his nose.

"I'm having an episode, dickhead," I spat.

"No, like booze and just . . . stank," he clarified. "We gotta get on the bus. We're late."

"I fucking know that, Stelle!"

"I'm gonna start throwing your shit in a bag."

I grumbled some sort of thank you as I splashed my face and ran a wet hand through my hair. I looked like hell. Guy tossed my shirt, suit, and tie at me in the bathroom. Bottles clattered on the floor as he walked through them.

"Jesus, you managed to drink this much while you were having an episode? I don't know what happened with your mom—"

"That's right. You don't."

He sighed, tossing some of the bottles in the trash. Through the two mirrors, I saw him take some money out of his wallet and leave it for the maid. "You talk to Jessie?"

"What do you care?"

"I'm worried about you, man. You missed breakfast. You never miss breakfast unless you're getting laid." Horror crossed his face. "Were you with someone?"

"No! I wouldn't do that to her!"

He leaned into the bathroom doorway as I got dressed. I was rushing so much I damn near zipped my cock into my pants. "But you'd yell at her when she calls you and dump her?"

"How do you—Kitty." Great. That meant Jessie was crying on Kitty's shoulder about me. And Kitty probably confirmed what a piece of shit I am, and I'd never have another shot at making it up to Jessie.

I was a fool for even holding out a hope that I could make it up to her. I didn't deserve Jessie, plain and simple. Love wasn't in the cards for me. My family didn't love me, and I'd been kidding myself to think that Jessie and I could be together after all the crap I'd pulled in the past.

Guy placed a soft hand on my shoulder. "We really gotta go, Mike." I'd just been staring into the sink. My head throbbed and my stomach was on the verge of another eruption. I pulled an Imodium out of my dopp kit and chewed it up.

"Are those chewable? Whatever," Guy said. "Come on. Let's go."

We were silent in the elevator, until he cleared his throat. "So, you wanna talk about it?"

"Fuck off."

"K." He looked the other way and fucking whistled like it was that casual. He'd always been a jokester when I was mad. Minus that one time I insulted Kitty, which I still regret.

We got to the arena in Jersey late, all because of me. Our flight was delayed, then our bus hit traffic. One game in New Jersey, one in New York, with a day off in between. A day off in New York would usually excite me. Well, I guess I used to use it as an excuse to get my dick wet, but that wouldn't be happening this time. Even if I wasn't with Jessie, I couldn't imagine finding any fulfillment in some random woman. I'd had the real thing. Maybe I'd just become a monk and never have sex again. I couldn't hurt anyone that way.

I put on my headphones and blasted the saddest music I could think of, remembering Jessie's sweet hazel eyes, how pretty she was when she lost it for me. The way at one point, I took the hurt away for her, getting her out of the bad situation with Cole. Holding her when she was scared. Becoming friends. Realizing what a big chance she was giving me by letting me try out love on her.

Then I just brought more hurt into her life. My ex-flings went on parade to show off how poor my choices had been in the past. Showing up at my apartment. Yelling at her at parties.

But it didn't matter. Because the love I'd known was a lie.

I made the mistake of checking my phone before locking in for the game against Jersey. No more messages from Jessie. Of course there weren't. I'd told her to leave me alone. Left her on read the night before.

I'd gotten what I wanted. She'd given up on me.

I slipped out to a bathroom stall where I lost it. I had to let her go. I had told her that I wasn't the guy for her and she still checked in on me. Too bad I was meant to be a loner. I'd always have my friends, but true love wasn't for me.

I wanted her so bad, but I just couldn't keep doing all that.

We were different types of people. She deserved more than what I could give her.

I'd figure out how to handle us living together when I got back. I didn't want to leave her high and dry financially, because she didn't deserve that either. Maybe I'd just move out and keep paying her rent. It would hurt too much to be in the same space as her and not be able to have her.

I didn't realize I was gasping for air until Sorrento was peeking under the stall.

"Open the door, Mikey," he said quietly. "It's gonna be alright, but you gotta let me in."

"I'm fine," I barked.

"I'm serious, man. Open the door."

I unlatched the door, where I was just sitting on the toilet with my full uniform on. His hand fell to my shoulder.

"It's gonna be fine, my man. Is this about Jessie?"

"No. Yeah. I don't know."

"She break up with you?"

"No, I did."

"Why?"

"Mind your business, Sorrento."

He chuckled a little. Fucking dick. "Bud, she'd probably take you back. She's a sweet girl."

"You think I don't fucking know that?"

"You cheat on her?" he asked.

"No! Why does everyone think that?"

"I just don't see why you dumped her. You're obviously upset about it."

I stood, getting in his face. "What part of mind your fucking business did you not understand, Dylan?"

He sighed, unfazed by me. "Alright. But you wanna go fuck up Jersey?"

"Let's fuck 'em up."

46

MIKEY

I was back in my room, mindlessly scrolling my phone after morning skate. Everyone else was headed out to do tourist-y shit. I just wasn't feeling it.

A knock came at the door. "Mikeyyyyyyy," came a raspy voice.

"Fuck off!" I yelled.

"You jerkin' it?"

"I said fuck off!"

"I'm not leaving," the voice taunted.

I scrunched my eyes shut and took a deep breath. I was willing to put money on it being Obi, being his annoying weirdass goalie self as usual. I opened the door to find that I was correct.

"What?"

He slung his arm around my neck and walked into my room. "Get some fun clothes on. We're going sightseeing. Stelle wants to take us to his favorite pizza place from when he used to live here."

"I don't want to go on Kitty and Guy's sightseeing extravaganza to see all the places they've fucked in New York," I grumbled.

"I heard that," came Stelle's voice from down the hall. He approached, along with Sorrento. "Come on, Mike. We're not letting you waste the day."

With the three of them crowding into my hotel room, I caved. They'd drag me out by my legs if I didn't go willingly.

The thing is, I ended up having fun. Guy fucked with me by pointing out places he and Kitty had allegedly fucked. We ate pizza. We walked around. We took stupid pictures in Times Square. We drank beers in a dive bar and played darts. My stomach actually tolerated everything. We ribbed each other constantly about anything and everything, though no one mentioned Jessie. Obi made us go to some bizarre-ass museum about magicians. Okay, fine, the magic museum was actually kind of cool.

We settled in for dinner at some sushi place that Guy liked.

"Kitty says hi," Guy announced after sending off our stupid selfie with a giant M&M in Times Square. My stomach sank, wondering if Jessie was with her. I thought of her in almost everything I saw. That would get easier with time, right? One day it wouldn't hurt so bad to know that I couldn't have her.

We drank too much sake at dinner, in addition to the beers we took in throughout the day while being ridiculous tourists. I was a little buzzed, reflecting on the good times. I had my phone under the table, scrolling through my camera roll. All pictures of Jessie. My beautiful Jessie Girl. Her smile. Her dimple. Her—

"Are those your girlfriend's tits?" Obi shrieked. "Jesus, why are you breaking up with her?"

"Stop looking at my phone!"

"When are you going to make up with her?" Obi asked.

I clicked my phone screen off. "I'm not."

"You can't take my mommy from me like that," he giggled.

"Someone cut this kid off," I growled.

"It's really not a big deal, man. You had one fight," Guy said. "You've made it up to her before."

Thankfully, our waiter came through at the right moment with our sushi boats (yes plural), and when she left, no one seemed inclined to pick the topic back up.

We found some bar with Skeeball and took turns trying to dominate each other. We got back to the hotel around midnight. I almost wished we were staying in New York longer. Going home and facing the reality of not having Jessie anymore was going to be torture.

A few minutes after I settled in my hotel room, there was a knock. Guy. "Can I come in?"

"This a booty call?"

"You wish," he said, pushing past me. "It's an intervention."

I busied myself with popping some microwave popcorn from the minibar.

"Why did you really break up with Jessie? Was it something she did?"

"No. She's perfect," I said. "She's just too good for me."

"Because of Sydney?"

I grumbled. "It's not just Sydney. One of my other old flings showed up at our apartment while I was gone. These people from my past just keep making her feel like shit. She wouldn't feel bad about herself if I weren't in the picture."

Guy shrugged. "So move."

"What?"

"Your exes won't be able to find you anymore if you move. So move."

I snorted, morose. "Sydney will still be around."

"Sydney sucks. I heard Leroy say he's not that happy with her right now either. I guess she got pretty irrational with him that night."

I blew out a breath. "Not surprised. She's something. I can't believe I fucked her. But I fucked a lot of people I shouldn't have."

Guy tossed a hand. "We all did. That doesn't mean you should give up on Jessie. She probably regrets being with Cole."

He had a point.

"Is that the only reason you dumped her? Your mom texted me today to ask if you were alright."

I rubbed my temples. "That's rich."

"Why? What does that mean?" Guy asked.

I explained what happened with my parents, and Laura.

"That's fucked up, man. I'm sorry. Like real sorry," he said.

"Don't exactly feel qualified to love anyone after that. My own family doesn't trust me."

Guy pulled the steaming popcorn bag out of the microwave, kicking it around like a hackeysack. "Gah! Hot!" Butter was flinging everywhere. I had to laugh. "Look, there was a time when I thought I couldn't be good enough for Kitty. I thought that because my dad sucks, and I'm just a shitty hockey player like he was, that I'd never be able to give her the love she deserved."

"Seriously?" It was hard for me to picture him, the most loving partner I'd ever seen, as feeling inadequate. "But your mom loved you, right? Like a lot?"

Guy cocked his head to the side. "Yours loves you, too, Mike."

I stared at the floor between us.

"It's gonna be alright, bud." He patted me on the back.

"They fucking betrayed me. Every one of them. Even Aunt Lori."

"I know it hurts, man. But don't turn away from a good thing with Jessie just because you got hurt."

"Every single one of them is a piece of shit."

"Maybe. But you're not." He looked at his watch. "It's late and we've got an early game. But just promise me you'll think about it. Let Jessie decide if you're good enough. Don't make that decision for her."

When I got up the next morning, I wasn't sure what I wanted to do. But I needed to at least start the conversation again.

I miss you

47

JESSIE

"Hey, Mom."

"Just calling to check on you. Haven't heard from you in a minute."

I was at the studio on Sunday, looking over resumes from potential candidates to fill my old position and packing for the on-location shoot that week. Mom's call gave me a chance to take a break.

I gave a small chuckle. "Yeah. Things have been busy." What an understatement.

"Well, you're the Hollywood star with the exciting life. Tell me what's going on."

"Um, I got a promotion! I'm the lead costume designer now."

"Oh, how wonderful! I bet Mikey's so proud of you. Did y'all go celebrate?"

My stomach dropped. "Oh, uh, he's out of town. And he . . . kinda dumped me."

"HEY! Get down off of there!"

"Huh?"

"Sorry, that damn cat's back and trying to piss in my spring planters. I only just got 'em out there. He dumped you? Why?"

I choked up a little. "I'm not sure."

"Oh, Jessie. I'm sorry. Are y'all still living together?"

"He's on the road now, but I packed my stuff to go."

"Bless your heart, honey. That's too bad. It's his loss, you know."

I really didn't feel like discussing it anymore. "How's Dad?"

"Oh, you know. Out getting ready for turkey season. I'm just a turkey hunter's widow."

My mother's dramatic streak was somehow comforting. My life was chaotic and stressful, but her biggest worry was the same worry she had every spring: being alone now and then while Dad hunted. I told her I needed to get back to work and that I'd call her later, truly needing to get back to it.

I combed the list of characters and scenes to make sure I had every single piece for each character. I was on my own. I had to get it right.

Rain pelted the wardrobe trailer. I'd gotten so used to not checking the weather in L.A. that I was shocked to walk outside to rain that morning. The barista at the coffee shop informed me that it was one of the spring storms coming in. I did my best to keep my AirPods in and not think about whether the storm was getting worse.

I was working a Sunday partially because I had to, and partially so I didn't have to deal with whether or not to watch Mikey's game. I'd spent Saturday finishing his suit and packing my stuff up at his place. Kitty had offered for me to stay there until I could find a place, and her place was closer to work than Mikey's.

I'd originally planned to stitch "Sweet Cheeks" or "Jockey" into the suit cuff, but it seemed too silly to do that under the circumstances.

Part of me felt stupid for being that heartbroken. We hadn't even been together that long. But we'd shared a lot, and not just physically. I felt really connected to him. Maybe it had just been a long time since I fell in love, not that he himself was that great.

But he was kinda great. He went out of his way to take care of me. He was so big and brawny and tough but so sugar-sweet underneath it all.

And wounded. I suspected the wounds were what made him break up with me, but I couldn't know since he left no explanation. "Find your relationship guy."

And yet, I woke up to a message from him in New York. "I miss you."

Maybe he was coming back around. But he couldn't just shut me out when stuff got hard. If he really wanted me, he had to get vulnerable. I knew deep down that this was injured child Mikey and not grown-up Ben, but I can't force a man to grow up. That's something he's got to do on his own.

I went from what I thought was a stable relationship to being cheated on, to a complete whirlwind romance where it felt like I was on a game show with the floor bottomed out. Floating on air, swept up in Ben with no grounding.

That lack of grounding came back to bite us. I needed to know how to be independent. I couldn't afford to screw up this time in my career either.

I had enough money at that point, between my new salary and a bonus they offered me to get me through the transition. I could easily put down money on a new apartment. I planned to look for my own place as soon as I got my replacement hired.

It was 7 p.m. by the time I felt confident that everything was coordinated for the week. I had emails out to a handful of candidates to fill the vacant position. I could head back to Kitty's for the night and be out early the next morning.

But right when I had my mind made up and everything tucked into its neat, uncomplicated mental box, I walked outside into a thunderstorm.

48

MIKEY

I played a great game in New York. I even scored a goal, which isn't that frequent for me. Assists? Sure. Goals? Not as much.

Moving on the ice pushed me back into myself. Guy was right. Why did it matter what had happened in the past for me? Jessie was willing to be with me as I was. I broke up with her, not the other way around. I wasn't my dad, or my mom. Why did it matter who I'd had sex with before? All those women were part of the process of learning what I wanted, who I am.

I got on the plane home with a new determination. I was going to get Jessie back. I'd apologize for clamming up. I'd finally tell her that I loved her. I'd show her that she was the only person for me. I'd commit to being the man she deserves.

She could say no. She could change her mind. But I had to try.

Because what's the point of living if you don't take a chance on love?

I made a lightning-fast stop to a corner store to grab some flowers, dodging raindrops on the way in. Apparently, we were lucky our game was at noon and we could fly back before this big storm hit. Figures that it would storm on the day I needed to make a dramatic comeback. How cinematic. And with how Jessie hated storms so much, I was determined to be there for her.

Our apartment was eerily quiet, the rain pattering the windows the only sound. My footsteps echoed in a way they hadn't before. Jess's bed was neatly made and Yarn Wad wasn't there, which isn't like her. My bed was neatly made, too, also without Yarn Wad. A really snazzy new cream-colored suit hung from the main hook in our closet. I touched the jacket, opening it to find a liner that stopped my heart. She'd found ocelot-patterned silk for the lining.

I wanted to laugh with her about it, to tell her how clever it was, but where was she?

Had she given up? Had she left? Was the suit my farewell present? I rushed into Jessie's room and opened her drawers. Empty. Her main sewing machine was gone, as was her suitcase.

Jessie had left. I don't know why I was surprised. I asked her to leave me alone. She just took me seriously.

The walls were closing in on me. The air felt tight and stale. She did the thing I'd feared most. She had really given up on me.

I slid down the wall in the hallway, not trusting myself to sit without just falling over. I pulled out my phone and dialed Jessie.

No answer.

I called Guy.

"What, Mikey? I just got home to Kitty. The roads are a mess."

I gasped in some air, my face wet. "Jessie left me. She's . . . she's gone."

Guy hesitated. "I'm sorry, man."

"She left. Her stuff is gone. Is she . . . is she there? With you?"

Guy sighed. "I feel caught in the middle here, Mike."

"So she is. I'm on my way."

"Mikey—"

I didn't hear the rest because I hung up. I grabbed a whole box of granola bars from my pantry on my way out the door because I was starving and didn't have time to think. My phone buzzed again, Guy. I didn't have time. I had to get to her. I didn't bother waiting for the elevator, tearing down the stairwell to get back to the parking garage.

Where the rain was light on the way home from the airport, it poured now. Jessie hated rain.

A crack of lightning whipped across the sky and I grew hysterical. Jessie hated storms. This was what her nightmares were made of. Did she feel safe at Guy and Kitty's?

"I'm on my way, honey," I said to no one in particular. I put my car into sport mode and went as fast as I could, being a dick and driving on the berm when I needed to get around an accident. I tried calling Jessie again, but she didn't answer. I needed to talk her down. Even if she was mad at me, I couldn't have her being alone with people who didn't understand her like I did. She needed me, even if she didn't know it.

The drive to Guy and Kitty's should have taken about twenty-five minutes, but I made it in fifteen. I ran through the pouring rain to their door, ringing the bell over and over. Jessie's car wasn't in the driveway, but maybe she'd put it in the shop like I told her to.

Guy answered the door in just a pair of sweatpants, his upper body red and splotchy.

"Fuck, man, were you fucking?"

"I . . . uh, yeah."

"Is she here?"

Guy rubbed his hand over his forehead. "No. She's not here.

But come in." I slipped off my soaked shoes on their doormat as Guy called out to Kitty. "Mikey's here, *ma puce*."

Kitty's "okay" sounded from the bedroom.

"Sorry, man. I just, I really, fuck. Where is she?"

Kitty walked in the living room with an oversized t-shirt and some sweatpants, too. Her expression was that of a funeral director. "Hey, Mike."

I couldn't help myself. I barged past her into the guest bedroom. Jessie's suitcase sat open on the floor. I stormed back out to the living room.

"She's been staying with you? What the hell? You could have told me, Stelle!"

"She's been working long hours and this was closer," Kitty consoled me, flopping on the couch. "She got the big promotion, you know."

My heart swelled. "She did? She didn't tell me."

Kitty's eyes turned murderous. "Well, I'm pretty sure you bitched her out and dumped her when she called to tell you, Michael."

"Easy," Guy warned, raising his eyebrows at Kitty. Kitty's attention was on her phone anyway, a soft "oh shit" issuing from her lips. She got up and went into the kitchen.

"Hey! What's wrong? I saw I missed some calls."

I rushed into the kitchen. "Is it her? Where is she?" I mouthed.

Kitty held up a finger to silence me. "Can you drop a pin? And slow down, it's hard to understand you. Is a tow truck coming?"

Of course. Her fucking car. And it was storming on top of it all.

Jessie's voice rushed through Kitty's phone. "Deep breaths, Jess. Are you safe? Are you on the 5?"

Muffled sobs came through, with a little shriek as thunder rumbled in the background. I heard a faint "I'm fine."

"Send me that pin. I'm leaving now," I said, racing for the door.

Kitty ran after me as I tore out the front door, grabbing my shoes as I went.

"You'd better have your shit together, Michael! Don't you hurt her!" Kitty raged. What was with these women in our lives who went absolutely apeshit when they were mad? Kitty was about as scary as mad Jessalyn.

"Hurt her? Are you fucking kidding me? Her car's broken down and she's afraid of fucking storms, Kitty! I'm going to help her!"

Guy held Kitty back. "Sweetheart, he's fine. Let him go."

The last glimpse I got of them was Guy holding Kitty from behind, both of them waving to me with worried eyes.

JESSIE'S CAR wasn't even fully pulled off the road, her hazards still on. It looked like some other car had side-swiped hers.

Oh, God. What if she was hurt?

I yelled her name, the rain somehow even harder than before. This storm business was no joke. I opened the passenger door and looked in, but she wasn't there.

I left the car and ran toward the overpass ahead of me, still yelling for her. I didn't see a person anywhere, but with the rain coming down so hard and people still driving by, I couldn't see anything. Under the bridge, I'd be able to look better.

Finally out of the rain, I searched for any sign of her. And there, up in the rafters, was a shivering figure. I ran, praying it was her.

It was. She was balled up with her knees under her chin, soaking wet and shaking as a rumble of thunder jostled the air.

"Jessalyn, baby, are you okay?"

She was stuffed up in that little corner where the bridge meets the overpass, in between two pillars.

"Can you come out of there, honey? I don't know if I can fit in there with you."

She cried harder, silent sobs wracking her.

"Let me take you home. Please."

Her voice came out as a shriek. "This is the safest place to be in a storm."

My heart shattered. She was terrified. "I'm coming in there. Just hang on."

"No! You can't shut me out and come walking back into my life! You dumped me!"

"I know, honey. I'm so sorry. A lot happened, but that's no excuse."

Another rumble of thunder boomed, and she sat, lips quivering as she cried.

"Hon, please let me be here for you now. I know I fucked up, but I can't watch you like this."

I flattened myself to the ground and army-crawled to get up next to her, then pulled her down a bit so I could hold her. Her eyes widened, resisting leaving her safe space.

"It's okay. We'll stay up high here. You're safe, Jessie."

I cradled her in my lap, letting her cry and shake and do whatever she needed to do. I had a better look at her car from that vantage point.

"Christ, did your front wheel just fall off?"

Jessie sniffled. "Yeah."

"We're going to get you a new car tomorrow."

She stiffened. "The tow truck's coming. They can fix it. I can get a ride to work."

I swallowed my frustration at her stubbornness. It wasn't going to help my case if I bossed her around at the moment. "When is it coming?"

"Couple hours, maybe. They had a few calls ahead of me."

I shook my head. "No, honey. We're leaving before that. We'll cash that one in and get you a new car."

She squirmed to try and escape my grip. "I'll wait for the tow truck."

I stroked my hand down her back. "Jessie, I know I screwed up. I know you're mad at me. And you have every right to be. But please let me help you."

"I can do this on my own, Benjamin," she said.

"I know you can. But you don't need to prove it to me. This is something I want to do for you," I said, catching her hazel eyes. The hurt in them told me it wasn't just about buying her a car. "Look, I haven't been doing okay the last week and I should have handled it better than I did."

She drew a shuddering breath. "You shut me out, Ben. You fucked up by calling it off, and then you fucked up some more by shutting me out."

"I know, honey. I'm so sorry. I knew how much I was hurting you, but I also couldn't stop. I wanted to protect you from all the dark stuff. I told myself I wasn't good enough for you. I feel like I've only brought trash into your life."

"But you didn't let me be part of that decision." She narrowed her eyes at me. "There's no getting around the dark stuff. That's what makes relationships real. If we only shared the good stuff, we'd never really know each other."

I chewed my cheek. "Guess I never really thought of it like that."

She stared off into the storm, then looked at me after another clap of thunder. "She didn't even scream, you know. She was just . . . gone."

"Your best friend?"

She nodded. "We were out for our little sunset-watching getaway. The storm clouds were starting to cover the sunset, but we thought we still had plenty of time to get back to the cabin. The air kinda changed at one point, and our hair stood on end.

We even laughed about it, not realizing the danger we were in. By the time we figured out that wasn't a good thing, it was too late." Tears streamed down Jess's cheeks. I stroked her back and let her keep talking. "I threw myself on the ground, and she fell on top of me. She took the brunt of it, and she saved me. But she was just dead. No goodbye. My best friend was gone."

She was quiet for a minute, but I could tell she wasn't done. Her lower lip wobbled. "Sometimes I wish I was in her place, Ben."

"Oh, honey," I said, kissing her temple. "I'm glad you're here. And I wish she could be, too. What was her name?"

Jessie cried harder, leaning into my chest. "Madeline. Madeline and Jessalyn."

"Bet you two were some hell-raisers."

She got a soft smile. "Yeah. I still think of her a lot. Not just in the nightmares. I miss her. I think I'll always miss her. Wonder what her life would have been like if we'd gotten more time."

I held her a little tighter. "Do you want to do something in her memory soon? Have a beach day where we talk about her?"

Jessie's eyes rounded. "That implies that we're still hanging out."

"Honey, I think I'll be around you as long as you'll have me. If I'm lucky enough for you to take me back, I don't want to live in a world without you. I don't want to screw up with you anymore."

She threw her arms around my neck, and I held her close. "I think you should screw up, but you should screw up and stay."

I had to laugh because it was so damn confusing. "What do you mean?"

She pulled back and cupped my cheeks. "Because we're both going to screw up. But you can't screw up and hide. You have to screw up and stay."

A bolt of lightning touched the ground not far from the bridge, both of us jumping at the flash of light and instantaneous thunder. Jessie's body seized up, clutching my wet shirt and balling herself up in my lap.

"I've got you, honey. Don't worry. I'll keep you safe."

I kissed her forehead and stroked her hair, her back, down her damp, cold arms. I rocked her in my lap, and before I knew it, I was singing our song. The rain slowly let up, and by the time I was done singing, it was down to a drizzle. Jessie was limp and relaxed in my arms.

"I got so scared I actually pissed myself." Jessie gestured to her soaked pants that indeed were extra soaked in the middle. She looked miserable.

"You know what, hon?"

"What?"

"You look so pretty in your pee pants."

She laughed, the first time I'd heard her laugh since everything fell apart. She cackled and wheezed, almost falling out of my lap.

"Are these the new fashion?" she asked on a gasp.

"If they're not, I'll make them the fashion. I'll wear pee pants to my next game."

That set her off again on another laughing jag, clutching her stomach like it hurt to laugh so hard.

"I love you, Mikey." She said it, then clapped her hand over her mouth. "Oh my God. Did I just say that?"

"I hope so. You know why?"

She winced. "Why?"

"Because I'm in love with you." Her eyes rounded, gaping at me. "I'm serious, Jessalyn. I've been so mad at myself because I threw away this beautiful love that you've given me. And maybe you didn't mean it like I do, but I love you, and I need you to know it."

Her smile was wide. "Yeah?"

I nodded, matching her expression. "Yeah. I love you. And I love your dimple. I love your pee pants. I even love silly old Yarn Wad."

She turned to straddle me in her pee pants, and I didn't even care. "I love you, Ben."

"I love you more, Jessalyn." I held us nose to nose, drinking in her smile. "Kiss for Daddy?"

Her warm laugh rattled out. "I think you've earned it."

49

JESSIE

Kitty threw her arms around my neck as we walked in at her house. Guy put on a kettle for tea. We'd run the heat the whole way there, but I was still shivering. My clothes were soaked, between the rain and my little pee accident.

"I'm so glad you're okay," she said. "I mean, are you okay? What the hell happened?"

"So, my wheel kinda fell off while I was driving on the highway."

Guy's hands were over his mouth. "During the storm, too? That's so scary!"

Ben held me from behind, trying to keep me warm as we caught them up.

"I'm okay now. This guy helped me out," I said, peering up at him. He kissed my hair and held me tighter.

"You're soaked to the bone. Go shower and warm up," Kitty said, pushing a steaming mug of tea into my hands.

I didn't have to be told twice, heading for the guest bedroom. Mikey walked along with me.

"Ay, Mike," Guy called. "Our shower's actually the better one for sex."

"Guy!" Kitty shrieked. "Jesus Christ!"

In the guest bathroom, Mikey helped me peel off my clothes, then had me hold my hot tea mug. He sat on the edge of the tub as the shower water heated.

"I feel like I should tell you some stuff, Jessie."

"I'm ready to hear it."

"I found out that my mom and Aunt Lori are lovers. She and Dad decided it was best if they still acted like they were together and Mom stayed in the closet. But my sister knew the whole time."

"Benny," I said, touching his arm.

"Yeah. I told myself that meant they didn't love me, to keep that secret for so long. It's still fucked up, and I don't know what to believe. But it really messed me up. I thought just Dad was the bad guy. But everyone had a little hand in it. I always saw my mom as the hero, but Dad said she made him leave because she fell in love with someone else. He just came back on weekends to spend time with Laura and with me at hockey."

I nodded, watching him.

"It's still a mess, but the point is, it made me feel like I don't know love, because all the love in my life was a lie," he said.

"That's a lot to take. I see why you shut down," I said. "But you do know love, babe. You know how your friends love you. You know how Guy and Kitty love each other, and Dylan and Jeanine. You know love. Just because what you got from your parents was complicated doesn't mean you can't love. And your parents do love you. They're just figuring it all out."

His eyes were fixed on the floor. "My dad was still super hard on me growing up. I was so convinced that if I just played hockey good enough, he'd be around more. I thought I was the reason he was gone. I kept fucking up in critical games because the pressure to get him to stay and be proud of me was too intense."

"Ben—"

"Hang on, there's more. I need you to hear it all. All my skeletons. Everything bad. I won't be able to trust that you love me until you've seen it all."

This poor, sweet man thought he was unlovable. It was soul-crushing. "Okay, baby. Go on."

"I have chronic stomach problems, IBS. I was having an episode when you called me and I told you to leave."

"I know, Ben. I mean, not that you were sick then, but I put the pieces together since we live together."

"That's so fucking embarrassing, Jess," he said, shaking his head.

"It's your body, baby. It's nothing to be embarrassed about. I love you and your body."

Ben was quiet, his eyes wet.

"That all?"

He gave a self-conscious laugh. "I mean, I slept with a lot of women. Like a whole lot. Like probably a bad number."

I bit my lip. That part did make me a little sweaty. "Are you sleeping with any of them now?"

"No," he shook his head vigorously. "Just you. I don't even care about all of them. None of them matter now that I have you."

"I'm not worried about your past, Ben. But I am worried about how we treat each other now, and how you treat yourself. I love you, but you need to know that you're worthy of love, too. You're worth it even if you have a bad game, or quit hockey, or screwed a bunch of women, or screw something up. You bring so much joy and love and care to the table. You know that, right?"

He didn't say anything, just crushing me into a hug where I sat on the toilet lid. He sat back and took the mug out of my hands, standing and guiding me to the shower. He still had his clothes on.

"You coming in?"

He got a little smirk. "If you'll have me."

"Get in here, Jockey."

I don't remember much about washing myself, because Ben did everything. Between every action, he covered me in kisses. On my mouth, on my skin, down my sides, between my legs.

I shampooed his hair, loving how thick the hair felt in my fingers. I spent extra time rubbing his neck and shoulders, his satisfied sighs a reward.

We got out of the shower, drying each other off. Ben radiated reverence, his eyes raking over my every feature like he was seeing them new for the first time. He held my hand walking me to the bed and laid down a towel for our wet hair.

"Lie down, baby," he said, climbing on the bed after me. He hovered over me, gazing down into my eyes. "I love you so much, Jessalyn. Whatever it takes, I'm willing to do."

I knew he wasn't just talking about sex. He was talking about us. "I love you, too, Ben."

"So you'll come home with me? Stop living here?"

I nodded, stroking his cheek. "I'll come home with you."

"To *our* home. It's ours, Jessie."

I smiled. "Yes. Ours."

And then we shut up. We kissed, all tangled up together, rolling each other to our backs. It was physical, yes, but like that day after the beach, it was so much more than sex. Kisses went everywhere. I worshiped him, and he worshiped me. There was pleasure and something even deeper: a quiet peace, a union, an iron-clad bond.

He entered me at last, his lips on my neck with whispered promises. To love me until I begged him to stop. To build a home together. To work on the hard stuff. And I promised not to leave. To be with him when life was hard. To be a partner, facing life together.

And for a while, we were silent, shared breath. He gazed into my eyes as he pressed into me, over and over. His hands alternated between grabbing and tender caresses. I held his shoulders, his waist, his hips. We came, him first with a soft whimper, and then me with a little help from his hand and his sweet words. "Be mine, Jessie. You're so beautiful when you let go for me. Let me have it. Let me take care of you."

He was still hard inside me, his release adding more wetness as he rolled his hips and brushed my clit with his thumb. I closed my eyes and squeezed him tighter as I came, overwhelmed with love for him. When I opened my eyes, he was smiling down at me.

"Thanks for taking me back, honey."

I grinned. "Thanks for coming back."

He laughed a little.

"What?"

"I can't believe the last guy didn't want to put a ring on you. I'm ready to do it all right fucking now," he said, nibbling my neck on the last words.

"Right now? You want to marry me right now?" I raised an eyebrow at him.

"Yep. Like Vegas Chapel of Love, wearing bathrobes because we're naked, married by Elvis. I would do it. Right now."

"Your cum running down my leg and everything?"

"Oh, definitely. That makes it even better. Then everyone will know you're mine."

"I think the act of getting married is pretty effective at that without compromising my dignity."

"What's undignified about my cum on your leg? Our love is beautiful, Jessalyn. Everyone needs to see it."

I sighed, and he laughed more. "I think maybe we should give it a minute before running for the chapel."

"What if I propose to you every single day until you say yes?"

I looked up into that dimpled smile, giggling. "You want me to marry you because you wore me down?"

"If that's what it takes to make this permanent, sure."

50

MIKEY

It had been two months since Jessie and I made up and said I love you. Things were so good with her. We occasionally ran into Cole, which was unsavory. I was kind of sad that Jessie still got irritated when she saw him. To me, that meant she still cared about him a little bit. She assured me it was just a constant nasty reminder of how much time she wasted with him. That made me feel better.

And anyway, I had a plan.

Her job had gotten so much better since she was promoted and found her replacement. She no longer had to get up at 4:30 since she had someone to share the load with more evenly. We had plans to go to Detroit late in the summer and stay with my family for a week, then to see her family for a week. I'd had some phone calls with my family where not much was said, but it was clear we all wanted to work on our relationship. We'd hit the bottom. Maybe we had a chance to go upward.

I was also taking Jessie to Japan after Guy and Kitty's wedding in July. I was grateful the Disneyland teacups weren't the thing she needed to be happy and that fresh sushi and ramen would make her more thrilled.

And yes, I still asked her to marry me every single day. She laughed me off and said the same thing every time: "Maybe someday."

Most days it was a joke. I knew we hadn't been together very long, or even known each other. But if she said yes any of the days, I would have gone for it.

I had her sew two little strips of fabric into all my pants pockets. I told her it was to tie my keys in, but really, it was to tie in the ring I got her. I was damn well going to be prepared if she said yes.

One Friday night after the first round of the playoffs, she came home to a box on our bed. I wasn't sure if this was the thing that would make her say yes or if it would upset her to no end, but it felt like a risk worth taking.

She gave a little squeal when she saw it. "Did you get a present, Benny?"

I was just a couple of steps behind her, excited to see her open it. It was kind of a risk, and I realized the whole thing could backfire. "It's for you."

She clapped her hands together. "Ooh! Lucky me!"

It wasn't uncommon for me to get her little gifts and she'd mostly stopped scolding me when I did. Most of the time it was truly small things that would make her smile, like a packet of salt one time because she was griping so much that a dish we got somewhere was undersalted. But I'd put in some work for this one. Jessie untied the ribbon on top and looked over at me with a grin.

"This is a bigger box than usual." Her silliness disappeared as she opened the box. "Ben."

She lifted the green velvet inside, holding the blanket out. She was silent, but her hands trembled. She crumpled it to her chest and dropped her head. Her shoulders shook and I feared this was all a terrible idea. She sniffed back a sob and looked back at me. "You remembered."

I nodded. "I did."

I put my hands on her shoulders and she leaned into me. She just kept crying. I still wasn't sure what was going through her head.

"Is it okay?"

She turned around to face me. "I can't believe you did that."

I swallowed hard and followed the path of her tear with my finger. "Yeah, I did. Jess, I thought it would be nice. I'm really sorry—"

She pinned herself to me. "I love you. So much, Ben. It's perfect."

The vise that had been squeezing my lungs released as I wrapped her up. "You like it?"

She cocked her head to the side, leveling me with a look. "Are you always going to follow me around noticing the things that mean something to me, then doing something about it?"

"I mean, I can't follow you everywhere, so no. I just like you to feel loved."

"You didn't know Madeline, but God, she would have liked you. I'd have had to fight her for you," she laughed.

"I would have been a little too old for you two at that time," I pointed out, "and I'm probably a better person at twenty-eight than I was at sixteen."

She shook her head with a little snort. "You help me keep her memory alive and Ben, it's . . . I . . . thank you."

"You're welcome, baby. She was important to you, so she's important to me."

She wiped her fingers under her eyes. "We're supposed to be celebrating you! You made it to round two!"

"We can celebrate that. The lady at the fabric shop just finished this and I couldn't wait until your birthday to give it to you."

She ran her hands over the satin edges of the blanket. "I

love how heavy it is. It's almost weighted." She turned to give me a stern look. "This doesn't replace my blankie, though."

I gave a warm laugh. "There's no replacing Yarn Wad. I'd never." She rewarded me with a tight hug and a nibble on my neck. "How about you wear one of your sexy little dresses to dinner with me?"

She cracked a grin. "Okay." She pulled me into a kiss. "Did I ever tell you that you're the kindest," she kissed me again, "most thoughtful," a deeper kiss, "sweetest man alive?"

My stomach was fluttering. I would never get enough of making her happy, of making her feel seen. Yet me being me, I couldn't leave well enough alone. "A simple 'thank you, Daddy' would suffice."

She laughed, bopping me with the blanket. "You're such an ass."

I ran my hands over her bottom. "You sticking with that answer?"

She giggled and bit her lip. "Yep. What are you gonna do about it?"

I hauled her over my shoulder and spanked her butt. "This."

She squealed and kicked her legs. "Put me down!"

"Not until you agree to go to dinner with me."

"I already did!"

I slapped her plump little butt again. "No attitude, missy! 'Take me to dinner, Daddy. I'll wear that dress you like.'"

"Take me to dinner, Daddy. I'll wear your favorite dress."

I slid her body down my front, catching her at the armpits to kiss her. "That's more like it."

Jessie had a devilish smirk as I put her down, that damn dimple that made me crazy popping out. "But I won't wear the heels."

She took off running and cackled as I chased after her.

WE WERE COMING to the end of round two of the playoffs. My dad and his girlfriend had come out to watch me play earlier in the series. He and the mom of his other kids had parted ways after the kids went to college. His new girlfriend was pretty nice, though. Dad and I had a good talk about what he expected of me. He didn't realize the expectations he was putting on me all those years, and felt really bad about it. We weren't 100% okay, but we were at least talking and working on having a better relationship. I was planning to work through stuff with Mom and Lori when we went to visit in the summer.

It was game six and we could move on that night if we won. I hoped we won that night because we were playing at home, and I'd have loved to be able to celebrate with Jess. She was being a real trooper about coming to my games even on her work nights.

"It's not every day that your boyfriend is in the playoffs," she said.

And thankfully, there were no further fights between any wives during away game parties.

I had really big plans for after the game, so I told her not to drive. I wanted to ride home together regardless of the game's outcome.

The game ended up being a barn burner. Florida played surprisingly hard, but we held them down. Obi was unstoppable. Sorrento, Stelle, and Beatty had a killer line, scoring two of our three goals. And for me, there was no sign of choking. I was comfortable, happy, excited to perform, rather than paralyzed by the pressure.

We were tied 3-3 with a minute to go in the third period. I snagged the puck from Florida's forward at center ice and kicked it to Leroy, who had just come in on a shift change. It was just the goalie on our end. This was our chance.

One of Florida's d-men made it between us, but Leroy deked on him and passed it over to me. I went in tight to the slot and cut the puck through the five-hole. The roof could have blown off the place it was so damn loud. So much for Fuck-up Mikey. I'd gone big when it counted. If nothing else good ever happened in my career, I'd have that moment. There were 26 seconds to play, and we were able to kill the clock.

Leroy and I exchanged perhaps the longest bro hug ever recorded, then yelled in each other's faces.

"You're alright, Mike, you know that?"

That would probably be the closest I'd ever get to a compliment from Leroy, and I'd take it.

The team got to move on to the next round in front of the home crowd.

The home crowd meant Jessie, in her WAG jacket, with her big smile. I had Kitty tell her the post-game celebrations would be at their house to throw Jessie off the scent of what I was about to do. Jessie ran into my arms after the game.

"JOCKEY!!!! YOU WON!"

I spun her around as her legs wrapped around my waist, kissing the living daylights out of her. "We might have won a little bit," I said with a laugh. "Thanks for coming to see me."

"Wouldn't miss you, baby."

I took her hand and led her to my car. Since she was expecting me to take her to Guy and Kitty's, she didn't even flinch that we weren't going home. She chatted like it was normal car ride, catching me up on her workday and what she and Kitty and Jeanine talked about during the game. I loved her little assessments about the players from the other team.

"That Segel is a real bruiser, huh? I got annoyed every time he stepped on the ice. Like how dare he," she said, crossing her arms.

"You think your man couldn't handle him?"

"No, I know you can. But I wanna handle him, too. Slap his stupid face and send him crying to his mama."

I cackled. "You and Kitty both get so into insulting the other team. It's hilarious."

"Excuse me, I beg to be taken seriously," she huffed. "Hey, I'm kinda hungry. Can we stop at that In'N'Out by their house?"

I chuckled. Like I'd ever say no to feeding her. "Of course."

We sat in my car, sharing a double-double with fries and a shake. She insisted on feeding me bites of the burger.

"You must be so tired after being such a big strong man on the ice," she said, squeezing my thigh. When I first met her, I never would have believed how silly she could be, especially when she was so grouchy with me in the beginning. Turns out, she was just unhappy in life then, and she's happy with me. She's a real spitfire now. Her hand got closer to my crotch, fingers stroking over my bulge. "A big winning strong man."

I grinned at her. "You proud of your Daddy?"

"Sure am," she said, pulling at my belt. Was she really gonna get frisky in the In'N'Out parking lot? I was definitely interested, but I also wanted to build some anticipation for the big surprise.

"Why don't you save it for the coat closet at Guy and Kitty's?"

After we ate, I got back on the road to our destination.

"Hey, didn't we just pass their house?" she asked.

"They told me to park down the street," I said, stomach jumping with nerves.

"But there weren't any cars out front," she said, turning in her seat to look back at their house.

"Huh. Maybe we're just the first here."

I pulled into a driveway of a house at the end of the cul de sac with a sold sign in the front yard.

"Mikey, we can't park here!" she started, then cut herself off.

Her mouth flapped open and shut. "Why are we parking here, Ben?"

I took a key on an old school hotel keychain out of my pocket. "Why don't you go find out?"

Her lower lip quivered. "Shut up. Stop it. What did you do?" She wrapped her arms around my neck. "Did you buy a house?"

I pulled back to look at her. "I bought *us* a house."

She held both my cheeks and kissed me, hard.

"Does that make you happy?"

She nodded, crying. "But what if, what if I hate it? Do you want me to pretend I love it?"

I laughed. Of course she'd think of that. "Then I'll sell it. You wanna go inside and find out?"

"Uh huh." She opened her door and waited for me at the hood of the car. She gave me a few quick kisses before dragging me to the front door. She unlocked it, but before she could walk in, I scooped her up.

"Aren't we supposed to do this?"

"I think only if you're married," she said.

"Well, I do keep asking you to marry me," I pointed out. I put her down inside the threshold and she looked around. She touched her hand to a wooden post by the stairs. Guy and Kitty's neighborhood was mostly midcentury homes, which I knew Jessie liked. She always talked about the cool features in their house.

"Ben, it's perfect."

I beamed. "Go look around, hon. It's ours."

She turned back to me, narrowing her eyes. "But aren't you going to be far from the arena?"

I shrugged. "Stelle makes it work. And you'll be closer, too. It's a compromise."

"But like, you make the money," she objected.

"It's not about the money, hon. Never will be. It's about us making a life together."

She jumped into my arms again, covering my face with kisses. "I love you so much, Ben Miknevicius."

"I love you more, Jessalyn Welsh." I swatted her butt. "Now go look around!"

She pulled me with her, looking in all the rooms. "Is this the master?"

I hugged her from behind. "This is our room, yep."

She drew a shuddering breath. "Say it again?"

"This is our room, baby."

She walked across the hall to a smaller room. "And this is another bedroom?"

My hands were shaky, so I steadied them on her hips. "I mean, it could be a nursery."

She sniveled, her eyes rounding. "You want that?"

I bit my lip, trying to read her expression. "If you do."

"Yeah. I'll want that."

My eyes welled a little, too. "We'll try to have a baby?"

"I think at some point, we should." We stared at each other, stunned and grinning like fools. Then she jumped at me again, peppering me with overjoyed kisses.

She started tugging at my clothes, unbuttoning my shirt as I picked her up. "Hold your horses, Sweet Cheeks. You haven't seen the kitchen yet."

I carried her in there, and as soon as she could see the vintage green cabinets, she started kicking her feet and screeching. I put her down and she folded over with a hand over her mouth. "You got me an avocado kitchen?!"

I couldn't stop smiling. I knew she'd love it. "You want to remodel it?" I teased.

"Are you fucking kidding?! Never, Benny! This thing is frozen in time! Look at it. It's gorgeous!" She looked back at me with teary eyes. "Do you like this house?"

"Yeah, I love it," I said. "Especially because you love it so much."

"But you didn't just buy it because I like stuff like this, right?"

I came closer to her. "I bought it because," I kissed her nose, "I love you," I kissed her forehead, "I'm obsessed with you," I kissed her neck, "and I want to share a home with you. Not just an apartment. Not a bachelor pad. A home. With you."

"Thank you," she whispered. "You didn't have to."

"I know. I wanted to."

"Right, but this isn't picking up takeout for dinner as a treat."

"It's me picking up a house as a treat," I said, knowing full well she'd hate that.

"You fucking dick," she growled, climbing up my body to kiss me. "I think you'd better take your clothes off."

"Ooh, Daddy buying you a house turns you on, huh?"

"Fuck yeah, it does."

"I think I owe you a fuck on the kitchen counter," I said. "And here, there's no one to hear you scream but me. And I'm going to need every single one of those screams."

I plopped her ass on the counter and grabbed her throat to her contented sigh. We could get to the team afterparty a little late. "You ready to christen every surface in this house?"

"Sure am, Daddy."

EPILOGUE
MIKEY

"Cheers!"

The four groomsmen clinked our whiskey glasses to Guy's. It was about an hour to the ceremony at the Greenbrier. Jessie filled me in on all the history around the West Virginia landmark on the flight to Charleston, thrilled to give me all her state pride facts.

"You ready to do this, man?" his old teammate Branson asked.

Guy cracked a love-struck grin. "Yeah. I've been ready since I was 21. I mean, it means more now, and we're in a better place as a couple, but I'm ready to marry her. She's fucking perfect."

"Damn right, she is," Kitty's brother Frank chimed in. He was the best man. I was only a little butt hurt that I didn't get picked. But I guess I'm not blood-related to the bride *and* a best friend.

"Can one of you run this gift to her? She told me not to see her until we're at the altar," Guy said.

"Isn't that some made-up shit left over from the 1400's?" Obi asked, lounging in a plush chair.

"I'm not taking any chances. I've waited this long to get my girl. I'm not losing her over a stupid superstition."

"I'll take it," I said. I wanted to see Jessie.

"I'll come with," Frank said. "I should mess with her hair or something to piss her off."

Once a big brother, always a big brother, I guess.

"Mel would probably appreciate it if I checked in," Branson said.

"Lies! You all just want to see your women," Guy said.

"I guess I could tag along, too," Obi said, jumping up.

"Traitors! You're really going to leave me alone on my wedding day?"

"Fine, I'll stay back," Branson said.

"Wait, who are you trying to see, Obi?" Guy narrowed his eyes at him.

"No one," he stammered. "I'm just being helpful."

"Okay, go," Guy sent us off. "But everybody hurry back."

The four of us walked across the courtyard between the bride and groom's suites. I caught a glimpse of Jessie fussing over the strap of a bridesmaid's dress through the window, her brow knit in concentration. My beautiful Jessie Girl.

Jessie wasn't a bridesmaid, but Kitty had asked if she could help out with styling everyone. She was operating as a wedding assistant of sorts as a wedding gift for her and Guy.

I knocked at the door of the bridal suite. "Boys coming in. Cover anything interesting!" I called.

"Come in!"

I opened the door to Kitty standing on a pedestal, Jessie fluffing the train of her dress.

"Lookin' good, sis," Frank said, stepping over to give her a hug.

"Aw, Kitty Cat, you look amazing," I said, truly taken aback by my friend in her finest. My eyes welled. It really was a long road for them, and I felt so thrilled that they were finally getting married. "I can't believe it's happening."

"Michael, no!" Kitty shouted. "You can't do that shit in here! I just had my makeup finished! This is a no-cry zone!"

"Okay, okay," I said, swallowing hard. "Well, Stelle wanted me to give you this."

I handed her the package, then watched her.

"Can I give you a hug?"

"Yeah, Mikey." Kitty extended her arms and I had to stifle the urge to cry again.

"You just look so pretty and I'm so happy for you. I've been rooting for you guys for years," I said into her shoulder.

Kitty's breath got choppy. "Michael," she sniffed. "Thanks for—well, you know."

I pulled away and she fanned her face. I wiped a tear that hung at the corner of my eye.

"Jessie, come get your man. He's a mess," Kitty said, then handed me a small package with a card. "And take this to Guy."

Everyone laughed. I noticed Obi and Annie, the maid of honor, having a quiet, but serious-looking conversation in the corner. So that's who he was after. I saw him do a dorky punch of her in the shoulder and her laugh. They were acting like middle schoolers. I'd definitely give him some shit later.

"Hey, Jockey," Jess cooed, "you look good."

I smooched her. "You're gorgeous, hon. Can't wait to dance all night with you."

"They did your hair," she said, messing her fingers through the styled-up strands.

"Is it bad?" I checked my reflection in a pane of glass.

"No, you're very dapper."

"Oh yeah?" I asked, coasting my hands down her backside, taking a handful, and pulling her close. I leaned down to give her a deeper kiss.

"Hey! Quit playing grab ass and go do my bidding, Mikey!" Kitty cried. "I'm the only one who gets to play grab ass today."

"Okay, Bridezilla," I shot, sticking my tongue out at her and giving Jess one last peck. "See you at the altar."

"Don't trip or do something stupid," Frank said.

"Frankie!" their mom barked. "You can't be nice to your sister for one day?"

I GAVE Guy a pat on the back as Kitty appeared at the end of the aisle.

"She's gorgeous, man."

Guy wiped a tear, then laughed as Kitty did the same. I looked over at Jessie, who was also wiping a tear as Kitty went to meet Guy. Then she looked at me, a beam of light coming through the chapel's window giving her an almost-angelic glow. I winked at her and she smirked. I hoped that one day, she'd say yes to my daily marriage proposal, and we'd get to do this ourselves. I knew it was kinda soon, but they say when you know, you know. And I knew with Jessie. So I was serious when I asked her every day. Usually, it was in a moment when I felt especially close to her. Sometimes I'd do it over morning coffee. Sometimes over text. Sometimes at night just before we went to sleep and said our last I love you's for the day. But I still got it in every day.

And every day, she said the same thing back: "Maybe someday."

During pictures, I noticed a tall man who looked something like Stelle, but with more gray hair, standing off to the side and sipping a Coke. He moved to stand next to me while Guy and Kitty got some solo shots.

"Beautiful wedding, huh?" I asked, trying to make conversation.

"It is," he said, accent thick.

"Did you come down from Quebec? I didn't know Guy still had family up there."

The man gave a wry smile. "He still has me."

Realization cracked over me. "Holy shit. Are you Gabriel?"

"I am."

I tensed, not sure if I should punch this guy out. I knew Stelle had a complicated relationship with his dad. Like, hadn't spoken in years, didn't go to his mom's funeral complicated.

"Don't worry. I was invited. We've spoken some in the last few months."

I saw Guy give a little wave to him between shots, proving his words true.

I nodded. "How's that going?"

"I made a lot of mistakes with Guy and his mother. I regret a lot of things. But he's a good man. He makes room for mistakes and forgiving. I'm lucky his mom raised such a good son."

"I know a little about complicated family relationships," I said. "Just curious, which of you reached out first?"

"He contacted me. One of the best things that's happened in my life." He finished his Coke and raised it to me. "Enjoy the wedding."

I stood, cemented to the spot. Things still weren't fixed with my family. But Guy's willingness to take his dad back, who had done some pretty fucked up shit to him growing up, made me look at my own life a little differently. I wasn't dreading seeing my family in a few weeks as much as I was before.

Dinner was served, glasses were clinked for kisses, the cake was cut, the bouquet and garter tossed, and Jess and I were enjoying a quiet slow dance. I'd long since shed my suit jacket, wearing suspenders and a bow tie with rolled-up sleeves. She played with the bow tie and booped my nose.

"I think the answer's yes," she said, peering up at me.

My heart raced. "What answer? The answer to what?"

"That question you ask me every day." She said it so casually, like she wasn't dropping really big news on me.

My stomach fluttered. "I didn't ask you yet today."

"Well, the next time you ask, the answer's going to be yes. So choose carefully."

"Really?"

Her smile was huge and her eyes bright. "Yeah. Really."

I pulled her into me, wrapping my arms tight around her. "Seriously? You're going to marry me?"

She looked up at me and raised her eyebrows. "Is that how you're asking?"

"No. No no no no no. This one counts. I wanna get it right. And I don't wanna storm on Guy's big day," I said.

"Smart choice."

"You're not even gonna see it coming, baby. It's gonna be like, the biggest left-field thing ever."

She grinned, her dimple popping out. "Is that so? So like, when you're balls deep in me?"

I shook my head. "More left-field."

"In the TSA line on the way to Japan?"

"Stop guessing, because you'll never get it. You'll just have to let it happen organically."

"You don't actually know, do you?" she teased.

"That's for me to know and you to find out."

"I love you, Benny."

"I love you, too, Sweet Cheeks. Every day. All the time."

She got a mischievous look on her face. "Come with me."

She dragged me by the hand inside, to the hallway by the bathrooms, pulling me into a little alcove. She slinked her leg around my calf and grabbed me by my shirt, locking her lips with mine. This was no wedding kiss. Jessie was starting something. I got lost in the kiss, biting her lips, sliding our tongues together, sucking. One of her hands went to my back, while the other went straight down my pants. I hummed in surprise, as Obi walked behind us and said, "Get a room!"

Jessie looked up at me, love-stoned, took her hand out of my pants, and pulled me up the grand staircase to an empty hallway. I pushed her against a door, the little plaque next to it reading "storage closet." I ground my hips against hers, letting my erection meet her center. I pushed down on the door handle and we fell inside, a loud moan meeting us.

"Wait, what the fuck?!"

There was Guy with his pants around his knees, Kitty's legs wrapped over his ass and her wedding dress shoved to her waist. I see Stelle's ass all the time, but Jessie does not. And I certainly have never seen Kitty and Stelle doing the deed. Jessie covered her eyes and backed away.

"Holy shit," Guy said, almost dropping Kitty, but swerving to put her out of sight.

"You're not shoving me off you this time, Guy-Guy! Keep me covered!" Kitty hissed. "And you, get out!"

"You took my closet idea!" I shouted at Guy.

"You told him about the closet?!" Jessie raged.

Guy looked over his shoulder with a smirk. "It's a good idea."

"OUT!" Kitty shrieked.

Jessie yanked me out by my wrist and slammed the door shut with a quiet "sorry!"

We sprinted down the hall, cracking up. Jessie tripped over her dress and landed on her ass, dragging me down with her. We sat on the floor, sides hurting from laughing. Jessie's smile was so pretty. Little laughing tears smeared her mascara. Her mini dimple pocked her cheek. Her chest was splotchy from the embarrassment. The strap of her dress slipped from her shoulder. And yet, she'd never looked more perfect.

And mine.

I wanted to laugh with her every day for the rest of my life.

My moment had arrived. I stroked her cheek with my finger and gazed into her bright eyes. Then I reached into my pocket and untied the ring that I'd been carrying for a couple of months.

"Jessalyn Welsh, will you marry me?"

And without hesitation, she said, "Yes."

CONTENT/TRIGGER WARNINGS

As a person with a hefty number of multi-initialed diagnoses to my name, I never want my characters to be walking diagnoses. I just want them to be people living with the things that people live with, because I genuinely believe we all have something difficult that we carry.

That said, Mikey has seemingly undiagnosed ADHD, and you'll see traces of that throughout the story. Jessie's childhood trauma left her with PTSD.

Potential triggers in this story include:

PTSD from childhood trauma (non-sexual, non-family, non-religious)

A cheating partner (not the MCs)

Anxiety and panic attack

Discussion of chronic health issues

Complicated family dynamics, including closeted sexuality

And explicit sex scenes featuring

- Dirty talk with ample praise and some degradation
- Anal play
- Double penetration (one partner)

- Cum play
- Spanking
- Squirting
- Choking
- Toy use
- Daddy/brat kink
- Semi-public sex

NEED MORE MIKEY AND JESSIE?

Ben, Benny, Mikey, Jockey, Benjamin Michael Jockey.

Jessie, Jessalyn, Sweet Cheeks, Jessie Girl, honey.

Whatever you want to call them, their journey's not over! Click here to receive a story from Mikey and Jessie's happily ever after.

Reading this on a physical page? Go to www.danigalliaro.com/puck-honey-bonus

And for the curious, Obi's next :)

ACKNOWLEDGMENTS

Thank you so much for reading Puck Honey. Mikey's story was a labor of love. I've never fallen for a character that I made up so much as I did for him. I hope I did him justice. It will be hard to top him in my heart.

Thanks as always to my favorite hockey teams for providing me the bloodsport that keeps this machine going and the teeheehees flowing from all your drama on the ice: Carolina Hurricanes, Seattle Kraken, and New York Islanders. May you all have great health and a good Cup run this year.

Thanks to the Redditors of r/BDSM and r/sex, where the best of my kink research is done.

To The Office Ladies, Jenna Fischer and Angela Kinsey. Your podcast put me behind the scenes of my favorite TV show in a way that made me feel confident writing this story. Your hours of spilling the details enriched my life and ended up informing Jessie's career.

To the Best Friends podcast with Sasheer Zamata and Nicole Byer for giving a picture of the other side of the Hollywood scene. And for keeping me laughing on long drives.

To the BookTok and Bookstagram communities, thank you for rising up to support me.

To my ARC readers and street teams, thank you so much for spreading the word about my writing and being so willing to go all in with Mikey-like zeal. I especially love getting to chat with many of you individually and finding out what speaks to you. Being an author can be a lonely experience, but knowing that

I'll eventually have readers to share with makes it all worthwhile. Some of you have been with me since Take Me Home, and it's such an honor to have you.

To Roxana, for your editing prowess.

To Joseph-Beth Booksellers in Cincinnati and Lexington, for genuinely supporting me since Take Me Home, and being the best bookstore ever.

To all my friends (MEV, Nan and Chrissy, the Gruhs, Skeeemp, Smellenkamp, Lizzy) who rallied around me when I confessed that this is what I do with my time. I could cry thinking about how wonderful all of you are and how happy I am that you've stuck with me for so long.

To Maude, for talking me off the author ledge time and again.

To Manda and Shannon, for creating such beautiful images of Mikey and Jessie according to my neurotic specs. I know I'm not an easy client, and I'm in deep gratitude for your patience with me as you bring my head children to life.

To Gee, for fielding my four million voice memos and giving me THE MOST DETAILED feedback. It's a buddy read on steroids and truly the greatest gift. Thanks for your beautiful art, and for always encouraging me to crank up the kink. You are the reason for my very favorite spicy part of this book. The best thing that's ever been MINE.

To Shelby, for going whole hog every time I write a single sentence and being all about it. You gossip about my characters with me like no one else does. One day, I hope to give you the Guy and Mikey why choose story of your dreams. Your support and enthusiasm mean so much, from the beta reads to the posting, to fielding my bonkers messages.

To Janney, Suze, and Brooke, thank you so much for reading my books before everyone else does and giving me the real talk. Climbing into the depths of your friend's brain is probably pretty bizarre, but y'all are fearless. I'm so honored to have you as critique people and as friends. Janney, I'm happy to have inspired you even a little bit to move for love.

To my parents, for continuing to keep my identity on lock.

And as always, to my darling husband, who doesn't have an alpha bone in his body (except in sports) and thinks Mikey is toxic, but who understands when I can't talk because I'm solving a plot problem.

ALSO BY DANI GALLIARO

Puck Funny (Guy and Kitty)

Coming Soon

Puck Money (Obi)

Puck Sunny (Leroy)

Puck Merry Chill (Sorrento)